LITERARY MURDER

Also by Batya Gur

The Saturday Morning Murder: A Psychoanalytic Case

LITERARY MURDER

A Critical Case

BATYA GUR

Translated from the
Hebrew by Dalya Bilu

HarperCollins*Publishers*

Grateful acknowledgment is made to the following for permission to quote from copyrighted material:

From "Samson's Hair" (p. 187), by Natan Zach, edited and translated by Warren Bargad and Stanley F. Chyet. Copyright © 1988 Indiana University Press. Used by permission.

From "Lament" ("See the Sun") (p. 263), by Schlomo Ibn Gabirol, in *The Penguin Book of Hebrew Verse*, edited and translated by T. Carmi. Copyright © 1981 Allen Lane Ltd. Used by permission.

HarperCollins books may be purchased for educational, business, or sales promotional use. For information, please write: Special Markets Department, Harper-Collins Publishers, Inc., 10 East 53rd Street, New York, NY 10022.

FIRST EDITION

Designed by C. Linda Dingler

Library of Congress Cataloging-in-Publication Data

Gur, Batya.
   [Mavet ba-hug le-sifrut. English]
   Literary murder: a critical case/Batya Gur; translated from the Hebrew by Dalya Bilu.—1st ed.
   p.   cm.
   "Aaron Asher books."
   ISBN 0-06-019023-X
   I. Title.
PJ5054.G637M3813   1993
892.4'36—dc20   92-56195

93 94 95 96 97 ❖/HC 10 9 8 7 6 5 4 3 2 1

LITERARY MURDER

B ecause it was led by Shaul Tirosh, the departmental seminar
was being documented by the media. In the small hall, the television camera and the microphone of the radio crew were
already in position. The camera clearly captured the nonchalant stance,
the hand in the pocket, and the red tones of the tie. The first shot on
the as yet unedited film would be a close-up of his hand, holding a
glass of water. He took a long drink of water and then ran his hand, in
the gesture so characteristic of him, through the pompadour of smooth
silver hair. Then the camera focused on the old book now in the long-
fingered hand, showing the pristine white cuff peeping out of the sleeve
of the dark suit, and moved in on the binding's gold lettering: Chaim
Nachman Bialik. Only then did it take in the table as a whole.

Glancingly it recorded Tuvia Shai's bowed head, his hand sweeping invisible crumbs from the green tablecloth, and young Iddo
Dudai's profile raised toward Tirosh's long, narrow face.

This isn't the first time, people in the hall were saying; Shaul
Tirosh has always been a media star.

"Fact," said Aharonovitz. "Would anyone have dreamed of recording an event like a departmental seminar for posterity unless Shaul Tirosh's name was connected with it?" And he let out a snort of contempt.

Even later, after it was all over, Kalman Aharonovitz wouldn't be able to hide his loathing for the eccentricity, the "cheap theatricality," that had distinguished Tirosh's every act. "And I mean *every* act," and he stole a critical and apprehensive glance at Tuvia's wife, Ruchama.

The technicians and the host of the radio literary program, the reporters and the TV people—for whom Ruchama had given up her usual seat on the right-hand side of the front row—were there for Tirosh's last departmental seminar.

The recording equipment, the TV lights, the cameraman who had been scurrying to and fro for an hour before the seminar started, stirred up excitement in her, beneath her trademark expression of bored indifference. From the end of the second row, Ruchama's view differed from the image recorded by the camera. She had to strain to see the group of lecturers beyond the intervening mop of curls belonging to Davidov, the host of "Book World," the TV program on which every novelist and poet dreamed of appearing.

Davidov's presence excited Tirosh too. A year earlier, he had quarreled with the television personality during a tribute on the occasion of his being awarded the Presidential Poetry Prize, and they had not spoken since. At the beginning of that program, after reading aloud Tirosh's famous poem "Another Sunset" and explaining to the viewers that it was his "visiting card"; after listing his various degrees and the prizes he had won; after repeating that Professor Tirosh was the head of the Hebrew Literature Department at the Hebrew University in Jerusalem and a patron of young poets, and after displaying the cover of the contemporary-literature quarterly edited by Tirosh, Davidov had turned to the poet dramatically and asked him to explain his silence during the past six years. This was a question no one till then had dared to ask him.

This program now also returned to Ruchama's mind, as Davidov's tangled curls obliged her to shift in her seat in order to attain an unimpeded view of the tall figure holding the book. She recalled Davidov's passing his hand over the four slim volumes of poetry scattered on the table in the TV studio and asking without any hesitation how Tirosh accounted for the fact that a poet who had broken new ground, established a new style, who was the undisputed spiritual father of the poetry that had been written after him . . . how had it happened that this poet had not published even one new poem in recent years—apart from a few verses of political protest, he added with a dismissive wave of his arm.

Ruchama well remembered the long interview, which had turned into a verbal duel between the two men, and as soon as she saw Davidov next to the cameraman this evening she had felt rising tension. Now she looked intently at Tirosh's face above the green cloth and pitcher of water that reminded her of cultural evenings in the kibbutz dining room, and she recognized the strained expression she knew so well, a combination of excitement and theatricality, and although she was unable to see his eyes clearly from where she was sitting, she could envisage the green gleam flashing in them.

When Tirosh rose to deliver his lecture, she too, like the camera, registered the movement of the hand smoothing the silver pompadour and then hovering over the book. At first she couldn't see Tuvia's face, which was obscured by the cameraman and by the radio technician, who was checking his equipment for the umpteenth time.

Afterward, when she was obliged to look at the unedited film, she was unable to stop her tears at the sight of the precision and clarity with which the camera had caught Shaul Tirosh's mannerisms—the seemingly relaxed posture, the hand in the pocket—and the red tones of the tie, so striking against the pure white of the shirt and doubtlessly chosen to harmonize with the bright red of the carnation in the lapel buttonhole.

She had always experienced difficulties in concentrating, especially when Tirosh was the speaker, but she succeeded in taking in the opening sentences: "Ladies and gentlemen, our last departmental seminar of the year will deal, as you know, with the subject 'Good Poem, Bad Poem.' I am aware of the excitement aroused by the theoretical possibility that this evening, from this platform, a set of principles will be proclaimed setting forth clear and unequivocal criteria for distinguishing what is good as opposed to what is bad in poetry. But I have to warn you that I am doubtful if that will be the outcome of our discussion this evening. I am curious to hear what my learned colleagues have to say on the matter, curious but skeptical." And the camera, too, caught the ironic, amused glance he cast from his lofty height at Tuvia's face, and after that the long look he gave Iddo Dudai, who sat with his head bowed.

Ruchama lost the thread. She was unable to connect the words and made no effort to do so. She gave herself up to the voice, to its gentle melody.

There was silence in the hall, where latecomers stood in the doorway. All eyes were fixed on Shaul Tirosh. Here and there a smile of excited anticipation appeared, especially on the faces of women. A young woman was sitting next to Ruchama, taking down every word. When she stopped writing, Ruchama became aware of the rhythmic sound of Tirosh's voice, reading one of the national poet's most famous works: "I Did Not Win Light on a Wager."

She heard Aharonovitz breathing heavily behind her and rustling paper. His pen had been poised to comment even before the entire audience had taken their seats. Aharonovitz's notepaper was resting on the shabby brown leather briefcase, resembling a schoolboy's satchel, that was one of his trademarks. A sour, old smell rose from him, mingling with the excessively sweet perfume worn by his neighbor Tsippi Lev-Ari, née Goldgraber, his promising young assistant, whose efforts to efface any traces of her Orthodox past were presumably the reason for the flamboyant colors of her clothing: flowing, brightly dyed garments about which Tirosh had been heard to remark that they were no doubt *de rigueur* in the cult she belonged to, for whose sake she had also changed her name.

On Tsippi's left, Ruchama noticed Sara Amir, a senior professor and one of the pillars of the department, who had not succeeded, even on this special evening, in disguising her housewifely appearance. Her best dress, encasing her heavy thighs in its floral silk and encircling the wrinkles of her neck with its brown collar, failed to dismiss the suggestion of chicken soup that followed her everywhere and was the basis of surprise when anyone who didn't know her perceived the intelligence she invariably displayed on any subject.

"I have read Bialik's poem to you in order to bring up, among other things, the question of whether a work of this standing is still a candidate for aesthetic judgment at all. Might we not be mistaken in taking it for granted that the poem articulates the process of creation in an original way? And is its originality, to the extent that it exists, a guarantee of its merit? Is the image of the poet quarrying in his heart, which we all understand as a metaphor, really . . . original?" Tirosh had taken a long sip of water from his glass before stressing the word "original," which caused an audible murmur in the hall.

People looked at one another and shifted in their upholstered seats. Davidov, noted Ruchama, signaled to the cameraman to focus on the audience. From behind her she heard the scratching of a pen: Aharonovitz was writing furiously. Ruchama looked back and saw Sara Amir's narrow brows arch and a frown appear between her eyes. The student next to Ruchama scribbled even more diligently. Ruchama herself couldn't understand what all the fuss was about, but this was nothing new. She had never succeeded in understanding the passion aroused in faculty members and their hangers-on by questions of this nature.

Dr. Shulamith Zellermaier, who was sitting in the first row of the semicircle facing Ruchama, had started smiling as soon as she heard the first words: a half-smile, with her chin resting on her thick hand, an elbow as always planted on her crossed knee. Her unkempt gray curls made her appear even more threatening and masculine than usual, in spite of the feminine two-piece outfit she was wearing. She turned her head to the right, and the lenses of her glasses glittered in the fluorescent light.

"I wanted to challenge a poem whose canonical standing is never questioned," were his next words—and again there were smiles in the audience, "because among other things, the time has come"—he took his hand out of his pocket and looked straight at Davidov—"for departmental seminars to deal directly with controversial subjects, subjects we never dare to bring up because we haven't got the guts, and so we escape into theoretical and so-called objective discussions, which sometimes lack all substance and are often so boring that our best students leave us, to yawn outside this hall." The young girl next to Ruchama was still writing down every word.

Again Ruchama stopped listening to the words and concentrated on the voice that held her spellbound with its softness, its melodiousness, its sweetness. There are some things, she thought, that cameras and recording equipment will never succeed in capturing.

Ever since she met him, ten years before, she had been enchanted by the voice of this man, the theoretician and literary critic, the academic with the international reputation, and "one of Israel's greatest living poets," as the critics, with rare unanimity, had been saying for years.

Once more she was seized by the impulse to stand up and announce in public that this man belonged to her, that she had just left his dim, vaulted bedroom and his bed, that she was the woman with whom he had eaten and drunk before he arrived here.

She looked around her, at the faces of the audience. The hall was flooded with the dazzling TV lights.

"I'll take on Bialik—that'll make them sit up," she had heard him saying, half to himself, while he was preparing his introductory remarks. "Nobody would expect an evening like this to open with Bialik of all people, and surprise is the main thing. They all assume I'll read something modern, contemporary, but I'll show them that Bialik can be surprising too."

Loud, sustained applause greeted the end of his lecture. Later she would be able to listen to a tape, or to the radio program, Ruchama consoled herself when she realized that the lecture had come to an end while she was absorbed in images of their afternoon, in memories of the afternoon before that, and the night last week, and their trip to Italy together, and the thought that next month it would be three whole years since their affair began, since the moment when he first kissed her in the elevator of the Meirsdorf Building and afterward, in his office, had told her that despite all the women he had known, he had always wanted her, her of all people, but had never believed that she would be interested in him. Her well-known reserve had prevented him from trying to break through the door. And he thought, too, that her devotion to Tuvia would make her inaccessible.

Again she stared dreamily at his hand holding the open book, at his long, dark fingers. The heavy khamsin hanging over Jerusalem tonight, dry and debilitating as nowhere else, had not prevented him from wearing his usual dark suit. And of course, the inevitable red carnation in the buttonhole, which together with the suit and the silver pompadour gave him the cosmopolitan, European air that had conquered so many women and made him a legend.

"Who washes Tirosh's shirts? How does a man who lives alone manage to look like that?" Ruchama had once overheard a female student wondering in the queue outside his office, after he had walked past and gone inside. Ruchama couldn't hear the answer, because she had hurried in after him, to take from him the key to the house, his house, where she would wait for him when his conference hour was over.

None of his students had ever dared to ask him a personal question. Even she didn't have answers to most of the questions, though, like Tuvia and the rest of the select few who had been permitted to cross his threshold, she knew that he kept the red carnations in his little refrigerator, their stems cut off, a pin stuck in each flower, ready for immediate wear.

His attention to minute details charmed her. Whenever she was in his house she would rush to open the refrigerator door, to see if the red carnations were still there in the small glass vase. There were never any other flowers; there wasn't even another vase. To her question as to whether he liked flowers he had replied in the negative. "Only artificial ones," he said with a smile, "or those that are utterly alive, like you," and he prevented further questions with a kiss. On the rare occasions when she had dared to ask him directly about his dramatic mannerisms, his style of dressing—the carnations, the tie, the cuff links, the white shirt—she had never received a serious answer. Only jokes, at most an inquiry as to whether she didn't like the way he looked, and once an explicit statement to the effect that he had begun wearing the carnations for fun and had continued to do so as an obligation to his public.

Tirosh had no accent to betray the fact that he was not a native of the country. "Born in Prague," it said on the back of his books; he had emigrated to Israel thirty-five years before. He told her about Prague, "the most beautiful of the European capital cities." After the war, he had gone with his parents to Vienna. About the war itself he never spoke. He had never told anyone how they survived the Nazi occupation, he and his parents, or even how old he was when they left Prague. Only of the times before and after was he prepared to speak. About his parents he had said on more than one occasion, "Delicate, spiritual people, who couldn't even survive the move from Prague, noble souls." In her imagination she saw a dark, slender woman, his mother, with rustling silk dresses, bending over the silhouette of a child. She had no clear picture of Tirosh as a boy; all she could envisage was a scaled-down, miniature version of him as he was now, playing on English lawns among flowers with intoxicating scents. (She had never been to Prague or to Vienna.) About his childhood he volunteered only a few details, mainly about a "series of nursemaids called Fräulein—you know, nannies, like the ones you read about in books. They actually brought me up, and I consider them responsible for the fact that I'm still a bachelor today." He had said that to her once in a rare moment of self-exposure, when she had wondered about his compulsive habits of neatness and cleanliness.

He was only twenty when he arrived in Israel, and nobody remembered ever seeing him dressed differently.

"And what does he do in the army?" Aharonovitz once asked Tuvia, not sneeringly but with a kind of sour admiration. "How does he maintain his sartorial style in the army? And it's not only the clothes I wonder about; his eating habits pose a problem too, the white wine with meals we hear about and the brandy in the appropriate glass at the end of the day. I ask myself what makes this important personality honor us provincials with his presence, instead of the world at large, in some real metropolis, such as Paris, for example."

And Ruchama remembered the noises Aharonovitz made then as he slurped his coffee, before going on to say with a smile: "On the other hand, in a place like Paris, nobody would notice every sneeze and yawn his honor deigns to emit, while in our tiny little country, in the words of the bard, the man becomes a legend, the press rushes into print to record the event whenever he sets foot in somebody's salon." Tuvia was then only a graduate student, not yet Tirosh's teaching assistant, and the relationship between them had not yet been established.

"The man's a foreign plant in our landscape, even though he's condescended to give himself a Hebrew name." This remark of Aharonovitz's had caused Ruchama to hide a smile. "Shaul Tirosh! I wonder if anyone remembers his original name. I have no doubt that remembering it affords its owner little pleasure: Pavel Schasky. Did you know that?" And Aharonovitz's red, blinking eyes turned to Tuvia. Those were other times, before people stopped talking about Tirosh in front of Tuvia, before they started treating him as if he were ill with a fatal disease.

"Pavel Schasky," repeated Aharonovitz with unreserved enjoyment, "that's the name he was born with, and he doesn't cherish the memory. Who can tell—perhaps he imagines that there isn't a living soul left who remembers his name. Those in the know aver that it was his first act on reaching these shores: changing his name."

Ruchama had never succeeded in taking Aharonovitz's statements seriously; she always had to stop herself from smiling. She couldn't decide whether his style of speaking was part of a deliberate act or if perhaps he hadn't noticed that other ways of communicating were available. She was particularly amused by the way in which he pronounced certain words in the old-fashioned, Ashkenazi way.

At the time, Tuvia had said: "What does it matter? Why worry about such insignificant details? What's important is that he's a great poet, that he knows far more than any of us, that he's the most brilliant teacher I for one have ever had, with an unsurpassed ability to distinguish good from bad. So let's assume he has some need to turn himself into a legend: why should it bother you?" That's what Tuvia said then, with the simplicity and directness that were so characteristic of him, before a huge, heavy shadow darkened his world, before he lost his way.

The conversation took place when Tuvia still liked Aharonovitz, when he still trusted him enough to entertain him in their home. "True, true, I won't deny it," Aharonovitz had replied, "but there are other problems too. I cannot endure the adoration he inspires in the fairer sex, the way they dance attendance on him, the fascination, the hypnotized expression in their eyes when he looks at them." And with a deep sigh, he added: "True, the man knows how to distinguish between a good poem and a bad one. True, too, that he plays the role of protector and spiritual father to the younger of our poets—but, my friend, don't forget, only on condition that they find favor in his eyes; only then. If they don't, God help them. If he in his wisdom decides to call a poet "mediocre," the miserable wretch might as well put on sackcloth and ashes and seek his fortune elsewhere. I once happened to witness this noble gentleman rejecting a supplicant for his favors. His face was sealed and his expression like stone when he announced: 'Young man, this isn't it. You are not a poet and you evidently never will be.' And I ask you, how could Tirosh know? Is he a prophet?" And here Aharonovitz turned to Tuvia with his eyes even redder than before, and a gob of spit flew in Ruchama's direction as he shouted: "You'll never believe who he did this to!" And he mentioned the name of a rather well-known poet, whose work had never appealed to Tuvia.

"And then there was that affair of the sonnet—have you heard about the affair of the sonnet?" And he didn't wait for an answer; there was no stopping him.

"After the appearance of Yehezkiel's first book, a literary party was given in his honor in the Habima Theater cellar in Tel Aviv. There were readings of his poetry, speeches, and afterward we retired to a café—the fashionable café of the hour, needless to say, habituated by the poets—and we were a large group of people, poets too; I could mention the name of someone whose poetry Yehezkiel very much admires."

"Who?" asked Tuvia.

"What do you mean, who? The gentleman under discussion, Tirosh, the object of your worship. Well, Yehezkiel was the happiest of men. But our friend is not the man to see someone else happy and hold his tongue, he has a sacred obligation to tell the truth, this is his claim to greatness, and for a glass of cognac he sold Yehezkiel's birthright and composed two perfect sonnets, one after the other, and all in order to prove that there is nothing remarkable in composing a sonnet."

"Just like that, on the spot?" asked Tuvia with undisguised admiration.

"Just so, then and there, after reading aloud Yehezkiel's sonnet and smiling his well-known smile. And after he smiled he announced: 'For one glass of cognac I'll write you a perfect sonnet, like this one, in five minutes, what do you say?' And the people around him smiled too, and he wrote, not in five minutes but in two, two sonnets according to all the rules, and everybody knew that they were in no way inferior to Yehezkiel's poems. Is it conceivable? And for whom? To impress people he himself calls poetasters?"

And Aharonovitz turned to look at Ruchama, who tried without success to look shocked, and then returned to Tuvia and asked: "And you still consider him worthy of admiration? Why, it's pure decadence!"

After sighing profoundly, Tuvia explained that the other side of the coin was the courage to expose himself that Tirosh possessed. The courage to state his opinion in university seminars, the courage to say the emperor has no clothes, to give his courses titles that any other lecturer would blanch at the very thought of. "And the fact that his classes are always packed, and the fact that he always presents a fresh, original, innovative point of view: these are things you can't dismiss," said Tuvia, and he got up to make more coffee, while Aharonovitz replied: "Theater, it's all theater."

"It doesn't matter," said Tuvia from the kitchen, "it doesn't matter. The important thing is that he's a great poet, that there's no one else like him, except perhaps Bialik and Alterman. Even Avidan and

Zach aren't as good as he is, and that's why I'm prepared to forgive him everything, or at least a very great deal. The man's simply a genius. And geniuses have different rules." And then he returned with the coffee and changed the subject to the examination for which he had been preparing for the past two weeks.

It was their first year in Jerusalem. Tuvia had requested a year's leave from the kibbutz in order to study with Tirosh, a request that was followed by a request for time to complete his M.A. He had already met Aharonovitz when Tuvia, still a teacher on the kibbutz, was studying for his B.A., and when they arrived in Jerusalem, Aharonovitz was a junior lecturer, teaching on a temporary basis in the department and trying desperately to obtain tenure. Tuvia had willingly acceded to his attitude of patronage and paternalism.

Now Tuvia stood up to speak. Ruchama hadn't been home when he left for the departmental seminar, but she had anticipated that he wouldn't change his clothes. His short-sleeved shirt revealed two pale, slender arms and barely covered his little paunch. Beads of sweat were visible on his high forehead, which was fringed with wisps of thinning hair of a nondescript color.

He had been chosen to give the first of the prepared lectures. The speaker after him would be Iddo Dudai, one of the youngest lecturers in the department, whose doctoral thesis, written under Professor Tirosh's supervision, had given rise to great expectations.

In comparison to Shaul, thought Ruchama, not for the first time, Tuvia looked like a skinny version of Sancho Panza. Except that Shaul, of course, was not Don Quixote. Even his voice, she thought in despair, his voice alone, was enough to make the difference between them.

The voice of her husband, who had begun to address himself to the topic "What Is a Good Poem?" was high, and it broke with the intensity of the pathos with which he read Shaul Tirosh's famous poem "A Stroll Through the Grave of My Heart." In this poem Tirosh expressed, in the opinion of the critics, his "macabre-romantic view of the world." The critics had stressed the "stunning originality of the imagery" and spoken of "linguistic innovations and new themes by means of which Tirosh revolutionized the poetry of the fifties. Other poets, too, contributed to this revolution, but Tirosh was by far the most striking and outstanding of them all," recalled Tuvia in his monotonous voice.

Ruchama looked around her. The tension in the hall had slackened, as if the lights had gone out. People listened with studied attention. On the faces of the women, including the young ones, the impression left by the previous speaker was still evident, and their eyes were still fixed on him. You couldn't say they weren't paying attention, but it was a polite attention to expected, predictable things. The poem chosen by Dr. Tuvia Shai, a senior lecturer in the department, was one you could have guessed in advance he would choose as a good poem to exemplify his argument. With half an ear, Ruchama listened to the learned asseverations she had already heard many times before when her husband held forth passionately about Tirosh's poems.

It would have been impossible to conceive of greater loyalty and admiration than Tuvia Shai felt for Shaul Tirosh. "Adoration"—that was the word, thought Ruchama. There were those who spoke in terms of an "alter ego," or a "shadow," but everyone agreed that you had better not utter a derogatory word, a word of criticism or mockery, about Shaul Tirosh in the presence of Tuvia Shai. Tuvia's cheeks would flush, a gleam of anger would ignite in his mousy eyes, if anyone dared to express anything less than reverence for the head of his department.

During the past three years, in which he had shared her with Tirosh, the gossip had grown, as Ruchama perceived by the silences that fell in rooms as she came into them and at parties given by faculty members, by the knowing smiles of such as Adina Lipkin, the department secretary. She also sensed an added dimension to the gossip: the outrage caused by Tuvia's persistent relationship with Tirosh.

But Tuvia did not change his attitude, not even on the day when he found her with Tirosh on the sofa in the living room of their own apartment, she with her blouse undone, buttoning it with trembling fingers, Shaul lighting a cigarette with an unsteady hand. Tuvia had smiled in embarrassment and asked if they would like something to eat. Shaul steadied his hand and joined Tuvia in the kitchen. They spent a quiet evening around the table, with the sandwiches prepared by Tuvia. Nothing was said about the hastily buttoned blouse, about the dark jacket lying on the armchair, the tie on top of it. They had never spoken of it, neither then nor later. Tuvia didn't ask, and she didn't explain.

In the depths of her heart, Ruchama enjoyed the thought that she was at the center of a mystery whose details the faculty of the Literature Department and literati all over the country would have loved to discover. No one dared to question the actors in the drama themselves. At the age of forty-one, Ruchama Shai still had a youthful, boyish appearance. Her cropped hair and childlike body gave her the air of an unripe fruit, one that was about to wither without ever having ripened. She had noticed the two deep lines that had begun to run downward from the corners of her lips, emphasizing what Tirosh called her "weeping clown look."

She knew that she did not look her age, thanks partly to the blue jeans she wore, the men's shirts, the absence of makeup. She was different from the "feminine women" with whom Tirosh had been associated before her. He himself never mentioned his previous affairs, or the ones he was still conducting. Not long before, she had seen him through the window of an out-of-the-way little café, running his fingers through his silver pompadour while gazing into the eyes of Ruth Dudai, Iddo's plump young wife.

How well Ruchama knew the look of suffering concentration on his face. The face of his companion, who was a doctoral student in the Philosophy Department, was invisible to her. He didn't notice her, and she immediately moved on, feeling like a voyeur.

Despite the intimacy of their relationship, there were some things about which she couldn't talk to him. She never discussed her feelings for Tuvia or her married life with him, and she never talked to him about his relationship with her husband and the exclusivity of the ties between them. The few attempts she had made to get him to say something about the nature of this special bond had come to nothing.

He simply didn't react. He would fix his eyes on the "invisible distance," as he called it (after a well-known book of poems), and say nothing. Once, when she was wondering aloud about "the situation," as she referred to the complicated triangle, he pointed to the door, as if to say: I'm not forcing you; you're free to go.

On social occasions, the three of them were always together, although once in a while she would go alone with Tirosh to his meetings with young poets. He spent a lot of time cultivating the latter— especially, some people said nastily, since he had stopped writing himself. These people, who were so careful in Tuvia's presence, lost all restraint with her. It was their way of compensation for not saying a word to anyone about her relationship with Tirosh.

The truth was that she was naturally reserved and that she lacked all interest in literature, as she had explained to Tuvia long before, when they were still living on the kibbutz. She read a lot, but not poetry. She was unable to derive from poetry the sublime enjoyment Tuvia experienced. Poetry was a closed world to her, enigmatic and unintelligible. Above all, she liked reading detective stories and spy stories, and she devoured them indiscriminately.

She had no close women friends, only colleagues, like the women she worked with at the admissions office of Shaarei Tzedek Hospital. Her ties with them were confined to office hours, and they tended to see her passivity as a rare gift for listening and empathy, and told her all about their family troubles.

Over the years, she had come to realize that the people around her interpreted her lack of vitality as a profound melancholy, and that many saw her as interesting and tried to solve her mystery. The women she worked with, especially Tzipporah, a buxom, motherly woman who plied her with cups of tea, apparently thought that this "melancholy" was due to her childlessness. But Ruchama herself was not grieved by it.

Until ten years before, when she first met Tirosh, she had lived with Tuvia on the kibbutz and worked wherever the member in charge of the roster put her, renouncing in advance any hope of the unexpected.

The move to Jerusalem, so that Tuvia, who had initially attended the Oranim Kibbutz Seminar and then the University of Haifa, could complete his studies at the Hebrew University, was the most dramatic event of her life, mainly because of meeting Tirosh, whose colorful personality had captured her heart. She immediately recognized that he was her polar opposite. Even his style of dress aroused her admiration, and when they grew close she often felt, like the heroine in *The Purple Rose of Cairo*, that the cinema screen had turned into reality in front of her eyes and the hero of her dreams had stepped out of it. Since she never shared her inner world with anyone, not even Tuvia, she remained a mystery to the faculty of the Literature Department. The presence of the mute, boyish figure who entertained guests in silence, who was always accompanied by Tuvia and afterward also by Tirosh, gave rise to the need for endless interpretations. "They're writing the Babylonian Talmud about you there," said Tirosh once, when he had asked her opinion about something and she silently shrugged her shoulders.

There were many attempts to breach the wall of silence, attempts by members of the faculty and by the poets into whose company she was dragged by Tuvia and Tirosh at the Tel Aviv café where she was referred to as the Mystery Woman, even to her face; to this, too, her only response was a smile. She never ordered anything there except black coffee and neat vodka—at first because pronouncing the words to the waitress gave her a thrill, and later on, even when she would have liked to order something else, because she found that the role she had established for herself obligated her and that she had become a captive to the silent, austere figure she had created.

Nobody wondered what Tuvia saw in her, but she was aware that many wondered, with incomprehension, envy, and hostility, why Tirosh was attracted to her.

She herself didn't really know the answer. Once, he told her that the colorlessness of her personality threw the colors of another into relief. She wasn't offended. For a long time she had suspected that the secret of her charm lay precisely in her passivity, which Tirosh called "the way you enable the person next to you to be reflected in the sharpest possible outline, as against a white background." With regard to her own motivation, she also had no answer. What attached her to Tuvia, to Tirosh, to anyone, to anything? What was the force binding the invisible cord thanks to which she went on existing? These questions went unanswered.

She was not a depressed person nor an apathetic one; she only lacked passion. "Alienation" was the word faculty members would have chosen to describe her way of looking at the world. "Defeatism," Tirosh himself once said, when he took the trouble to try to explain her lack of any wishes for herself, her renunciation of any goal whatsoever.

At first Tuvia had directed her life. It was he who had chosen her, and she consented because he had persisted more stubbornly than others, who had despaired of her reserve and retreated from the field. It was Tuvia who had led her, who had brought her here, and now there was Tirosh. If he wanted her to change her life, she once said to him, he would have to pull the leash. That's how things had been until recently, when something began to crack.

"What's happened to you?" was Tirosh's response when she asked him why he didn't want to be with her all the time. There was a note of astonishment in the question. Ruchama had never expressed a wish or desire before.

"The text describing the vision, in the poem before us. . . " She heard Tuvia's voice and realized with a shock that he had been speaking nonstop for twenty minutes without her taking in a single word. "Is a hermetic text, in the simple meaning, which is close perhaps to the original meaning of the word: it is composed as a secret text, an occult book—like the hermetic literature of the Egyptian priests. But what distinguishes this poem by Tirosh is the fact that the secret text is not a recipe for a potion conferring immortality, a set of instructions for the construction of a golem, or a secret formula governing the structure of the spheres; it is not a schematic outline but a detailed description. More than that, it is a description of a view, and the reader can follow it and construct in his imagination the whole picture, move in its space and time, which are detached from any concrete reality, populate it with characters and a hero, and sense through it the spiritual and emotional and even the social and political condition. The poem moves with great tension between the concreteness and the sensuality of the materials and the abstraction and spirituality of what is produced by their combination: especially between the 'secretness' of the text and the 'revelation' of the vision it describes. The situation of the reader in relation to the text is one of constant effort. As he reads, his understanding is constantly perfected. The structure of the text forces him to perform a complete transformation of his modes of relating to words. And thus, gradually, the theme is developed: this is a poem about the spiritual and existential situation of a human being."

To her surprise, Ruchama realized that her husband's words about Tirosh's poem interested her, were almost comprehensible to her, and she remembered Shaul's once remarking that Tuvia was the only person who interpreted his poems correctly. Tuvia now took a sip of water, and the young girl sitting next to Ruchama shook out her hand, which had been feverishly noting down every word uttered, took off her glasses, and wiped the lenses vigorously. She resumed writing as he said:

"In conclusion, all I have to say is this: The question is not whether this is a good poem but as what and in relation to what a poem is a good poem. In other words, from the outset there is no point in talking about immanent value, value that is context-free; and this is one of the basic mistakes of those who seek absolute value in a work of literature. I'm not saying anything new when I say that in order for anything to have value, it has to be related to something else, something different from itself. The statement that value is relative does not diminish it. On the contrary, relativity is what makes its existence possible. The question 'As what is this poem good?' is concerned with subjects such as genre, type, cultural tradition, and linguisitic tradition on the diachronic axis, and subjects such as the poetics of a particular poet in relation to his period—the specific cultural and historical context of the poem—on the synchronic axis. The words 'good' or 'very good' in relation to what has been said about 'A Stroll Through the Grave of My Heart' are indeed applicable to what I chose to stress in the poem, and they turn what has been said about it into a value judgment; but this evaluation does not derive from the poem itself, it is not logically connected to it. The word 'good' is imposed on the descriptive statements from the outside and transforms them suddenly into value judgments: it creates an ostensibly causal connection between description and judgment."

Davidov leaned toward the cameraman and muttered something. Ruchama saw Tirosh's green eyes peering at her husband with intense concentration, as if he didn't want to miss a single word, and she saw Iddo Dudai's face, whose pallor she ascribed to his excitement at his approaching lecture.

Ruchama turned and caught sight of Sara Amir, listening with great interest. The expression of concentration on her face grew, Ruchama noticed, as Tuvia went on talking. "In my opinion, there is no point in trying to establish a general criterion for the quality of a literary text, either relative or absolute. Every text presents a new case for judgment. I have no rules for the future. I can say which work *is* good in my opinion, but not which work *will be* good in my opinion. 'There's no arguing about taste' is a nonsensical statement. Taste *should* be argued about. And arguing, in fact, is all we can do about it." Tuvia sat down with an air of exhaustion, and a faint smile appeared on his face at the sound of the applause and the words that Tirosh whispered in his ear as he patted his hand, and again silence descended on the hall as Iddo Dudai stood up to speak.

Later it would be possible to see and hear what the camera had clearly recorded: the terrible trembling of Iddo's hands, the beads of sweat on his forehead, the shaking and stammering of his voice. Ruchama would remember having noticed the glass of water he swallowed in a single gulp.

Although Iddo Dudai was only a doctoral candidate, his position in the department was assured: Tirosh predicted a brilliant future for him, Tuvia praised his perseverance and diligence, and even Aharonovitz, in his perpetually complaining voice, spoke warmly of "a true scholar, a *talmid haham* in the Talmudic sense of the term."

This was not the first lecture he had delivered to an academic audience, and Ruchama thought that his extreme nervousness must be due to the presence of the TV cameras, although Tuvia argued heatedly against this on their way home, at the end of the evening: "You don't know him. He's not interested in things like that; he's a serious scholar; it's silly to think that that's the reason. I knew from the word go that it was going to be a catastrophe. I sensed it. He's not the same person since he came back from America. We shouldn't have let him go. He's too young."

But Ruchama, still under the vivid impression of the drama that had taken place in the hall, was unable to see for herself the terrible change that had occurred in Iddo, apart, of course, from the fact that he had defied Tuvia's guru, who was also his own supervisor, and by so doing had endangered his status in the department.

At the beginning of his lecture, Iddo read a poem by a Russian dissident whose work Tirosh himself had published and brought to attention as a sensational example of the preservation of the Hebrew language in the Soviet labor camps. The subject of Iddo's doctoral thesis, Ruchama to her surprise later recalled, involved underground Hebrew-language poetry in the Soviet Union.

Then he went on to say that there were three levels in literary research. "The first is descriptive poetics," he said, wiping his brow and looking expressionlessly at the audience. "This is the objective level, whose goal is research," and once more Ruchama's mind strayed, and when she began to listen again she heard the words: "The most subjective pole is the pole of evaluation and judgment. And the poem I have just read is one that was written in the tradition of the poetry of allusion—in other words, poetry that relates to an earlier text, in this case a biblical text, and it is impossible not to feel that it fails to transcend the banal and the expected in its description of the figure of Heraclitus the Obscure. Beauty that is easily acquired is not beauty," said young Dudai, and he paused to take a breath.

A faint stir ran through the audience. Ruchama saw Shulamith Zellermaier smile her ironic half-smile, one hand ceaselessly fingering the brown wooden beads encircling her thick neck. The student next to Ruchama stopped taking notes.

"The poem ingratiates itself by means of kitsch," Iddo continued rapidly, "and in this case the kitsch lies mainly in its adaptation of isolated elements from symbolist poetry and the plastic art associated with it, *art nouveau;* in other words, the kitsch lies in the poetic anachronism. This is not a symbolist poem but a structure borrowing external elements of an earlier period, in order to take advantage of the regressive tendencies of the reader."

"Bravo!" cried Shulamith Zellermaier, and the academic audience began to buzz. The noise in the hall grew louder. Everyone knew how much Tirosh had admired these poems that had reached him by an obscure route and that he had edited and published. Davidov murmured something to his cameraman, who directed his lens to take in the faces of the other participants: Tuvia's lowered eyes; the expression of surprise and the spasm of anger, immediately suppressed, that crossed Tirosh's face. Ruchama turned to look behind her and saw the glitter in Aharonovitz's eyes, the smile of alarm on the face of Tsippi, the assistant lecturer, and the expression of calm surprise on Sara Amir's face. The girl on Ruchama's left had resumed writing. And then Iddo continued: "However, in favor of the poem, we have to take into account the fact that it was written in a labor camp, that it was written by a man who had not been exposed to the European culture of the past three or more decades, who never completed his formal education in Hebrew—and this is what makes it remarkable. The circumstances in which it was written, the period, and so forth. If this poem had been written here, in this country, in the fifties or sixties, would anyone of you have considered it a good poem?"

The hand busily writing on her left came to a momentary halt. Ruchama looked behind her and then turned her eyes back to the pale face of Iddo Dudai, who now took off his square-framed glasses with their thick lenses, placed them carefully on the green cloth, and said: "It goes without saying that I agree with Dr. Shai: this is a subjective matter, dependent on circumstances and context, a question of evaluation, taste, and so on." And then he put his glasses on again and read the latest political poem by Tirosh, a poem that had been published in one of the literary supplements at the end of the Lebanon war and had even been put to music and turned into a mournful ditty that had joined the string of familiar songs sung on memorial days. Iddo read "It's All the Same to Us" in a dry, monotonous voice.

Ruchama couldn't concentrate on the tortuous sentences with which Iddo interpreted whatever called for interpretation in the text, but she remembered the concluding sentences vividly: "This is a poem that betrays its actions. A political poem should never be precious or ironic. A poem of political protest cannot at one and the same time be aware of the act of the poem and of the intellectual virtues of its writer. His cultural assets are of no value when it comes to a poem of political protest. The question is: where is the power that existed in Tirosh's lyric poems? Where are the deeper levels? Is the man who wrote 'The Girl with the Green Lips' and 'The Moment When Black Touched Black' the same man who produced the posturing poem before us?"

Tuvia sprang up from his chair—Tirosh had buried his face in his hands, as the camera would testify—seized Iddo's arm, and almost forced him to sit down, saying in a voice trembling with agitation: "Mr. Dudai doesn't understand. I disagree with him. The context—he doesn't understand the context! The context is manifestly political; it refers to all kinds of slogans that appear in the literary supplements and mocks them. It mocks them in their own language." Tuvia wiped his forehead with his hand and continued passionately: "This isn't a poem of political protest in the conventional sense, against the Lebanon war. On the contrary! Mr. Dudai has missed the point! This is a protest poem against the usual run of protest poems and their lack of substance! It's a parody of protest poems! That's what you failed to see!"

Iddo Dudai looked at Tuvia and said quietly: "I think that a parody that doesn't clearly read like a parody fails to make its point. All I can say is that if the poem was intended as a parody, then it doesn't come off."

The uproar in the hall began to make itself felt. Professor Avraham Kalitzky, the only authority recognized by his colleagues as competent to evaluate the bibliographical basis for any argument whatsoever, raised his hand, rose to his full dwarfish height, and cried in a shrill voice: "We must examine the original meaning of the word *parō idia* in Greek and not use it irresponsibly!"

But his cry was swallowed up in the growing commotion. All eyes, as the camera recorded, were fixed on Tirosh, who with "admirable restraint," in Tuvia's later words, calmed the disputants ("Gentlemen, gentlemen, calm yourselves. It's only a departmental seminar, after all"). But the camera also caught the stunned look he gave Iddo, as the latter sat down and stared in front of him while Tirosh, in his capacity as chairman, rose to his feet, summed up in a few sentences, glanced at his watch, and said that there was only a short time left for discussion and questions from the audience.

None of the faculty or students of the department said anything, nor did any of the regular members of the audience, those who were never officially invited but never failed to show up at the departmental activities open to the public: three elderly women school teachers who broadened their intellectual horizons by regular attendance at such events; two literary critics who had left the academic world but went on faithfully attacking its members in the slandermongering literary columns of obscure newspapers; and a few Jerusalem eccentrics and culture vultures. No one said anything. Even Menucha Tishkin, the oldest of the three teachers, who always asked something after a long introduction setting forth her professional problems—even she didn't open her mouth. Something had happened, but Ruchama didn't know how to define it, and she certainly had no idea of what it portended.

The technicians began packing their equipment and Iddo Dudai left the platform. Violently shaking off the hand Aharonovitz put out to grip his shoulder, he almost ran out of the hall.

Ruchama stood to one side of the exit. As the audience filed past her, she caught snatches of conversation, half-words, but they didn't sink in. Tuvia still stood behind the table, crumpling the green cloth with his fingers, and from where she stood, he looked to her like one of the Labor party lecturers who used to come to the kibbutz, sitting in the dining room behind a table that had been covered with a green cloth in honor of the occasion. She had detested them.

The water pitcher was empty, and Tuvia, leaning on the table and nodding constantly, listened attentively for several minutes as Shaul Tirosh spoke to him. Finally Tirosh stood up, and together they began making their way to the door. Tirosh smiled at her intimately and said: "Well, did you enjoy it?" Ruchama didn't reply, and he went on: "Someone should have enjoyed the drama. Tuvia thinks it was an Oedipal rebellion, Dudai's attack. I disagree with him, although I have no other explanation to offer. In any case, it was certainly interesting. I've always thought he's an interesting fellow, young Dudai, but Tuvia doesn't agree." Ruchama caught a new expression in the green eyes, one she had never seen there before, perhaps anxiety, and she herself was suddenly overcome by a feeling of obscure fear. Tuvia said nothing, but his face was clouded and angry.

Together they went down in the elevator to the underground parking garage. Even now, ten years after coming to Jerusalem, Ruchama was unable to get around the campus unaided. The round arts faculty building, each wing of which was painted a different color in order to distinguish it from the others and help people locate themselves, filled her with dread. She only knew her way to the Meirsdorf Building, the university guesthouse, and the elevator to the parking garage. Even when she had to get to the Literature Department wing, she would go there through the labyrinth of the Meirsdorf Building, the only way she knew to reach her destination.

Shaul declined their invitation to come home with them for a late cup of tea, and they accompanied him to his car and then turned toward their own light-colored Subaru, which was parked in a dim corner.

In the underground parking garage, too, Ruchama was always overcome with dread: spaces like these, and also crowded department stores, gave rise to powerful anxieties in her, which were expressed in an immediate nausea. This time the anxiety took on new dimensions. At the sight of the figure suddenly looming up in the corner, she was unable to stifle the scream rising in her throat, and she was reassured only when she recognized the intelligent face of Iddo Dudai. "Tuvia," said Iddo, "I have to talk to you," and despite the businesslike gesture with which Tuvia opened the door of the car, whose inside light went on and illuminated Iddo's tense features, Ruchama sensed the anger, embarrassment, and discomfort in his voice when he said: "Good. I really think we should talk, especially after this evening. Are you free tomorrow?"

"No, tomorrow's too late. I have to talk to you now," said Iddo, and listening to the panic in his voice, Ruchama knew that her husband would not be able to refuse. "Then follow us and we'll talk at home," Tuvia said.

Iddo looked at Ruchama. She quickly lowered her eyes, and Tuvia said: "Don't worry. Ruchama will leave us alone. Right?" He turned to her, and she nodded.

In the car, Tuvia spoke without pause, trying to guess what could have been behind Iddo's behavior. "We should never have let him go abroad," he said heatedly. "For two weeks now, ever since he came back, he hasn't been the same." Ruchama said nothing. She was tired.

Her curiosity was momentarily aroused by the sight of the distress on Iddo's face as he entered their second-floor flat in the big apartment house on French Hill, but then her weariness overwhelmed her, and she said good night and retired to their little bedroom. She heard Tuvia's shoes shuffling and the clatter of Iddo's sandals as he followed him into the kitchen; she even heard the rattling of the cups, and after that Iddo's question: "How do you turn it on?" but by then she was already in bed, under the sheet, and even that was superfluous, the night was so hot. The open window didn't help. The air stood still in the yard, dry and oppressive. The last sounds she heard were those of the television sets in neighboring apartments, and then she fell asleep.

Do You Have a Regulator?" asked the title of the lead article in *Diving News*. Michael Ohayon looked at the magazine and smiled. No, he didn't have a regulator, nor was he going to have one. *He* had no intention of scuba diving.

Superintendent Ohayon, head of the Criminal Investigations Division in the Jerusalem Subdistrict, may have been staying at the Diving Club in Eilat, but he was there "strictly as a father," as he said firmly to his childhood friend Uzi Rimon, director of the club, when the latter tried to persuade him to take the course. "Water exists for drinking, to wash with, and at the most to swim in. I'm a Jerusalemite," he said, looking with dread at the blue depths in front of them.

"That's not what I heard about you. They didn't tell me you've turned into such a coward," said Uzi with a sly smile.

"And what *did* they tell you? *Who* told you?" Michael smiled in embarrassment.

"Don't ask. They say that ever since you got divorced, all the husbands in Jerusalem are keeping their wives locked up at home, and I also heard that when you're on a case, hardened police officers shake in their boots. They say you're tough. Pity there isn't some dame around to see what you really are—chicken!"

And indeed, only those closest to the tall man, whose jutting cheekbones gave his dark, deep eyes a melancholy expression that had melted many hearts, were acquainted with his anxieties. In the view of the others—the men he worked with in the police force, his commanding officers, his casual friends—Michael Ohayon was a strong, clever, cultured man and a dedicated womanizer, whose reputation attracted women in droves. And it was true that even hardened policemen paled at hearing the tapes of some of the interrogations he had conducted, though, as was well known, he never used physical violence against suspects. The loyalty and relaxed atmosphere among the men on his staff was a tribute to the civility and respect with which he treated everyone, to his lack of arrogance, and to the modesty he radiated. His close friends argued that it was precisely his humility that was responsible for his rapid rise on the police force.

Uzi, too, surrendered now to the shy, embarrassed smile that lit up Michael's face, and he patted him on the shoulder and said: "And who's ever heard of a Moroccan Yiddishe mama?"

Michael's buried anxieties, a never-failing source of amusement to those close to him, mainly entailed his only son.

When Yuval was still a baby, his father knew that the moment would come when the boy would leave for the annual school hike, want to ride a bicycle, dream of a motorbike, join the army. The first nights after Nira came home from the hospital with Yuval, he couldn't fall asleep for fear the child would stop breathing. When Yuval was a year old, there were already legends about the Moroccan-born father who behaved like a Polish Holocaust survivor. "We've exchanged roles," Nira explained with mocking coldness to their friends. "It would have been logical for me to behave like that. What reason does he have?"

Michael Ohayon found no difficulty in waking up at night when the baby cried, and changing the diapers was actually an enjoyable task. And when they were still married, Nira's complaints about Yuval's emotional demands found no echo in his heart.

Hardest of all was watching his son's first steps to independence and freedom, the ever-present consciousness that life indeed hung on a thread, that his control over outside disasters was minimal, and that it was his task above all to keep the child alive and well.

He never expressed his anxieties to Yuval, and the boy began going to school by himself in the second month of the first grade, in spite of the heavy traffic on Gaza Street, and joined the Scouts without suspecting what it cost his father every time he left on a hike with his friends. Yuval was six when his parents separated, and his father consequently lost what little control he had over the dangers lurking at every corner. He had the boy twice a week and every other weekend, until Yuval himself rebelled against the rigid schedule imposed by his mother and began coming to his father's house whenever he felt like it.

The passion for scuba diving that had taken hold of Yuval was the realization of all his father's fears.

In reply to the question "What do you want for your birthday?" the boy had asked him to pay for a diving course. "Just the course and the essential equipment; I've already saved the fare from working last summer, and it may even be enough for part of the gear," he said when he saw the expression on his father's face and thought that the problem was the money.

Michael Ohayon had to call on all his reserves of inner strength when he instructed himself to respond quickly and as calmly as possible: "That's an original idea. Where do they hold these courses?"

"All kinds of places," said Yuval, and his face took on an expression of pure pleasure. "But I want to go to Eilat. I thought of taking the bus on Friday morning and missing school in honor of my birthday; anyway, it's the end of the year. Or else I could leave after school and hitch down."

And that, of course, was the straw that broke the camel's back. The longing on Yuval's face was joined by a trace of cunning, and Michael wondered if he had really succeeded in hiding his fears. The boy looked at him expectantly.

"Are you thinking of going with friends?" Michael asked cautiously, and when the boy said that he hadn't thought about it yet, the solution came in a flash, the same stroke of genius that had saved the situation before, on the first trip Yuval had ever taken that involved sleeping away from home.

"We could spend the weekend together, and I could go down to Eilat with you. I've got a friend there I haven't seen for years."

There was a new suspicion in Yuval's eyes when he asked: "In your car?" Michael nodded.

"Just the two of us?" asked Yuval, and Michael replied: "Why, is there anyone else you'd like to come with us?"

"No," said Yuval hesitantly. "I just thought that maybe you might want to bring someone else along." And then the delight began to break through the suspicion: "And I'll dive, right?"

"If you want to, why not?"

"And you're sure we can go from Friday morning till Sunday?" asked Yuval, and Michael started to argue about missing classes at the end of the school year, but in the end he smiled and said: "Okay, you only turn sixteen once. We'll celebrate it the way it should be celebrated. The way you want to, anyway."

Yuval asked no more questions, but the words "you might want to bring someone else along" reawakened Michael's need to speak to him about Maya. In Eilat; I'll talk to him in Eilat. On the beach, thought Michael, and calculated that there were still two weeks left before Yuval's birthday. A lot of things could change in two weeks, he thought despairingly. Perhaps Yuval would catch a cold.

And now they had already spent two in Eilat. Michael lay on the beach and leafed through *Diving News*. He even read the advertisements, ignoring the books he had brought with him. The sun was at its zenith, and the heat made him drowsy, but he couldn't surrender to it because of the feeling of unfocused uneasiness that had accompanied him since they set out from Jerusalem.

When he woke up that morning, he had told himself that the first day was safely over, that Uzi was taking care of Yuval personally, that he had the finest apparatus available, that there was only one more dive to go, and that tomorrow it would all be behind them and he would be able to drive home with an easy mind.

But then he saw the title "Do You Have a Regulator?" and he began to read the article below it. "There are no rules governing the examination of the tank valve and the regulator; the sole responsibility belongs to the diver," it said. He went on reading to the end of the article and decided to show it to Yuval as soon as he came out of the water. ("During the dive, immediately after the diver had executed the underwater somersaults, a fault in the air supply was discovered, necessitating an emergency haul to the surface, while I gave him buddy-breathing," reported the diving-instructor author of the article, and Michael found himself reading with intense concentration. "Observation of the underwater pressure gauge showed a drop in atmospheric pressure from 100 lbs to close to zero, during inhalation from the regulator.")

Michael Ohayon looked at his watch: the practice session was due to end in fifteen minutes. He stood up and approached the sea. The Diving Club was crowded. No father had ever abandoned his son to his fate like this, he thought in a panic, and then he saw the figure in the black rubber suit being carried from the boat by two people and laid on the beach.

The first thought, of Yuval, was immediately dismissed, because the youngster removing the diving mask from the supine figure was not Guy, the diving instructor who had gone out with Yuval, but Motti, to whom he had been introduced the previous evening. With him was a woman in a diving suit, one of the students in the course, Michael thought. From where he was standing he was unable to see the expressions on their faces, but something in their movements, as they bent over the figure in the diving suit lying on the sand, proclaimed catastrophe.

The premonition of disaster immediately turned into a certainty when he saw Motti rapidly pulling out his knife and ripping open the recumbent figure's diving suit. The woman ran in the direction of the office, a small stone building on the beach not far from where Michael had been lying.

Motti began mouth-to-mouth resuscitation, and Michael couldn't take his eyes off the spectacle. Without knowing how he got there, he found himself standing next to them, waiting for the chest to rise and fall. But nothing happened. Together with Motti, Michael counted the breaths to himself.

It was a young man. His face was pink and swollen.

Superintendent Ohayon, who had seen a lot of corpses during the course of his career, still hoped that one day he would achieve the callousness of the police investigators and private detectives on television. Every time, he was astonished anew, always after the event, by his feeling faint, by the nausea, the anxiety, and sometimes the pity too, that he felt in the presence of a corpse, precisely when scientific detachment and attention to detail were called for. Nothing at all would be demanded of him here, he consoled himself when he realized that all the attempts at resuscitation would be unavailing.

The woman came running back with a young man who held a doctor's bag. Michael drew closer, silencing the inner voices reminding him that he was on holiday and that it was none of his business.

People began to gather around the diver lying on the sand. The doctor freed the body from the buoyancy compensator, laid the rubber mask on the ground, ripped off the diving suit, and set to work.

Now Michael could see the neck, swollen and bloated as the ankles of old women carrying baskets from the market. The doctor, with swift, sure movements, touched the neck with his finger and let go, pressed again and let go. By now Uzi was standing next to him, and he cried out in a panic-stricken voice: "Let's get him into a recompression chamber," and the doctor, without looking at him, shook his head and said: "It won't help. You need a big recompression chamber, where he can be given artificial respiration as well. Look how dilated his pupils are, look at his neck—subcutaneous emphysema has already set in, I'm sure that all the inner organs are ruptured."

And to his horror, Michael saw a thin line of blood breaking from the corners of the blue lips and trickling down the chin, and afterward he heard, through rising waves of nausea, the doctor saying something about inserting an intratracheal tube. "I doubt if it'll help, but what can we lose?" he said as he deftly inserted the tube into the windpipe, and Michael—like Yuval, who in his childhood had been obscurely attracted precisely to the things that frightened him most—moved up closer and saw the dilated pupils clearly, and he saw the trickle of blood too, clearly, and the cut the doctor had made to insert the tube: he saw everything, and it was all new to him.

He had never seen the dead body of a diver before, he said to himself, and tried to overcome the nausea by means of the "scientific mechanism" a pathologist had once described, which dissociated the humanity from the dead body and made it possible to "get on with the job." That's what the pathologist had said the first time Michael, then an inspector in the police force, had watched a postmortem being performed. But his nausea increased: the diver's body was wet and bloated, the skin looked as if it had been replaced by some spongy material, and the pink face—a surprising color for a dead man's face, thought Michael—was turning blue. Finally the doctor knelt down next to the young man's head and with an effort closed his eyelids. Then he wiped the sand off his hands and put the instruments back in his bag.

All this time, Uzi stood in helpless silence. When the mobile intensive care unit arrived, he shook himself and helped to carry the water-saturated body into the vehicle on a stretcher.

The doctor in the mobile unit exchanged a few words with the other doctor, and Michael looked alternately at the deep blue-water and at his watch, while pricking up his ears, out of habit, to hear the conversation taking place behind the open ambulance doors. "I don't know what to say to you—he was completely pink; you can still see the redness in the mucous membrane of the mouth. . . . I don't know, it looks like carbon monoxide poisoning to me; but maybe I'm wrong. You'd better check it out."

Michael heard the answer without taking it in, except for the last sentence: "We'll have to check and see." The professional terminology, as usual, meant nothing to him.

The ambulance doors closed, and the siren began to wail with a noise that startled everyone on the beach, as if such sounds belonged only to a main street in a busy town. Michael shuddered, and he asked Uzi, who was standing and kicking at the sand, what had happened.

It had been twenty years since he had last seen Uzi Rimon. The director of the Diving Club had been his classmate at school, and his future had been forecast by their teachers in the grimmest terms. Despite all the years that had passed, Uzi had not lost the boyish, enthusiastic expression Michael well remembered from their school days, when he, Michael, had been a boarder, while Uzi had been what they called a "Jerusalemite," attending school during class hours—not with any great regularity—and then returning home. Michael was often invited there, and to this day he remembered the awe that had overwhelmed him when he first met Uzi's parents: his father was a famous painter, with people coming from all over to worship at his shrine, and his paintings of the sea hung in all the museums in Israel as well as in the finest ones abroad. Uzi himself treated his father with a mixture of distant reverence and tactful compassion, the meaning of which Michael did not then understand.

The mother was much younger than her husband, and she often referred to the fact that she was only eighteen years old when Uzi was born. She welcomed with undisguised delight the friends Uzi brought home and involved herself in her son's social life to a surprising degree.

At the beginning Michael was invited there on Saturday afternoons, to a ritual of coffee and store-bought cake. Uzi's father would sit behind a vast desk in the living room, while his mother reclined on the red-upholstered sofa along the wood-paneled wall opposite the desk. She reminded Michael of a young Roman matron.

The atmosphere was exceptionally cultured. The walls were lined with a fine library in four languages, in all of which Uzi's father was fluent, as his mother never failed to mention. On the shelves behind the desk stood big artbooks, which Michael longed to look at.

There was always music too, music which was unfamiliar to Michael, and it was in this room that he was first overcome by miserable embarrassment at his ignorance, when Uzi's father looked at him in disbelief, in astonishment, and asked: "You really don't know that? At your age?" after he had hesitantly asked what the music was that was playing in the background.

To this day he couldn't hear Tchaikovsky's *Swan Lake* without that old embarrassment flooding him again.

The conversation was always discreetly directed by Uzi's mother. She would draw out her husband, who would finally respond by producing reminiscences about his European childhood and his travels around the world. Both parents' reminiscences contained stories about poverty told in a lighthearted, humorous vein. Michael Ohayon, who was then Yuval's present age, would return from those visits charged with contradictory feelings: thrilled by the intimate, personal contact with a new world, so different from the world in which he had grown up, and with these two people—the great artist, who was revealed as a man of almost childish innocence, completely lacking in self-importance, shy and at the same time friendly; and his wife, who gave off signals of frank sexuality and aroused feelings of discomfiture and attraction in him.

Today it all had faded. The tempestuous emotions of those days had turned into touching memories. But then! What fierce envy Uzi's home had aroused in him, and what incomprehension at the outbursts of his friend's inexhaustible rage against his parents, at how Uzi could come from a home like that and be so alienated from it.

How baffled he had been by Uzi's tense and angry attitude to his mother, an attitude Michael was incapable of understanding. On the rare occasions when his own mother came to parent-teacher meetings, he was aware of her awkwardness, of the way she gazed in silence at his teachers, of the poor Hebrew in which she replied when she was asked a direct question, lost and in need of a translation, straightening the scarf tied round her hair, smiling her warm smile. He, who felt shame, and helpless anger at himself for being ashamed, and at his teachers and friends for witnessing his shame, thought then that if only he could have brought Uzi's mother to meet his teachers, or his eminent father, his life would have been completely different.

It was years before he could correctly interpret the tensions to which Uzi was subject, the heavy burden of his famous father, the loathing he felt for his mother and the love with which he could not cope, the drive to destroy their expectations and the inability to conform. In the end, reflected Michael, holding his towel as Uzi mumbled something about being in shock—Michael himself felt detached from everything that was happening—in the end Uzi had become, in his own way, a conformist. For years now he had been living in Eilat, managing the Diving Club. He had become an expert on marine life in the Red Sea, even though he had never taken the trouble to study anything formally.

It was true that he went from one woman to another—Michael had met the latest of them the day before—but even in this he followed a pattern. The women in his life maintained friendly and concerned relations with him even after they parted, and it was always they who broke off the connection. Noa, his second wife, the one who had given birth to their only son, had once taken the trouble to come to Jerusalem and seek Michael out. Uzi had told her so much about him, she said apologetically, and she had never understood why they stopped seeing each other. And thus, to his surprise, he learned that Uzi still thought about him. Until the meeting with Uzi's second wife, Michael thought that his old friend had uprooted him from his consciousness, felt nothing for him but shame and anger. In the little café where he sat with Noa, he heard for the first time that Uzi spoke of him with great feeling, and she, for her part, couldn't understand "why you haven't met over all these years, as if there's some terrible secret between you. It's so mysterious!" Michael said nothing and offered her his most charming smile, and she was, indeed, charmed and stopped pestering him with questions.

He still remembered, with painful clarity, the day when Uzi discovered—quite by chance, of course—the fact that his mother, who was then younger than they were today, not quite forty, had been the answer to Michael's prayers for an older, experienced woman to come and, in the words of the little books he read in secret, "rescue him from the torments of his virginity."

Even at the meeting with Noa, fifteen years after what he called "the carpet scene," Michael couldn't smile at the memory of Uzi's face as he stood paralyzed in the doorway of the big room, looking down at the heavy carpet and at his best friend and his mother, and slamming the door behind him without uttering a word.

Even though Michael had repeatedly explained to himself then that he couldn't possibly have known that Uzi—who had gone off to the western Galilee after their final exams, to relax and "let his hair down" at the beach at Ahziv—would come back the same day, even though he consoled himself with the thought that Uzi had no way of knowing that the affair had been going on for a year and a half, he couldn't look him in the eyes again.

It was only after the meeting with Noa, who complained to him about Uzi's reserve, about the fact that it was impossible to have a warm, open relationship with him, that he was barricaded inside his own world of fish and marine vegetation, cut off from people—only then did Michael think that it might be possible for him to meet Uzi again one day.

He heard the pleased surprise in his old friend's voice when, with trembling fingers, he had called the Diving Club in Eilat the week before, five full years after the conversation with Noa in the Jerusalem café. They spent the first evening in laughter, bringing each other up-to-date. Uzi's parents were scarcely mentioned. Of his father's death Michael had heard ten years before, a slow, agonizing death from cancer. He had heard too, from a former classmate, that his wife had cared for him devotedly, that she had remarried, and that she had gone to live in Paris.

Uzi himself did not mention his mother, only his father's death, to which he referred in passing, and Michael, who was longing to bring up the subject and had imagined, almost in detail, how they would discuss it and explain it and resolve everything between them, felt profoundly disappointed. Uzi avoided emotional subjects, and all Michael's attempts in this direction were rebuffed with jokes, which were usually pointless. Even the bottle of wine they polished off with the delicious meal Uzi had cooked for them didn't help.

For the first time, Michael noticed the resemblance between Uzi's features and those of his mother—the shape of the lips, the slanting eyes—and he even hoped to recapture that marvelous smell of hers, which he had sought ever since in every woman he met, and found finally in Maya. But Uzi's smell was the smell of the sea.

Michael couldn't deny the relief he felt, after the tension and initial joy of the reunion, when he noticed that Uzi had put on weight and even begun to go bald. There was something consoling about it. Time had not spared even this eternal youth, despite his vigorous way of life, despite his tan, despite the luxuriant beard and the eyes that were almost always laughing. The eyes that were now veiled with panic.

"What happened?" Michael repeated his question, and Uzi explained that that was precisely the problem, he didn't know what had happened, and he pointed to the diving apparatus lying on the beach. "They took the air tanks," he said. "We'll see; maybe there was a leak. I asked him routinely before the dive, and he said he checked the equipment two months ago. I don't know what happened, but he wasn't alone; he was with an instructor. We'll have to wait for the results of the examination. Things like this are really rough on one. Now I'm waiting for everyone to come out. Here comes your kid."

And Michael remained where he was and watched his son sit down on the sand a little way off and begin removing his mask, his regulator, his flippers, and finally his black diving suit, listening attentively all the while to his instructor, Guy, who was standing next to him and rapidly taking off his gear, talking and gesturing vigorously with his hands. Now, seeing his son alive and alert, Michael realized just how frightened he had been.

"Who *was* the fellow who drowned?" he asked Uzi, and Uzi replied distractedly: "Some guy from Jerusalem, but not originally. His name's Iddo Dudai, a bit serious but okay, someone who always wanted to do it but didn't have the dough. He began the course a year ago, but he got stuck for money; one of those university types. I'm still hoping he'll come out of it. I'm waiting for them to call me; the instructor went with him. What can I tell you—he's got a wife and a little girl. Well, maybe he'll pull out of it," he said in a weak voice. "It's not our equipment; he got it from someone as a present when he began the course, I don't know who. I don't know anything about the tanks either. Maybe there was a leak."

"And maybe there was something wrong with the regulator," said Michael, seeing in his mind's eye the article in the magazine that he held folded in his hand, and Uzi looked at him appraisingly and asked: "Since when have you become an expert on diving apparatus? Are you planning to specialize in that, too, now?" Michael handed him the magazine, and suddenly he remembered, vividly, the rage that would flare up in Uzi when they were studying together for their final exams, especially the history exam; and thick, tedious books they had to read would inspire in his friend a mighty desire to sleep in the middle of the first book, while he, Michael, had already read all five of the texts for the second time.

Uzi began telling Guy the details of the accident, and Yuval listened tensely. Guy, a red-haired young man, became increasingly upset. His round freckles grew more and more pronounced as his face grew paler.

Michael scrutinized Yuval's face, which, at first radiant with the thrilling experience of the dive, was becoming grave, and as words like "atmospheric pressure" and "diaphragms" began to fly around them, all Michael could think of was whether Yuval would forgo the last dive of the weekend. It was hot and he was longing for a dip in the deep-blue water, but he knew that in the circumstances it would look like a demonstration of indifference to what had happened, like something indecent.

The question of the last dive was settled when Uzi announced that there would be no more diving this day and assembled the instructors—four tanned young men who looked as if someone had cast them in bronze in their bathing trunks, as if they had never worn anything else in their lives—and accompanied them to the office, where he sat next to the telephone, biting his nails in a way that flooded Michael with a wave of acute longing for the boy he had once been, for his mother and father, and even for Tchaikovsky's *Swan Lake* and the whole experience of that first encounter with European culture, which had been so powerfully transmitted to him through the delicate filter of Becky Pomerantz, Uzi's mother.

They sat in the office, waiting for the telephone to ring. Uzi refused to budge, and Michael waited with him. The two of them smoked in silence, the stubs mounted in the ashtray, and at four o'clock the phone finally rang. Uzi let it ring twice and coughed deeply before he picked up the receiver. Michael heard the words "Yes, I understand" and then pricked up his ears as Uzi said: "How do you want me to handle it?" and after that: "I don't mind going up there myself. I feel responsible, anyway." Finally he replaced the receiver and asked with downcast eyes if he could drive back to Jerusalem with Michael that day, "actually, now, if you wouldn't mind cutting your holiday short," and Michael went to look for Yuval, who didn't protest and, on the way to collect their belongings from Uzi's flat, said to his father: "I spoke to him a bit and he seemed a really okay guy, that Iddo. He told me he taught literature at the university." Apparently it came as a surprise to him that anyone who taught literature could be interested in a sport like diving.

After Michael let Yuval off outside his flat, he offered to accompany Uzi to Ruth Dudai's address, to inform her of her husband's death in a diving accident, "in unclear circumstances," as he would say in the living room of the Ramat Eshkol apartment, with the Saturday evening television news as accompaniment, to the woman with big brown eyes that stared at them in horror from behind round spectacles.

Uzi, in the briefest of shorts, with "biblical" sandals on his feet and a wild, unkempt beard, looked like a desert creature transplanted to a zoo, as if he was completely out of his element and didn't know what to do with his body.

So, once again, Michael Ohayon found himself playing a role to which he was accustomed, and he broke the news.

She didn't cry, the plump little woman who tightened her hands on the flimsy stuff of the shift she was wearing. Because of the heavy khamsin that had descended on Jerusalem a week before and had still not relaxed its grip, the windows, which overlooked the street, were wide open, and the noise of the cars and buses driving past on Eshkol Boulevard sounded as if they were coming from inside the apartment. The sound of the television set, which nobody had thought to switch off, merged with the din from the street and the voices coming from the televisions in the apartments surrounding them.

"What's going to happen now?" asked Ruth Dudai in a dreamy voice, and Michael recognized the signs of shock. Quietly, slowly, he began to explain to her that they would have to wait for the results of the postmortem examination in order to discover the cause of the accident, and only then would it be possible to make the funeral arrangements. "It will be necessary for someone to identify him," he said carefully, "and you should have someone close to be with you now." And then he asked gently if she had any family. "Only my father and his wife, and they're in London now, and someone will have to tell Iddo's parents—oh, God!" And only then, it seemed, did the news sink in, and she burst into tears.

Uzi stood there in horrified embarrassment, and Michael made her sit down in the only armchair in the room and handed her a glass of water that he had quickly brought from the kitchen. As she sipped the water, he asked her who could be with her now, immediately, and she said "Shaul Tirosh" and gave Michael the telephone number, which he made haste to dial.

There was no reply from the home of the man of whom even Uzi, who was blatantly uninterested in literature, had heard. Michael remembered him clearly from his university days; he had taken some classes with him when he was studying for his B.A. As he dialed the number, he conjured up the image of the dark suit, the carnation in the buttonhole, and especially the yearning looks of the female students. Discreetly he asked if Tirosh was a member of the family. "No," said Ruth, and her ponytail swayed as she shook her head, "but he's close to Iddo. He was Iddo's supervisor for his doctorate, and I thought. . . " She burst into tears again. "We can't tell Iddo's parents over the phone; they're old and sick, and his father's recovering from a heart attack, and his brother's traveling in South America, and I don't know what to do."

Michael leafed mechanically through the telephone book lying next to the phone and asked again whether there was anyone she would like to have with her now. "Perhaps a close woman friend?" he asked. In the end she gave a name, Michael dialed the number, and the woman on the other end promised, in a shocked voice, to come right away. After that he called Eli Bahar, the inspector he had been working with for years, gave him the information he had extracted from Ruth Dudai, who between bursts of crying had answered all his questions in a matter-of-fact way, and asked him to notify Iddo's parents, "with a doctor; they're old and there's a heart problem."

Afterward Ruth Dudai asked them to inform the secretary of the Literature Department, Adina Lipkin, which Michael did, and finally, when a forceful young woman called Rina arrived, embraced Ruth—who remained frozen in Rina's arms—with a dramatic expression on her face, patted her on the shoulder, and announced: "I'm going to put the kettle on," they left. Outside, Michael brushed aside Uzi's thanks aside impatiently, never imagining for a moment that this was not the end of the affair.

3

The telephone rang next to Ruchama's ear with a shrill clamor. She hastened to pick up the receiver, still almost in her sleep. Then she noticed that Tuvia was not in bed and assumed that he had fallen asleep on the sofa in his study, as he frequently did. She heard a trembling, hysterical voice at the other end of the line. Ruchama saw that it was not yet half past seven in the morning. "Hello," said Adina Lipkin again, this time in a firmer voice, and Ruchama replied with a weary "Yes?"

"Mrs. Shai?" inquired Adina, and Ruchama envisioned the rigid waves of the department secretary's hair and her plump hands stirring cucumber into a container of yogurt.

"Yes," said Ruchama. She kept her relations with Adina on a strictly official level, never exchanging recipes or health information or personal experiences with her, with the result that Adina never dared to call her by her first name.

"This is Adina Lipkin, the department secretary," said Adina, as she had said to Ruchama almost every morning for the past ten years. Ruchama had never done anything to break the familiar pattern.

"Yes," she said, with businesslike brevity, hoping her tone would prevent any attempt at a conversation.

"I wanted to speak to Dr. Shai," said Adina with a certain despair.

"He's sleeping," said Ruchama, and waited for the usual explanation.

"Ah," said Adina, and sure enough began to explain that it was convenient for her to call at this early hour since she had a lot of work waiting for her during the day, "and later on, you know, all the lines are busy." Ruchama said nothing.

"Perhaps you can help me yourself?" and Adina went on without waiting for a reply. "I'm actually looking for Professor Tirosh. I've phoned and phoned, and there's been no answer at his house since yesterday. I need him urgently, and I thought that perhaps you might be able to help me by telling me where I can find him."

"No," said Ruchama. Her head began to clear, and at the same time she felt the oppressive uneasiness of the past few days returning. When Adina Lipkin said that something was "urgent," as Ruchama knew only too well, it predictably meant that it could, and usually did, wait for weeks.

"All right. Thank you, anyway. I'm sorry to have bothered you. I only thought that perhaps Dr. Shai would be able to tell me where I could find him. In any case, if Dr. Shai's coming in today, and it seems to me that he is, would you please ask him to contact me first?"

"Yes," said Ruchama and she put down the phone.

Adina couldn't have known that ever since the departmental seminar, ever since Wednesday night, Ruchama's world had collapsed around her. Even Shaul Tirosh, who had broken with her without any warning on Thursday, the day after the seminar, couldn't have known. He had hardly been conscious of her then. There was a strange fire burning in his eyes as he examined his well-manicured nails and then looked at her, his head on one side, and, in a lighthearted tone that contradicted the fire in his eyes, said that she must have noticed that for some time now the relationship between them had lost its flavor and become routine, the kind of routine he had been trying to avoid all his life. "That's the way it goes," he concluded. "In the words of the poet: at first it's 'I loved you more than I could say,' and in the end it's 'Then we came to town and Havazeleth pinned me down,' if you understand what I mean."

Ruchama didn't understand, but she thought of Ruth Dudai. She didn't know what poet he was quoting; she had no idea of the process described by the poem. Her incomprehension was apparently evident on her face, and in response Tirosh indicated the book by David Avidan that was lying on his desk and, drawing her attention to the poem "Personal Problems," said that reading poetry could be very helpful in one's life and that she ought to try it.

Ruchama had often, in dread, imagined their parting. But she had never guessed that it would hurt so much, never envisaged, despite all she had been told, despite all the signs, how cruel he could be. "What have I done?" she wanted to ask, but she choked back the question when she saw him resume examining his fingernails and sensed that her presence was superfluous.

She counted to herself the days that had passed since then: "Thursday, Friday, Saturday, Sunday—and Sunday's only beginning."

Since Thursday afternoon she had been in bed. Tuvia had informed the hospital that she was sick and had taken care of her with distant concern. Behind the familiar domestic gestures she was aware of a new energy, of something she had never sensed in him before. Something that spoke of rage and despair.

Shaul's name was not mentioned between them. Tuvia went out and stayed away for hours on end. She didn't know where he was. On Friday he went to a department meeting at eight in the morning and came home late at night.

She had spent the days since Shaul's farewell ceremony in continuous sleep, interrupted only by drinks of water and trips to the bathroom. When she awoke for a moment, the feeling of loss would return to torture her with such intensity that she felt as if her body could not bear the separation. The pleasure she had known since meeting Shaul, the physical pleasure, had become an addiction, and she did not know how she would overcome it.

When Tuvia urged her absentmindedly to eat something, she shook her head. It was hard for her to talk, and Tuvia did not try to draw her out.

For once, Ruchama wanted him to break through the wall, to help her. And precisely now, of all times, she felt that he was relieved by her withdrawal, her lack of interest in his activities. He had spent the whole of Saturday in his study. Now, after Adina's phone call, she went there for the first time since Friday and found him lying on the sofa with his eyes open, staring at the ceiling. On the threadbare carpet at his feet lay scattered all the volumes of Tirosh's poetry.

Ruchama began to wonder if Tuvia was actively participating in her intimate grief at no longer having a place in Tirosh's life.

She put the thought into unspoken words; surely Shaul couldn't have told him; surely he wouldn't have dared. Surely Tuvia couldn't possibly know. She looked at him. His eyes went on staring at the ceiling and then slowly turned to her. They terrified her. There was something lifeless in them. Disengaged.

"That was Adina," she said quietly. Of all the words in the world, these seemed the safest.

"What Adina?" asked Tuvia, and then she saw that he had disconnected the telephone on his desk.

"Adina. On the phone, looking for Shaul," said Ruchama uncertainly.

"Why's she looking for him here?" asked Tuvia.

"I don't know. She hasn't been able to find him since yesterday. Has he gone somewhere out of town?"

"I don't know," said Tuvia, and he sat up.

"What's wrong?" asked Ruchama, and got no answer. "Anyway, she said you should phone her before you go in. She said you were supposed to be there today. Have you got a class?"

"It's the last big class of the year," said Tuvia, his voice wearier than usual. "This is the last week of the year. I've only got two more seminars to give."

"Good. Then talk to Adina. I think I'll go back to work today."

Tuvia didn't react. He went on staring absently.

Ruchama looked at him in growing panic. He must have told him; there was no other explanation.

Tuvia shook himself and straightened his legs. The little room was crammed with books—on the shelves lining the walls, on the desk, on the floor. Some were open, others had bits of paper sticking out of them. Every book in the room looked as if it had been handled repeatedly. "Felt books—they're always being felt," Tirosh had once said affectionately to Tuvia.

Ruchama saw that he had slept in his clothes, and there was a sour smell in the air of the room. His face was pale and strained when he said: "All right, then, I'll phone her. Otherwise she'll be after me all day. I really haven't the strength to talk to her."

The moment the telephone next to Tuvia's sagging white sofa was plugged in, it began to ring deafeningly. Tuvia lifted the receiver and held it far from his ear. His faded, thinning hair was rumpled, and his scalp was exposed. The sight revolted her.

At the other end, a man's voice, a voice Ruchama knew, could be clearly be heard, shouting into the phone. Standing next to the door, she made out almost every word.

"Where is Tirosh?" shrieked Aharonovitz, and, without waiting for an answer: "Have you spoken with Adina this morning?"

Tuvia said in a whisper that he had not yet spoken to anyone.

"So you know nothing of what has occurred?" shouted Aharonovitz.

His voice anxious, Tuvia asked what had happened. He pressed the receiver to his ear, and the small veins on his face turned blue as he listened in silence to what was being said at the other end of the line. "Okay. Tell her I'll be there right away," he said, and slammed down the receiver.

Suddenly he looked at Ruchama, as if for the very first time in his life. He looked at her in wonder, with a remoteness she had never seen in his eyes before, and said: "Iddo Dudai has been killed in a scuba-diving accident."

Ruchama stared at him uncomprehendingly.

"Yes. He was taking a diving course and he had to complete two more dives to get his diploma. He went down to Eilat the day before yesterday, right after the department meeting. It happened yesterday—I don't know the details. If anyone wants me, say I'm at the secretary's office. She's been trying to get hold of Shaul since last night."

"Who? Who's been trying to get hold of him?" asked Ruchama with a feeling of obscure dread.

"Ruth Dudai notified Adina, in the end, and Adina tried to reach him last night, from home, but he wasn't there." Tuvia began feverishly searching for his car keys, and finally he found them under the typescript of the first chapter of Iddo Dudai's doctoral thesis. He shuddered, muttered something about irony, and left the house.

For a while, Ruchama remained standing where she was, and then she sat down on the sofa. She hadn't taken off the long T-shirt that served her as a nightgown since Thursday. She looked mechanically at her exposed, bony knees. Slowly and dreamily, as if she had been sedated, she placed her hands on her knees and stared at the short, slender fingers. "A child's hand," Shaul would sometimes say and kiss the wart that habitual sucking had left on her thumb. Ruchama now stuck her thumb in her mouth. The old sweet, soothing taste had disappeared. Then she began to look around her, as if she were in a strange place.

Gradually she became aware, at one end of the sofa, of the titles of Shaul Tirosh's poetry books: *The Sweet Poison of the Honeysuckle, A Stubborn Nettle, Necessary Poems.*

The titles rang meaninglessly in her ears. The colors of the books' covers, two of which had been illustrated by Yaakov Gafni, Tirosh's favorite painter, seemed unbearably bright.

Without knowing why, she began to collect the books into one pile. When she knelt down, she saw another book, not by Tirosh, hidden under the edge of the cushion. *Poems of a Gray War* was the title, with the words "by Anatoly Ferber" underneath it and, at the bottom of the cover: "edited and with an introduction by Shaul Tirosh."

He's told him: the thought flashed through her mind. Shaul had told him everything. Confessed. And Tuvia was considering whether to break off relations with him. And perhaps also with her. Ruchama stood up. Her knees were dusty. It was months since Tuvia had cleaned the room. There were woolly balls of dust in the corners and next to the desk. Absentmindedly she began gathering them into one big ball.

The telephone startled her. At first she didn't pick it up; it went on ringing persistently, stopped, and then began again, as if it intended to go on ringing forever. Finally she picked up the receiver, which was still damp and sticky from Tuvia's hands, always sweaty.

"How are you feeling, Ruchamaleh?" asked Tzipporah with motherly concern.

"Better," said Ruchama, and she pulled down the hem of her T-shirt, sank to her knees, and began collecting a new ball of dust in her free hand. In her imagination she saw the black telephone, the admissions office in Shaarei Tzedek Hospital, Tzipporah's hand polishing the Formica countertop as she spoke.

"Do you still have a fever?" she inquired, and Ruchama saw the heavy body, the swollen feet, the ankles blue with the effort of bearing the body ("Varicose veins, from the first time I gave birth, that's what I got from them," said Tzipporah once, at the time her son brought his girlfriend home and announced his intention to marry her. "What's his hurry, he's only twenty-three years old, and getting married already. What good will it do him? What good did it do me?"), and replied that no, she didn't have a fever.

"Are you taking anything? Aspirin—listen to me—aspirin and lemon tea and a lot of chicken soup," said Tzipporah, and sniffed. Ruchama said nothing. She wasn't going back to work today, she decided. She was staying in bed.

"Well, I don't want to disturb you any longer. Go back to bed, that's the most important thing, not to get up too soon; you can't imagine the complications that can come of it. What we've seen here in the past few days! Only yesterday a young girl came in, hardly more than a child, a soldier, I don't know what they're thinking of there in the army."

And Ruchama began paging through the book of poems by Anatoly Ferber, "one of the outstanding dissidents in the Soviet Union since the Stalin era," as Shaul Tirosh wrote in his introduction. "Born in Israel, then Palestine, in 1930, he emigrated to Moscow with his mother at the age of sixteen, and died in 1955, under unclear circumstances, in a labor camp in the town of Perm, in the Ural Mountains," she read, and suddenly she heard Shaul Tirosh's voice thundering behind Tzipporah's, as if he were reading the introduction aloud to her.

The alarm that seized her galvanized her into saying, in a weak voice that miraculously penetrated the stream of Tzipporah's words: "I'm tired; we'll talk at work tomorrow. Goodbye for now, Tzipporah." Then, gently, she replaced the receiver, let the big ball of dust fall from her hands, and lay down on her back, staring at the ceiling. Finally she closed her eyes, and when she awoke, it was three o'clock in the afternoon.

The house was quiet, the windows were closed, there was a smell of dust in her nostrils. Tuvia was nowhere to be seen. Neither in the kitchen, the shower, the bedroom, nor the little living room, sparsely furnished with items they had brought with them from the kibbutz, which, until she met Shaul Tirosh, had looked elegant enough to her. Suddenly she remembered that Iddo Dudai had been killed; Tuvia had said so before he went out. The phrase "Iddo Dudai has been killed" echoed in her mind, but it didn't melt the block of ice that enclosed it. Later she remembered the words "in a scuba-diving accident" and she gripped her throat tightly as she saw the deep-blue water before her eyes and thought of the lack of air. She was standing in the kitchen, with the bread knife in her other hand, but she didn't have the strength to slice the hard, stale bread. Tuvia hadn't shopped. She looked at the big clock on the wall, a present from Tuvia's parents. It was ten to four, and she thought that after Shaul's confession, perhaps Tuvia wasn't ever coming back. This thought no longer caused her any anxiety. Again she fingered her throat. Something else, not Tuvia's absence, perturbed her. She didn't know what it was; she only felt that it was hard for her to breathe, and she sat down on a vinyl chair. She buried her face in her arms, resting on the kitchen table, a Formica surface covered with dust, and struggled against an image of Shaul Tirosh's face, with the mocking smile growing ever more twisted until the mouth gaped in a scream and turned into the dead face of Iddo Dudai.

4

The Literature Department faculty came into the secretary's office, one after the other, all morning, and Racheli could tell by their faces whether they had heard the news or not. Tuvia Shai's face gave her gooseflesh. His watery eyes were bloodshot, as if he had spent the night on the town, but even Racheli, the department secretary's assistant, knew that Dr. Shai did not spend his nights on the town. His bursting through the door, the haunted, desperate look in his darting eyes, and the broken voice in which he asked if they had heard any more details, confused Racheli.

This quiet man, normally so unassuming as to be boring, now seemed exposed, as if he were naked. His rumpled clothes appeared to have been slept in, a gray stubble covered his cheeks, his thin hair cried out for a comb. Adina Lipkin registered his appearance but refrained from comment—after all, she would probably have said, a tragedy had taken place.

It wasn't her sense of humor that saved her, said Racheli to Dovik, who had found her the job, when he marveled at the fact that she had stuck it out for so long. "Ten months! In the past two years Adina's had five assistants. Nobody can stand it," said Dovik, who worked in the university's personnel department.

A sense of humor wasn't enough to cope with Adina Lipkin's compulsiveness for almost a year. Greater ironists than herself, argued Racheli passionately, had broken down in the office and screamed with rage the moment they left it. "It was only scientific curiosity, the fact that I got permission to take part in the psychopathology tutorial, my seminar paper on the compulsive personality, that made it possible for me to put up with her," she explained.

Racheli, a third-year psychology undergraduate, continued apologetically: "And it's a convenient job, really: I'm free to attend classes. In any case, she doesn't like anybody else to be in the office during consulting hours. But what I really can't stand is the pitying looks of the other secretaries on campus. Whenever I go into some office and say that she sent me, people panic and get rid of me as fast as they can, and afterward they look at me as if I'm returning to some gulag."

Actually, Racheli noted to herself in an attempt to remain detached from the catastrophe, Adina's functioning today had been exemplary. At eight o'clock in the morning she had already pinned up a prominent notice: DUE TO UNEXPECTED CIRCUMSTANCES THERE WILL BE NO CONSULTING HOUR TODAY. Then she locked the door. Racheli sat behind her desk in one of the five corners of the office with a pile of green files—which had been there since Friday—in front of her. This morning she was supposed to continue erasing the names of the courses and their computer codes, which Adina always recorded in pencil at the beginning of the year, and rewrite them in ink. Needless to say, Adina regarded the computer as an appliance introduced for the express purpose of making her life difficult. ("At the beginning of the year they haven't really made up their minds, and they change courses, and I write it all down with a pencil, so as not to have to spoil the page. But later on, if they comply with the requirements and hand in their papers, I correct it in ink, because otherwise it fades, the pencil, that is, and it's true that it doubles the work, but this way the file stays clean, which you won't find in other places I could mention." A

meaningful glance at the window, overlooking other university buildings, accompanied the explanation of the task, and Racheli sat down
and addressed herself to the files.)

The green covers had greeted her this morning when she entered
the room. Adina was already there, naturally enough; she always
arrived at seven. Her eyes were red, and her desk was empty, all the
papers cleared away. She hastened to inform Racheli of the news and
added: "I won't be able to get any work done today. I never closed my
eyes all night. What a loss! Such a promising young man!" Racheli
warned herself not to condemn Adina for her clichés. She had to
accept things as they were and hold her tongue.

She sat at her desk and admitted to herself that although she had
liked Iddo Dudai and was shocked by his death, the news had not
upset her to the extent of incapacitating her for work. After all, she
had only met him in the department office, and she had never spoken
to him about anything that wasn't connected to her work there. She
assumed a diligent look, an effort that turned out to be redundant,
since Adina didn't even look her way.

The department secretary herself did not succeed in sitting still for
a minute. Every time she sat down, it was only to jump up from her
chair again. Her desk stood to the left of the only window in the
room, opposite the door, at which, and every couple of minutes,
someone knocked. Three students who risked everything and came in,
one after the other, to inquire about something were greeted initially
by the usual lecture: "First of all, this isn't the consulting hour, please
come during the consulting hour, what have we got a consulting hour
for?" followed by the special addendum: "Apart from which, there
won't be any consulting hour today, as it says right here on the door."

The facial expression of the last student sent away empty-handed
remained etched in Racheli's mind as that of someone confronted by
bureacratic whims presented as *force majeure*, one who knows he has
been tricked and should protest but remains helpless in the face of
ostensibly logical arguments. The departmental secretary always made
her actions seem logical and always spoke politely to her victims.

When it came to the junior members of the faculty, to the teaching assistants, the arguments took on a more personal note: "I'll have to ask you to wait outside until I finish talking on the phone. I can't talk and think about you and your problems at the same time. No. You can't sit down and wait inside; it makes me nervous."

She caused the most eminent professors to assume an expression of Christian humility before they even crossed the threshold. When she saw them in the doorway her voice would grow shriller, her eyes become panic-stricken, and a ritual would be enacted: First she ostentatiously cleared her desk (there was always a neat pile of papers and files on the corner, which she had every intention of tackling "as soon as they let me get on with my work"). Then she would place her soft hands on the desk in front of her and raise her eyes, as if to say: Here I am, at your disposal; all I want in the world is to attend to your needs. But nobody was taken in by this performance: the hidden message shrieked through the apparent one: Get out—you're disrupting my routine.

Racheli would be reminded then of her aunt Tzesha: of the plastic sheets spread over her living room furniture, of the two children forced to spend most of their time outside the house, so as not to ruin or dirty anything inside it. Sometimes Racheli would find herself letting out an actual sigh of relief when the tension relaxed with the departure from the office of an eminent professor.

The previous week, Aharonovitz had stood in the doorway like a timid student and hesitantly asked if he could trouble her, and at that moment, Racheli decided on the subject of her seminar paper: "The Effects of a Compulsive Personality on the Behavior of Colleagues in the Workplace." This morning, trying to predict how the department secretary would react to the unusual circumstances, she had assumed that Adina would cling to her daily routine even more desperately than usual; but she was wrong.

Adina's expression conveyed an abandonment of any attempt at normal functioning. She must be exceedingly upset by the news, thought Racheli. And after all, Iddo Dudai had enjoyed a special status in the secretary's office. He had aroused Adina's maternal feelings. He was also the only one who had listened with interest to her stories about her grandchildren, who had exchanged ideas with her about medicinal herbs, potted plants, and recipes, especially dietetic recipes. Adina had forgiven Iddo his slovenly attire and had even allowed him to stay in the room when the telephone rang.

This morning the department secretary looked as if she had resolved to be efficient, quiet, and, above all, discreet. She dealt firmly but patiently with the students who attempted to invade the office despite the notice displayed prominently on the door, and she showed them out without so much as mentioning the accident. The container of yogurt and the cucumber she customarily allowed herself until lunch she pushed into a bottom drawer with an expression of disgust, and Racheli remembered a remark Tirosh had once addressed to the room at large on catching sight of Adina's cucumber in its neatly secured plastic bag: "For twenty years I've known her, and for twenty years she's been on a diet." And then Racheli's thoughts wandered to Tirosh, whom Adina was still feverishly trying to locate. "I tried until midnight, from my house, even though I had guests, and I've been here since seven this morning, and I haven't been able to get hold of him yet." Again Racheli wondered at Adina's state of calm, which even the stormy entrance of Tuvia Shai failed to undermine. To him too, for the tenth time that morning, she gave the same explanation, speaking calmly and slowly: "We don't have any details. I'm in contact with Ruth, and his parents have been informed. The cause of death is still being investigated. They suspect there was a fault in the diving apparatus. But they're checking it. I don't know anything about the funeral arrangements; they'll let us know as soon as they can." Her expression was serious, even solemn, as if to say: You see, when something really terrible happens, I can be businesslike and efficient. And then came the obsessive question about Tirosh.

Everyone looked at Tuvia, and he said that the last time he had seen Tirosh was on Friday, when they had lunch together after the department meeting. "I think he said something about going to Tel Aviv, but I'm not sure."

Racheli, who persisted in her observation games, convinced that she was doing important scientific research, noticed even then that

Tuvia "was not himself," that he was both detached and uncharacteristically efficient, as he began speculating, in a voice louder than usual, firmer than usual, about how they might locate Tirosh. A few faculty members were already in the room when Tuvia burst in, and Racheli noticed especially his uneasy reaction when Aharonovitz, who was unusually quiet, even withdrawn, said that perhaps Adina should go into Tirosh's office and see if he hadn't left a message there.

It seemed to Racheli that they had already spent hours in the department office, a room too small to hold them all, on the sixth floor of the purple wing in the Humanities Building on Mount Scopus, one of the insane edifices housing the Hebrew University, of which Tirosh said, in an often quoted remark: "The man who designed this building should be shot, hospitalization won't help here; the only thing that will do any good is murder." Until that Sunday, it was quoted with a smile, whereas afterward it was repeated with an accompaniment of statements full of hindsight about fate and about tragic irony, a concept with which Racheli had became familiar in the secretarial office of the Literature Department.

From time to time someone left the room and returned with a cup of black coffee; from time to time the murmurs were interrupted by a hesitant knock on the door, and a student's head would peep in, see the assembled lecturers, and quickly disappear before Adina managed to get in a word about the cancellation of consulting hours.

They gathered as if by chance, the department teachers, having come to hand in examination forms, to collect seminar papers, but they all remained in the little room, bound by their shock and sorrow for Iddo. The usual tensions seemed to have vanished. Everyone liked Iddo, Racheli knew. Occasionally someone broke the silence. Sara Amir asked how Ruth was going to manage—"the baby's not even a year old"—and Dita Fuchs, who had taken off her purple hat and was now sitting on the edge of Adina's desk, because there weren't enough chairs for everybody, once more demanded to know: "What did he need it for, that diving?" On any other day Adina would have told her off for sitting on the desk, but today she heroically ignored it. Racheli looked at Dita Fuchs with interest, breathed in the scent of her perfume, and remembered the rumors that she had been Tirosh's longest love affair. Years ago, Racheli had heard, they were always at each other's side, and even when the affair was over, they remained close. Dita Fuchs's face showed lines of suffering and traces of feminine charm, a combination that produced, especially this morning, an expression of pathos that contradicted the patronizing amiability with which she treated everyone around her.

It was there, in the department office, that Dita Fuchs first heard the news. Racheli had witnessed the unrestrained weeping, she had seen the slender hand holding her throat as she repeated: "I knew it would end in catastrophe, that diving of his. Such a gifted boy! What did he need it for?" Adina had made her a cup of strong tea and even stroked her arm. Normally their relationship was one of unmitigated hatred, which was expressed by the saccharine cordiality with which they treated each other, and by the highly sophisticated bureaucratic difficulties that Adina heaped on Dr. (as she was always careful to call her) Fuchs's students. By the time Tuvia arrived, Dita Fuchs had calmed down, and when he came into the room she was sitting on the corner of Adina's desk, her hands ceaselessly smoothing invisible creases in her narrow skirt. "Where's Shaul?" she asked helplessly, and Racheli thought that they needed some kind of big daddy to "take charge of things," to make all the "arrangements." It wasn't clear to Racheli exactly what the arrangements were that had to be made, but something of the general malaise infected her, too, and clouded the lucid judgment of which she was usually so proud. It was terrible to see mature, adult people in such distress, not knowing what to do or say.

Sara Amir was the first person in the room to mention the name of Ariyeh Klein. With her famous directness, she exclaimed in a moment of silence: "What a shame that Ariyeh's not here. He would know what to do. Thank goodness he'll be back the day after tomorrow." Dita Fuchs sighed, and Adina chimed in with her automatic response to the mention of his name: "What a mensch!" repeated three times.

Racheli had yet to meet Professor Klein, who had been on sabbatical at Columbia University in New York for the whole of the academic year that was now drawing to a close. Hardly a day had passed during the ten months, from September to June, that she had been working in the department, without Adina mentioning his name. On days when a letter arrived from him, and especially when the letter referred explicitly and personally to Adina, Racheli could leave the office for a cup of coffee without any danger of being picked on for it. Adina would smile to herself as she read the letter over and over again, sometimes even reading passages aloud.

Thanks to the happy smiles that broke out on people's faces whenever his name was mentioned, Racheli had begun to admire Professor Klein in advance. "He's due back the day after tomorrow?" confirmed Aharonovitz, and he added: "In that case, he may be in time to attend the funeral." Again the oppressive silence descended on the room, and Tuvia Shai ran his fingers through his hair—a gesture that was so graceful in Tirosh and so grotesque in Tuvia, whose pink hand raked the mousy, thinning hair and left it sticking out in all directions.

Shulamith Zellermaier's heavy tread, even in her trademark padded sandals, was audible even before she entered the room. Racheli held her breath as she waited for the woman she privately called the Dinosaur to appear. Although she thought she had once read that dinosaurs were not aggressive, Racheli had always been afraid of them, even in pictures. Zellermaier terrified her, with her bulging eyes, her sharp tongue, her unrestrained outbursts, her perfectionism. Even when she lingered in the office to relate an "anecdote," as she called it, Racheli would wait tensely for the punch line and her deliverance. When the woman came in now, closed the door behind her, and contemplated her colleagues in silence, Racheli let out a sigh of relief. Shulamith Zellermaier had already heard the news and was quelled. Her head on one side, without the sarcastic half-smile, she said only: "It's terrible, just terrible." Racheli immediately stood up, to free her chair for the heavy body, which lowered itself with a sigh.

Again the door opened, and in came two teaching assistants, Tsippi Lev-Ari, in a translucent white caftan, and behind her Yael Eisenstein, who as usual caused Racheli to feel elated.

"It's not just ordinary prettiness," she would say to her friends before calling their attention to the "phenomenon," as she called her. "Well, what do you say?" she would ask immediately after they had seen her. And she was always furious at the male response. All the women were properly admiring, but the men recoiled. "How could you touch her?" said Dovik. "She'd break. Why doesn't she eat?" Even Tirosh treated her with an uncharacteristic gentleness: in her presence, his voice became soft and protective, and he never flirted with her.

Yael was slender as a stalk, her face was white and pure, her blue eyes held all the sorrows of the world, and her big, fair curls, "completely natural," as Racheli would emphasize to anyone interested, fell to her shoulders. Today, as always, her slender body was draped in a thin, flowing black knit dress, and her slender, nicotine-stained fingers were holding a cigarette, whose strong smell filled the room. "She smokes only Nelsons, constantly, and she constantly drinks black coffee. I've never seen her eat, and she only travels in taxis: she's afraid of crowds. Her family's very rich." So Racheli had been told by Tsippi, who was striving to reach "the ineffable spiritual quality that girl possesses. She's pure spirit, without a body. Once I was at her house, trying to persuade her to join our group, and I peeked into her refrigerator. There were two yogurts and some goat cheese, that's all. And don't think she ever wore anything else, either. I've known her from the beginning, from her first year as a student, and she never wore anything else, and nobody dared speak to her. One day I simply started talking to her, and she's really a nice person. Not in the least snobbish, only shy and lacking in self-confidence. Ever since I've known her, and ever since I first set eyes on her, years ago—an unforgettable occasion—she's never worn anything but those black outfits of hers. Even when the fashion was short and wide, she wore a narrow black knit skirt, and those blouses, thin sandals even in winter, and always Nelson cigarettes, and she never hung out on the lawn, she was always in the library, she only went out to smoke, and breaks in the cafeteria she spent at a table in the corner, and never with anything but coffee. What can I tell you? She's really something!"

It was obvious, as Tsippi entered the office, that she hadn't heard the news. She waved the papers in her hand and announced: "That's it! No more classes for me this year! I swear I'll never teach bibliography again!" And then she registered the silence in the room and the grave faces, and she asked: "What's everyone doing here? I only came to hand in the exam questions. What's up—has something happened?" and she advanced into the room, followed by Yael.

Both were in the midst of writing their doctoral dissertations. Tsippi's was about the status of women in folklore, and she was "Aharonovitz's," as they put it in the department. Yael, whose subject was the Hebrew *makama,* the comic medieval narrative poem, was regarded as the exclusive property of Ariyeh Klein.

Of the ten doctoral candidates in the department, only four had been chosen as teaching assistants. Although they dealt with different subjects, all had been told that as a result of budget cuts, only one of them would be able to follow the smooth course of a tenured academic career. The senior lecturers saw them as their spiritual heirs and particularly as concrete expressions of their own success as scholars. And though all knew that only one of them would be appointed to the post of lecturer in the department upon completion of their Ph.D.s, they succeeded in sustaining close, warm relations and never put each other down. Racheli had often asked herself if this might not offer a subject for scientific study.

Sara Amir smoothed her floral dress. Her intelligent brown eyes looked at Tsippi and then rested on Yael—Racheli noted the glint of anxiety in them—and finally she said, without taking her eyes off Yael: "Iddo's gone."

"What do you mean, gone?" demanded Tsippi, and her hands began to shake, but everyone was looking at Yael, whose white face had become translucent and whose eyelids had begun to flutter. "She's not too strong psychologically," Racheli remembered Dita Fuchs once remarking, and she looked around at the people in the room, who seemed to stop breathing when Sara Amir said straight out: "He's been killed in a diving accident."

Adina opened her mouth, and Racheli prepared herself to hear again the familiar lines about not knowing the details, etc., but Adina changed her mind under the annihilating look Aharonovitz gave her. He then took Yael's arm with uncharacteristic gentleness and led her to the open window, which no breath of air traversed. He propped her against his shoulder and gently patted her arm, while Adina hurried into the corridor for a glass of water. Nobody took any notice of Tsippi, who dropped the papers she was holding and burst into loud, harsh sobs. At the window, Yael stood still and silent, her body frozen. Adina uselessly held out the water to her and after a while turned to Tsippi to make her speech about the details and the funeral. She concluded by asking her whether she had seen the department head. Tsippi shook her head and mumbled through her sobs: "I'm looking for him too. I've just come from his office, but he's not there and the door's locked, and we had an appointment this morning."

With a single movement, Yael extricated herself from Aharonovitz's hold, and in her bell-like voice—Tirosh had once said in Racheli's presence that it was a pity Yael hadn't studied singing, adding that if he closed his eyes when she spoke, he could hear the pin aria from *The Marriage of Figaro* through her words—in that bell-like voice she said: "But there was a bad smell there, near his office." Racheli began to suspect that Yael was just plain crazy after all, and here was the proof.

In the ensuing silence, Tuvia Shai looked at her in terror, then asked: "What are you talking about?" and Racheli felt her eyes darting from one face to the other. Suddenly they all resembled giant vultures ready to swoop on an unknown prey; Yael, in her black dress, looked like a lost gosling as she elaborated: "I don't know; a smell like a dead cat." And as usual it was Sara Amir who recovered first; she stood, picked up her chair, put it next to the window in the narrow space between the wall and Adina's desk, and sat Yael down on it. Then she turned to the desk and decisively opened the drawer. Adina didn't even have a chance to protest when she took the keys from the place where everyone knew they were kept, though no one ever dared to lay hands on them. Rapidly she selected one of the keys, turned to Adina, and asked her in a clear, forceful voice: "This is the master, right?" Adina nodded her head and, distractedly, told Avraham Kalitzky—

whose funny little figure was now blocking the doorway, and whose confused face, the face of a Talmudic scholar detached from this world, looked even more confused than usual when he saw that the room was full—to come in immediately and shut the door behind him, because there was a draft and everyone would catch cold. Though the khamsin had already lasted for a week, and there wasn't a breath of air in the room, nobody smiled.

It was only then that Adina said: "I don't know, I've been phoning everywhere I could think of, since yesterday, and until I got through . . . And now it's one o'clock already, and I haven't heard a word from him. But I don't dare go into his room without permission; he doesn't like it at all, you know yourselves, and afterward I'll have to take the responsibility. I phoned all the colleges and publishers, and nobody's seen him anywhere, and now I just don't know."

"Good," Sara Amir said. "Now it's not your responsibility any longer. I want to know where to get hold of him and who's with Ruth Dudai now. We have to put a notice in the paper, we have to look after Ruth, and maybe he left a note in his room. We have to start doing something; we can't go on sitting here and twiddling our thumbs. Tuvia, are you coming with me?" she asked impatiently. Tuvia Shai started from his seat as if from a dream and looked at her in alarm. "Don't look at me like that—you know his office better than I do— and Adina had better come too—I'll take the responsibility, Adina. We've got an emergency on our hands. Do you understand, Adina? An emergency!" Tuvia Shai looked around him with a dazed expression. Racheli remembered how fond he had been of Iddo, and suddenly she was flooded with pity. Perhaps, she thought, Iddo had been a substitute for the son he never had; Tuvia looked like a person who had lost his son and had not yet taken in the news. The burst of energy that he had shown earlier had died down completely, she noted, and he simply made her want to cry as he stood there, helpless and paralyzed, until finally he moved from the corner where he had been leaning against the wall and submissively followed Sara Amir and Adina Lipkin, whose distress was evident in the fact that she failed to close the door behind her.

Shulamith Zellermaier cocked her head and sighed; her protruding eyes glittered for a moment with the pure spite that Racheli had dreaded from the moment she walked into the room. "He's probably shut up in some house or other, pursuing his affairs," she said in her hoarse voice, but Dita Fuchs gave her a new, threatening look. Dr. Zellermaier stopped talking, the spiteful gleam faded, and the only sound in the room was that of her heavy breathing as she took a cigarette from the packet of Royal filtertips in the pocket of her wide skirt and lit it. The cigarette had a sweetish smell that Racheli found repugnant.

Again Racheli looked around at the people in the room, and her eye fell on Professor Kalitzky, who still stood next to the door, completely at a loss. Racheli noticed how tiny his feet were in the padded sandals he wore. His toes wriggled inside his thick socks, and she remembered the stories she had heard about him, about his notorious pedantry when it came to recording bibliographical details, about the student who had once shouted in Adina's office that the two points Kalitzky had taken off the grade of his seminar paper, because of some fault in one item in the bibliography, was the only thing preventing him from going on to do his M.A. Helpless in the face of Kalitzky's obduracy, the student had raised his voice and demanded to know how he could improve his grade. Kalitzky had looked past his shoulder, ignoring the question, and resumed studying the form in his hand with the same vague look, through the thick lenses of his horn-rimmed spectacles that he now directed at Racheli, who, for the first time since she had started working in the department, felt sympathy for him too. He suddenly seem so human in his helplessness, his sorrow and shock, and then in the childish question: "Where's Professor Tirosh?" She shook her head to indicate that she didn't know, and she turned to look at Tsippi, who was sitting cross-legged on the floor in a corner of the room, sobbing without restraint and occasionally wiping her nose, and then to look at Yael, sitting motionless on the office chair at the window. Behind her stood Aharonovitz, and Kalitzky addressed his question to him, and his answer was interrupted by a scream.

Although nobody had ever heard her scream before, they all knew that the scream came from Adina Lipkin, the department secretary. And indeed, she was standing and screaming continuously at the open door of Shaul Tirosh's office. It was close to the secretarial office, just beyond the first turn in the corridor, on the opposite side, the one that overlooked the view of the Old City. Racheli raced to the spot, but she was overtaken by Aharonovitz, who pushed her aside and caught Adina in his arms as she said: "I feel sick—oh, God, I feel sick," and proceeded to vomit all over Dita Fuchs, who was standing between her and Racheli. She didn't even apologize, before being carried back to her office in Aharonovitz's arms. Racheli, who stood rooted to the spot for a moment without understanding what had happened, entered Tirosh's office. She saw the sight before Sara Amir seized her brutally by the arm and pushed her out of the room. As Sara Amir led her away, Racheli saw Kalitzky peering into the room with a curious, frightened expression. She saw his face turn green and then saw Tuvia Shai burst out of Tirosh's office and rush past them. All along the curving corridor, doors began to open, people began popping out, their faces full of alarm, and asking questions, which Sara Amir ignored.

In the fog that enveloped her, the fog in which only the painful grip of Sara Amir had any reality, Racheli sensed a constant stream of movement, a terrible din of voices, and then she found herself back in the department secretary's office, where Tuvia Shai was shouting into the telephone, "Get an ambulance, the police, hurry!" and only then did the smell begin to haunt her.

For some minutes the interior of the room was blurred, and then the fog began to lift, and Racheli saw Aharonovitz, his lips pursed and a look of horror in his eyes, holding out a glass of water to Adina, who was sitting slumped in her chair with her legs stretched out in front of her. Adina's eyes were closed, and drops of water trickled down her thick neck and rolled onto her large bosom, which was tightly enclosed in a blouse made of fine tricot, now soiled with vomit.

Shulamith Zellermaier's face twisted when she heard what Dita Fuchs said to her; she stood up and gasped for breath, and her eyes bulged more horribly than ever.

It was impossible to stay in the little room, and it was impossible to stand outside it in the dark corridor, whose curves now looked so terrifying, and all Racheli wanted was to get away from there. But she didn't have the strength to stand and wait for the elevator, or to descend the six flights of narrow steps to the parking garage. And next to the door, Kalitzky was still standing, and the smell, which would remain with her for months to come, began to grow palpable, to cling to her body, and Dita Fuchs, who was leaning against the wall with a gray face, kept saying: "What's going on? What's it all about? I don't believe it," and she began screaming hysterically that she had to get out of there. Sara Amir held her and murmured unintelligibly, and it was clear from her voice that she was frightened too, and only Yael went on sitting, without saying a word, like a Madonna Racheli had once seen a picture of in a book about the Middle Ages. Dita Fuchs walked over to the window and took a deep breath, and Tuvia Shai went on shouting into the telephone, in bursts of words that sounded to Racheli like a foreign language, and then the sight she had seen in Professor Tirosh's large, elegant office came back to her in all its vivid reality, causing her to collapse on the floor, next to Tsippi Lev-Ari.

A crowd of people had gathered outside the door, demanding to know what was going on, but nobody answered them, and in the midst of the uproar a tall, fat man, who looked like a giant to Racheli from her vantage point on the floor, pushed his way into the room and roared in a jovial voice: "Adinaleh! What's everybody doing in here? I've only been away ten months, and just look at the mess!" And when Adina raised her head, opened her eyes, looked at him, and burst into tears, Racheli knew that Ariyeh Klein was back.

Tuvia Shai looked at the big man in astonishment and cut short his telephone call. The receiver was still in his hand when he said: "But what are you doing here? You wrote to me that you were arriving the day after tomorrow."

"All right, if you object to my coming home early I'll go back immediately." And then he realized that something was wrong, and in an alarmed voice, from which all the joviality had disappeared, he asked: "What's happened here?"

They all looked at one another in silence. The people at the door waited in suspense. In his reedy, nasal voice, which was more breathless than usual, Kalitzky announced: "Iddo Dudai was killed yesterday in a diving accident, and Shaul Tirosh has just been found dead in his office." Although he was standing close to Ariyeh Klein, his pointy head almost touching the larger man's chest, Kalitzky spoke in a shout. Outside the room, cries of astonishment and horror were heard, and Ariyeh Klein looked around him incredulously. Then he sprang to Adina's desk, raised her to her feet, gripped her by the shoulders, and shook her, as he asked in a strangled voice: "Is it true, what he says? Tell me, is it true?" And Adina looked at him and blinked.

"I want to see," said Ariyeh Klein, and he looked directly at Aharonovitz, who shook his head and said quietly: "Believe me, you don't. He looks—" and his voice broke.

Klein opened his mouth, his thick lips quivering as if he was about to protest, but at that moment university security officers appeared in the doorway, followed by two uniformed policemen and two men in green gowns, and the security officer in charge of the Humanities Building, well known to Racheli, asked: "Where is he, Adina? In his office?" Tuvia Shai replied for her and left the room after the new arrivals. Gently pushing Ariyeh Klein aside, he elbowed his way through the crowd outside the door, as security officers demanded: "Everybody clear the corridor. Go back to your rooms and stay out of the way." Doors began to open and close along the adjacent corridors, and Ariyeh Klein, who seemed uncertain and looked at Aharonovitz again, said: "I'm going there anyway," and made for the open office door, coming face-to-face with the tall, handsome man to whom Racheli raised her eyes, and in spite of everything, she thought in dismay, she even noticed his dark eyes, which scanned the occupants of the room. In a calm, authoritative voice, he asked: "Excuse me, did anybody here report a death? We're from the police," and Klein said: "Follow me," and waited a few seconds for the policeman, who looked around him, his eyes resting particularly, as Racheli noticed, on Yael, who had not stirred from her seat, as if her spirit were wandering in some other place.

5

There was no doubt in Superintendent Michael Ohayon's mind that Shaul Tirosh himself would have been horrified at the thought of looking like that. As for the stench, even the neatly ironed handkerchief Ohayon held to his nose did not succeed in keeping it out.

It was impossible to connect this bloated body, the blurred features of the face, the trickles of blood that had stained the white shirt and the gray suit and had congealed under the nose and earlobes, with the figure that Michael, once a student in the History Department, taking a course in the development of poetry since the period of the Hebrew Enlightenment, remembered so well—the long, elegant figure standing on the platform in that striking pose, hands at his sides, utterly relaxed, and speaking fluently, without looking at his notes, in the big lecture hall in the Mazer Building on the old Givat Ram campus.

In the corner of the room where the ruins of that glory were now revealed, a withered brown carnation lay on the floor in grotesque testimony to the aesthetic perfection once possessed by the bloated corpse now revealed to the experienced but still unhardened eyes of the policeman.

"That skull had a tongue in it, and could sing once," thought Michael, and for a moment he feared that he had spoken the Prince of Denmark's words aloud, but it was Ariyeh Klein, his thick lips pale and quivering, who broke the silence of the encounter with death. Wordlessly, and without quoting anybody, the literature professor uttered a throttled cry and stumbled out of the room.

Superintendent Ohayon signaled to Eli Bahar, who went out and came back and reported that "they're all on their way." Michael stood in the corner of the room, next to the window, which he had already opened carefully, wrapping his hand in the handkerchief that he removed from his nose, holding his breath as he did so.

On this side of the corridor the offices were larger and grander; they were probably the preserve of the most senior professors, he thought as he looked outside and breathed in the hot air and looked at the golden dome of the Al-Aksa mosque and at the Old City, which seemed to be lying right under the window. Then he stole another look at the corpse, shuddered, and immediately turned back to the view.

"They'll have to take him down to the parking garage in the basement," said Eli Bahar. He was standing on the threshold and holding the door open a little, in the evident hope of getting a bit of air into the room. "There are elevators nearby," said Michael dryly. "They won't need to walk far."

Holding his nose, Eli Bahar gingerly approached the corpse, which was still lying between the big desk and the radiator. Crouched behind the shoulder of the pathologist, who was bending over it, he took a look from close up. "Don't touch!" warned Michael mechanically, without turning his head—knowing that his words were superfluous.

Long moments passed before the young doctor—whose face grew greener all the time, until it resembled the color of his pale-green gown—opened his mouth. And then, at last, he said in a whisper:

"Someone really went to town here," and Michael, who had not met him before, saw the youthful face and its lack of experience, and felt compassion and affection for the pathologist, who had not yet learned to protect himself by using professional terminology. After a while the pathologist said that they would certainly find fractures of the skull, and with his eyes still fixed on the corpse, he asked if they had noticed that the victim's tie had been used to strangle him, "among other things, although it's clear that that wasn't the cause of death, I can say almost definitely, even before the autopsy, that this man didn't die of suffocation, not by strangulation, anyway. Look, you can see over here," and he turned to Eli Bahar, who looked obediently at the neck, which was swollen around the tight knot of the tie, and immediately averted his face and nearly tripped on his way back to the door.

From his position by the window, Superintendent Ohayon observed the pathologist's face closely. He saw the little creases at the corners of the eyes and realized that the man couldn't be as young as he had supposed, and in a quiet voice he asked him how long, in his opinion, the body had been lying there, and the pathologist replied: "Okay, we still have to do all the tests, but if you want a rough estimate"—Michael nodded—"then I'd say about forty-eight hours at least," and he pointed to the suit, which looked small and shrunken on the swollen body. Michael asked if he had indeed been physically assaulted before death. "It looks like it. I'd say someone hit him in the face, maybe with his fist, although I'd be inclined to think with a blunt instrument or perhaps a chair." The doctor wiped the beads of sweat off his forehead with a rubber-gloved hand. He looked at Michael, a trace of anxiety in his eyes, and Michael was about to ask for more medical details when the door opened.

The brisk smiles on the faces of the mobile forensics team—who in the course of their work had seen everything—froze even before they saw the corpse. Michael could tell that his expression betrayed the horror of the sight—that this time he had not succeeded in putting on what Tzilla affectionately called his "poker face"—when he exchanged glances with Pnina from the Criminal Identification Division. Behind her, Zvika, the photographer, bounded in, and the wisecrack he had been about to deliver was nipped in the bud and turned into a sharp whistle, accompanied by a hand flying up to block his nose.

By the time the measuring and photographing were under way, all the "brass," as Eli Bahar called them, were already there: the Jerusalem Subdistrict commander, the Jerusalem police spokesman, and the departmental investigations officer. They crowded in and stared at the corpse, and they even bore the stench with heroism, anything "to be in the picture," and Ariyeh Levy, the Jerusalem police commander, remarked that "there's never been anything like this before, a murder at the university. Maybe it's the work of terrorists— what do you say, Ohayon?" And Michael, whose throat was parched, replied, "Maybe," and waited impatiently for the corpse to be removed from the room, asking himself if the sweetish smell of decomposing flesh would ever disappear from this room, whose window overlooked the most beautiful view he had ever seen. He knew that it would certainly take days for the smell to go away and that it would linger in his own nostrils for a long time, because he had once known him, the dead man, because he had often enviously remembered his easy posture as he lectured, his long, elegant silhouette.

The mobile lab people were busy taking fingerprints. He watched them, dimly aware of their voices, as they worked, noticed the expression of concentration on Eli Bahar's face, heard the murmur of the pathologist, who finally replaced his instruments in his bag and left the room. The lab crew were still busy with the fingerprints, and then, in flagrant violation of the unwritten rule that demanded his presence at the scene of a crime as long as the forensics people were still there, Michael went out to the corridor, where he leaned against the wall and waited for them to finish their job. Actually he hoped that outside the room with the corpse in it, he would be able to breathe. But the long, angular hallway was airless. He walked along it until he came to a juncture of three corridors, which, like a traffic island, constituted a kind of little square surrounded by purple walls, and he sat down on a wooden bench, on the other end of which sat Ariyeh Klein, his head buried in his hands.

Klein raised his head and looked at the policeman. The professor's eyes were gray, deep and wide-set, and their expression was sad and fearful. Michael Ohayon lit a cigarette and offered the pack to the big man sitting next to him. Klein seemed to hesitate, and then he shrugged, took a cigarette, and leaned toward Michael, who lit it for him. For a few seconds the two men sat and smoked in silence. It was surprisingly quiet. There were no doors in the purple walls, only mailboxes, bulletin boards, and two benches. Michael felt as if a part of him had separated off and was standing enclosed in one of those balloons that hold the words spoken by the characters in cartoons. This miniature version of himself looked at him and at Professor Klein sitting and smoking, their faces clearly reflecting the secret solidarity of people who had not yet succeeded in putting up the barrier against the feeling of fear, which was stronger than anything else.

Ariyeh Klein's massive, sturdy body shifted uncomfortably on the narrow bench, and his face turned toward Michael, who found himself looking into his eyes and also at his lips, which began to move. When he finally heard the voice of the professor of medieval poetry, which had once thundered in the biggest hall in the Mazer Building, it was whispering: "It's never possible to imagine correctly what's going to happen." And then, as if he had heard the policeman's mute question, he went on to say: "I would have imagined I would feel pain and sorrow, maybe shock too, but more than anything I feel fear. Just like a child, as if that corpse had a vitality, a strength of its own, and it could get up and jump on me. I don't understand it."

Michael stretched his legs out in front of him and said nothing. He looked straight ahead, but he knew that Klein knew he was listening to every word. "There's nothing that resembles him, Shaul, as I knew him as a living man. He's not even someone else, only something else. That's why we're so afraid, I think," said Ariyeh Klein, and he ground his cigarette into the standing ashtray, a tin cylinder covered with paper that matched the wall. Michael reflected in silence. "What I mean is that I saw the man I've known for so many years, and all of a sudden he's a repulsive, stinking corpse, and all the suits and carnations in the world won't help him anymore. And he didn't even have a child. And I can't feel any sorrow. Only fear, not sorrow. A man looks out for himself, and above all he fears death. And I don't mean the end of life; I mean the actual encounter with the dead."

Michael couldn't find it in him to take advantage of the moment in order to gather what the professional jargon called "preliminary information." He preferred not to break the spell of the intimacy, the accord he felt with this bulky man who had always looked to him like one of the founders of the first Hebrew colony. "I suppose," said Klein, rising to his feet, "that a policeman who comes across things like this in the course of his work has ways of defending himself against the fear."

"You're wrong," said Michael, as he, too, stood up. "Certainly not in the first moments." They were the same height, and their eyes met again. Michael nodded his head, put out his cigarette and returned to the room with the corpse.

He watched them taking measurements and notes, combing every centimeter for evidence. And soon it was all over. The Jerusalem Sub-district commander left the scene of the crime, followed by his entourage. The stretcher was brought in, and the lab crew put away their instruments and collected objects from the room in big plastic bags; the corpse was removed, and the police filed out and began making their way to the Humanities Building's superintendent's office, descending narrow, winding flights of stairs that looked as if they led nowhere yet led to a different floor in another wing. Michael Ohayon suppressed a smile at the unexpected thought that the place looked like the background for a drama of international espionage, an association that made him wonder at himself.

Again he thought of the old Givat Ram campus. Of sitting on the lawn on sunny days, of the miniskirts, of his ex-wife Nira's legs and the impulse to stroke them one warm spring day, when both of them were sitting bent over their books on the lawn—an impulse that had been the direct cause of Yuval's birth. He often thought of his first years at the university, almost always with longing for the lawns of Givat Ram, for the intimacy of the buildings. In his imagination he could see the cover of the basic textbook by La Monte, on which all the students in the History Department were tested. How many marriages, he wondered, had sprung from that medieval-history exam? He asked himself how on this campus on Mount Scopus, with its marble and stone buildings that the sun never penetrated, couples came together. And the cafeteria, he thought . . . they didn't even have a decent, crowded cafeteria here, like the one on Givat Ram; there were only spaces for drinking coffee, supposedly inviting but actually alienating, like everything else here.

He felt hot in his faded jeans, the last of the clean ones in his closet. Listening to the rapid, clattering footsteps of the procession at the end of which he walked, he looked alternately at his shoes and the back of the Jerusalem police spokesman, Gilly, who preceded him, squeezed into his khaki uniform, the chief inspector insignia gleaming on his shoulders. The university security officer strode among the policemen, like someone who had finally found his true vocation. Before going into the superintendent's office, in the blue wing, the C.O. gripped Michael's arm. The thick hand on his flesh was oppressive, but the commander's words were even more so. "Ohayon," said Ariyeh Levy without removing his hand, "this isn't an ordinary case. I want a special SIT," and Michael, combating the weariness that was already spreading through him, refrained from remarking that a special investigation team was special by definition.

The weariness was familiar, the immediate response to the sense of being at a loss, of not knowing where to begin. It would come after the second wave: the dread that assailed him with every new case, the feeling that all his previous achievements had been wiped out, vanished into thin air. The first wave was always a reaction to the ugliness, the atrociousness of the death itself. At the beginning of every case he would be filled with the terrible certainty that this time there would be no solution. And then came this weariness, accompanied by voices that reminded him of the futility of life, the futility of death, the fact that in the end someone would be punished and that this would solve nothing. But he covered all this up with the question he addressed to his commander: "Sir?"

Major General Ariyeh Levy, commander of the Jerusalem Subdistrict, replied: "I think you should head it; I'd like you and Bahar to make up the team. We'll have the university president breathing down our necks, and the press and the whole bloody world. I need it wrapped up quickly."

Superintendent Ohayon nodded automatically. The text was so familiar. It was always a special case, it always had to be wrapped up quickly, although the head of the Investigations Division was not always asked to head the special task force in person. Someone knocked on the door, and the police spokesman, whose task would be more delicate than usual this time, as the commander had warned him, opened it. The president of the university stepped inside.

Ariyeh Levy treated him as if he were still the Israeli ambassador to the United Nations, and Michael looked at the dark-blue tie lying against the blinding white shirt and wondered how the man managed to look so cool and flawless on such a scorching day, while he himself felt sticky in his jeans and his open-necked light-blue shirt, which he had ironed only that morning and which already felt as if it had been dragged out of the laundry hamper. The room filled with the smell of expensive shaving lotion, and Michael breathed it into his nostrils, in the hope of effacing that other smell, which still pervaded everything. President Marom's face was pale, and there was a look of panic in his light eyes. Michael asked himself how Marom would have reacted to the sight of the corpse, and he squirmed with embarrassment at the pompous manner of the C.O., who introduced himself by name and rank, looking at once self-important and obsequious. Ariyeh Levy's attitude toward institutions of higher learning was one of the main reasons for his habitual outbursts against Michael. Eli Bahar enjoyed quoting the sentence, "This isn't a university, you know!"—the invariable conclusion to Levy's fulminations against his subordinate, ever since his early days as an inspector on the force.

But this *was* a university—the university—and with increasing embarrassment, Michael listened to Levy's words: "Our investigating team will be headed by Superintendent Michael Ohayon, who was once a big star over here—history, wasn't it, Ohayon?" And the university president looked at him with an expression in which politeness vied with anxiety, and straightened the tip of his tie as he nodded at Levy, who couldn't seem to stop talking.

Avidan, the departmental investigations officer, introduced himself to the president and then began to consider various possibilities. A security-related crime was the first on the list. They began to discuss the security arrangements on the campus. They spoke of the hours when the gates were locked, the fact that a person could stay in his office for the entire weekend without anyone noticing. Finally the spokesman commented that they could make no real progress until the hour of death was determined. Then, said the departmental investigations officer, they would be able to speak to the security officers who had been on duty during the relevant shift. The president stared at them, and then he asked quietly what the other possibilities were.

"Well," said Levy grandiosely, "there *are* other possibilities, of course, such as nationalistic motives or, of course, personal, sexual ones."

The university president looked at the people surrounding him, with an expression of anxiety, and Michael clearly read the disbelief on his face. Only then did the other incident surface in his mind, and he spoke for the first time in a quiet voice, listening to the silence that descended as he began talking. "Last night," said Michael Ohayon, "I drove back from Eilat. I had been a witness to a diving accident there."

They all stared at him. Ariyeh Levy was about to protest, but before he had a chance to do so, Michael addressed himself directly to Marom: "A young man by the name of Iddo Dudai—does the name mean anything to you?" The president shook his head, and Ariyeh Levy opened his mouth again.

The spokesman, the departmental investigations officer, and Eli Bahar waited for Michael to continue.

"I understood that he, too, was a lecturer in the Hebrew Literature Department here. And I can't help but ask myself if the two things aren't connected. Two people from the same department, on the same weekend."

"It hasn't been brought to my attention yet," said the president, with diplomatic discretion. "But I can make inquiries, of course." He looked hesitantly at Ariyeh Levy, and after Levy nodded, he picked up the telephone and spoke to his secretary. She confirmed the fact that Iddo Dudai, a lecturer in the Hebrew Literature Department, had died in a diving accident. "She said that the autopsy is yet to be performed—the funeral will not be held until tomorrow. I knew nothing about it, of course," he said, glancing apologetically at Michael. "But surely that's something entirely different? A diving accident in Eilat and a violent death here."

Ariyeh Levy looked at Michael with interest. Then he said decisively: "Yes, we'll have to go into the question of a possible connection between the two events. How many people are there in the Literature Department?" he asked Marom, who replied apologetically that he didn't know exactly but that the administration office would of course provide all the information they needed. He estimated that there were twenty, "including teaching assistants," and then he looked at Michael with a worried expression and said hesitantly: "Although it's very tragic, of course, terrible, I can't see why there should be a connection between the two incidents, especially since one of them took place here, inside the university, and the other in Eilat."

And suddenly the policemen constituted a united front. No one answered the lean man fingering his tie, the only necktie in the room. Traces of perspiration became visible on the white shirt. Ariyeh Levy passed his hand over his short, frizzy hair, wiped his forehead, and said in a soothing tone: "Maybe there's no connection, but it has to be checked. Two incidents in the same weekend. From the same department. We can't ignore it."

Pnina from Forensics peeped into the room. Her bouncy joie-de-vivre had disappeared, and her usually rosy cheeks were pale. "We're finished," she said, looking at Ariyeh Levy, who nodded. Even she can't take it; I'm not the only one without defenses. Not much consolation, thought Michael as the door closed behind her and Marom set about making the contacts that would "help you in your work," as he put it. He phoned his secretary again, at her home, he explained, as if hoping to win their appreciation for his efforts. They would receive every possible assistance, he promised. By then they could hear the commotion outside, and they exchanged looks of despairing resignation. Finally Levy nodded at Gilly, the Jerusalem police spokesman, and said: "Okay, you'd better go out and say something. Tell them we're investigating the security angle, but keep it cool; we don't want a panic. Make it clear from the beginning that's only one possibility, before the politicians begin to scream. They'll have something to say in any case. The ones on the right will say that Mount Scopus has to be made safe, that the Arab students should be expelled, and the ones on the left'll say that the campus should never have been moved here after the Six Day War. There'll be an uproar, for sure."

"How did the reporters get here so quickly?" asked Marom in surprise.

"I don't call that quick," said Ariyeh Levy, glancing at his watch. "It's already five o'clock. They usually arrive as soon as we do, but we only began radioing for our intelligence officer half an hour ago, and if they've come he'll be here soon enough. They tune into our frequency, you know, and anyway, there's no way we can hide the facts."

Marom looked doubtfully at Gilly. His youthful face, his wide blond mustache, his smiling eyes, apparently failed to inspire confidence in the veteran diplomat.

Gilly noticed, and the hint of a sly smile appeared on his face as he looked the university president up and down, from his gleaming black shoes to his cold blue eyes, and then asked if he should talk to them immediately. "Yes. Talk to them and get rid of them. Tomorrow—tell them we'll have more information tomorrow," said Ariyeh Levy impatiently, and then the door opened and in burst Danny Balilty—his paunch was growing more evident every day, thought Michael—tossing juicy profanities at the group clustering around the door. "And this," explained Ariyeh Levy to Marom, who straightened his tie again, "is our intelligence officer, Inspector Balilty," and he scowled at Danny, who tucked his T-shirt, drooping over his paunch, into his trousers, wiped his red face, and apologized for his late arrival, offering some vague explanation about having just come back from a professional meeting. He looked around him, and gradually his face relaxed. He hasn't seen the body, thought Michael.

"So what's going on?" inquired Balilty, breathing almost evenly. "What happened here?" Levy briefly reported the facts.

"Tirosh . . . isn't he some sort of poet?" Balilty asked, and he looked at Michael, who had seated himself behind his C.O. and was holding an unlit cigarette.

The president now directed the same expression at the intelligence officer he had used on Gilly when he went out to speak to the press. Michael asked himself how much confidence someone who looked like Balilty—with his bald head, his red face, the belly bursting from his grubby trousers—could arouse in someone who looked like Marom.

Balilty spoke. "But during the weekend, all the buildings on campus are locked from Friday afternoon to Sunday morning, and to get in you have to contact the security officer and ask him to open up for you, and then call him to open up again so you can get out." He looked at the university security officer. Michael Ohayon, whose voice rang hollowly in his own ears, said quietly that this was indeed the case, unless the murder had taken place on Friday morning, "or somebody remained here in the building until Sunday morning, when the gates are opened and anyone can come and go as he pleases."

Danny Balilty scratched his scalp and said: "Okay, there's no point in talking until we know the time of death. And I suppose we have to discount the security aspect first? Does anyone know anything about Tirosh's politics?"

Michael had read the poems published in the literary supplements of the Friday papers. He had not been impressed by their power, and so he said: "On the surface, I'd say a parlor pink."

"He was from the university, wasn't he?" said Balilty brutally. "Couldn't avoid being a bit of a pinko, could he?" He looked at Marom. Except for Michael Ohayon, who suppressed a smile because he knew that Balilty meant every word he said, everyone there thought that he was being ironic.

Dryly, the president replied that all shades of political opinion were represented at the university.

"In the Hebrew Literature Department? A poet? In nineteen-eighty-five and not on the left? Give me break!" Balilty tilted his sweating head and threw the president of the university a mocking glance.

Michael saw the president, tie and all, feel the ground slipping beneath his feet. There were beads of sweat on his forehead when he asked if his presence was still required. "Whom should I keep in touch with?" he then asked, and Ariyeh Levy, with the expression of a man too busy to be bothered, replied: "We'll contact you the minute we know anything new. If you want anything, or come into possession of any information that might be helpful, you can contact Superintendent Ohayon, who'll be in charge of the investigation from now on. You can always locate him through our control center. But you'll have to be patient," he warned in a didactic tone, and Michael knew just how superior Levy was now feeling.

For a moment Michael vacillated between his enjoyment at the embarrassment of the president, who aroused what he called "my Foreign Office antibodies"—by which he meant the resistance aroused in him by the suave smoothness, the tie, the ability not to perspire in stressful situations, the noncommittal remarks, the well-camouflaged but explicit message: "I know how to tell the genuine article from the imitations, I know what wine to drink with every dish"—and his own embarrassment at being associated with the self-important C.O. He decided in favor of enjoyment.

Even though he had sworn to Maya that ever since he had met her, at the home of the ex–cultural attaché to Chicago (who at the time was home between postings, on his way to Australia), nothing about the Foreign Office could surprise him, he could not help feeling the old rage, and also—he had to admit—the envy, that these people had been born with a silver spoon in their mouths, which later, as he explained in all seriousness to Maya, turned into a silver tiepin.

On the other hand, he said to himself—as Ariyeh Levy escorted the university president out of the room and silenced, with a loud, authoritative voice, the gentlemen of the press who were still besieging the place, and who now turned from the spokesman to the two figures emerging from the door—on the other hand, how was it possible not to respond with polite chilliness and almost undisguised contempt to the obsequious affectation of his commanding officer?

But then they began discussing whom to co-opt onto the SIT, besides Ohayon himself and Eli Bahar, and Avidan asked whether Tzilla was still in bed—she was pregnant and experiencing complications—and was told by Eli Bahar that she wasn't: "She got up two weeks ago, but I wouldn't like her to start running around at night and so on, even though as a team coordinator she's the greatest, of course. I really don't know what to tell you," and he looked inquiringly at Michael. "If Tzilla agrees, she could be coordinator," said Michael, "but she'll have to have help," and then Levy came back into the room and shut the door behind him. His face had resumed its usual sour expression, and his little eyes, which always reminded Michael of two beads, dulled as he said: "Okay, you've seen for yourselves the kind of person we'll have to deal with, and that's even before the commissioner's stuck his oar in, never mind the district commander and everybody else in the world. Balilty! You three are joining the SIT, and I think I'd better add two more men to the three of you if we want a quick solution."

Michael looked at the marks his teeth had made on the filter of the unlit cigarette he had been holding and now lit. "Tzilla could be useful," he remarked. "She knows some of the people here. She spent two years as a student at the university before she joined the force." Levy squinted in his direction and asked: "And who else?"

"I don't know at the moment, unless we decide to take Raffi off that Jaffa Gate case."

Ariyeh Levy nodded and suddenly smiled as he said: "You're a conservative, Ohayon. You like working with the same people all the time, eh?" Michael did not reply, but thought of Emanuel Shorer, who had headed the Investigations Division before him, the man who had "groomed" him and taught him all he knew, and he wished with all his heart that Shorer would come back and be over him, that he himself wouldn't have to take the responsibility for solving a case that didn't seem to offer a single clue.

The team had been decided on before anyone had spoken to Tzilla, and Eli Bahar's face was clouded. Bahar's wife had almost lost a baby, Michael remembered, but he hardened his heart, thinking that he didn't have the strength to teach a new person the subtleties only Tzilla knew. He would insist, he decided. There was no reason why a woman in the third month of pregnancy, who had now been allowed to get out of bed by her doctors, shouldn't be able to sit in an office and coordinate activities from there.

There was no escape; in spite of the relentless khamsin, in spite of the hour, he had to return to the little room where the Literature Department faculty were still sitting. Despite their protests, reported by the sergeant who had been posted outside the door, they had not yet been allowed to leave the building. The same sergeant had also kept out the reporters, four in number, who were waiting there and who pounced on the two men about to go inside. Michael knew three of them. The fourth was an attractive young woman, the television police reporter, who gazed at him seductively as she waved to the cameraman standing behind her to aim his camera at him, causing Michael to protest.

He ordered the reporters to make themselves scarce. They retreated down the corridor, issuing their usual protests about the right of the public to know, and Michael called after them: "The public will have to wait until there's something for it to know."

"Chief Inspector Ohayon," shouted the veteran reporter from the most widely circulated daily in the country, and Eli Bahar quickly corrected him: "Superintendent, Shmaya; it's time you got used to it. Superintendent, okay?"

Without knocking, the two men entered the room.

Despite the open window, the air in the room was stuffy and full of the undefined body odors that were always present, thought Michael, when frightened people were crowded into a closed space.

Among the smells Michael distinguished a trace of a sweet perfume and, above all, the odor of decomposition that had pervaded everything since he had been in the room with the corpse.

He looked around him in silence and within a few seconds had taken in the picture in all its details. Sometimes he felt at these moments like a cameraman obeying the instructions of the director of a well-made movie.

Opposite the door he saw Yael, still sitting next to the window, in the same position as before, and behind her Klein, standing and with his thick lips quivering. Adina Lipkin sat at her desk, rhythmically wiping her face with a tissue that she had apparently taken out of the open drawer on her left.

The only people in the room whom he remembered from his university days were Ariyeh Klein, the medieval-poetry professor, and Shulamith Zellermaier, who specialized in popular literature and folklore. She sat there, her heavy legs spread, her dark skirt drawn up to her knees. Her feet in their padded orthopedic sandals stamped on the floor as she began to protest. She was the first to speak, and with a restraint that failed to hide her anger, she asked if they could leave now. When he did not reply at once, she burst out in a loud, breathless voice, delivering a speech that began with the words: "This is an unheard of outrage! Detaining people for hours like this, without water or air or any way of notifying their families, and it's already five o'clock!" When she paused to take a breath, Michael cut her speech short by asking if any of them had seen Tirosh on Saturday.

Zellermaier fell silent, and in an instant the room's atmosphere of shock and depression changed into something else. Michael sensed the electricity, the new energy galvanizing the people in the room. But no one answered his question.

They looked at each other, and finally Adina said: "I tried to contact him on Saturday night to tell him a terrible accident had happened, but I couldn't get hold of him," and she crushed the tissue in her hand and burst into tears.

Nobody had seen him on Saturday: they all shook their heads no or blinked their eyes, and Kalitzky pronounced the word "No." Balilty and Raffi were already on their way to Tirosh's house, thought Michael, and wondered whether he should begin with the personal questions at once, before the tension relaxed. He asked if anyone had seen Tirosh on Friday.

Adina said that there had been a department faculty meeting on Friday. "Anything special?" inquired Michael, and was told that there was a faculty meeting every three weeks, "always on a Friday," said Adina.

Michael looked at her and asked if anything unusual had happened at the last meeting.

"I don't know. I haven't had time yet to read the minutes; the secretary doesn't attend the meetings."

Michael recalled the stories Tzilla used to tell about the department secretary, and he almost smiled. Adina Lipkin's face expressed bitterness at not being in a position to control all areas, but it also showed determined resignation.

"But I saw him, of course, before the meeting and after it. Only Professor Klein didn't see him; he only returned from a sabbatical yesterday," and Adina again burst into tears, issuing loud sobs between which fragments of sentences were audible: "What's going on? . . . Is everyone going to die . . . one after the other? . . . There's someone here among us. . . . I'm afraid to be here at all. . . ."

"There's no connection, Adina, there's no connection," said Sara Amir sharply, but Aharonovitz blinked his eyes, looked at Adina in horror, and said: "Is it conceivable? Could there be some conspiracy?"

"And who," asked Michael, rapidly scanning their faces in order to register as many reactions as possible, "who else saw him after the meeting?" And again it was Adina who replied, saying that Dr. Shai had had lunch with him.

"She means me," said Tuvia Shai from his place next to the wall.

Michael had taken note of the bluish veins on this man's face when he first opened the door. Now he signaled Shai to step outside with him. "When was this?" he asked him. A police sergeant stood behind them, at the ready, in the corridor, opening his note book.

"I think it was about half past eleven, because we finished the meeting at eleven, and it took a while until we got moving. We ate here, in Meirsdorf, and he said something about going to Tel Aviv, but nothing definite."

"And how long did your lunch take?"

"Until half past twelve."

"And after that? You didn't see him again?"

"No. I went up with him to his office for a minute, to get something, and I left him there."

Michael looked at Tuvia Shai for a moment, the lifeless voice in which he had spoken echoing in his ears, and asked him what time he had parted from Tirosh.

"A few minutes after half past twelve, I think, or maybe closer to one."

Michael called Eli Bahar out of the room and whispered something in his ear.

"Did anyone here see Tirosh or speak to him after one o'clock on Friday?" Bahar asked the people in the room.

Tuvia Shai stood in the doorway, and Michael walked past him into the room. His eyes again rapidly scanned the faces. They all looked at one another; nobody said anything. Shulamith Zellermaier sighed loudly. "Maybe I'll be next?" she asked, and Michael noticed the sharp look Dita Fuchs gave her, and he also registered that there had been no irony in her voice. She really looked frightened, and as if to excuse herself, she added: "It's too much to take, two violent deaths at once."

"Did he have a car?" asked Michael, and again he noted the change in the atmosphere, as if he had drawn their attention to a detail they had not yet considered.

"Yes," said Tuvia Shai, and everyone looked at him. "I suppose he came in his car. You'll probably find it in the university car park downstairs—you can't miss it, it's a 1979 Alfa Romeo; there are only two of them the whole country." Dita Fuchs burst into tears, and Michael noticed her pallor, her swollen eyelids, when she said between sobs: "He loved that car. Perhaps you could let us go now? The policeman outside the door wouldn't let us leave. I'm thinking of my children. I just want to go home," and Michael was aware of the suppressed hysteria, the fear hidden in the childish tone.

Eli Bahar opened the door and murmured something into the ear of the uniformed policeman who was still standing beyond it. Before the door closed, Michael saw the policeman hurrying off in the direction of the blue wing.

"What was he going to do in Tel Aviv?" Michael had turned again to Tuvia Shai, who said in embarrassment: "I don't know exactly."

He looks like a corpse himself, thought Michael.

"Something to do with gender, no doubt" said Kalman Aharonovitz dryly, sitting up in his chair. You could see fear giving way for a moment to malice.

It was only then that Michael asked if Tirosh had a family.

"A confirmed bachelor," replied Shulamith Zellermaier, "with not a single relative in the country."

And then he asked the inevitable question that always made him feel like a television detective: "Can any of you think of anyone who might have wished him dead?"

There was a tense silence in the room. Again Michael glanced from face to face. Some expressed hesitation, others disgust, and still others knowledge they had decided to withhold. But behind the facial expressions Michael perceived the true, hidden feeling: fear. He looked straight into Adina Lipkin's eyes, which reflected a mixture of outrage and discretion.

Who? his eyes asked the secretary, and she clasped her damp hands and said: "I really don't know," and looked imploringly at the others.

"Do any of you know anything about his political opinions?" asked Eli Bahar, and the tension relaxed as Shai replied: "I imagine everybody knows what his political opinions were, everyone knows he was active in Peace Now and wrote political poetry."

Michael asked if he was an important figure in the movement, if there had ever been threats against his life.

"Enough!" groaned Shulamith Zellermaier impatiently, raising herself to the full height of her corpulent body. "A lot of people would have been glad to see him dead, and I don't understand why we're all so silent all of a sudden. There are students he tormented and women he had affairs with, and their husbands, and poets and writers he humiliated, and there are dozens of people who would have been only too happy to see him dead. We're taking leave of our senses here—

there's no connection between the fact that both of them are dead, him and Iddo. It's a coincidence! Nothing but a coincidence, can't you understand?" Silence ensued.

Tuvia Shai stared at her in dismay, opened his mouth, and propped his skinny body against the wall again. Ariyeh Klein looked at her as if she had gone mad, and he said in a trembling bass voice: "I think we'd better try to restrain ourselves, Shulamith; as you see there's quite enough drama here already. No need to add any more. Maybe there are a lot of people who might have thought they would be glad if he were dead, and maybe there are some people who really will be glad to hear that he's dead, but I can't think of anyone who would actually have done it with his own hands, and you'll agree with me: that's a significant difference. And finally"—he turned to Michael —"we didn't do it, none of us murdered him, so maybe you'll let us go now and ask us for our help later in a civilized way?"

Eli Bahar looked at the people in the room and then at Michael with a critical expression. "You break all the rules," he had once complained to him. "Why do you question witnesses in a group, together? Why don't you wait and question them one by one?" But Michael glanced at his watch, quickly calculated his plans for the rest of the day, and looked questioningly at Eli Bahar. Eli nodded. "Okay," said Michael in a tired voice. "Please leave your addresses and telephone numbers here and be available during the next two days. This evening, or tomorrow morning at the latest, we'll get in touch with you and let you know when each of you will be invited to come in and be interrogated."

"Interrogated?" said the gentle voice of Yael Eisenstein, and everyone in the room looked up. Michael too, who had grown accustomed to seeing her sitting still as a statue, staring straight ahead as if blind and deaf to everything, was startled.

"Interrogated, questioned, have a statement taken—you can take your pick," said Michael slowly, without taking his eyes off her, his hand on the door handle.

"What does it mean? And where is it done?" asked Yael in a whisper, and even when she whispered, her voice rang like an alarm bell in

Superintendent Ohayon's mind; he answered her immediately in a voice that sounded horribly brutal to him: "At the police station in the Russian Compound. You'll be told the exact place."

The sergeant who had been standing outside the door came in to report that the university security officer had found no sign of Tirosh's car in the car park. Michael was about to leave, when Yael slipped off her chair and dropped to the floor like a rag doll.

"When she comes to," said Michael roughly, "take all their particulars. She'll help you," and he pointed to Adina Lipkin, who was bending over Yael, muttering that she probably hadn't had anything to eat or drink all day. Yael recovered consciousness and opened her blue eyes, and Michael hurried out of the room and crossed the corridor to press the elevator button. As he drove the Ford Escort out of the underground garage and onto the main road outside the university, the windows wide open, he took a long breath and said half to himself: "We've emerged from Hades."

"What?" asked Eli Bahar. "What did you say?"

"Nothing; something from Greek mythology. Like coming out of hell. I keep on having these mythological thoughts—it's probably because of the Literature Department. We have to make contact with Eilat, first thing, and find out if the two cases are connected. Let's think who we know there."

"Just a minute," said Eli Bahar, "just a minute. Don't you think we should bring one of them in for questioning today? The one who saw him last, who had lunch with him, for example?"

"It's half past six; I still have to meet someone from Eilat. What's the point of starting interrogations tonight, before the pathologist's report, before we've spoken to Forensics, before we have a report on his house? On second thought. . . " Michael picked up the transmitter and asked them to find out if Balilty had finished his search. A few minutes passed before Control called back: "They haven't finished; you're invited to join the party. You want the address?" Eli pulled a crumpled paper out of his pocket and laid it on the dashboard, and Michael said: "Not over the radio. It's okay. We've got the address."

"Okay." Eli sighed. "We'll wait for the reports from Forensics and the pathologist. You're always slow at the beginning. I always have a hard time getting used to it. I know, I know." He sighed again, loudly. "You have to understand the essence of things first, the milieu, get to know the characters—all those ideas of yours. Don't tell me, I know, and I hope the pathologist will give you enough 'essence of things' to get up some speed—I can't stay in first gear too long. And will you speak to Tzilla, or should I?"

"Why shouldn't Avidan speak to her?" said Michael ingenuously.

"If you're frightened of her too, then I needn't worry," said Eli without smiling. "I thought *you* knew how to get around her."

Michael smiled without replying. They had worked together five years, and Eli Bahar was only beginning to express in words, roughly, the intimacy that existed between them.

It was seven o'clock when Michael parked in the picturesque artists' quarter of Yemin Moshe, next to Balilty's Renault 4 and the forensics van. He stretched. Eli Bahar examined the crumpled paper and said:" "Okay, let's begin looking."

But Michael Ohayon looked around him and asked: "Do you know Amichai's poem about Yemin Moshe?" Eli Bahar shook his head. "It begins with the line: 'In Yemin Moshe* I held my beloved's left hand in my hand.' What do you say to that?"

Eli Bahar looked at him in silence for a while; then he said: "I don't see what it means. It's like saying: 'In Kerem Avraham† I kept my wife's orchard in my pocket.'" Michael burst out laughing.

"And the khamsin has broken," said Eli Bahar as they began descending the broad steps leading into the quarter.

*Literally, Moses' right hand; the neighborhood is named for the nineteenth-century Anglo-Jewish philanthropist Sir Moses Montefiore.
†Abraham's Vineyard; another Jerusalem neighborhood.

6

The khamsin had indeed broken, the haze having cleared as if from one moment to the next. A sudden breeze bore the scent of flowers as Michael hesitantly descended the wide steps into the romantic quarter that had been taken over by artists and celebrities. He stopped opposite the Music Center, while Eli Bahar, who had gone on ahead, waved his arm and broke the silence with a cry of "Here it is." Michael looked at the houses, at the neat gardens, at the "Art Gallery" signs, and wondered what Tirosh's house would be like.

In the little yard in front of the house, which they entered through a dark iron gate, there was no garden. Only a few rosebushes and three statues dotted the expanse of white gravel.

"He didn't owe anybody anything. A free man, without even a garden to encumber him," said Michael aloud, but Eli Bahar didn't react and opened the door, upon which an Armenian tile said, in Hebrew, English, and Arabic: TIROSH. The heavy brown wooden door scraped as if there was a bit of gravel stuck underneath it, then it opened onto a large, vaulted room, whose arched windows overlooked the Hinnom Valley.

The last light of the day colored the room in gold and crimson and lent it a magical, almost fairy-tale air. The walls were lined with books, and this, noted Michael, was the only warm thing about the room. A narrow white storage unit held a stereo system and a collection of records and tapes. Michael glanced at them and saw thick albums of all the Wagner operas and operas by Richard Strauss. The bottom shelf was devoted to church music. Dvořák's *Stabat Mater* and Britten's *War Requiem* were there, as well as a piece he had never heard of, whose composer and title, printed in curved gold letters on the spine, he deciphered with difficulty: Janáček—*Glagolitic Mass*. There was no chamber music in the record collection. Michael looked at the cassettes as well, noticing the exemplary order in which they had been arranged, those Tirosh had himself apparently copied carefully labeled with titles and the names of composers and performers. There was no television set.

Only two paintings hung on the walls, and one of them sent a shiver through Michael, because of the coincidence. Between the two big windows hung a painting of an angry, stormy black sea; Michael knew who the artist was, even before he looked at the signature: A. Pomerantz—Uzi's father.

Encountering this painting in Tirosh's house, the threads connecting Uzi, who had reappeared in his life after twenty years, to the death of Dudai, to Tirosh, aroused Michael's anxiety. It was only later that he located the source of this anxiety in the feeling that coincidence was taking control of his life and that there was some mysterious law behind the coincidences. But when he was standing in front of the painting, all he felt was the anxiety, the wish to be rid of it, and a powerful urge to understand the world into which he had been thrust.

The second painting was smaller, a charcoal sketch of a nude woman. He did not recognize the signature.

The furniture itself was strictly functional: two cold, pale armchairs, an angular sofa, and a coffee table—mosaics in a gleaming nickel frame. There were no vases, ornaments, or any other kind of decoration in the room. On the mosaic table was a large ashtray, made of blue Hebron glass, and a copy of *The New Yorker*. Michael paged through it absentmindedly, still preoccupied by the painting he had seen on the wall.

Balility and two men from Forensics emerged from another room. The house had two bedrooms and a small kitchen, in addition to what Balility called the salon. One of the bedrooms served Tirosh as a study, and it was from this that the three men had come. To Michael's regret, Balility switched on the light, and the magic disappeared. The illumination from the large white fixture suspended from the vaulted ceiling emphasized the whiteness of the walls, the coldness.

"You can smoke inside. Come and see something," said Balility impatiently, and Michael followed him obediently to the study. There was a large chest of drawers, all five of its deep drawers open, all of them overflowing with papers and notes. Then Balility directed Michael's attention to the desk, its four drawers, too, open and over-flowing with papers. Next to the desk stood a stack of cardboard files, each of them labeled in an exquisitely neat handwriting: "Enlighten-ment, Hebrew," "Bialik, criticism," "Structuralism, articles," and so on. A large notepad lay on the desk, and next to it an ordinary ball-point pen. Michael bent over the pad and tore off the seemingly blank first page. He looked closely at it against the light and read "Shira—the last chapter."

"Yes," said Balility impatiently, "I've already seen that; he pressed the pen hard, but you can't really make it out. We haven't found the page he was writing on."

Michael looked around him. He glanced at the pile of books on a corner of the desk but found no clue there.

"We'll worry about it later," said Balility, and looked at the stack of files again.

"I took them down from that wall, fifty of those files, and there are files full of newspaper articles, and a million books, and there's no safe in the house, and the bedroom's full of books and notes too. And if I know you," said Balility in a complaining tone, "we'll need two years to go through it all thoroughly."

"Letters? A diary?" asked Michael briskly, as if to forestall any further complaint.

"Follow me, sir, please," said Balilty, leading him into the bedroom.

For a while Michael gazed at the wide, low bed, at the bookshelves on either side, at the single arched window, full of a soft light, overlooking the Hinnom Valley, at the bottle of wine on the little brown bedside chest, the two glasses, the copper candlestick with the stump of candle stuck in it, at the soft white rug. A volume of poems—by Anatoly Ferber, a poet he didn't know—lay open on the foot of the bed. Balilty opened the closet door wide. Dark suits, gray suits, white shirts, hung there by the dozen, and three pairs of soft, dark leather shoes stood underneath them on the floor.

How empty and pathetic the decor looks without the main actor, thought Michael.

Eli Bahar shuffled around him impatiently and cut through his reflections with a question: "Well, what do you want to begin with?" and Balilty pointed to the little bedside chest, which was locked. Michael sat on the bed and stroked the silk kimono lying on the pillow.

"Is there a key?" he asked, and tapped ash into the little ashtray lying clean and empty on the chest.

"I haven't found one. The most personal thing we found in the study was his bank statement. And I can tell you right now that he didn't do too badly for himself: he's got money invested here and there, and royalties from his books, and an accountant, and reparations money from Germany and money he inherited, and he's very well organized; he's got a file for everything. I can't tell you if there's anything suspicious in the money department; there's no copy of a will or anything like that."

"Okay, let's get it open," said Michael wearily. "Let's not waste any more time. Meanwhile, Eli, call Control, from the phone here, and find out if they've made contact with Eilat. Maybe the pathologist's report on Dudai's ready. Maybe. And ask them to get in touch with the Institute for Forensic Medicine at Abu Kabir and the Marine Medicine Institute in Haifa, where they sent Dudai's diving gear."

"Where's the phone?" Eli asked Shaul from Forensics, who had entered the room, and Shaul led him to the kitchen.

Balilty broke open Tirosh's bedside chest with a little screwdriver he had taken out of his pocket, removed three deep drawers from it, and set them on the floor at the foot of the bed. Michael straightened up and announced: "I need coffee. I'm dead on my feet." Balilty ignored this remark, spread the silk kimono out on the bed—Michael noted the green dragon pictured on its back—and emptied the contents of one of the drawers onto it. Michael reached for the ashtray, and suddenly there was an explosion as the bottle of Riesling that had been standing next to the ashtray on the bedside cupboard fell and shattered, and the room filled with a sour smell of wine. Balilty looked at the bottle on the floor and said: "Lucky we've already taken prints—from the glasses too; we've fingerprinted everything in the room," and only then did Michael notice the traces of the powder. Balilty went out of the room "to get a rag, to clean it up so it won't stink." Again Michael tried to dispel the sweetish stench of decomposition from his nostrils, taking a deep pull on his Noblesse cigarette, whose aroma overcame the wine smell as well.

The drawer had contained photograph albums of the old-fashioned kind, the covers and pages tied together with cord, and inside them yellowing family snapshots against a background of foreign, European scenery. On the first page of one of the albums the single word "Schasky" was written in a rounded script. Michael saw a picture of a young woman holding the hand of a little boy in a sailor suit, who was looking straight into the camera with serious eyes. Under the picture the words "Prague 1935" were written in blue ink in a masculine hand.

He paged slowly through the album, and the child grew from page to page. In the second album Michael traced the boy's features in the face of a youth. The sailor suit had given way to a man's suit and a tie, and the youth in the yellowing snapshot stood in a relaxed pose, his hands at his sides and, in his eyes, the serious, lusterless expression that Michael recognized from the lectures on the history of Hebrew poetry from the period of the Jewish Enlightenment to the present day. Under one of the photos, the young Tirosh standing behind the same woman, who had aged in the interim—she in a heavy armchair, her hair drawn back in a bun, he looking straight at the camera—were the words "Vienna 1956," they, too, written with a fountain pen in Roman letters, this time in a round, feminine hand.

There's a whole life history here, thought Michael, even material for research into European Jewry and its vicissitudes.

Balilty came back into the room with a rag, went down on his knees, and cleaned up the wine stain and the broken glass. Michael returned the albums gently to the drawer and emptied the contents of the second drawer onto the silk kimono. Three notebooks bound in black leather hid the red flames bursting from the dragon's mouth. Now they'll have historical value, thought Michael, and remembered the portable typewriter on the desk in the study. All Shaul Tirosh's poems seemed to be there in the notebooks, handwritten in ink, in elongated Hebrew characters with vowel points. Michael leafed through page after page and found poems he knew, lines that he remembered by heart, combinations that had stunned him when he first saw them. "What a field day the scholars will have when it's all over. There are even different versions of the same poem here— there'll be many papers written!" he said out loud.

"What is it?" asked Balilty impatiently.

"Poetry," replied Michael, and recited aloud: "'To what base uses we may return, Horatio! Why may not imagination trace the noble dust of Alexander, till it be found stopping a bung-hole?'"

Danny Balilty looked at him in amazement for a moment, then he smiled and tapped him on the knee. "My dear Ohayon," he said, "we're not crazy about *Hamlet* in the police, you know. We like action, not hesitation."

"You know it?" asked Michael, and felt foolish when Balilty answered with a good-humored smile: "Come off it, Ohayon, don't be a snob. I studied *Hamlet* in high school too—in English, what's more, hours of learning speeches by heart. It's just that it took me a while to understand what you were talking about. As soon as I hear 'Horatio,' I know that it's from *Hamlet*. My brother learned *Julius*

Caesar by heart, and my sister *Macbeth*, so as far as Shakespeare goes, I'm okay. Which doesn't mean that I go around thinking about *Hamlet* during working hours. A very negative type, old Hamlet. Unhealthy. Can we get back to business now? Are those poems important? For our case?"

"Everything's important for our case," said Michael.

Balilty emptied the contents of the third drawer onto the bed.

Notes, rhyming lines, snapshots of Tirosh himself, Tirosh with women, Tirosh in a large group of people, reviews of his poetry neatly cut out of newspapers, a photograph of a long article about the award of the Presidential Prize, old menus from restaurants in Paris and in Italy, old programs, official invitations, letters and diaries.

"This is what I was waiting for," said Balilty, and the two of them began paging through the diaries. "I don't believe it!" said Balilty after a while. "So many women! And all with names and addresses! What are you blushing about?" Michael handed him a page of the letter he was reading.

Balilty glanced at it and then read it in silent concentration, holding out his hand for the rest of the letter, which graphically detailed the reasons why the author, who signed her letter only with initials, was interested in meeting Tirosh again.

Balilty finished reading and whistled. "Okay, we'll have to take this with us. According to this, our poet's technique wasn't bad, eh?" And again the sight of the corpse and the battered face appeared before Michael's eyes. He went on working through the letters in silence. He always felt embarrassed and curious, even excited, when he was delving into the intimate lives of subjects of an investigation.

"Shaul, Zvika!" roared Balilty from the door. "Come and pack!"

"There are already some bags in the hall, and there'll be another one here. We'll need an entire team to go through all this stuff!" said Shaul with uncharacteristic resentment.

"What's up, Shaul? Is anything wrong?" asked Michael.

"Nothing, except that my wife's going to kill me. Today's our anniversary, and I promised to be home by six. We're supposed to go out to a restaurant. I didn't have the guts to call her, and it's almost nine already. You know how many times a year we can afford to go to a real restaurant on my salary?"

They went into the kitchen. "Good," said Michael, putting out his cigarette in the sink and dropping the wet stub carefully into the empty garbage pail underneath it, whose contents had already been emptied into one of the official bags.

"What's so good about it?" said Shaul sourly. "Look how much material we've got here."

"It can wait till tomorrow. How many years have you been married?"

"Ten," said Shaul, looking somewhat appeased.

"Ten?" said Balilty. "You deserve a weekend in Eilat, something serious, not just a restaurant."

"Yeah?" retorted Shaul angrily. "And who'll cover my overdraft? You? And who'll look after the kids?"

Balilty sighed and nodded. "Okay, we all live like that, don't we? What do you think, that we all drive down to Eilat for the weekend? You think we've all got friends who run diving clubs?" And he slapped Michael's shoulder with a sweaty hand.

"Where's Eli?" asked Michael.

"Back at the office. Control said the pathologist's report from Eilat is in, so he went to check it out for connections," said Zvika. The door of the little refrigerator on which he was leaning suddenly opened, and Shaul, who was facing it, gazed inside and said: "Take a look at this," extracting a glass jar of red carnations with truncated stems.

Balilty looked and burst out laughing: "The guy was one big act, no? Ohayon, come here and quote a bit of *Hamlet*—now's the right time for it."

"And I haven't said anything yet about the French cheeses and salamis and the bottles of wine," said Shaul. "Nothing but foreign goods in this house."

"Shaul," said Michael wearily, "call home, so you don't ruin the evening entirely. And then get going—you wanted to go, no?"

It was situations like these that Michael particularly loathed. His indignation had been roused by the signs of preening and pampering that greeted his eyes wherever he looked, starting with the suits and ending with the bottles of perfume and Italian shaving lotion he found in the bathroom cupboard, on the way to the kitchen, and the French cheeses. But Danny Balilty's frank envy—which he translated into jokes—and the crudeness he had revealed upset him too. Phrases such as "respect for the dead" and "violation of privacy" went through Michael's mind, stirred into life by the hostility and contempt expressed by Balilty. But more than anything else, he longed for a simple, satisfying meal and a cup of steaming black coffee, something to efface the refinement he saw all around him.

"Refined, you know, is another side of negative." He suddenly remembered this line from a poem by Natan Zach and felt that now, for some reason, he understood it better than ever, and also that he had finally entered the "essence of things," although he still had a long way to go, he thought as he listened to Shaul trying to pacify his wife over the telephone.

This business of the "essence of things," which was often mentioned with a smile in all the investigating teams he had worked with, was his personal contribution to an unusual style of detective work. He needed, he felt, to become part of the environment that he was investigating, to sense the subtle nuances of the murdered person's world.

The literary associations that had been coming into his mind ever since he saw the corpse were part of this involuntary, uncontrolled process, the attempt to penetrate the milieu of the Hebrew Literature Department. He felt that he was penetrating deeper and deeper into the soul of Shaul Tirosh. He clearly sensed loneliness, emptiness, something false and overcultivated, and he knew that he was not the only one to feel it, except that Balilty and Eli Bahar resisted, expressed open revulsion for Tirosh's world, while he followed his feelings, allowed them to take control of his consciousness, wanting the subterranean currents of Tirosh's life to overtake him.

"Can we go?" asked Balilty, interrupting his thoughts.

"Not yet," said Michael. "Has the place got a storeroom?"

"Behind the house; nothing unusual: a few tools, boxes, some papers, bottles of wine, and a bit of old furniture," said Zvika. "I took photographs."

"Okay, then, we can lock up and leave," said Michael with a sigh, but at the door he stopped and said to Balilty: "On second thought, I'd better take another look in the bedroom too."

"You said it was just a bunch of poems," protested Balilty.

"Never mind, give me an empty bag anyway," said Michael to Zvika, and returned to the bedroom, where after putting the note-books and the albums into the bag he looked at the bed again. The silk kimono was no longer there; the lab people had packed it up. For a few seconds he gazed around the room, and then he picked up the book of poems by Anatoly Ferber, which lay on the bed. I'd better have a look at it, he thought wearily to himself; it was presumably the last book Tirosh read before he died.

Michael joined the others and placed the extra bag carefully in the Forensics van. There was no sign of the Ford Escort in the parking lot. For a moment he was alarmed, and then he remembered Eli Bahar. He got into Balilty's Renault and sat down next to him. The radio began sending out signals.

"Where are you?" said the officer on duty in the control room when he heard Michael's voice. "Danny Three's looking for you."

"On my way," replied Ohayon, and lowered the volume of the radio. After lighting a cigarette—"one for the road"—he raised the volume again and announced that he would be there in a few minutes.

"Be back in a minute," said Balilty when they arrived at the Russian Compound headquarters, and, as usual, he disappeared.

Eli Bahar was standing in the control room and saying: "So get me Ariyeh Levy—what is this bullshit? What do you mean, you can't let me have a copy?" When he saw Michael, he turned to him: "The bureaucracy's unbelievable—I'm telling you it's unbelievable. The idiots don't want to give me a copy of the autopsy report. That's what you get for going by the book with them—they can drive a person crazy."

"Who doesn't want to give it to you?"

"In Eilat they don't want to, and the pathologist I talked to at

Abu Kabir gave me a whole song and dance about it too," said Eli furiously, and concluded with a juicy curse in Arabic.

Five policemen were sitting at the switchboard and answering incoming calls without missing a word of their superiors' conversation.

"Just a minute," said Michael. "Before you get onto the C.O., get me Abu Kabir again. Who's the pathologist there?" Eli Bahar mentioned an unfamiliar name, and Michael said: "No, don't put him on; wait a minute. I'm going up to the office—come with me." And finally, as always, Eli calmed down after Michael put the phone down in his office and said quietly: "That was Hirsh I just spoke to. They'll send us a copy of the pathologist's report in the morning. But he's going to phone back soon and give us the gist of it."

Michael smoked silently, and Eli Bahar went out and came back with two cups of coffee. When the phone rang, Michael picked it up immediately and listened attentively to what was being said at the other end, making rapid jottings on the paper in front of him and saying, "Aha," innumerable times. Then he thanked Hirsh, a pathologist who had been working with him for eight years now, asked him how his son, the soldier, and his daughter, the student, were getting on, sent affectionate regards to his wife, and replaced the receiver.

"Well?" said Eli Bahar. "Is there any connection? Is there anything?"

"Is there a connection!" Michael gulped down the rest of his coffee. The painting of the sea in Tirosh's house reappeared before his eyes, together with Dudai's body lying spread out on the sand. "Iddo Dudai died of carbon monoxide poisoning. Carbon *monoxide*, CO, not CO_2, the carbon dioxide we exhale, but the poisonous gas that comes out of car exhausts. All those suicides in America in a closed garage with the car engine running? That kind of thing."

"But," said Eli with a big question mark on his face, "poisoned how? By himself? By someone else?"

"He explained to me, Hirsh, that in our bodies. . . ," and Michael began speaking slowly and patiently, as if explaining to himself, as well, that oxygen attaches itself to the red blood corpuscles, which contain hemoglobin. And hemoglobin contains an atom of iron, to which the oxygen we breathe attaches itself. When there's carbon monoxide in the blood, the hemoglobin in the lungs can't take hold of the oxygen and convey it to the tissues of the body. This gas, CO, attaches itself to iron even faster than oxygen, and anyone breathing it in quickly suffocates, loses consciousness without even feeling it. He stopped speaking and looked for a moment into Eli's green eyes, which were narrowed in concentration.

"That's why Dudai's body looked the way it did: his face was completely pink, and all his internal organs were ruptured from the dive. Apparently he'd dived to a depth of thirty meters. His lips were completely blue. They call it—" Michael bent over the paper on which he had jotted down his notes—"cyanosis. They found a lethal amount of CO in the postmortem. A really lethal dose. Now I understand the sentence I heard there on the beach, next to the ambulance," he said slowly.

Eli Bahar asked, his eyes wide: "But where did the gas come from?"

"I don't know exactly how, but someone must have let compressed air out of the air tank and replaced it with CO. They sent both tanks to the Marine Medicine Institute for examination; I thought you talked to them."

"There was no reply. It seems they go home sometimes. But I don't understand," Eli went on, "how anyone can introduce CO into an air tank. How's it done?"

"It seems that's not such a big problem, though you have to be a genius to think of it," said Michael, and tapped his cigarette ash into the dregs of his coffee. "Every diving tank has a valve, and the CO cylinder has a valve too, or you can screw one onto it. So all you have to do is attach the valve of the compressed-air tank to something like a soda siphon containing the poison gas and squirt it in."

"But"—Eli looked thoughtful—"couldn't he tell, Dudai? The gas has a smell, no?"

"No," replied Michael, and looked at the frown between Eli's eyebrows. "There's no smell. You suffocate gradually, without feeling a thing."

"What is this?" exclaimed Eli Bahar in horror. "Are we dealing with a chemist here, or what?"

"All that's needed is creative thinking. Anyone can get hold of CO; every chemical plant has cylinders of it, every decent lab. It's not a problem. All you have to worry about is making sure that the tank isn't lighter or heavier than it would be if it were full of compressed air."

"And he died on Saturday," said Eli, as if to himself.

"Ten past twelve on Saturday," Michael specified.

"So now we're looking for two murderers?" Eli sounded despairing.

"Or one murderer who murdered twice. And it's not only us; the Dudai case belongs to Eilat, and they're looking too."

Danny Balilty burst into the room, puffing and panting, talking a mile a minute, but as usual his words were obscure, and nobody could make out where he had been. "Why don't you offer a person a cup of coffee? And why are you sitting here as if a mountain just fell on top of you? What's going on?"

Michael told him briefly.

"It's getting complicated." Balilty sighed.

"It is indeed," said Michael. "Let's take a break and have something to eat, then go over the list of people to question tomorrow. Or better still, let's take the list to Meir's and go over it there, and maybe we can pick up Tzilla on the way, if you have no objections."

Eli Bahar looked at his watch and muttered that it was eleven o'clock, but he dialed anyway and whispered something into the phone. "We'll pick her up on the way," he said, replacing the receiver.

After they had left the room, Michael called home. He let the phone ring for a long time. Maya didn't come, he thought with a mixture of sadness and relief. Yuval was at his mother's, helping her prepare for her father's seventieth birthday celebration tomorrow. And with the voice of Youzek, his ex-father-in-law, ringing in his ears with sentences such as: "It's going to kill us, this divorce of yours," Michael hurried to join Balilty and Bahar, who fell silent as soon as he got into the car and didn't open their mouths until they reached the restaurant.

Meir's was located in the heart of Machane Yehuda Market, in the "accursed house." Years of work with Tzilla had accustomed Michael to seeing this restaurant as the only possible place for rest and recreation after the discovery of a body, after tensions at work, after watching an autopsy.

The three young men who acted as cooks, waiters, and cashiers always welcomed Tzilla like a long-lost sister. Michael they treated with such deference and respect that he once curiously asked Tzilla what she had told them about him. "I told them that you were from the fraud squad, that you worked hand-in-glove with the income tax authorities," she replied with a wink, and ever since, Michael had felt awkward and embarrassed whenever they presented his check made out with an especially scrupulous correctness. He would raise his eyes to the wall above the cash register and contemplate the picture of the sainted Baba Sali, then he'd look over at that of Rabbi Sharabi, whom rumor credited with having recently laid a curse on the building. The picture over the register was intended to remove the curse from the restaurant.

Nobody knew which of the three who worked in the restaurant, sometimes wearing skullcaps and at other times bare-headed, was Meir. As always, they greeted Tzilla with enthusiasm, then quickly restrained themselves when they caught sight of the tall figure behind her.

To Balilty's question "How's business?" they replied: "Thank God."

"And three portions of fries," called Tzilla to the unshaven youth who was writing down the order. He smiled at her when she explained: "The khamsin's over, and my appetite's back."

They sat in the inside room. Michael looked out through the plate-glass window into the dark, neglected yard. Rabbi Sharabi's curse had emptied the building of its tenants, and Meir's restaurant provided the only source of light in the ghostly darkness all around. For the first time he noticed the fern trailing down the wall opposite him, and he wondered how it stayed so green in the perpetual gloom. He remembered Nira's many attempts to cultivate ferns in their student room after all the other plants had withered and died, leaving behind them only dry yellow stalks. Tzilla followed his eyes, and as if reading his thoughts, she said: "That fern is plastic, and so's the other one," and she pointed to the wall behind them. And when she saw his eyes following the direction of her finger, she said with a smile: "And how about this?" and she stretched out her hand to the wall of dark-red bricks at the right of her chair and delicately peeled off the corner of a brick, exposing the gray concrete underneath it. "It's wallpaper, did you know?" and Michael, who felt sure that if anyone had asked him he would have said that the wall was whitewashed, was slightly embarrassed and raised his eyes to the wooden rafters on the ceiling and then looked at the caricature of Peres and Shamir, dressed as belly dancers, on the wall facing him and the big bull's horns hanging next to it, and Tzilla laughed out loud and said: "You've been here a million times. And to think of the way not a single detail escapes you when it comes to a case! But here you're off duty, right?" And Michael hastened to protest, claiming that he remembered the poster of Shamir and Peres very well, but Tzilla stood her ground: "My point is that you don't see anything when you're not on duty. Tell me, did you see the big picture at the entrance?" Michael nodded uncertainly, and she cocked her head and asked provocatively: "Can you describe it?" Michael started to turn his head, but she forbade him to look behind him. "Something with Bedouin, a biblical picture perhaps?" he said, and Tzilla laughed and said: "Now you can turn around and look." Michael stood up and walked into the front room, where he examined the huge, brightly colored picture from close up. It portrayed a palm tree and a tent in which a number of figures who looked like shepherds were crouching, with a campfire next to the tent. Michael studied them all and returned slowly to the table, where, sitting down, he listed all the features of the picture to her satisfaction, after which he added: "And there's another plant there too, and it's not plastic." "Big deal, it's a wandering jew," said Tzilla contemptuously. "They grow anywhere, under any conditions," and at this point the unshaven youth arrived and wiped the brown Formica surface with a wet cloth and asked if they wanted salads. They all nodded, and Balilty was the first to fall upon the Turkish salad and the Moroccan carrot salad. Tzilla sprinkled lemon juice on the finely chopped vegetable salad and delivered a speech on the art of making a proper salad. "You see, they don't season the salad or put the lemon on it beforehand, so that it'll stay like this, like it's supposed to," she explained to Balilty, who nodded and reached for the pitas and remarked with satisfaction that they had been warmed up. After that Balilty explained how healthy beets were for the digestion and tipped the little saucer of them onto his plate. Until the main courses arrived, while Balilty helped himself liberally to the salads and the pitas, Eli filled in his wife on the details of the case. Michael sipped his beer and watched the couple with enjoyment and also with a sadness he could not understand.

Tzilla and Eli had been working with him for a number of years, and their courtship, slow, tortuous, and full of vicissitudes, had taken place before his eyes. Eli Bahar had turned thirty a year before his marriage to this determined young woman, who had fought for him with praiseworthy persistence. Michael had observed the stage at which she pretended to have given up, and he'd wondered whether Eli, who had often declared that he had no intention of tying himself to "any woman, never mind how I feel about her," would break down and surrender his freedom. Now, seeing his tender gaze fixed on Tzilla as he described the latest developments to her, Michael felt gratified and at the same time suddenly old. They hadn't confided in him. And he had never asked, only looked on with interest, as if he were watching two children reading a story whose ending he already knew. He was glad when they finally got married, even though he privately predicted that their life together would not be easy. Eli was withdrawn, and Tzilla bubbled over with life and tireless energy. Anyone who looked into her eyes, which were always wide open, light and clear, could see the secrets of her heart made manifest.

It had been a few weeks since he last saw her, and now he peered intently at her face, which was paler than usual, at the faint shadow of anxiety. He knew how much she wanted a child. For years she had kept her hair short, but in recent months she'd let it grow, and the brown waves now reached her shoulders. She had a fuller, more womanly appearance, even though the pregnancy was not yet evident except in her breasts, which swelled up out of the low, round neck of her dress.

He thought of the changes that had taken place in her, of the flimsy dress she was wearing instead of jeans, of the slender shoulders and arms, now rounded, and concluded to himself that she had indeed grown more attractive. He complimented her aloud on her hair.

"Yes, I knew you'd like it," she said with a sigh, "but I feel as if all my thirty-two years are obvious to everybody," and she lifted her slender legs onto the empty chair opposite her.

"A woman of thirty-two"—Michael smiled—"is only beginning her life. The only thing more attractive than a woman of thirty-two is a woman of thirty-three."

"Oh, Michael, don't start; I know your line. You can't see a woman without saying something to her. And believe me, you don't have to say a word, all you have to do is look—and stop with that smile already."

The smile broadened and then died. Ever since her marriage, Tzilla, who always was a bit inhibited with him, had grown bolder, her remarks more and more personal, as if some threatening barrier between them had fallen. Sometimes he shrank from the sharpness of her tongue.

Thirty-two years old, thought Michael as the main course arrived, and his hunger vanished. He stared at the meat on the skewers: shashlik from prime beef done to a turn, piquantly flavored lamb kebabs, and to crown it all, *muledjas,* Tzilla and the waiter called something whose origin they refused to disclose. He longed for black bread and goat cheese, for onion—the foods that had whetted his appetite as a child reading books about poor peasants. Nevertheless he sampled the finely chopped salad and the fresh, golden fries, which Tzilla had oversalted, and finally, when Balilty remarked that you could taste the arak in which the meat had been marinated before it was grilled, he dipped a cube of shashlik in the tahina salad and chewed the soft meat. And as he chewed he turned Tzilla's last sentences over and over in his mind.

Thirty-two, thought Michael, a cruel age. The age when sobriety sets in and real knowlege of the virtue of compromise begins. He thought of Maya, about how he would have preferred to be with her now. Tzilla was not eating with her usual gusto. She, too, was picking at her food. Balilty did not say a word. All his attention was devoted to the meat, which he ate with steady concentration, and when he was finished he patted his stomach and grunted his appreciation of the quality of the food.

"Okay," said Tzilla with the arrival of the coffee. "Am I on board or not?"

"You're on board," said Michael, ignoring Eli's worried look, "on condition that you do exactly what you're told and don't initiate any activities outside the building, unless specifically requested to do so. I want to become a godfather. And this time you can't complain that you're only the coordinator, because there are good medical reasons for it." He looked at Eli out of the corner of his eye and then handed her the list of teachers in the Literature Department. From their testimony, he told her, they would get a picture of Tirosh's way of life. "And perhaps," he said hesitantly, "of Dudai's too. I feel that the two cases are connected, as if it's all staring us in the face and I can't see the picture."

"It's too early to see the picture," said Balilty, and belched.

And in the end they mapped out their schedule. Balilty would get on with his intelligence work—"and don't disappear for three days," warned Tzilla. "Tomorrow you'll call in at the end of the day and make contact with me." They agreed on which of the people on the list to question first in the morning, and Michael and Eli divided them up between them.

"So we'll only meet the day after tomorrow?" said Tzilla an hour after midnight, when the restaurant was about to close. Michael remarked that they would have to schedule a meeting late the next day, "even if it's late at night, to plan for Wednesday interrogations according to the information we collect tomorrow." And after he had dropped Eli and Tzilla at the entrance to their small apartment in Nachlaot, he drove home to Givat Mordechai.

The apartment smelled of dust. He opened the windows wide and breathed in the cool air after the heat of the week-long khamsin. He calculated that he would have only four hours' sleep and recalled the face, the dead eyes, of Tuvia Shai, whom he was to meet the next morning. There were still faint traces of Maya's smell in his bed, but it was the form of Adina Lipkin, the department secretary, that appeared before his eyes, and her voice that echoed in his ears, although the words did not suit her at all: "Thirty-two years under Your heavens are enough for an intelligent person to judge the quality of Your mercy," were the words Michael Ohayon heard before he fell asleep.

7

Racheli looked at the dark man sitting opposite her; at his long, restless fingers playing with his pen and cigarette pack, at his smooth-shaven cheeks and his jutting cheekbones, and, finally gathering her courage, straight into the dark, deep eyes that never left her face. But only for a second, after which she again glanced at the bare room—the old wooden desk, the two chairs, the metal cupboard, the window overlooking a backyard in the Russian Compound—and then peered once more into the dark-brown eyes gazing at her steadily.

She had a profound sense of being preferred. Out of them all, she had been chosen to be first. He had called her, this tall man whose dark hair had threads of silver in it, out of the whole group, and she didn't know why.

Adina Lipkin had paled and almost protested when Racheli was invited to go inside, but he had pretended not to notice her anger. Dr. Shai had not stirred, his expression had not changed. When Racheli arrived, obeying a telephoned request of the night before, at the

Criminal Investigations Division in the Russian Compound a bit before eight o'clock in the morning, Tuvia and Adina were already sitting in the anteroom, on shaky wooden chairs. Like patients outside a doctor's office, thought Racheli, or students waiting for the results of some fateful exam. Tuvia Shai looked as if he had resigned himself to the worst.

She succeeded in glancing at her watch without the man opposite her noticing. She had been sitting in the room only a minute, during which nothing had been said, and suddenly she was seized by a terrible fear that she was going to be accused, like Kafka's Joseph K., and by a feeling of uncertainty: perhaps she really had done something wrong. The tall man proffered the pack of cigarettes, and she shook her head. Her throat grew even dryer, and her hands trembled.

Then he began to talk. His voice was soft, quiet. First he asked about her job in the department secretary's office, about what she did outside the office, about her family.

She found herself responding in order to please him. Again she stole a glance at her watch; five minutes had passed, and he already knew everything. About her studying psychology, about her flat in Bnei Brith Street, about her roommate, about her ex-boyfriend, and even about her parents' wishes to see her happily married at her "advanced age." He smiled at the expression and nodded as if his parents had been the same. She asked herself if he was married. He wasn't wearing a ring, but Racheli already knew, at twenty-four, that not all married men wore rings.

She didn't notice exactly when they began to talk about Tirosh and the department. Somehow he had succeeded in managing things so that within a few seconds she found herself telling him all about Adina Lipkin. He was listening attentively, she felt, was really interested in her description of her difficulties, really interested, too, in her observations about the department faculty. He didn't ask about her relations with Tirosh, only asked her to describe his personality as she saw it.

Racheli felt transfixed by the dark eyes of her interrogator, spellbound by his soft voice, and she responded to them: "He had a lot of charm. I've never met anyone like him. I've been a fan of his poetry ever since high school, and my first meeting with him gave me a real thrill. And his outward appearance, and his knowledgeableness about everything, and the way everyone admired him. But I wouldn't have wanted to be close to him."

As she spoke, she sensed that the policeman agreed with her, felt as she did, so she didn't hesitate when he asked: "Why?" It was clear to her that he really wanted to know why she, Racheli Luria, did not want to be close to Shaul Tirosh, and she answered without thinking: "I was afraid of him. He frightened me."

In the same interested tone, he asked: "In what way?" and Racheli, embarrassed, replied: "There was something dishonest about him, but that's only a feeling; actually, I don't mean dishonest, but insincere, not genuine. I couldn't have trusted him. I sometimes used to see him making eyes at people, like flirting, but you could never tell—I could never tell—if he meant it."

The man leaned toward her from the other side of the table. She noticed his long, dark lashes, his thick brows, and then, in a coaxing, authoritative tone, he said: "Give me an example; describe a situation that involved you."

"I can't explain exactly, but there were times when I was alone with him in the office, and once, when they were repairing a leak in the radiator in his office, he held his conference hour in the department office and for a while I was the only person there—Adina was recovering from a minor operation; otherwise she's always there—and we started talking. He behaved toward me then as if he was really interested in me. I remember that I felt as if something really special was happening: he, the eminent professor and poet and everything, was talking to me, the mere student, as if I was a real woman." She stopped talking, but the policeman didn't take his eyes off her as he waited for her to go on.

"And at the same time, I had the feeling that I was watching a movie, a movie I'd already seen. He stood next to the window, looked outside, and talked as if he was talking to himself, about himself. He said that at his age he asked himself if he had any real friends, and something about human loneliness in general, and he quoted a poem by Natan Zach: 'It's not good that the man should be alone, but he's alone anyhow,' and he asked me if I'd ever thought about the meaning of these lines—that's how it began. After that he spoke about the real friends, and I thought: Why is he telling me this, what does he want of me? And I had the feeling that if I let myself be dragged into this conversation, something terrible would happen to me, that he would—how can I put it?—that I would be attracted to him. That's it. He was so attractive, I almost went up to him, to console him, but something stopped me. I sensed that it wasn't really me he was talking to, but I was just someone who happened to be there. After all, he didn't know the first thing about me"—she sounded apologetic—"but what really frightened me was that fascination of his, the power that drew me toward him, just to touch his terrible, infinite suffering, which I couldn't do anything about: I would give him all of myself, and he wouldn't give me anything back, he had nothing to give me. I don't know how to explain it."

"You explain it perfectly," said the policeman with a sober, encouraging expression, and Racheli blushed, and since she didn't want to show how much the compliment had meant to her, she went on: "That lecture about loneliness sounded so strange to me because of all the stories."

"Stories?" asked the policeman, and he put out his cigarette, which gave off a strong smell, in the tin ashtray at the edge of the table, as he scribbled something on the sheet of paper in front of him.

"Well, there were all kinds of stories," said Racheli in embarrassment. "Rumors."

"Such as?" he asked softly.

"All kinds of things," and again Racheli felt her throat contracting and her feet in their biblical sandals beginning to sweat, but the man wouldn't let go. His look said: Trust me; I want to know.

"There were stories about him and women and about other poets and all kinds of people."

"Did you think, when he was talking to you, that he was really lonely?"

"Yes and no. Mainly I thought that it was like a line from a novel, or a movie. I don't like that kind of empty declaration. And that business of standing next to the window, as if he'd chosen the most flattering angle for his profile. And at the same time, there was something convincing about it, I believed him too, and that's what frightened me so much. I didn't think it all out then; it's only now that I can put it into words."

"Who was the person closest to him in the world, in your opinion?" And again Racheli thought that she was being given an important and central role, that she was being asked to offer the fruits of her long and patient observation.

"Well, his relationship with Dr. Shai was considered to be close," she said hesitantly.

"But?" he asked, and waited patiently.

"But I couldn't stand the way Dr. Shai abased himself—he simply hero-worshiped him. And then that story with his wife."

"His wife?" asked the policeman, and Racheli looked at his brown arms in the white shirt and thought that she knew exactly what his skin would smell like, a clean smell, and she felt herself blushing.

"Dr. Shai's wife, Ruchama. I hardly know her; I've only seen her a couple of times, and I've talked to her on the phone, but still. . . " She searched for the right words, and in the end she said: "Everyone talked about it; it was obvious that they were together."

She couldn't get the words out quickly enough to express what she wanted to say, clearly and eloquently, about the strange triangle that had been the talk of the department, the students, everyone. Except for Adina, of course, who never said a word about it.

"Together?" he asked. "You mean Ruchama Shai and Professor Tirosh? They lived together?"

"No, but it was as if the *three* of them lived together. Everybody knew about it, and in my opinion Dr. Shai knew too; a lot of people think so, anyway. It went on for years, but lately. . . " Racheli looked at him and hesitated, but he nodded as if to say: "I'm all ears," and she went on. "Lately something seemed to have changed." The policeman remained silent.

"She would look for him, and he would disappear, or ask us to say that he wasn't there; to other people too—that is, it wasn't as if he told us to tell just her, but I felt that things weren't what they used to be between them, as if he was avoiding her."

Racheli couldn't stop herself. She, who had been observing these people for months, who had heard about them ever since she began studying at the university, and who had kept her impressions to herself all this time, suddenly felt a tremendous need to tell him everything, and for a minute, a second, she heard herself from the outside, and she couldn't believe her ears. She asked herself if the urge to talk stemmed from the wish to come close to this man, whom she wanted to touch her, to smile at her pleasantly, with the smile that made her talk on and on; or whether, perhaps, it came from the feeling that at last she had a listener, someone who would take an interest in her long labor of observation and appreciate her perceptiveness.

"And why do you think that Dr. Shai knew?"

"Because in the first place, *everyone* thought he knew, but also because of his subservience to Tirosh. And Tuvia Shai isn't a fool or a blind man, and everyone else saw, and he was in the office more than once when his wife called, looking for Tirosh. They didn't even try to hide it. There was something frightening about it; I didn't understand why he—Dr. Shai, that is—stayed with her, why he didn't divorce her."

The telephone rang. He lifted the receiver and said: "Yes."

His face changed. The soft expression with which he had listened to her disappeared, and tensely he jotted down a few words. But he kept his eyes fixed on her, and by now she felt brave enough to face his look.

"Between two and six?" he said in a hard voice, a different voice. "Okay, I'll get in touch again later, in a little while." He replaced the receiver and lit another cigarette.

Then he asked about Iddo Dudai, and Racheli said: "He was a nice guy, pleasant; even Adina liked him. But he took himself too seriously, in the professional sense, I mean—for example, he'd never say anything off the cuff—but everyone respected him anyway and liked him."

"What about Tirosh?"

"With regard to Iddo, you mean? I think he also respected him; his attitude toward him was paternal, though he mocked him a bit too. Not actually mocked, really, but he made fun of his seriousness, of the way he examined everything under a microscope. But there was no ill will in it."

"Did Tirosh dive too?"

"You mean scuba diving?" And Racheli sensed that the policeman knew something she didn't know, that now he was directing the conversation. "No; why should he? He always laughed at sports and said that life was too short for suffering. 'Only skiing is worthwhile,' I heard him say once, 'but only in Switzerland, in the Alps, not on Mount Hermon.' But I can't imagine him skiing either—if you ever saw him, in his suits, you'd know he wasn't the type for outdoor sports, despite his tan. He said he loved the sea, but I don't believe he dived. It was Iddo who was mad about diving." She didn't dare ask him why he wanted to know, she had the feeling that there was something else here, something she knew nothing about.

"And apart from Mrs. Shai, did you notice any other changes? Did anything unusual happen lately? Did Tirosh seem strained? Different?"

Racheli hesitated before answering. She remembered Tirosh's pallor and air of weariness after the departmental faculty meeting on Friday, when she had first noticed the traces of age, the deep creases in his cheeks, the heaviness in his tread.

"Anything at all," said the policeman. "Whatever comes into your head."

Racheli reported the changes and summed up: "On Wednesday night there was a departmental seminar, and afterward everyone behaved as if a catastrophe had taken place, but I couldn't understand what had happened. I wasn't there, but I heard from Tsippi, a teaching assistant, that Iddo attacked Professor Tirosh and there was a big scandal. But they're always having scandals over things like that; it's all political. They carry on as if one word of theirs can change the face of literature in Israel, and sometimes they even imagine they can influence the whole world." She was taken aback by her own bitterness and hostility.

"And Iddo? Were there any changes in Iddo?"

"Ever since he returned from the United States—he was there for a month, on a grant—he wasn't the same person," said Racheli, who realized that she was quoting something she had overheard Tuvia Shai say.

"How would you describe the change?" asked the policeman, and once more he leaned forward and fixed his eyes on her as if eagerly anticipating her reply.

"I don't know exactly; as if he was upset about something, uneasy, angry, and he avoided Tirosh. But that may have been connected to what he heard when he came back."

"What did he hear?"

"I don't know if it's true, but people talked, and I saw them in Meirsdorf, having lunch in the guesthouse restaurant—Iddo's wife, Ruth, and Tirosh. And I don't know, maybe that's the way Professor Tirosh behaved with any female, but it seemed to me that there was more to it than just a friendly lunch. He had that agonized expression on his face—the one I told you about, when he was standing next to the window—and afterward I heard from Dr. Aharonovitz. . . ." And Racheli stopped to take a breath, and also in order to convey that she didn't like Dr. Aharonowitz—he sensed it, she knew, just as he sensed everything else. "He didn't tell me, he told somebody else, in the line at the cash register in Meirsdorf, and I heard him, because they didn't see me, he said"—and she looked at the ceiling, she could hear his voice, the ugly innuendo in it—"'And so we behold our great poet snaring yet another woman in his net. Gullible fools.'"

"You think he was sleeping with her? With Iddo Dudai's wife?" asked the policeman. "And that Iddo knew about it?"

Racheli nodded, then she said: "And Iddo wasn't the type to go along with it, like Dr. Shai."

"Why do *you* think"—and Racheli's heart swelled at the emphasis—"that Dr. Shai went along with it?"

"I don't know," said Racheli, and though she started hesitantly, the words turned into fluent, full sentences: "I thought about it a lot, because Dr. Shai's such an honest, decent person. You could even like him, really, but I think he admired Professor Tirosh so much that he couldn't bring himself to object even to that. I heard him say more than once that true genius was a force he couldn't resist. When he came back from Europe, from a conference, at the beginning of the year, he talked about Florence, about the statue of David. He was talking to Iddo, in our office, and I've never heard anyone talk about a work of art like that before. As if he was talking about—" Racheli searched for the word while he waited patiently. "—as if he was talking about a woman, or something," she finally announced, and she bit her lip.

"And did *he* dive?" the policeman asked, and then lit another cigarette.

"Who? Dr. Shai? Not on your life. Have you seen him?" And she refrained from asking why he was so interested in diving, because it was obvious that she wouldn't get an answer.

"Did anyone else in the Literature Department go in for diving?"

Racheli stared at him incomprehendingly and shook her head. After this she obediently answered questions about her movements since Friday and what she had done over the weekend. She explained that she had finished work at noon on Friday, that it had been her turn to clean the flat and do the shopping, that she had been expecting her parents to come on a visit from Hadera, and that they had arrived at four o'clock.

"So you're from Hadera?" he asked as he wrote, and she nodded and suddenly realized the purpose of his questions. Gathering her courage, she asked him if he was checking her alibi.

Again he smiled the smile that narrowed his eyes to slits and emphasized his cheekbones, and he said: "You don't have to call it that, but yes, more or less," and in the same breath asked her if she had any ideas about who murdered Shaul Tirosh.

She shook her head. She had thought about it all night, she said— she couldn't sleep because of the sight of the corpse, and the smell— but she didn't have a clue. None of the people she knew looked to her like a murderer.

"And in the departmental seminars," he said, and she sensed that he was about to tell her she could go, "does anyone take notes of the proceedings?"

"No; it's quite a mass event; sometimes they publish the lectures. But it was apparently a very unusual evening; I heard that they recorded it for the radio and for television, Tsippi told me the next day." Racheli sensed the change that came over his face; as if a curtain had descended, there was a different atmosphere in the room.

"Television?" he asked, and a glint came into his eyes. "Is that routine? Do they always have television reporters at the seminars?"

"No," said Racheli. "Of course not; there's a seminar every month. It was because of Professor Tirosh: they call him the darling of the media."

"Who, for example, calls him that?"

"Aharonovitz, I think. He always ridiculed Professor Tirosh, but never in his presence."

"Did Aharonovitz have any particular reason for ridiculing Tirosh?"

"Not that I know of. Maybe just pathological jealousy. But he never laughed at his poetry. Next to Tirosh, Aharonovitz always looked so repulsive; he's unattractive in any case, but next to Professor Tirosh it was even more conspicuous." And Racheli felt terribly tired; she knew with despairing certainty that the man sitting opposite her wasn't going to get closer to her, and she didn't have the strength to say another word.

As if he knew what she was feeling, he stood up and said that he might require her assistance again during the course of the investigation, but for now she was free to go. For a moment the dark eyes rested on her face, but he was no longer with her.

A young woman with wide blue eyes opened the door with a brisk, determined movement and said: "Listen, Michael—" but then she noticed Racheli and abruptly stopped talking.

Michael, thought Racheli, of course his name is Michael. And although the woman waited for her to leave the room and didn't say another word, Racheli could sense the intimacy between them, the equality, and her heart shrank inside her as he opened the door wide and said: "Thank you very much."

Without replying, she hurried out into the narrow corridor, where she noticed the frightened expression on Adina's face as she stood up and took a step toward her from the corner where she had been sitting. But Racheli fled; she didn't have the strength to face Adina Lipkin and answer her questions about what had happened there, inside the room.

Racheli ran along the corridor and hurried down the stairs leading to the ground floor, and from there to the backyard of the Russian Compound and into Jaffa Street, running all the way.

Outside the building, the strong sunlight hit her in the face, making her blink and rub her eyes. At the window of the Jordan Bookshop, she stopped at the sight of Ariyeh Klein's latest book, *Musical Elements in Medieval Poetry.* Her legs trembled as she waited for the Zion Square traffic lights to change, and the news dealer on the other side of the street looked resigned as she stood and gazed at the headlines of the morning papers, reporting the murder, and at the picture of Shaul Tirosh emblazoning them all. Then she bought a paper and made for the Café Alno, on the pedestrian mall, where she sat down at a table. The waitress stood there impatiently until she said, "Coca-Cola with lemon." Then she tried to read the story, which continued on an inside page and included a description of the body and a biography of Shaul Tirosh, as well as details concerning the head of the special investigation team, Superintendent Michael Ohayon, who owed his fame mainly to the solution of the murder, two years previously, of the psychoanalyst Eva Neidorf. It said nothing about his private life or his age. Racheli looked at the man sitting at the table on her left, eating his breakfast, and then at the elderly couple at another table nearby, drinking coffee and talking nonstop, and finally she looked at the big clock on the wall opposite her and saw that it was eleven o'clock and realized that the statistics examination had begun at nine and would be over in half an hour. For a minute she panicked, and then she told herself to calm down, she would be able to take the exam later, but she didn't calm down, and her hands trembled so hard that she had to put her glass down on the table. The man eating breakfast paid and left, and the waitress collected the dishes and put a copy of the daily *Ha'aretz* on her table. On the front page, next to the picture of Shaul Tirosh, there was a photo of the man she had spent the morning with, Superintendent Michael Ohayon. He held his hands out in front of him as if holding someone at bay, and his lips were parted. Staring at the picture, Racheli picked up her glass and slowly sipped her drink.

8

W hat did you do to her? A child like that," said Tzilla as she sat down opposite him.

"She's not such a child. She's okay," replied Michael absentmindedly as he compulsively redialed a number on the outside line, which had continued to be busy.

"And pretty too, no?" said Tzilla in the coquettish tone she sometimes used when they were alone. Sometimes Michael would respond, but this time he ignored her amused, inquisitive expression and, as he redialed yet again, asked: "What's up? What's new?"

Sighing loudly, Tzilla began briefing him: everyone had already been told to come in for questioning, the intelligence information had been gathered, there was nothing out of the ordinary about any of the people in the Literature Department.

"What does *that* mean?" Michael was increasingly irritable as the telephone continued to emit the busy signal.

"I mean that they've committed traffic offenses, that Iddo Dudai took part in an unlicensed demonstration, and that Aharonovitz once complained about the noise in the house next door. Are you listening to me?"

Nodding as he dialed yet again, he said: "On Wednesday last week they had a departmental seminar, and there was a TV crew there. There's a film, and I want to see it—today."

Tzilla stood up and walked to the other side of the table, and while Michael kept talking and dialing, she took a sheet of paper and a chewed pen out of the top drawer and scribbled something down. Her arm brushed against his, and he breathed in her smell, a delicate astringent perfume. Tzilla drew her arm quickly away.

"And please get hold of Tuvia Shai's wife for me, ask her to come in for questioning, and Iddo Dudai's wife too."

"I told you yesterday," said Tzilla as she resumed her seat opposite him, "that if you started looking for all the women he ever slept with, you'd waste your whole life on it."

But then someone answered the phone, and Michael spoke to Dr. Hirsh at the pathology lab, while he drummed his fingers on the table. Tzilla went out and came back with two cups of coffee, and by then the paper in front of Michael was crowded with words.

He sipped the coffee, pulled a face, and went on talking into the mouthpiece. A few minutes passed before she realized that he was talking to somebody else now.

"What's the problem? It shouldn't be difficult to find such a rare make." And afterward: "Really! How do you think you're going to find it on the computer? What dead person reports a stolen car? A white 1979 Alfa Romeo GTV. Comb the whole university area, Mount Scopus—I don't have to tell you how to work!" He slammed down the phone.

"She's waiting outside, the department secretary—I forget her name. She looks as if she's about to have a heart attack. What did Hirsh say?" asked Tzilla, who knew that from now on there would be no flirting.

"The report won't be ready until the day after tomorrow; he couldn't begin the autopsy until the court order arrived, and the absence of family complicated things. Eli was there while Hirsh was doing the postmortem." Michael looked at the sheet of paper in front of him, knowing very well what the expression on Tzilla's face would be when he raised his eyes. And indeed, her mouth tightened and her eyes flashed, but she didn't say anything. Michael preferred to avoid autopsies, and Tzilla was always angry at him for shirking this unpleasant duty and relying on Eli's report instead. But Michael was not willing to experience the ordeal with each new case. He almost told her: When Eli's the head of an SIT, he'll be able to send someone else too. Instead he looked at the paper again and said: "The cause of death was a double fracture at the base of the skull, apparently from the fall onto the radiator. The pathologist on the scene already pointed that out: there were marks on the radiator. Hirsh says that he was unconscious from blows received before the fall, which is why he fell. There were fractures of the ribs, too, and internal bleeding."

"I didn't know he was beaten," said Tzilla, and Michael remembered that she had not seen Shaul Tirosh in his office. "His face was squashed flat," he explained. "I presume someone hit him with something commonly found in a university lecturer's office—a paperweight or a heavy ashtray or a knickknack. Forensics said that the only bloodstains were the ones on the radiator. There was nothing on any of the objects in the room. And nothing without fingerprints. So maybe the assailant used something that was there, or maybe he brought the instrument with him, but now it doesn't look as if we're talking about a premeditated murder, so the weapon probably was something in the office."

"What prints did they find?" asked Tzilla. "Did anyone refuse to be fingerprinted?"

"No; everyone agreed; there was no problem. We took them yesterday, and we've already eliminated anyone with a legitimate reason to be there. Tirosh's prints were all over the place, and everyone who went into his office on Sunday, and some unidentified prints. Students went into his office too, don't forget, so who knows who was there."

"Do you think," asked Tzilla thoughtfully, folding her hands on her stomach in the way of pregnant women, even at the beginning, when their stomachs are still flat, "that a woman could have done it?"

Michael looked at her before replying wearily: "I don't know. People sometimes have demonic strength, especially when they've gone berserk." He leaned backward, stretched his legs out in front of him, and lit a cigarette. There were investigation teams working on other cases, there was his ongoing work as head of the Investigations Division, and Azariya, his deputy, was in the hospital, recovering from back surgery. Michael wanted to lay his head on the table and abandon himself to Tzilla's caressing hands. They were both careful to avoid any physical contact, but there was something so soft and appealing about her now. She was wearing the dress she had worn the night before, and her arms looked smooth and soft.

Michael sat up in his chair and said: "Tell Raffi that the estimated time of death has now been increased to between two and six on Friday afternoon. I think the murder took place closer to two than six, because the security officer didn't register an entrance or exit after the gates were locked."

Tzilla stopped taking notes and looked at him questioningly.

"Anyone who wants to be on the campus at night on weekdays, or after four on Fridays, has to register in advance with the security officer. It's a simple procedure, but it's documented. You have to phone 883OOO and inform them. And please tell the C.O. that I want a meeting with him today. And tell everybody there's a team meeting at seven o'clock tomorrow morning."

"And when do you want the television film?"

Michael silently reviewed the day's schedule and replied: "Late this evening." And after thinking, he added: "And we can decide about tomorrow's schedule then, when the whole team's there."

Tzilla rose, her movements slower than usual, and when she reached the door he said: "Please send the Literature Department secretary in," and switched on the tape recorder. He had to push aside the oppression he had felt since the end of his conversation with Racheli.

Adina Lipkin was wearing her "good dress," he noticed with a smile, the dress that he assumed a respectable woman felt she should wear on important occasions involving contact with the authorities.

But such occasions were apparently rare in Adina's life, he thought, since the dress, which was made of a dark, thick material, was at least one size too small for her, making her stomach stick out and emphasizing her heavy arms. Her face was flushed, her head thrust forward. She sat down, breathing heavily, on the chair he indicated. Her hands gripped the handles of the black patent-leather bag in her lap, and when she stared reproachfully at the cigarette he was about to light, he put it down, unlit, on the desk.

When he asked her about her movements on Friday, she looked at him with round, bulging eyes, her expression that of a schoolgirl facing an oral examination for which she had been preparing for an entire year. "Do you mean after the faculty meeting?" she asked. Michael replied that he meant everything she did on that day. "Aha," said Adina Lipkin, as if everything was now clear to her, and she even nodded her head firmly, without disturbing a single stiff curl. "If I remember rightly—and I can't be sure; there are always things that we think we remember, but we don't get the details right—in any case, if I remember rightly, I was already in the office at seven o'clock in the morning, because I had a lot of work to do, we're at the end of the year and the students are very nervous about their exams and in a hurry to hand their papers in, really, I ask myself, why do they always leave things to the last minute, but that's already a different question." Here she activated her lip muscles, but the smile she produced had nothing mirthful about it, only the anxiety of someone eager to please and wishing to know if she was going about it the right way. Michael maintained his reserve but could not help nodding in response to the smile. "In any case, I was already in the office at seven, and there were a few telephone calls, because I take advantage of the hours when the university's empty in order to get everything out of the way before the consulting hours, because of course Friday is a very short day, and even if officially there's no consulting hour, there are always a few students who come to find something out, and even if I don't usually see students outside consulting hours, sometimes there are special cases, but in any event it interrupts the sequence of work. In any case, there were a few calls to make. I think I phoned Dr. Shai to find out something about a student who handed in a seminar paper very late, and then I called Dr. Zellermaier, she's always easy to reach in the mornings, because I had a question about typing her exam questions, and afterward I called Professor Tirosh because there was a question about the budget that he was the only one authorized to deal with," and here she paused at last to take a breath and also because she had remembered the new state of affairs, and she went back to listing the things she had done after she had made the phone calls, and Michael felt like the sorcerer's apprentice who had set the brooms in motion and couldn't stop them. The spate of words flowed on, while an expression of satisfaction spread over Adina Lipkin's face, as if she felt she was passing this test with flying colors, and the exhausted Michael was seized by a feeling of utter helplessness and the certainty that if he stopped her she would lose her power of speech. From time to time he would scribble a note, an act that caused her to look at him with a gratified expression but did not interrupt her monologue. Michael had lost his ability to distinguish the wheat from the chaff, and it was a full twenty minutes before he pulled himself together and acknowledged that she didn't actually control him. She was in the middle of describing the events of the afternoon. "The children were supposed to be coming for the weekend, even though my grandson had a bit of a fever and my daughter wasn't sure because her husband wasn't feeling too well, and he spent the whole of yesterday and today having tests," and on and on, in her shrill, jarring voice. When she began describing her daughter's visit, he succeeded in bringing himself to utter the magic words that arrested the verbal torrent: "Excuse me just a minute," and she silenced herself immediately, her face anxious but full of good will. Then he asked about her relations with the department faculty.

Her view of the staff of the Hebrew Literature Department was restricted to their administrative functions. All her opinions and feelings about the various lecturers related exclusively to the manner in which they performed their duties in handing in grades, examining papers, and completing forms. Michael quickly learned that Dr. Shai always treated his students' seminar papers seriously, grading them fairly and not procrastinating. "Of course, I'm not setting myself up as an expert, but everything goes through me, the student hands the paper in to me, and I pass it on to the lecturer, and so we avoid problems, because it's already happened that a student has complained that he handed in a paper and the lecturer lost it, and what do we need problems for?" she said, straightening her hem.

All questions about the personalities of the teaching staff, about changes in their relations, gave rise to anxiety and confusion and disrupted her smooth delivery.

"I'm not interested in gossip," she said firmly when he asked her about Tirosh's relations with Tuvia Shai's wife. "Dr. Shai does his work properly, he's always in order." And she quickly added: "As far as I know, in any case."

When Michael had understood—only at the end of half an hour—what it was possible to ask her, he learned that Shaul Tirosh did not always meet his departmental obligations. But Michael grasped that even though Tirosh didn't consistently hand in his students' grades in time, she was somewhat intimidated by him, a little in awe of him. Sometimes the students complained that he didn't make any comments on their papers, and some said that they didn't think he even read them, "but that's not my department, I can't make any comment on that," she stated firmly, as if to say: It wouldn't be fair to demand information from me that's not included in the material set for the examination.

Iddo Dudai, said Adina in a voice full of pathos, a solemn expression on her face, "was such a nice boy, he took such an interest. There are a few people, not many, who appreciate your work when you make an effort, and Iddo was one of them. He always thanked me and always praised my responsibility and always...," and Michael let her sob, and blow her nose loudly on the tissue she extracted with an effort from her patent-leather bag.

Michael reflected silently to himself, while maintaining his inscrutable facade, that sometimes people are even more stereotypical than the stereotypes you store in your head. Adina Lipkin personified all his prejudices about the classic secretary who identified totally with her role. And you can't tell, he went on reflecting, if she was always like this, or if during the course of the years the border between herself and the role she performed had grown more and more blurred. He raised his eyes from the paper at which he had been gazing and looked into her face with renewed interest.

Soon after she had entered the room, Michael learned that the only object of her unqualified admiration was Professor Ariyeh Klein. "He's a real mensch!" she said three times, each time with the stress on a different word. "You won't hear a bad word about him from anyone. And what a wife he's got! And what daughters!" And inclining her head to one side, she said in a confidential tone: "I'll give you an example. You know how sometimes it's the little things that show you who the person is?" Michael nodded. "He's never come back from a trip abroad," she continued, "without bringing me something—something small, but just the fact that he thought about me . . . This last year when he was away has been so difficult for me."

Her answers were more to the point when he asked her about the department faculty meetings. She had never taken part in them, but the minutes were all in her possession. And he could certainly have a look at them, on condition, of course, that she received the proper permission.

No, she had never read the minutes; she only took care of them. The minutes were usually taken by a junior lecturer or a teaching assistant.

No, she didn't attend the departmental seminars either; she worked so hard during the day, she said, that in the evenings she was worn out. "And also," she added, "I don't like leaving my husband alone at night. There are some women who don't care"—she paused here as if to give him time to consider which women these might be— "but I like spending my evenings at home." And then, in a special effort to share her life experience with him: "There are some days when the pressure is terrible. Everyone hands in their examination questions at the last minute, for example, and they want them copied immediately, and then there's pressure from the students, and a person who doesn't understand, a person from outside," she said, and giving him a subtle look of rebuke, added: "If you'll forgive me, I don't mean you, but people in general, the students too, in any case, someone from outside can't understand why I'm so strict about having everything in writing, about the consulting hours, because he doesn't see the difficulties, I can't talk on the telephone when there are students in my office during consulting hours, and it makes some people angry," she said in a tone of incomprehension, confident that he would see things from her point of view.

It was impossible not to see her as a stereotype, and Michael suddenly realized that he was thinking, angrily: I know the type. After two hours he gave up in despair. He was bone-weary, impatient and irritated. He couldn't mobilize even a grain of humor to soothe him.

She had not noticed any change in Tirosh's behavior, not after the faculty meeting on Friday either—he had only looked tired. Iddo looked tired too, "but it was the khamsin; it exhausted me too." Finally Michael asked her about the objects in Tirosh's office. She looked at him perplexed. "Do you mean furniture? Books?" she asked.

"You've got a phenomenal memory," said Michael with the right smile, "so I thought you might be able to describe the things in his office to me, as you remember them. What, for example, did he have on his desk?"

A few seconds passed before she replied in embarrassment: "But I never went in there when he wasn't there."

"But you must have been there with him," Michael encouraged her. "We all know how it is—sometimes it's easier to go into a person's office than to telephone."

She nodded. "Ah, just a minute, let me think," she said, and a frown of concentration appeared on her forehead. Then she turned to him with shining eyes and said: "Okay, I think I've got a mental picture."

Michael knew that now he would let her talk to her heart's content. No one, he felt sure, would draw a more accurate picture of Tirosh's office than Adina Lipkin.

She described the full bookshelves, the separate shelf for poetry (although disclaiming knowledge of titles and authors), and the "standard furniture," as she called it. Michael wrote feverishly. Then there were the "other things": the Mexican carpet—her daughter had brought something similar back from Mexico, even though she herself didn't like carpets, if you asked her opinion, all they did was collect dust, and in our climate they were superfluous, especially in summer, in winter it was something else again, especially in Jerusalem; the Indian statuette, something made of bronze, very heavy, she had once held it in her hand to move it away from the edge of the desk—and again, she said, it was a matter of taste, of course, but she couldn't understand why anyone would want to keep something like that in an office, which was a public place whether you liked it or not, and although everyone said that Professor Tirosh was a man of taste, she, at any rate, didn't think it was very appropriate, she wasn't saying it was ugly, or worthless, but it was out of place, if he understood what she meant. He understood. She described the location of the fire extinguisher, and she didn't forget to mention the telephone. Finally she was silent. She had covered everything. If she remembered anything else, she said, she would be happy to help. And then: "I hope I've been of some assistance, of some use, I've never had any dealings with the police before." Michael murmured a few words to the effect that she had been very helpful and stood up before she could say another word. He accompanied her to the door, where he parted from her with a practiced politeness that brought an embarrassed smile to her lips and a blush to her cheeks. As soon as the door was shut he fell on his cigarettes, then switched off the tape recorder and dialed the number of the forensics laboratory. A few minutes passed before Pnina informed him with absolute certainty that no Indian statuette had been found in Shaul Tirosh's office on Mount Scopus.

As he was putting the phone down, Raffi Alfandari burst in. Michael looked up in surprise; Raffi was supposed to be in the middle of an interrogation. And so he was.

"Come and see for yourself," he insisted in reply to all Michael's questions. His fair hair was falling over his forehead, and he was breathing rapidly, as if he had been running. "Everything was okay with Kalitzky and with Aharonovitz, until I got to her. But come and see for yourself."

In the narrow hallway, Tuvia Shai was sitting and staring in front of him, his eyes lifeless. Michael ignored him and followed Raffi to the room where Yael Eisenstein sat, dressed in a black knit outfit that emphasized her pallor. The room was small and seemed crowded, though it contained only a table and three chairs. She sat with her legs crossed, one knee over the other, and her ankles looked white and delicate in their slender black sandals. Her big blue eyes gazed at him serenely.

Her beauty stunned him. He caught his breath. For a few seconds Michael looked at the white skin—so white it seemed never to have been exposed to the Israeli sun—at the red lips, at the nose, arched just enough to give an aristocratic air to the narrow face, at the neck, which looked as if it had been painted by Modigliani. He was afraid that he wouldn't be able to speak.

"She won't talk," said Raffi Alfandari, "without her lawyer."

"Why not?" Michael's eyes had not left her face.

"It's my right," she replied softly, the softness of her voice in sharp contrast to the firmness with which she uttered the words. She took a final deep drag on the cigarette she was holding. Her delicate fingers were stained yellow with nicotine. Her other hand supported her arm. Michael glanced at Raffi, who hurried out of the room.

"You know," said Michael Ohayon after he, too, had a cigarette going, having seated himself in Raffi's chair, "you're a surprising person."

"What do you mean?" asked Yael. A spark of interest appeared in her eyes, and she lit another cigarette from her stub.

"On the one hand, you faint and everyone protects you, and on the other, here you are, demanding a lawyer. Have you done anything wrong to make you want a lawyer?"

"Nobody's going to ask me personal questions and get an answer. My private life is my own business."

Again he was struck by the contradiction between her delicate, aristocratic beauty and her assertiveness. And then he was overcome by anger and heard himself saying: "My dear young lady,"—in the particular quiet voice he always used, so he was told, when he was angry—"maybe you think this is a movie, but we're conducting an investigation into a murder here, not acting in a French film, so perhaps you'll be good enough to get off the screen. You want a lawyer? A psychiatrist? No problem!"

"A psychiatrist?" asked Yael, uncrossing her legs. "What's a psychiatrist got to do with it?" Her voice was still soft, and before Michael gave way to the temptation to retort with some witty, sarcastic remark, he looked at her face and realized that he had unintentionally touched a sensitive spot.

"We're not in the Middle Ages," he said after a moment, "and you're not a murder suspect yet, even if you *are* in therapy. I'm quite willing to let you phone your lawyer, if you have one, right now. I simply think it would be superfluous. At this stage, anyway."

"It's not a question of therapy," she said, and burst into tears. Michael let out a sigh of relief. Tears were something more familiar; at least they were human. Between sobs she said: "That man who was here before, he was so rude to me, he asked me right off why I'd fainted, as if it wasn't obvious, and if I'd had an 'affair' with Professor Tirosh."

"And had you?" asked Michael, quickly deciding to gamble.

"Not really; just something years ago."

"What do you mean by 'something'?" Michael looked into her eyes.

"I read his poetry when I was very young, and I wrote him a letter, and then I met him. When I was in the army I even ran away to him once. I stayed in his house for a few days."

"Until they discharged you?" asked Michael, in what seemed like a fortuitous intuition but was actually the product of a story he had once heard from a friend, a history student, who was in love with a girl who had gone absent without leave to be with Shaul Tirosh. Now the two stories connected, like the other threads that were connecting, and he felt anxiety rising in him again, like the dread he had felt in Tirosh's house. But the woman in front of him—now he remembered, too, how his fellow student had raved about the beauty of the girl so many years ago—had no idea of the source of his information, and two dark-red stains flushed her cheeks as she asked: "How do you know? Everything's in your files, isn't it? Why do I even bother to ask?" And again she burst into tears.

"I wouldn't have thought," said Michael, "that it would matter to a woman like you if that information was known. I wouldn't have thought that you cared about military service—*or* public opinion."

"I don't. But I do care, very much, about my private life, and I'm not prepared"—her voice, delicate and bell-like, rose for the first time—"for every policeman in this ugly place to know everything about me."

And Michael remembered the whole story and asked: "And you were hospitalized again later, right?" and the blue eyes looked at him in dread. The red patches on her cheeks disappeared as she shook her head, and then she said: "No, that was the only time." (Rely on the computer, on the intelligence people! thought Michael. They'll always tell you that there's nothing special—computer never lies!)

"And how long did that hospitalization last?"

"Two weeks. Just for observation. It was the only way to get out of the army, and it goes without saying that there was no way I could stay in the army. I couldn't stand the ugliness."

She shuddered and lit another cigarette, this time with a gold lighter from the little gray leather bag that hung from her shoulder.

Again Michael examined her exquisite beauty, which seemed so extraordinary and out of place in the mean room; a beauty not of this place, thought Michael, and remembered Tirosh's house, which was somehow connected to this beauty, to the slender ankles and the eyes, to the voice. He looked at the large, round breasts and the slim body and thought of the Black Madonna. He couldn't take his eyes off her but at the same time felt no desire to touch her, and even began then to wonder why her beauty aroused no physical attraction in him, only the wish to go on looking. Aloud he asked: "And who's treating you now?" and immediately regretted it.

A curtain seemed to descend over her face, her expression freezing and then becoming calm, as it had been when he entered the room. She didn't bother to reply. I was in too much of a hurry, he thought; I should have waited. When she spoke again, her voice was soft and her words blunt: "It's none of your business. That's confidential information. In any case, he wouldn't speak to any of you. Haven't you ever heard of medical confidentiality?"

"Tell me, were you at the department faculty meeting, the one that took place last Friday morning?" he asked, and the wind went out of her sails.

She was.

"And did you see Professor Tirosh?"

"Yes, of course. He was at the meeting."

"Did he seem as usual?"

"What do you mean? What's as usual?" she demanded, and launched into a serious lecture, in the same soft voice, to the effect that nobody had a usual appearance, everybody had a different appearance every day.

Michael looked at her as she spoke, at the red lips without a trace of lipstick, and asked himself again why he felt no desire to touch her.

She lacks human warmth, he concluded, and then he asked: "And when was the last time you saw him?"

"At the meeting, at the Friday meeting," she said nervously, prompting him to ask: "And not after that?"

The soft voice repeated the words "After that?" and Michael was silent. "What do you mean?" she asked with growing nervousness.

"Perhaps you saw him after the meeting? Perhaps you heard from him? Perhaps you were in his office?"

"On Friday, after the meeting, there was a taxi waiting for me, and I went to my parents'."

"Where do your parents live?" She didn't reply. He repeated the question. Again she didn't reply.

Michael looked at his watch: one o'clock already. Without a word, he went out the door. Raffi Alfandari was in the next room. Michael filled him in briefly. "Don't spend the whole day on her," he said. "Just try to get her parents' address out of her, and what time the taxi came to pick her up from the university on Friday, and what she did later that day. And tell her we'll be asking her to take a polygraph test, and the subjects she'll be questioned on. As far as I'm concerned, she can come with her lawyer."

At the door of his office, he bumped into Danny Balilty, who was sweating and out of breath. "I've been looking for you; let's go in for a minute," said Balilty, as Michael stole a glance at Tuvia Shai, still staring apathetically in front of him.

Inside the office, Balilty said: "I've got a few things for you. First, they found Tirosh's car. In the parking lot of the Hadassah Hospital on Mount Scopus. My guess is that someone, the same person who murdered him, moved it there to delay their looking for the body. The keys were in the car, and that solves one problem—Forensics couldn't stop talking about the missing car keys. Second. . . ," and Balilty tucked his shirt into his belt and wiped away the sweat that trickled down his face. "Professor Ariyeh Klein arrived in the country on Thursday afternoon and not on Saturday; he came without his family, who did arrive on Saturday night. Third, one of them, Yael Eisenstein, was discharged from the army, on psychiatric grounds, while she was still in basic training, and she was involved with Tirosh then." And Balilty gave Michael a triumphant look and waited to be congratulated. "Well, well," said Michael, and smiled. "Have you got any details?"

Balilty promised to bring a copy of the psychiatric reports "within a couple of hours." Michael didn't ask how the intelligence officer would get his hands on the confidential information. Years of working with Balilty had accustomed Michael to his elegant ways of getting around the law, and he preferred to turn a blind eye, which did not now prevent him from saying: "I'd like to know if she's still in treatment, and with whom."

Balilty threw him an offended look: "Who do you think you're talking to? Have I ever let you down? By the end of the day you'll have the whole picture."

"Nevertheless," said Michael, knowing that his words would be like a red rag before a bull, "quite a few years have passed since she was discharged from the army."

"Fourteen and a half," said Balilty, and as he spoke he picked up the coffee cup on the desk and tilted it. "Someone didn't stir your sugar for you," he said with a smile, and went out of the room.

The black interoffice telephone rang. "Ohayon," said the Jerusalem Subdistrict commander, on the other end of the line. "Sir?" responded Michael. Even in his C.O.'s moments of grace, Michael never let himself be tempted to disrupt the delicate balance achieved by means of this formal mode of address. "I want to see you for a minute," said the C.O. Michael listened to the buzz on the line and made a face, but he left the room immediately, pausing only to light a cigarette.

Tuvia Shai still waited in the hall. "I'll be with you in a minute," Michael said to the colorless face that looked at him blankly; then he ran up the stairs to the second floor. "Levy's Gila," as they called her, was sitting at her typewriter in the little anteroom to the police chief's office. "He's waiting for you," she warned, and followed this with: "When are you going to come and have a cup of coffee with me?" as she slipped a piece of carbon paper between the two white sheets in her hand.

"What's up?" asked Michael, putting out his cigarette in the ashtray on her desk.

"Don't ask me. All I know is that I've been on the phone to Eilat all morning. When are we going to have that coffee?" she asked, and contemplated her long nails—which he never failed to admire in view of the many hours she spent at the typewriter. They were painted a gleaming silver. "As soon as I've got a spare second," he replied. "Is everything okay with you? The kids?" She nodded. All you have to do is relate to her, thought Michael, and for a long moment he felt self-revulsion, especially when she smiled trustfully at him and replied with a deep sigh: "Everything's okay. Thank God."

Behind his big desk, Ariyeh Levy sat drumming his fingers on the large sheet of paper in front of him. The desktop was otherwise empty, except for a round stone on one of the corners. "Ohayon, come and sit down," said his chief, and Michael tried to identify his mood. No effort was needed: something was clearly making him angry. Michael waited patiently for the string of curses to die down, while he digested the information they contained: the Marine Medicine Institute and the Institute for Forensic Medicine had informed the Eilat people that Iddo Dudai had been murdered. An SIT had been set up in Eilat, and it would be beefed up with extra investigators from the Negev Subdistrict. The main reason for Ariyeh Levy's anger was the decision to set up a new SIT, manned by people from the national Major Crimes Unit. "In short," said Levy with one last profanity, "they want you to interrogate the witnesses and send them the conclusions, and they'll take care of the Dudai murder."

Michael Ohayon was too familiar with the procedures to lose his temper. In his imagination he could see the whole picture: the request for assistance from Eilat to the Negev Subdistrict, the application to the Southern District, the application to National Police HQ. The only thing that surprised him was the speed with which it had all taken place.

"What's the rank of the station head in Eilat?" he asked.

"Chief superintendent," said Levy with a snort of contempt. "And they've got one forensics technician but no lab; that's why they asked for help from the subdistrict on Saturday. When the first doctor from the hospital in Eilat told them that it was an unnatural death and there was a suspicion of carbon monoxide poisoning, they applied to the Marine Medicine Institute, and they sent the air tanks and all the diving apparatus there."

Several moments passed before Michael said reflectively: "But they'll soon discover that it all begins here, in Jerusalem, and when they do, we can safely predict that they'll apply to the departmental investigations officer of the Southern District, and at last they'll pass it all on to us."

"Yes!" Levy raised his voice to a shout and banged his fist on the desk. "That's just it! It's exactly the 'at last' that worries me! All that time they're going to waste, when it's obvious the investigation should be conducted here. And the credit they'll take after we do their job for them!" He spread out his little hands, which had wisps of fair hair sprouting on their backs, and looked at the wedding ring glittering on his thick finger.

Sometimes Michael tended to forget that behind the hefty figure of the subdistrict commander lay something deeper than a placard. He remembered the stories about him, how he had supported himself as a boy, how he struggled to complete his education. He was fifteen years older than Michael—that is, fifty-five—and he would climb no higher than he had already reached in the police hierarchy. "I don't have to remind you who the departmental investigations officer of the Southern District is now, or do I? In short, I want you to put pressure on your old pal, Commander Emanuel Shorer, to use his position to talk some sense into the people down there."

As soon as he heard the emphasis on the word "you," Michael knew what was coming. "And I also want to point out to you," continued Ariyeh Levy, "that even though you may be the pet of the media, it doesn't mean that five minutes after I appoint you head of the SIT you have to run straight to the television cameras to say something clever."

Michael lit a cigarette to gain time and then asked what, exactly, his chief was referring to.

"You didn't see the news last night?" asked Levy. The bitterness in his voice softened slightly when Michael said that he had worked until the small hours.

"So ask and you'll hear all about it. A close-up of you all over the screen, with your whole CV, on the twelve o'clock news! 'Superintendent Michael Ohayon, in charge of the special investigation team, the man credited with successfully solving this and that murder.' Ohayon, you don't work alone!"

"I didn't chase them," Michael began to say angrily, but the C.O. wasn't interested. "If you want credit," he went on furiously, "you'd better get this case out of the hands of the Southern District and into ours, exclusively! And don't think I'm going to go crawling to your ex-boss, Shorer, who's grown so big for his boots that his secretary told Gila three times that he wasn't in his office! Three times! What am I supposed to think? That as long as he was here, under me—" The sentence was cut off by the opening of the door. Gila came in with two containers of orange juice; she smiled at Michael as she left.

"Right, I'll speak to Shorer today, but I think that one word from you would be enough. I know he regards you very highly," said Michael, and Levy's suspicious look bored into him for a long moment, until it softened and he said in a damp, juice-saturated voice: "Anyway, it's your case, and you have to see to it that you're fully in the picture." Michael nodded, and then, as if he had just remembered, Levy asked: "What did she want, that girl of yours, what's her name, when she came in before?"

"Who—Tzilla? I asked her to see you today because Azariya's going to be in the hospital for a few weeks and I don't know who's going to coordinate all the other teams; not that I want to be completely out of the picture, but we have to be realistic." Michael, his voice worried, looked directly at Ariyeh Levy, who rolled his pen between his fingers and scribbled something. Then he said absent-mindedly: "Okay, I'll speak to Giora; he can transfer the information to you, but you have to stay in the picture, understand?" And he wiped his thin mustache with the back of his hand and carefully stroked his bald spot.

It was only after Michael had left the room, and smiled at Gila, brushing her cheek with his finger, that he remembered: the sentence with which Levy usually concluded their conversations ("This isn't a university, you know!") had not been uttered even once, and for some reason this omission worried him. Perhaps, he thought, his chief had begun to regard him as a normal human being—a possibility that had its advantages, but not a few disadvantages too.

Tuvia Shai still sat outside Michael's office door, his face buried in his hands and his elbows propped on his knees. After arranging a meeting with Commander Emanuel Shorer, his predecessor as superintendent, Michael emerged from his office and invited Tuvia Shai to come inside. He had to touch his shoulder in order to awaken him from his trance; startled, the man got up and followed Michael into the room. For a moment, his face became animated, but then it immediately resumed its mask of detachment.

9

Tuvia Shai sat opposite Michael Ohayon and answered all his questions. His answers were brief and to the point, his language clear and precise. In a monotonous voice, he described the hours of that Friday that he had spent with Shaul Tirosh. At first Michael focused on lunch. Tirosh had eaten vegetable soup and schnitzel with potatoes, reported Tuvia Shai, blinking his eyes; he himself had eaten only clear soup. He had no appetite because of the khamsin, he explained in reply to Michael's question. He remembered that it had been half past twelve when he accompanied Tirosh back to his office. He went inside, he said, again in reply to a question, because he had to get something.

When Michael asked him exactly what it was that he had to get, he didn't hesitate, didn't protest or ask "Why is it important?" but answered promptly: it was an exam Tirosh had prepared for his students, "because Shaul had asked me to give it to Adina on Sunday to be copied." To the question of whether he would be ready to take a polygraph test, he replied indifferently: "Why not?"

But despite the direct, to-the-point answers, Michael experienced an increasing tension as the interrogation progressed. He had the almost physical sensation that Tuvia Shai wasn't there. The man sat throughout in the same posture—body slumped, hands on the table—and didn't look at Michael even once. He stared at the little window just above the policeman's shoulder, as if he were listening to other voices, as if there were another, parallel conversation going on. Michael felt there was a shadow sitting opposite him, the body of a man whose nature was a mystery. Things Michael said, such as: "I'm told that you were very close to him," were answered with a noncommittal nod. Even when he said, "In that case, the murder must have affected you very deeply, no?" Tuvia Shai didn't move a muscle, except for the same mechanical nod.

When Michael asked about diving, Shai produced a tired smile and shook his head. He had never dived. After an entire hour spent in an effort to get Tuvia Shai to be present and involved, he decided to try shock tactics.

"You know," he said, and lit a cigarette, registering the fact that his own voice, too, had begun to sound lifeless, "Iddo Dudai's death wasn't a tragic accident." He looked at Shai and noticed that his shoulders shrank, narrowed, as it were, and then he raised his voice and added: "He was murdered!"

There was no sound in reaction to Michael's bombshell other than Tuvia Shai's breathing.

"Was this information already known to you?" asked Michael, aware of a growing nervousness that made him clamp his jaws. Shai shook his head.

"And what do you feel now that I've told you?"

Tuvia Shai didn't reply.

"Don't you want to know the details of the murder?"

Shai bowed his head.

"Or perhaps you already know how Iddo Dudai was murdered?" Michael, angry now, had to restrain himself from shaking the man's shoulders. But then Shai raised his head and looked into his eyes for the first time.

Michael saw the tears behind the thick lenses of Shai's glasses. They did not blur the terrible expression in his eyes, which seemed to see in Michael's eyes the image of Iddo Dudai's death, his fight for breath, the body spread out on the sand. He groaned but said nothing. Then, ineffectually, he inserted a skinny finger behind one and then the other thick lens to wipe his eyes.

When he listened to the tape later, Michael discovered that the silence lasted only half a minute. At the time, in his office, it seemed endless. But all his waiting was in vain. Tuvia Shai was not tempted to speak.

"On second thought," Michael finally said, "you don't have to know how to dive in order to introduce carbon monoxide into a tank that is supposed to be full of compressed air. Do you have any background in chemistry?"

Shai shook his head. When he finally spoke, his voice came out in a muffled croak: "You don't understand, I was very fond of Iddo."

"You were very fond of him," repeated Michael, and then he asked: "And you have no idea who wasn't very fond of him?"

Again Shai shook his head. Then he said: "I don't know who murdered him." The dampness disappeared from his eyes, and they went back to gazing behind his interrogator's shoulder.

"What, exactly, happened at your departmental seminar?" asked Michael, and Tuvia Shai sat up in his chair. Again his eyes burned for a moment and flickered out.

"The subject was 'Good Poem, Bad Poem,' and Shaul Tirosh, Iddo Dudai, and I were the speakers."

"And did anything special happen?"

"What do you mean, 'happen'? It was a departmental seminar— maybe I should explain what a departmental seminar is?" said Shai, and a hint of vitality came into his voice.

Michael shrugged his shoulders as if about to say "Go ahead," then silently scolded himself for the childish impulse that prompted him instead. "That won't be necessary. I once lectured at one myself, on my M.A. thesis, which by the way was highly praised and won a couple of prizes. . . ." He was usually obliged to forgo what he called "narcissistic gratifications." As a rule, when he exposed himself he did so consciously and deliberately, in order to impress a witness or a suspect, and sometimes in order to instill respect and confidence in a subject prejudiced against the police. His present failure to restrain himself was due to his assumption that the university people related to him with a certain contempt, although simultaneously it was clear to him that Tuvia Shai would not be impressed by his academic past.

"The departmental seminar," Shai proceeded to say, in a businesslike manner, "is the forum in which theoretical subjects are dealt with. People can present articles before publication, or a chapter from a doctoral dissertation or an M.A. thesis. We hold the seminar once a month, more or less." Suddenly Michael could imagine Tuvia Shai in front of his students, how he succeeded in arousing their interest and even spoke with passion.

"I understood that there was something special about the last seminar, the one that took place Wednesday," said Michael. "The TV and the other media were there, no?"

Tuvia Shai looked relieved. It was only later, after Michael had seen the film footage and watched the events with the hindsight provided by the deaths of two of the three speakers, that he understood why. The unedited footage made Shai's explanations superfluous. Seeing the film, Michael felt for the first time sympathy mixed with pity for Tuvia Shai, but at their first meeting, when he was questioning him, he didn't understand him, and couldn't tell for certain whether the expression he noticed *was* one of relief.

"Yes, the media," said Shai thoughtfully. "That was because of Shaul. The media, as you call them, were very fond of Shaul." And then he sank back into himself again and stared at his feet.

The misery surrounding Tuvia Shai, like impenetrable armor, again aroused Michael's helpless anger. The desire to hurt turned into a decision that he could find a dozen rational reasons for, but even then Michael was aware that the wish to hurt came first, without any apparent reason. Something in the man's reactions—he didn't know what—gave rise in Michael to embarrassment and confusion. Perhaps, he thought afterward, it was the lack of horror at Iddo Dudai's murder.

Though it was evident that the information was new to him, it did not arouse his anger or dread, as if he knew the principle but not the facts.

"But it seems," Michael said—and his voice sounded sharp to him, loud and hard, "that you weren't so fond of Tirosh."

Tuvia Shai didn't react immediately, but then he lifted his eyes to Michael again, and there was a flicker of interest in them.

He's got some curiosity, at any rate, thought Michael, and waited for the question that didn't come. "Perhaps it was you who murdered Shaul Tirosh?" asked Michael, looking at the thin arms, the narrow shoulders, the slack body.

"You're at liberty to think so, of course," said Tuvia Shai wearily. "But I've told you the exact facts."

The obvious question: "What motive could I have had for murdering him?" was not asked, and Michael, for a reason not clear to himself, put off the question of motive for the time being. When the rest of the team listened later to the tape and saw the draft of Tuvia Shai's statement, which Michael had scribbled down—and Tuvia Shai had signed without even reading—they all commented, in their different ways, that Michael had been too soft with him, that he hadn't brought up the question of motive at the right time. "Well, that's *your* method," said Eli Bahar doubtfully, "to seem soft at the beginning. Why is it so important to you to seem soft?" he asked in an aggrieved voice. "In the end it seems more cruel to me than my method—to start right in on the motive."

But Michael Ohayon put off the question of motive and asked instead: "Did anyone see you leave the university?"

Tuvia Shai shrugged his shoulders and said indifferently: "I don't know."

Again there was a silence, which Michael broke by asking: "Perhaps you can tell me what usually stands on Tirosh's desk on Mount Scopus?"

And without a word about the irrelevance of the question, Shai began to list the items: the little Persian ashtray, the square paperweight, the big office diary, the seminar papers in the right-hand corner, and, finally, the Indian statuette.

"What statue is that exactly?"

"The god Shiva, quite ancient, about the size of a forearm, made of bronze and copper." Michael examined the expression on Tuvia Shai's face carefully and was unable to detect any change in it, or in his voice either. "And what did you do afterward?" he asked, and again he noted that Shai made no attempt to evade the question, that he didn't ask, "After what?" or try to gain time.

"I went to a movie."

"Where?" asked Michael, and began to scribble something on the paper in front of him.

"At the Cinematheque," said Shai, as if it should have been obvious.

"What film did you see?" asked Michael, his pen poised.

"*Blade Runner.*" A light flickered in Shai's eyes for a moment.

"Whom did you go with?" asked Michael, pressing his ballpoint pen on the paper.

"I went by myself."

"Why?" asked Michael.

Tuvia Shai looked at him incomprehendingly.

"Why did you go alone?" Michael repeated the question.

"I always go to the Cinematheque alone on Friday afternoon," he said, and then, as if to explain: "I often go to the movies alone. I prefer it."

"And the film you saw, *Blade Runner*—was that the first time you saw it?"

Shai shook his head. "No, the third," he said, and once more the light went on in his eyes and immediately died.

"I gather that you like the film," remarked Michael casually, and saw him nod in confirmation.

"And who sat next to you?"

Tuvia Shai shrugged his shoulders. "I really don't know."

"Didn't you meet anyone there? Did anyone see you?"

After some thought, he said: "I didn't notice."

"Perhaps you kept the ticket?"

"No," asserted Shai.

"How can you be so sure?" asked Michael.

"Because it bothered me all through the movie, and finally I threw it away."

"Maybe the usher remembers you? The ticket seller? Somebody?"

"I don't know. I shouldn't think so."

"Why not? You go there often, you say."

"Yes, but it's not a social occasion," and Shai dropped his eyes.

"In any case, we'll look into it," warned Michael, and Tuvia Shai shrugged his shoulders.

"When did the movie end?" asked Michael.

"Half past four, a quarter past four, I don't remember exactly, but you can check the theater."

"Yes. We will. And what did you do after the movie?"

"I went for a walk," said Shai, and staring at the window behind Michael's back.

"Where?" asked Michael impatiently. Though the man didn't offer any information without being asked, there was no sense that he was holding something back, only the ominous feeling that he wasn't present.

"I went home on foot, I walked up past the Jaffa Gate and all the way to Ramat Eshkol."

"What about your car? Do you have a car?"

He did, a Subaru, but that morning he had left it at home, in the parking lot.

"Do you always walk to the university?"

Not always, but sometimes he walked on Fridays.

Michael waited for additional explanations—about physical exercise, about the city's visual splendors—but they weren't forthcoming.

"I want to understand. You walked on foot from Mount Scopus to the Cinematheque and then from the Cinematheque home?"

Tuvia Shai nodded, then he replied to the next question in the same mode, without any anger. "I didn't meet anybody. But perhaps I didn't notice." Then: "I don't remember exactly what time I got home. In the evening. It was already dark." He lowered his head again and stared at the space between his feet and the table. Michael saw only the fair lashes, the pink, inflamed eyelids, and the sparse, colorless hair. "My wife was home, but she was sleeping," he replied to the next question.

"And speaking of your wife," said Michael, "how did you feel about the special relationship between her and Shaul Tirosh?" He had lit another cigarette, hoping it would cover the eagerness with which he asked this question. From his point of view, the interrogation was only now beginning. He was prepared for the man sitting opposite him to jump up in protest, for indignant, dramatic questions.

To his surprise, Tuvia Shai did not protest. He did not query the term "special relationship," he did not demand clarifications and explanations. He was silent, but he raised his head and looked at Michael with a expression of contempt—for the simplemindedness of the human race in general and of this policeman in particular. His compressed lips twisted for a moment.

"How did you feel about it?" repeated Michael. "Did you know that your wife was having an affair with Shaul Tirosh?"

Tuvia Shai looked at him and nodded. In his eyes Michael read utter despair, in addition to the contempt that might have extended to the subject of his question.

"And how did you feel about it?" he asked again.

When there was no answer, he said quietly: "You know, that's a common reason for murder, if we want to talk about motive." Tuvia Shai looked at him and said nothing.

"Dr. Shai," said Michael Ohayon, "I suggest you answer my questions if you don't want to remain here in detention. I'm telling you that you had a motive to murder Tirosh, and the opportunity too. You have no witnesses, you tell me you went to a movie, that you walked around the streets, that you didn't meet anyone, that nobody knows you. The time has come for you to take this seriously. Or do you really want me to arrest you?"

Tuvia Shai nodded as if to say: I understand.

Michael waited. "How long did the affair between your wife and Tirosh go on?" he finally ventured, and Tuvia Shai replied: "A few years. I'd prefer that you not use the word 'affair.'"

"And when did you find out about it?" asked Michael, ignoring the last remark, which had made his anger flare up again. He felt that he didn't understand anything about the man sitting opposite him.

"I think I knew right from the beginning, although I only actually saw them together in that way two years ago."

"And what did you feel about it?"

"My feelings were complicated, naturally, but they have nothing to do with his death."

"And whom did you talk to about it?" asked Michael.

"I didn't talk to anyone."

"Not even your wife?"

"No."

"And Tirosh?"

"No. I didn't talk to anyone. It's my own business."

"You'll agree with me," said Michael, wondering at the formal turn that the conversation was taking, "that such matters are commonly considered to have some bearing when a murder has occurred?" Tuvia nodded.

"Dr. Shai," said Michael in despair, feeling as if he were calling on a dead man to rise from his grave, "do you love your wife?" Shai nodded, not in affirmation, but to indicate that he understood the question.

"These are more complex matters than the ones you commonly come across. We are not conventional people, apparently," said Shai, and Michael stared at him in astonishment. At the moment when he was least expecting a detailed, voluntary answer, it was being voluntarily given.

"I don't expect you to understand. My wife and I never spoke about it to each other, and Shaul never said anything to me, but if I were a police investigator, I would ask myself: Why should he suddenly murder him, after all these years?"

This time Michael was silent. He looked at the man opposite him and thought that in a newspaper article he would be presented as a nonentity, a wretched creature who accepted the "situation" for lack of any alternative, but Michael himself sensed the strength of the man, beyond the despair, beyond the silence. Get out of your mind-set, said Michael to himself during the silence; different laws apply here; try to see it from his point of view. If he accepted the fact that his wife was having an affair with Shaul Tirosh, what fact wouldn't he have accepted? What would provoke him to murder?

And aloud he asked: "Dr. Shai, you were probably aware of the fact that Tirosh had a special relationship with Ruth Dudai as well?"

Tuvia Shai made no attempt to hide the anger that suddenly flared in his eyes as he said: "No, I didn't know. But why are you telling me?"

"I'm telling you," said Michael Ohayon, weighing every word, "because if the fact that Tirosh was your wife's lover didn't make you hate him, maybe the fact that he left her was too much for you to take. Maybe for you that was a motive for murder."

"And who says that he left her?" and Shai continued: "Shaul was capable of carrying on a number of relationships at once."

"Nevertheless, you're angry," Michael announced, and looked into Tuvia Shai's eyes. He noted with satisfaction that the expression of contempt had vanished without a trace.

"Yes," said Shai, as if surprised at his own reaction, "but not because of what you're hinting at."

"Perhaps you can tell me what I'm hinting at?" said Michael, leaning forward on the table.

"You think that I identified so strongly with Ruchama that I would have murdered him if, as you say, he had left her. That's an interesting view, even a profound one, I'd say, but not correct." And again the interest faded from his eyes and his face resumed its dead expression, and again he bowed his head.

"So would you mind telling me what you are angry about?" prodded Michael, and Tuvia Shai shrugged his shoulders and replied: "I'm not sure. I was very close to Shaul."

Michael noted that Shai had failed to connect the closeness to the anger, and he asked: "But?"

"There aren't any buts. Shaul Tirosh was beyond good and evil, to use a Nietzschean term. But I don't think you'll understand what I'm talking about."

"Dr. Shai," said Michael deliberately, "are you prepared to take a polygraph test today?"

Tuvia Shai nodded. He didn't look threatened.

Michael asked him to wait in the next room and switched off the tape recorder.

It was almost four o'clock when he passed Tuvia Shai on to Eli Bahar for further questioning and asked Eli to brief Shai on the polygraph test. "If we give him twenty-four hours to stew about it, he'll be ripe for the polygraph tomorrow afternoon, I hope," he said, trying to overcome his feeling of impotence. He sensed that Tuvia Shai was telling him the truth but at the same time that he, Michael, had failed fully to understand the truth he was being told.

Knowing that there would be a polygraph test brought a measure of consolation. He had been well aware, when he asked Shai if he would be ready to take the test that same day, that it required coaching: the SIT prepared the suspect for the subjects on which he would be questioned, and the person giving the test prepared him again, making certain that the questions were understood.

"Tzilla's got a sandwich for you. You must be dying of hunger, no?" asked Eli Bahar, passing his hand over his dark curls.

Michael replied that yes, he was hungry, and added that again he wouldn't find time to pay his electricity bill. "They'll cut me off," he said. "I never seem to make it to the bank."

Eli Bahar clucked sympathetically and lifted the receiver of the black phone, which was ringing. "Yes, he's here. You want him?" he asked. Looking at Michael, he listened for a few seconds and then replaced the receiver.

"They've brought in Ruchama Shai, Dr. Shai's wife, as you asked. Tzilla says she's waiting in the conference room."

Michael looked at his watch; it said one minute past four, and like a video on "Fast forward," there rushed through his mind electricity bills; Yuval, who was waiting for him at home; Maya, who hadn't called or come over for several days now—"life outside," as Tzilla called it when they were in the midst of an investigation. The world outside the building made him feel a pang of longing, as if it were a world to which he had no connection, a world remote and inaccessible. Since this morning, he thought, he had met four new people and come to know them quite intimately, ascertained their views and their habits. And now he had to confront one more side of this complex geometrical figure.

There were two hours until his anticipated meeting with Shorer in a café. Aloud he said: "I'll begin interviewing her, and please send Raffi along later to check if I need him to continue the questioning."

"Tzilla said to tell you that she's arranged for the film to be screened at ten. Do you want us all to see it?"

Michael nodded. "If you've still got the strength after the autopsy," he said, aware of the note of guilt that had crept into his voice. Eli Bahar did not respond directly. He began a lengthy description of the results of the pathological examination, summed up by confirming what Hirsh had told Michael over the phone, and went on to describe the results of the analysis of the stomach contents. "They never found any poison," he said, answering the question that had been troubling Michael. "So should we pick you up a bit before ten?" he ended by asking.

"No, I'll get there under my own steam," said Michael, aware of the fact that the despair he had sensed in Tuvia Shai had infected him too, along with apathy and extreme fatigue. Words seemed superfluous to him as he returned to his office and asked Tzilla on the internal line to bring in Ruchama Shai, wondering as he did so where he was going to find the mental energy to question her.

10

And that's all I think I know at present," said Michael at the end of his summary to Emanuel Shorer, who stared at the ashtray full of butts and bits of matchsticks and now broke another match in half.

They were sitting on the crowded garden terrace of the café in the Ticho House. Inside the building, which housed a gallery where the works of the Jerusalem artist Anna Ticho were on display, there were a number of tables on the ground floor, but despite the overcrowding, everybody sat on the terrace that overlooked the large garden, enjoying the cool evening air after a hot, dry day. Above the circular terrace the sky was dark and starless, and from where he was sitting Michael could see the tall cypresses and pines in the garden; they looked black and threatening. At the adjacent table, two middle-aged women were whispering and laughing unpleasantly, adding to his nervousness, the nervousness of a tired child who refuses to admit its fatigue and reacts to every well-intentioned gesture with furious protest.

Emanuel Shorer gulped down the dregs of his beer, wiped his lips, and asked: "When, exactly, did he break up with Ruchama Shai?"

"Thursday morning. Her fingerprints were in his office, on his desk. He couldn't even wait to meet her somewhere else."

"Maybe he was afraid of a scene," said Shorer, and Michael muttered that if Emanuel took a look at the woman for himself, he would know that it was impossible to imagine her making a scene. "That business with the air tanks," Shorer continued. "Have you found out yet where you can get hold of pure carbon monoxide?"

"I have. In any of the chemistry or physics labs at the university. And you can also easily order it from chemical suppliers."

"And there hasn't been any breaking and entering in any of the labs recently?" asked Shorer, and while he was waiting for their young waitress to unload the coffee from her little tray, Michael remembered the café next to the Russian Compound, where the two of them had sat on scores of occasions, stirring hundreds of cups of coffee. Emanuel Shorer would pluck his thick mustache—he had shaved it off two years ago—and utter a few sentences or casual remarks whose importance Michael understood only later, when he was alone.

He stirred the sugar round and round and replied that no burglaries had been reported as far as he knew. "But," he said, leaning over the table, "nobody would call the security arrangements at the university foolproof. I spoke to one of the chemists in charge of the laboratories there; he told me that many people have keys, many people go in and out. I don't think there would be any need to break in."

He spoke absentmindedly: part of him was still with Ruchama Shai. To keep up the conversation now, he was obliged to invest a tremendous effort, which seemed to exhaust his last reserves of strength. She hadn't been frightened; her reactions were those of someone in shock, which prevented her from concentrating on the questions. There was no way of getting through to her, not in the first hour, anyway. Only when he referred for the fourth time to the "delicacy" of her husband's position had she begun to blurt out, one after the other, answers to his questions, in a mechanical, laconic manner that reminded him of Shai himself. From her answers he understood that relations between her and Tirosh had been broken off. ("Whose initiative was it?" he had asked, and she had lowered her eyes and said "His." And when he asked why, she had mentioned Ruth Dudai.) Then she told him that she had slept from Thursday morning to Sunday afternoon almost without a break. She didn't know, she said, if Tuvia was at home during that time.

Despite the shock, Michael sensed, she hadn't been surprised to hear of Shaul Tirosh's murder, as if there was some sort of logic behind it. When he asked her about it, she reacted with incomprehension; she didn't know anything about it, she repeated stubbornly. He mentioned a polygraph test, and she shrugged her shoulders. "I've got nothing to hide," she said, and as with her husband, Michael had felt that she wasn't there. He asked himself several times what a man like Shaul Tirosh could have seen in her. When she spoke, her hazel eyes were empty and expressionless. He looked at her thin arms, her slender neck, her drooping lower lip (almost like a a weeping clown's), and her skin, which was smooth but so thin (almost transparent) that you could imagine it suddenly shriveling and peeling off, exposing another skin, lined and wrinkled, underneath it, and again he concluded, as he now told Emanuel Shorer, that some things were beyond his comprehension, and one of them was "the way of a man with a maid."

The thought of driving to the television studio and viewing the film footage filled him with tension, and he tried to intensify it in order to overcome his fatigue.

"You drink too much coffee," Shorer scolded him, "and you also smoke too much. At your age it's not a joke anymore; you have to look after yourself. Why don't you stop smoking? Look at me: if you offered me a cigarette now, I wouldn't be able to enjoy it. I haven't touched a cigarette in four years."

Michael smiled at him. Manifestations of Shorer's paternal concern for him always went to his heart.

"It's true I've put on weight since I stopped smoking," said Shorer plaintively, touching the tire of fat that encircled his waist, "but I'll take it off again." And he stuck a half-matchstick into his mouth and fell silent. Then he took it out and waved it at Michael like an admonitory finger as he said: "You know, it's not so simple to let compressed air out of a tank and fill it with carbon monoxide to the same weight, and don't forget we're talking about two tanks here. I would look for someone who had access to a chemistry laboratory first, or who ordered carbon monoxide from a chemical supplier. You can worry about the motive later; the first problem is the execution."

"I've thought about it, and I've begun looking, but so far I can't see that anyone had a connection to a chemistry lab; anyway, half the SIT's busy on it right now. I do know one thing: Tirosh was at the Dudais' house, and twice he went down to the basement—once when Iddo was abroad and once after he had come back. They had problems with the electricity, that's what Ruth Dudai said, and he fixed it for them, and that's where Dudai kept the air tanks and the rest of his diving equipment."

"The problem is," said Shorer after a moment or two of silence, "that the cylinder could have been tampered with long ago, without any connection to times and alibis."

"It could even have been Tirosh," said Michael suddenly.

Shorer looked at him, and finally he smiled and said in a tone of rebuke: "Do you know something that you haven't told me? Otherwise why the hell would Tirosh murder his star student? According to you, anyway."

"I don't know; it just came out," replied Michael absently.

"It didn't just come out. First you mentioned the basement, that he was in the basement," protested Shorer, looking sorrowfully at his empty beer bottle.

"I don't know," said Michael hesitantly, "but he's the only one who we know was in the basement, apart from the people who live there. And besides. . . " Michael fell silent.

"And besides?" Shorer persisted.

"It doesn't matter. As you say, the question of motive can wait."

Shorer resumed his former line of questioning and asked again about Tirosh's family and the women in his past. "You can never know if there wasn't some marriage. You have to ask someone who knew him when he first arrived in the country. From the way you describe him, it figures that he would have married at the age of, say, twenty and then disappeared. Maybe there's even a child, maybe an illegitimate child," and he began scribbling lines on a paper napkin with a burnt match he had removed from the overflowing ashtray. Michael mentioned Ariyeh Klein and said that Aharonovitz, too, had known Tirosh from those early days, but they had never been on familiar terms. "I understand that Tirosh had a lot of respect for Klein, even reverence, and there was a time when he used to go to his house a lot and even eat meals there. But I haven't yet spoken to Klein."

Shorer gave him a disapproving look. "Why haven't you? Didn't you say that you found out he returned to the country on Thursday, and not on Saturday, as they thought in the Literature Department?"

"The fact that he notified them he was coming back on Saturday doesn't mean a thing," said Michael, smiling. He glanced at his watch: nine o'clock—they had been sitting there for three hours. "If you'd seen the way they jumped on him, you'd understand why he'd want to keep his time of arrival to himself. Are you coming with me to see the film?"

"Now we can talk about Tirosh again, in the matter of the air tanks," said Shorer as they left the television studio. The streets were dark, with only a few cars driving past the blinking yellow traffic lights. Michael stopped in front of Shorer's house, and the two of them sat in silence.

"He was at the Dudais' two weeks ago, after Iddo came back from America," Michael explained. "Iddo wasn't home. There was a short circuit, and Tirosh went down to the basement to change the fuse. Ruth went with him; they weren't there long. We searched the place thoroughly, but we didn't find anything."

"What did you think you'd find? A carnation?" asked Shorer, grasping the door handle.

"That's not the point; I didn't think he'd leave his signature. But now if we find his fingerprints there, they have no significance."

"So we're back to the need to learn if he got hold of any carbon monoxide," said Shorer, beginning to get out of the car, "because it's obvious that something happened there between them."

"I don't know if I've already told you, but we found Dudai's fingerprints on a bottle in Tirosh's house."

"You didn't tell me," said Shorer tensely, and resumed his seat in the car. "What bottle?"

"It was chocolate liqueur."

"Chocolate liqueur!" repeated Shorer in disgust.

"That was the only drink Iddo would take. Ruth Dudai told me that he drank no other alcohol, not even wine. We never found a single print of his in the whole house apart from that bottle."

"Well?" grumbled Shorer impatiently.

"So I heard from Ruchama Shai that Tirosh never touched the chocolate liqueur. He only kept it for guests. And what I think is this: Dudai came back from America two weeks and one day before he died, and during this period, or maybe before he left the country, he was at Tirosh's house. In any case, some time ago, because the only prints we found there were the ones on the bottle. So either the place was cleaned after that, or I don't know."

"I can't understand why you didn't tell me. When did you say he was there?"

"That's just it: there's no way of knowing," said Michael quietly. "His wife has no idea where he went in the evenings recently; he came and went, and God knows where. But before he left for the U.S., everything was okay; she still knew where he was going. And she also says that he wasn't in the habit of dropping in on Tirosh at home; it wasn't a usual event."

"That means," said Shorer decisively, putting his hand on the door handle again, "that they met before the departmental seminar but after Dudai returned from America, that there was a confrontation between them then."

Michael was silent, and Shorer added: "And you saw Tirosh's face in the film? The expression of surprise? As if he was in shock from what Dudai said."

"I had the impression," Michael said hesitantly, "that it was more fear than surprise, as if he wasn't expecting it in that forum. . . ."

"Okay," said Shorer impatiently. "I say again that the only way of knowing if Tirosh tampered with the tanks is to find out if he got hold of the carbon monoxide." He opened the door, and when he stood outside the car he put his head in through the window and said with a smile: "We've done more difficult things in our lives. Have a good night," and he gave the dusty roof of the car a slap as if to send it on its way.

At one o'clock in the morning, Michael Ohayon parked his car in the lot next to his apartment building and got out slowly. The voices were still echoing in his ears. He remembered the gray cover of Anatoly Ferber's book, which now lay next to his own bed, and asked himself what had motivated Iddo Dudai to endanger his whole academic future by adversely criticizing Shaul Tirosh's political poetry. And to choose the departmental seminar to do it in, he thought as he locked the car door, realizing that there were hours of poetry reading ahead of him.

It was impossible to see lights from most of his building from outside. The building was on the side of a hill, overlooking the wadi, and only the kitchen windows faced the street. Like many in the Jerusalem suburbs, his apartment, which was reached by descending a flight of stairs, was flooded with light in the morning.

This was his third apartment since the divorce. He had been living in it for four years, and he did his best to see it as his home. When he left Nira, he knew that he might never have a home of his own, and ever since, he had tried to consider every place he lived in as home. Although he had no plants, he thought, as his eye fell on the cactus in the entrance lobby, which one of the residents watered scrupulously, his apartment was always tidy, there was always something to eat in the refrigerator, and the furniture, acquired bit by bit, had given Yuval, too, the feeling of home.

There were three rather small rooms, with the living room opening onto a wide balcony that overlooked a stretch of greenery. The living room contained a brown sofa and two armchairs he had bought on sale even though their color didn't coordinate with the sofa and they were too heavy for such a small room. But they were comfortable, he thought, and one day he would replace the fabric. Next to the blue armchair stood a reading lamp, on the floor was a large, thin rug his mother had given him after the divorce, and a small storage unit in the corner held the stereo system and the television. A small bookcase next to the blue armchair held the books to which he was particularly attached (all of le Carré, in English and in Hebrew; *Poems from Long Ago* by Natan Alterman, *Practical Poems* by David Avidan, *Various Poems* by Natan Zach, and *White Poems* by Shaul Tirosh; *Madame Bovary*, two volumes by Florinsky about czarist Russia, stories by Chekhov and Gogol, a few volumes of Balzac in French, Faulkner's *The Sound and the Fury, Past Continuous* by Yaakov Shabtai, and copies of the historical quarterly *Zmanim*, in one of which was an article he had written about the Renaissance guilds). Under the telephone were the water and electricity bills.

In the blue armchair sat Maya, her legs tucked underneath her and her knees peeping out under her light cotton skirt. Only the reading lamp was on in the room, and in its light he saw the reddish tint of her hair and also the threads of gray. She looked at him without saying anything. And in the absolute silence of the flat—she hadn't even switched on the radio—Michael knew that something had happened.

Only when she slept was her body still and relaxed. At all other times it was in a state of constant activity. She tapped her feet to music—she listened to music all the time—and cooked even when she had come only for a short while, or she talked without stopping and cooked and listened to music simultaneously. When she was waiting for him in his apartment, he would find her in the kitchen or in bed, knitting her brows as she read a book, her fingers playing with the sheet. Sometimes, when she was tired, he would find her sitting in the blue armchair watching television, a book in her lap. He had never before seen her sitting still with her legs tucked underneath her, staring at the window opposite, as she was now. On her face was an expression he had seen only a few times in all the years he had known her, but then it had come and gone unexplained. Now it was frozen. It was an expression of despair and calm at once, as of a person facing a catastrophe against which there was no defense. Her expression paralyzed him.

He sat down in the other armchair, the floral one, and put the keys on the little coffee table. He did not dare approach her. For seven years he had been with her, and still there were moments when he did not dare approach her. He lit a cigarette. And he waited. A few moments passed before he asked her what was wrong. When he heard the coldness of his voice and felt the tremor in his hands, he knew how frightened he was.

Maya looked at him dully and moved her lips several times before she succeeded in saying that they would have to stop seeing each other for a while. This was the first time that she had initiated a break. It was always Michael who tried to cut himself off from her, because he couldn't cope with the double life she led, the stolen moments with which he had to be content.

Right at the beginning of their relationship she had made it clear to him that they would never talk about her husband, her married life, or even about the reasons why she would never live with him. Only her daughter, Dana, who was three years old when they met, would she sometimes mention. Michael knew, of course, where she lived, and he even knew her husband's voice from the times when he renewed contact with her after he had broken off relations. On the first evening they met, he had looked her up in the telephone directory. "Wolf, Maya and Dr. Henry, Neurosurgeon," it said, and ever since, he had imagined their luxurious apartment on Tivonim Street in Rehavia, and her husband, perhaps silver-haired, perhaps older than she was, but without a doubt impressive-looking. During the first year of their relationship he had even been secretly proud that from her magnificent home in Tivonim Street and her surgeon husband (he could even hear the sound of the piano), she came to him, she preferred him.

After a year he even told her about it, mocking himself. She laughed but didn't dismiss the picture. He never told her about the times he had stood on a corner of Tivonim Street and waited, about the one and only time he had seen her emerging from the front door arm in arm with a short, thin man who walked slowly, or about going to the neurosurgical ward at Shaarei Tzedek Hospital, where her husband worked, and looking at the name tags on the doctors' chests, without finding him.

Looking back, he couldn't pinpoint the moment when Maya had changed from an agreeable adventure into his heart's desire. Looking back—and he never stopped looking back during the long nights that he had begun increasingly to spend alone, tired of the effort of seeking someone to replace her—he sometimes thought that already on that first night, however innocent it was, but also strange, Maya had become the woman of his life. But even he knew that it was only with hindsight that he could recognize the structure, the processes, the reasons, the patterns of behavior. At the time, when it was actually happening, he could not have been able to predict where it would lead. And to the question "And if you could have predicted the future, would you have changed anything?" he would answer immediately, without having to think, that then, too, everything would have happened in exactly the same way.

Now he heard himself asking her coldly if she would like a cup of coffee and saw her shaking her head.

She didn't want anything. Only his full attention. Things were difficult enough anyway, she said, plucking at the hem of her skirt. It was about her husband.

Michael was stunned. Maya never before used the words "my husband," nor did she ever refer to him by name. Michael, too, usually managed to avoid the subject. He had always felt that beneath her gaiety when she came to him there was a deep sadness, that behind the experienced, assured woman was an anxious little girl. But there was nothing unusual about that, he thought. Take any self-assured woman, you'd always find a frightened child. Nevertheless, Maya was different. Underneath the childish insecurity he could clearly sense the presence of another layer, which aroused deep fears in him, a layer of strength and the capacity to endure the worst of all. What "the worst of all" was, he didn't know, but the perception that she possessed some tragic strength was absolutely clear to him. And this perception now received a verbal, concrete expression.

"Multiple sclerosis," said Maya, in a detached, scientific tone. "Up to now the progression has been very slow, but he's been in a wheelchair for a year, and now it seems that he'll never get out of bed again."

The filtertip cigarette Michael was holding in his hand had no ash left on it. He stared at her in disbelief.

"You can't possibly not have known," she said. "We live in Jerusalem, a provincial town where you can't not know things. I was sure you knew, that you pretended not to know for my sake. After all, you're a detective. Although perhaps because of the fact that he's a doctor, and because of his position, and because of a thousand and one things, it wasn't really so well known."

"And when we met?" asked Michael. She nodded.

"Ten years. A slow deterioration. He's forty-seven now." So Maya was ten years younger than her husband, Michael quickly calculated, and was immediately ashamed of himself.

"But I wouldn't have left him even if he hadn't been so sick, even if he were well, although perhaps I wouldn't have allowed myself to enter into such a deep involvement with you." Michael hated the word "involvement" and thought of the arrogance of people who imagined that they could control the depth of their love, but he maintained his poker face and resisted the temptation to speak.

"Don't ask me why, but I don't intend to move him out of the house. I'll look after him at home, for as long as possible, anyway. And I don't know if I'd be able to take the transitions from there to here, not to speak of the guilt."

He had rarely been as paralyzed as he was at that moment, thought Michael afterward. And again, as in a movie, he ran the scenes of their time together through his mind, from their first meeting on. The opening picture was always the same: One night he was driving from Tel Aviv to Jerusalem, and after the turn at Shaar Hagai he saw a car at the roadside, with a woman leaning against its fender. It was one o'clock in the morning, and Michael Ohayon, a newly promoted inspector in the Major Crimes Unit, young and divorced, satiated with sexual adventures but still open to a smile from a woman, stopped and approached her. She smiled, and his headlights illuminated the golden glint in her eyes and the fullness of her cheeks. Then he saw the curved white knees and the wedding ring on her finger. When he asked what the problem was, she explained that she had run out of gas. She didn't add any of the conventional feminine apologies. For a moment he wondered if he should transfer gas from his tank to hers, but the thought of the taste of the gasoline he would have to suck up at the beginning made him nauseous. There was no gas station open at this hour of night. He offered her a lift home, to Jerusalem, leaving her car where it was. "I'm attached to my Peugeot, the champion of them all," she said and patted the car as if it were a noble racehorse. "I hope it will be here in the morning." He hoped so too, he said politely, and opened the door of his car for her. To this day he remembered the autumn air, growing cooler as they approached Jerusalem, the full moon—she said that the moon aroused base desires in people, that you couldn't be indifferent to it—and the utter darkness beyond his lights.

Michael fell in love with Maya then without being in the least aware of it, although he should have known. The minute she closed the door, the car filled with her smell, a mixture of lemon and honey, the smell he had been searching for for years, ever since he was eighteen years old. Already then he should have known that there would be no way back. She was wearing a wide blue skirt and a white blouse with wide sleeves, and her face was broad and full of freckles. Her straight brown hair fell to her shoulders, and her voice was slightly husky. She told him, between Shaar Hagai and the Kastel, about her work editing manuscripts at a publishing house, about the concert she was on her way back from (the violinist Shlomo Mintz was "so young and such a devil, a real demon"). He smiled all the way, as if to himself, and by the time they reached Abu Gosh he felt that he had to know if the smell came from her hair, her perfume, or her skin itself. Next to the School for the Blind in Kiryat Moshe, at the entrance to the city, opposite the blinking traffic light, he bent over her and smelled her hair. Then he parked the car in Kiryat Moshe. She stopped chattering, and her face was very serious, but in her eyes—in the light of the streetlamp he saw that they were brown—the golden glints were still twinkling. And when he opened his eyes in the middle of their kiss he saw that her eyes were open too. He wanted, but he didn't dare, to ask her if she used perfume, and then he took her home. She always afterward reminded him with a smile that he had asked permission to touch her hair, and then permission to kiss her. "I thought people only asked questions like that in the movies and that everyone in the real world was sponta-neous," she said that night, and later on, the remarks about lack of spontaneity returned and became a bone of contention between them. ("Why do you have to ask me? If you don't know after seven years if you can or not, what are we doing together? To ask your woman per-mission to kiss her! That's not good manners, that's insulting. It means that there's no intimacy between us.") He returned to his apartment that night happier than he had ever been in his life. He didn't know her name, and naturally nothing had been said about their next meeting, but Michael knew that there were no meaningless, accidental events in the world, and he did not doubt that now, having once met her, he would meet her again. But it never occurred to him that it would hap-pen so soon. Three weeks after the drive from Shaar Hagai, he was obliged to attend a private concert given by Tali Shatz, the daughter of the professor who had supervised his M.A. thesis at the university. It was no longer autumn. The rain beat against the windows of the large salon in the new house in Ramot, where, he later learned, the former Israeli cultural attaché in Chicago now lived. Professor Shatz said some-thing about the host being his second cousin. Tali played the violin and her new husband the piano in Beethoven's Kreutzer Sonata, a work Michael particularly liked.

When the door opened and Michael heard her voice, he thanked God that he had come alone. She arrived without an umbrella, soak-ing wet, and left wet marks on the pale carpet covering the vast floor of the salon from wall to wall. The hostess, who assured her that she hadn't done any damage ("It's only water"), followed her progress anxiously. Now he could see her in full, bright light. She was wearing a simple black dress gathered at the waist, with a low round neck and long sleeves. You couldn't say that she was beautiful in a conventional sense, but there was something graceful and appealing about her movements, and something radiant about her face. She even smiled warmly at the host, who was standing and rubbing his hands together in a way that reminded Michael of Anna Sergeyevna in Chekhov's "The Lady with the Dog."

She doesn't recognize me, thought Michael. He was introduced to her next to the large, gleaming table in a corner of the salon. On the table stood an elaborate dessert, and the hostess, with a well-oiled smile, repeatedly informed her guests that it was a "charlotte russe, something I learned to do in preparation for our next posting." There was a tea set too, "Rosenthal," the hostess said with veiled reproach to Maya when she dropped a cup of hot tea onto the carpet, though without breaking it. Hurrying to dilute and dry up the spilled tea, the hostess was too busy delivering a lecture on Rosenthal china, and how hard it was to replace, to notice Maya staring at Michael and frowning in an apparent effort of memory, her nostrils expanding and contracting as if they had a life of their own. And suddenly, seeming just to have remembered, or decided how to react, she smiled, and the golden glints danced in her eyes. Michael, sipping his coffee deliberately, noticed that his hand trembled. This in itself, he said to himself, wasn't anything special. I always get excited and tremble when I meet a woman I want. It's the same "thrill of the chase" that I've felt dozens of times.

They escaped from the private concert before wine was served, a few minutes after the music was over. After ascertaining, in a café, what she called "the circumstances of his life," she had asked him simply and directly why they shouldn't go to his place. She was sure, she said, that he wanted her. "Are you married?" he asked then, looking at the ring on her finger. She nodded but refused to elaborate.

That same evening she told him that her married life was irrelevant. "You won't find the explanation there," she said, and Michael didn't press her. "But you should find the situation convenient and unthreatening," she commented, and only the laugh that accompanied this remark reduced its aggressiveness.

She left his apartment late that night, without anything having been said about their seeing each other again, but with a radiant smile, full of promise and confidence. When she phoned the next morning, he couldn't understand how she had found the number.

And now she sat in the blue armchair, her legs tucked up underneath her. She had not changed her position since he entered the room, and Michael looked at the curved knee and wanted to touch it, but didn't dare. He thought about what Tzilla had said to him in Meir's restaurant, about how he had no gift for detection outside the criminal situation, that in "life," as she put it, he was actually rather naive.

"Haven't you got anything to say? Nothing at all?" asked Maya, and Michael heard the sob behind the harsh voice and replied that he was thinking what to say to her, how to put into words the confused torrent of emotions that made him seem unfeeling. "And also," he said slowly, "I'm wondering whether breaking off relations with me is what you need now, and asking myself if I'm really incapable of helping you, but mainly I'm thinking about how for the past seven years you've hidden this from me, and I thought we were so close, and all the time you were keeping this terrible secret from me, and. . ." Michael contemplated the irony of the picture he had built for himself of her glamorous social life, her harmonious existence, her superior husband, but of this he said nothing.

"What are you thinking about?" asked Maya after a long pause, and Michael replied: "If there's an involvement, as you call it, between us, isn't there anything I can do for you except to break it off?"

"Only for the time being," said Maya desperately, and Michael thought that multiple sclerosis could go on for twenty years, but about this, too, he said nothing.

He looked at the exposed knee, at the slender hand resting on the arm of the chair, and suddenly he filled with rage, which he made no attempt to hide.

"You're shouting," said Maya, half questioningly, half fearfully. "Why are you shouting at me?"

"It's a trap," shouted Michael again. "What can I say in the face of your guilt? Naturally you make the rules—you always have—but you've never hurt me so much before, and you've still got the nerve to call me unspontaneous! Who gave you the right to say you loved me when all the time you were hiding a thing like this from me? What did you take me for? A baby? Did you think that I wouldn't be able to 'cope'? Another one of your favorite words. But what right have I to say anything? I'm not your husband, I'm only your lover, and I thought we were friends too, but now you suddenly throw something like this at me, and it turns out that for all these years I've been nothing but your playmate."

And Maya, after opening her mouth a few times and spreading her wide skirt over her knees, took advantage of the moment of silence to shout back: "You're the famous detective; if you wanted to know you would have known; you think it's a coincidence that all these years you've never dared to ask anything? Isn't it you who always say that there's no such thing as coincidence? How come you didn't know?" And the tears that had choked her voice as she spoke began to flow, big and transparent, and the childish gesture with which she wiped her cheeks with the back of her hand pierced his heart, and despite the waves of anger again engulfing him, he stood up and went over to her, lifted her, sobbing, from the chair, embraced her with all his strength, and even wiped away her tears with his lips. But then she said: "Don't make it hard for me, Michael, please don't make it hard for me. Let me go and I'll come back, you'll see, I'll come back." And he no longer said anything, because the voices inside him clamored with anger and pity and love and hate, and especially the stinging sensation of having been deceived.

He couldn't fall asleep. Whenever he closed his eyes, a new wave of rage attacked him, followed by self-pity, and finally, when he saw that it was three in the morning, he gave up all attempts at sleep and returned to the armchair. ("What did you do all month?" Maya asked him once, after one of his attempts to break off with her. "I drowned myself in work," he had said. He could still remember what she was wearing then.) Pulling the chain of the reading lamp, he leafed through the book by Anatoly Ferber that he had found on Tirosh's bed, and stared at the black letters in the short lines. He remembered Iddo Dudai's face as it had been in the television film, and as it had been on the beach in Eilat, and then he thought about Emanuel Shorer's remark in the café, and he knew that the key lay in Dudai's behavior at the departmental seminar, in the battle that had taken place on the screen. Again he looked at Tirosh's introduction to the book by Ferber, the poet he had discovered and whose poems he had had published, and he remembered how Ruth Dudai and Ruchama Shai—and he himself—had reacted to the sight of Tirosh's body. He felt a similar sensation now, and he said to himself aloud: "You're in shock," and the sound of his voice echoing in the room frightened him, and again he felt the helpless rage against Maya, and then a wave of pity for himself and for her and even for her husband, and he tried to pull himself together and rose from the chair. His body felt heavy. The sky was beginning to grow light, and he went into the kitchen and put the kettle on the stove, and then he found himself in the shower, shaving slowly and staring at his face, which looked like the hard face of a stranger, and at the little lines next to his eyes. The kettle whistled, and again he thought that he should buy an electric kettle, which wouldn't get on his nerves like this one, but he let it go on whistling until he had finished drying his face with the little towel, which was as hard as sandpaper, and he heard Maya's voice lecturing him, "It's impossible to launder anything in Jerusalem without a softener, the water's so hard here," and he tried to stop the tears as he made his strong black coffee and spooned sugar into the black liquid, his hand trembling. The clock on the kitchen wall, which Yuval had bought him on a trip the boy had taken with his grandfather to Switzerland, showed five; the sparrows started their chirping outside, and in one of the neighboring apartments a baby began to cry. Michael drank his coffee standing up, at one go, despite the searing sensation he felt on his palate and his tongue—he even welcomed it, at least it was a clear, sharp physical sensation—and then he washed the white cup, put it away in the little cupboard above the sink, and left the house.

11

They're all here," said Tzilla with a worried expression. "He wanted details about the film footage we saw last night and said that today's Wednesday already and moved everyone into his office. I told him you were on your way, but he's in a mood, and now he's reading the file." They were standing at the door to Michael's office, and the tension in her voice and movements made him quicken his step and hurry after her in the direction of the C.O.'s office. The little anteroom was empty, the typewriter covered, and Tzilla went straight through.

"Here goes," Michael said aloud, in a voice that betrayed his depression, and stepped into Ariyeh Levy's office.

Again they were all at the morning conference, again they pored in silent concentration over the detailed file prepared by Tzilla—the pathologist's report, the photographs, the comments by Forensics, the list of questions to be asked in the polygraph tests, the typed copies of the interrogations, the signed statements of the witnesses.

Raffi Alfandari put down the paper he was holding and looked intently at the photograph of Tirosh's body, then at a photograph of the Indian statuette, which had been found in the Alfa Romeo. "What's this statue?" he asked, and took a long gulp from the paper cup in his hand.

"It's the god Shiva," said Michael, "and Forensics say there aren't any prints on it. It's completely clean. But someone brought it from Tirosh's office to the car, a very strange thing to do, as if to give us a clue, to tell us that it was the murder weapon. And if you read the pathologist's report carefully, you saw that traces of metal were found on the facial skin and that he was, indeed, apparently beaten with it. There are no prints in the car either, but the office itself is full of them. They've all been checked out. They're mainly Tuvia Shai's, but also Yael Eisenberg's—she claims she wasn't there that day and may in fact have left them the day before—and the cleaner's, the guy we spoke to yesterday—"

"You mean the Arab? The one Bahar questioned?" asked Balilty suspiciously, and Michael nodded and went on: "But I think we should talk about Ariyeh Klein now."

"It's a bit pornographic to keep in an office, no?" remarked Balilty, raising his eyes from the photograph of the statuette and looking at Tzilla, who did not react to the sly twinkle in his eyes.

"I don't know what's pornographic and what isn't, but it's certainly literary—meaningful, as they say," said Michael, and he grimaced.

Ariyeh Levy, the Jerusalem Subdistrict commander, raised his eyes from the file he was studying and took off his reading glasses, but his disapproving look was wasted on the air, and he replaced the glasses with a sigh and again immersed himself in the contents of the file. Michael thought of the countless hours he had spent with these people in similar circumstances and asked himself why he was not deriving his usual comfort from the very fact of their intimacy, their familiar gestures, their predictable reactions. This morning everything irritated him. Perhaps, he thought, it was because of the absence of Emanuel Shorer, who had always acted as a buffer between himself and Ariyeh Levy, but he knew that this morning not even Emanuel could have saved him from his feeling of loneliness. He looked deliberately at his watch, and Balilty, surprisingly, registered his mood and mumbled: "It's only eight o'clock in the morning, Ohayon." Tzilla fanned herself with the copy of the report in her hand.

In spite of the early hour, it was hot and stifling in the large room, whose windows overlooked the main entrance, and the dusty ivy covering the facade of the building and creeping in through the window created only the illusion of shade.

Gilly, the Jerusalem police spokesman, asked hoarsely if he could "release the photograph to the press," and Michael replied "Not yet," quietly but with a firmness that brooked no argument. Balilty sighed and Raffi began to brief them on his questioning of Ariyeh Klein. The C.O. put the file down on the table with a thud and looked around him silently. His eyes came to rest on Michael, and his expression soured. He dropped his reading glasses to his chin and began nibbling the earpiece.

Raffi Alfandari went on talking: "If you look at the copy of his statement, you'll see that he came back on Thursday night and decided not to let anyone outside his family know. He rented a car at the airport and drove straight to Rosh Pinna, where his elderly mother lives. He returned to Jerusalem on Saturday night, after picking up his wife and three daughters at the airport. They came back Saturday night; we checked. So I think he's out of the picture."

"How did you check it?" asked Ariyeh Levy.

"Well, we asked his mother, one of those old pioneers from way back; you can see on her face that she wouldn't tell a lie. Anyway, that's what she said." He pushed an invisible lock of hair off his forehead, lowered his eyes uneasily, and went on: "The interesting thing— we've only got it on tape so far—is that he met Dudai in America twice—once when Dudai arrived and once just before he left. And what he told me is that Dudai was in a very bad mood before he came back to Israel."

Balilty looked at Raffi Alfandari and said with a smile: "That's the longest speech I've heard from you all year."

Michael ignored Balilty and asked: "Why?" and Raffi, who since the day he had begun working on Michael's team had demonstrated unbounded admiration and loyalty toward him and maintained, as it were, a dialogue with him alone, said in embarrassment, which gave him a youthful and innocent air: "Klein said that Dudai was having a serious crisis about his doctorate, but he didn't want to go into details; he asked if he could talk to you about it."

Levy laid his reading glasses on the cover of the file.

"What is this, a cafeteria? Everyone can order what he feels like?" protested Balilty, but Michael cut his protest short and asked if Klein, too, had been invited to take the polygraph test today.

Tzilla nodded her head vigorously and said: "Yes, at four. And he asked if you would be here then, and I didn't know what to tell him."

"I don't know if will be here," said Michael, "but you can tell him that I'll contact him."

Ariyeh Levy rested his hands on the table and raised his eyebrows, as if he couldn't take any more of this nonsense. Michael picked up the signals and knew that an outburst was on its way, but he chose to ignore it, saying to himself: This isn't your day for sitting with the team; you'd better get out of here; you sound as pompous as Ariyeh Levy and about as agreeable.

But then Balilty suddenly asked: "And have I told you that he was once married?" and looked triumphantly around the table until his eyes fell on Michael's furious face, when he said in a serious, businesslike voice: "In 1971, Professor Tirosh went on a sabbatical to Canada. He was apparently very lonely there, because a month later he was joined by Miss Yael Eisenstein, who was then aged eighteen and a half, and I want to remind you"—here he smiled lasciviously—"that he himself was then forty-one, and when she got there he married her, even if it was only a civil ceremony, without a rabbi. And exactly six months later he divorced her."

Levy looked at both of them, first at Balilty and then at Michael, with an expression of satisfaction, as if to say: Even you can't control him, and returned his attention to the file. "Get in touch with Forensics and tell them to add it to her polygraph," said Michael to Tzilla.

"But what does it mean?" Eli Bahar spoke up for the first time that morning. "So what if he was married to her a thousand years ago? Why should she suddenly wake up now?"

"It's a fact that her fingerprints were in his office, and the Arab had cleaned on Thursday because of course he's off Fridays," said Balilty. "Who says that relationships end with a divorce? The world is full of all kinds of things, and the main thing here is that there was an unusual relationship between them, and nobody knew about it, and we have to talk to her about it."

"But I checked her story after Raffi questioned her, and she really did take a cab from the university at half past twelve on Friday, and she doesn't have a driver's license," said Eli Bahar aggressively, and Balilty retorted, "How do you know?" and again there was a silence, which was broken by Ariyeh Levy, who said paternally: "If we didn't know they had been married, there might be other things we don't know about too, like a Canadian driver's license, and people can take a cab and go back later." Eli Bahar opened his mouth to speak, but Levy stopped him with a raised hand: "I'm sure you checked—never mind the details; just check again in the light of what we've just heard. Remember the case of Dina Silver, who claimed she didn't know how to shoot, and then it came out that she'd won first prize in a sharp-shooting contest abroad. Some people think that anything they do outside the country's a secret. Obviously it has to be rechecked. And in general, you're dragging your feet and treating them with kid gloves!" His voice rose and the paternal note disappeared. "I don't understand why you don't arrest Tuvia Shai and his wife; in my opin-ion, they were in it together. There are cases like that, with rich, lonely people. And I don't know about you"—he glanced mockingly at Michael—"but from where I stand, Tirosh was a rich man, and this couple, the Shais, got their hands on him through her, the wife, for the money, and then Tirosh kicks her out and spoils their plans."

Michael remarked that the Shais had not benefited financially from Tirosh's death, apart from which, he added, there was nothing in the C.O.'s theory to explain the death of Dudai. As he spoke, he saw the glint of anger in Levy's eyes, and he knew what the C.O.'s next words would be. "This isn't a university here, whatever some people think!"

roared Ariyeh Levy, banging his fist on the table, and no one dared to smile. "And the only reason I'm not ordering you to arrest them right now is that you haven't got any proof, because any judge would see the fact that he was screwing his wife as a good enough motive, and he had plenty of opportunity too—his alibi's useless."

"I intend to talk to him again today," said Michael.

"How are you going to get him in here? He's teaching all day; I've got it written down here," said Tzilla.

"Mount Scopus isn't on the moon," said Balilty, "and so what if he's teaching? What's the big deal if he doesn't teach for a couple of hours? Would it be better for him if we arrested him? If he didn't teach for the rest of his life?"

"And what about the chemists?" asked the C.O. matter-of-factly, his outburst forgotten. "From what Dudai's wife said, the tanks and all the diving gear were stored in the basement of their building. She's got a key, but from what it says here, the door was often left open, and anyone could have tampered with the tanks, and as I understand it, Dudai didn't have any connections with chemistry laboratories and he didn't know anything about gases. Not that I think we should do their work for them as far as Dudai's concerned, let them break their heads over there in the Negev, but still, we've decided the two cases are linked, and in the meantime we haven't come up with anyone else in connection with the diving tanks."

"Aharonovitz," said Eli Bahar.

"What about him?" asked Michael.

"He wanted to be the head of the department, and Tirosh was against it; they had a special faculty meeting about it on Friday morning. But Aharonovitz told me that he had said at the beginning of the meeting that he had to be home at one o'clock. He kept saying it. I asked him why and in what connection and so on, but he wouldn't tell me. Finally he said his wife was sick. So I went around to his address—he lives in Kiryat Haovel, on Rabinovitz Street, where they've got those villas—and I spoke to the neighbors. He's got a wife and two grown kids, the son's okay, studying medicine and all that. The daughter's a mental case; she's been hospitalized for years in Ezrat Nashim, and they bring her home on weekends. I thought, from the way he looks, that he would live in a dump, but. . . " Eli's voice trailed away, and he dropped his gaze. "Never mind, it's not important," he said hesitantly.

"Go on," said Balilty.

"No, it's nothing. Just that he's got a nice house, with a garden that his wife cares for herself, and she's like refined looking. You couldn't call her beautiful—she's over fifty—but a real lady."

"Well?" said Balilty. "What's the point?"

"Somehow"—Bahar ignored Balilty and spoke directly to Michael—"I never had the time to tell you, but it changed my whole perception of him. And he's no fool either."

"Nobody said he was a fool; the question is if he's a suspect," said Ariyeh Levy suspiciously.

"I don't know, but after the meeting on Friday he went to the hospital to bring his daughter home for the weekend. We checked. It's only that he really hated Tirosh. Boy, did he hate him!"

"But could he have been in Tirosh's office before that or not?" asked Levy impatiently.

"I don't know what to tell you. At the hospital, they said he arrived at about one, that he always gets there around one. He doesn't have a car. He says that he took two buses—he's against taxis. It doesn't look to me as if he had the time."

"Did you ask him about the notepad on Tirosh's desk—the impression of those words?" Michael asked Eli Bahar.

Eli nodded.

"Well?" asked Balilty.

Eli ignored Balilty. "He said that the first word had to be read with the old Ashkenazi pronunciation rather than the way we talk now. So it's not *shira,* poetry; it's Shira, a woman's name. And then. . . " Eli blushed and reached for his coffee cup.

"What's all that rubbish? What does it mean?" Balilty asked.

"He said: 'Young man, it doesn't hurt to learn something. Go and see what Agnon changed in *Shira.*' I didn't know what he was talking about."

There was an uneasy silence in the room. Ariyeh Levy drummed his fingers on the table. Michael stared at the wall opposite him.

"So what's it all about?" Levy finally barked in Michael's direction. "Perhaps our educated colleagues can tell us?"

Michael said unwillingly: "It's a novel by S. Y. Agnon, published after he died. It isn't finished. I seem to remember that the last chapter is missing."

"Did you ask him what Tirosh was getting at, in his opinion?" Ariyeh Levy asked Eli.

"He said something about leprosy and corruption. Half the time I didn't even understand him. I really don't know what to tell you," said Eli in embarrassment.

"Is there anything there about leprosy? Corruption? Do you know the book?" Levy asked with increasing haste, and looked at Michael.

"I don't remember, but he did write one story about leprosy," replied Michael thoughtfully.

Ariyeh Levy opened his mouth to say something, his face flushed and his expression ominous. "That's not what I asked," he said menacingly, "and I don't want any lectures now."

"I really don't remember. The book is five hundred pages long," protested Michael, looking at his sandals.

"So what's it got to do with anything?" said Ariyeh Levy. "I don't think there's any connection."

"Maybe he was busy writing an article about it," said Michael without looking at anybody.

"And he left no notes? said Balilty doubtfully. "A person who's writing something throws papers into the wastepaper basket, makes rough drafts and tears them up, stuff like that. No?" he asked Michael, who nodded in confirmation.

"So in the meantime, as far as I can make out, our educated colleagues haven't got a clue either. It's a good thing I never wasted a few years over there," said the C.O. with ostentatious satisfaction.

"But the way he hated Tirosh. . ." Eli looked around him uneasily, then he opened his mouth, had a second thought, and shut it again. Michael looked at him and said irritably: "Well, what is it?" and

Eli said, slowly and hesitantly: "I don't know, but just take a look at the photo of Tirosh's storeroom; it's not very clear. . . ."

"Well?" Michael prodded him.

"It seems to me," said Eli, "as if there's something behind the tools that looks like a gas cylinder. I think we should go back there and see."

"Didn't you search the storeroom?" asked Ariyeh Levy threateningly, and Michael shrugged his shoulders and looked him in the eye as he said: "Perhaps we didn't search it thoroughly enough."

"So check it out today, if it's not too much to ask," snapped Levy, and Michael nodded.

"First make sure it's not for an ordinary domestic gas balloon," said Balilty. "That character with his Hungarian sausages," he added with a sneer in what purported to be a Hungarian accent, "probably kept a gas balloon handy."

Eli Bahar looked at him belligerently and said in a whisper: "I don't take my orders from you."

Then Michael said in a conciliatory tone: "Check it out this morning, please."

"What can I tell them in the meantime?" inquired the spokesman, Gilly, desperately, wiping the perspiration underneath the fair hair that fell onto his forehead. Ariyeh Levy threw him an impatient "Just a minute" and turned his attention to Michael, who had begun outlining the tasks for the day. "They're waiting outside; they're getting fed up. There's a foreign correspondent too; the guy was an international figure—have you seen the headlines in the past couple of days?" Gilly persisted.

"You bet I saw them," replied Balilty, though it wasn't he who had been asked. "'Lethal Lit'—that was a good one!"

"Let them write more feature stories," said Michael firmly. "In the meantime Tirosh's books are selling like hotcakes—not that I know who'll get the money."

"The article 'Serial Deaths in the Literature Department' is more worrying," said Eli. "They're all shaking in their boots! Kalitzky asked for a bodyguard. Zellermaier said that she's too frightened to sleep at night. It's not funny—don't you think one of them might really need guarding? Who'll be next? That's what they're asking."

There was a thoughtful silence, and as usual it was broken by Balilty. "There are some people," he said reflectively, "who don't believe they'll ever die. Tell me how, with all that money, a man who was alone in the world didn't leave a will."

"You checked it out?" inquired Levy, and Eli Bahar mentioned the name of Tirosh's lawyer.

"So maybe someone else has it?" ventured Ariyeh Levy, but Eli said stubbornly: "I checked. There wasn't any will in his papers either."

"And there's no family?" asked Levy disbelievingly.

"An old aunt in Zurich," said Michael, and once more there was silence in the room.

"So what are you looking for now?" asked Levy, and Michael responded carefully: "We're looking for someone who left Mount Scopus between two and six, with a small statue the length of a forearm, driving off in Tirosh's Alfa Romeo. The statue doesn't fit into Tuvia Shai's briefcase, and he says he wasn't even carrying a briefcase that morning. But the statue could fit into any biggish plastic bag, and there couldn't have been a lot of blood on it. It could have been taken out in a plastic bag. We examined all his wife's bags, Ruth Dudai's, everyone's; there wasn't a trace of blood. The guard at the parking garage entrance doesn't remember seeing the car leave, but it was hot, he was sitting inside his kiosk, and he could have raised the barrier without looking. In short, it's not going to be easy, and as you read in the file, there are a lot of candidates, a lot of people would have liked to see him dead. Just thinking about his dramas in that café is enough," he concluded sourly.

"What café?" asked Tzilla, who had been usually quiet this morning.

"Didn't I tell you?" said Michael impatiently, then noticed her worried look. "For the past few years he had a kind of ritual. He would arrive at a café in Tel Aviv, called Rovall, I think—but it's written down; you typed it yourself."

"I didn't do all the typing myself," protested Tzilla.

"So what happened at the café?" asked Ariyeh Levy impatiently.

"Every Monday he would sit in the café between four and six in the afternoon, and young poets would bring him their manuscripts for criticism. He would just sit there with a cup of coffee, and read them one after the other, and decide on the spot—thumbs up or thumbs down."

"What do you mean, thumbs up, thumbs down?" said Levy.

"He edited a very prestigous literary magazine—it's called *Directions*—and there in the café he would decide whom he was going to publish in it."

"But I told you, there were dozens of people there, and there wasn't any discrimination—he humiliated them all; no one was special," said Balilty sharply. "I've got a list, and we're checking it; most of them were women, young girls, there were a few guys, but none of them would have had the strength even to pick up that statue."

"I don't understand," said the C.O. to nobody in particular. "Why would anyone be prepared to let somebody do that to them? Nobody could have made me. . . ."

Michael responded, "Well, it's a different world, with different laws, the world of poets. They thought he was a first-rate poetry critic." He looked into Ariyeh Levy's eyes defiantly, but Levy kept quiet.

"They have different standards," remarked Balilty venomously. "They think that we're illiterate or something."

"It's important," said Michael reflectively. "It's important to us because it's important to them. Just as you'd go and find out about diamonds if there was a murder about diamonds, you have to try to enter their world and—"

"I haven't got any plans to start reading poetry magazines!" said Ariyeh Levy, banging his fist on the table. "You can get that out of your head!"

"The point is that for a poet to get published in a magazine like that means attention and recognition and respect and all the things that exist in other worlds too, and Tirosh had the last word on the subject," explained Michael quietly.

"Okay, we get the point, and now I'm asking you again," said Levy, passing a thick-fingered hand over the back of his neck, as they all got up to leave, "have you discarded the security aspect? The political background?"

"We have," pronounced Balilty, and Levy looked at him doubtfully. At the door, Michael reminded them that by evening they should have the results of the polygraph tests.

"Where will you be all day?" asked Tzilla anxiously when they were outside the room.

"First on Mount Scopus," said Michael, "with Tuvia Shai again, maybe we'll come up with something new." He hesitated and wiped his face as he said, "I'll call you from there when I'm finished."

"Will you take someone with you? To stay in the car and record the interrogation?"

"Come along, Alfandari," Michael called to the far end of the corridor. "You're coming with me."

Alfandari drove the station wagon, which was equipped with remote, wireless recording equipment. "Why don't they put air-conditioning in here? Do they want this delicate equipment to be damaged?" he asked rhetorically as they settled into the stifling car. Michael, whose eyes were hurting in the glaring light, said nothing. For the thousandth time he contemplated the majestic entrance to the Russian Compound and wondered at the mixture: the facade of the Russian palace, whose interior was partitioned by thin walls into offices, and opposite it, glittering silently in the sun, the Russian church. On Sundays the voices of the Orthodox nuns would rise from it, and sometimes he would hear them singing as he walked or drove past. The sound always moved him, and it would take him a few minutes to realize that it was Sunday. Sometimes he would be next to the guardhouse when he heard the singing and would note with satisfaction the expression of wonder on the faces of others, before they shook themselves and went back to their business. He looked now at the big barrels fencing off the parking lot, at the wooden guardhouse, and at the green domed roof of the church, shining in the sun, and saw opposite him the hostel that Prince Sergei of the house of

Romanov had built for the Russian Orthodox pilgrims, a building that now housed the office of the Society for the Protection of Nature and a department of the Agriculture Ministry. He glanced around the whole of the Compound, at the large, splendid Russian palaces that had been adapted without too much effort to the needs of the Israeli bureaucracy, and the conjunction of the offices with the vision of Prince Sergei made him marvel yet again at people's ability to lead prosaic, day-to-day, taken-for-granted existences in Jerusalem.

He found a pair of dark glasses in the glove compartment and mechanically followed their progress in the car.

They were standing in the corridor outside the department secretary's office. Tuvia Shai wiped his forehead with one hand. In the other he was holding a thin booklet and a cardboard file. He said impatiently: "It's the last class of the year and I can't possibly cancel it."

"Not even after everything that's happened here? You cancel classes for far more trivial reasons—just take a look at the board." Michael pointed to the bulletin board hanging on the wall just beyond the bend in the corridor and said: "Family reasons, or no reason at all. Why can't you cancel it? What if you suddenly took ill?"

"Don't say 'you,'" said Shai angrily. "We're not all the same, and I never cancel classes without a very good reason. The students weren't notified in advance. Why should I suddenly start treating them with contempt?"

"Because two of your fellow teachers were murdered," said Michael simply, and Tuvia Shai suppressed his anger and looked as if he had just remembered, as if he had been doused with a cold shower.

"Everything I've been talking about all year was supposed to be tied up today. I've been working toward this class all year," said Shai. "So wait another hour and a half, that's all it will take. You can talk to someone else in the meantime—why do you have to talk to me so urgently now? I spent all day yesterday talking to you."

"You're the last person who saw him alive," Michael reminded him, and after a moment's thought he added: "And you were also particularly close to him, as I never stop hearing from the others."

Shai waved his hand; at last he said: "You can't compel me to cancel my last seminar. Yesterday I canceled my poetry tutorial because of you."

"What makes you think your students will turn up? They must be scared out of their wits too."

"They phoned to ask me if there would be a class and I said yes. We decided not to cancel anything, neither classes nor exams. It's the end of the year."

Michael was silent for a few seconds and then said: "Okay, I'll wait for you in the class, if you have no objections."

"I can't understand why you should want to sit in on a class where you have no idea of what's going on. I've been trying to explain to you that I'll be tying up the threads of something we've been examining for a whole year. Apart from which, we'll be dealing with a particularly difficult text. . . . Well, do what you like."

Michael followed him in silence. They descended to the floor below and walked along a corridor. Doors appeared at unexpected angles, and Michael imagined them leading into narrow labyrinths, but the door that Tuvia Shai opened led into a well-lit, pentagonal space, where a group of students were sitting and waiting. A buzz arose in the room when the door opened; the students stared at Michael curiously for a moment, and he thought that he could recognize fear on their faces.

Fifteen women, counted Michael, most of them young, two with the headscarves of the observant and one wearing the kind of turban (it had slipped slightly to one side) worn by ultra-Orthodox married women. There were two young men and an older man who looked very tired and supported his chin on his hand. The students were seated at rectangular tables arranged in a horseshoe, with booklets of typed texts and Bibles open in front of them. Michael sat next to the older man, who was in the second row, not at a table but on a chair with a writing arm. On the arm lay a closed booklet, on the cover of which Michael read the title *Elements of Lyric Poetry*. When Tuvia Shai took his place at the teacher's table, at the open end of the horseshoe, the man next to Michael roused himself, opened his booklet, then began paging through the Bible lying on his knees. Michael peeped into the booklet, read the words "Samson's Hair," then read the lines below the title.

I've never really understood Samson's hair:
its immense secrecy, its ascetic mystery,
the prohibition (perfectly understandable) against talking about it,
the constant fear of loss of locks, the endless dread
of Delilah's light caress.

But I have no trouble at all with Absalom's hair.
Obviously it's beautiful, like the sun at high noon, like a red
vengeance moon.
Its fragrance is sweeter than the perfumes of women.
Conniving cold Ahitophel can't bear to look

when he sees before him the reason for David's love:
It's the most glorious hair in the realm, the perfect motive
for every uprising and afterwards the terebinth.

Tuvia Shai looked out and said: "The class has begun," and he read the poem aloud. The room was still: apart from his voice, there was no sound to be heard. Michael looked at the face of the man reading. He immediately noticed the color spreading over his cheeks, and his voice, no longer monotonous. Michael understood that Shai loved the poem, and soon he also knew that he loved teaching as well.

He finished reading and turned to the students. The matter-of-fact way with which he had opened the lesson prevented them, Michael sensed, from thinking about the events of the past few days and made it possible for them to come immediately to grips with the material.

"What is it that sustains this poem? What is its deep structure? What does it rely on?" asked Tuvia Shai. A hand went up hesitantly, and one of the young men, the bespectacled one, began talking before being given permission to do so. "There are two references to biblical stories here, two allusions," he said in an eager, animated voice.

The young woman in the turban interjected: "Judges thirteen to sixteen and Samuel Two, chapters thirteen to nineteen."

Tuvia Shai nodded and enunciated: "So what do we do with it? We've had poems with allusions before, but this time we've got two biblical texts in one poem; where do we go from here? We've identified the allusions—what now?"

"We should discuss interpretations of the texts alluded to," said one of the older women after examining the papers spread out in front of her.

"Remind me," said Shai, and for a moment his face assumed the empty, lifeless expression so familiar to Michael. "Who undertook to prepare something?" He dropped his eyes to the papers in front of him, and Michael glanced at his watch. Only ten minutes had passed. Again he looked at the poem before him; it aroused his curiosity, he even liked it, but he didn't know why. He understood hardly anything about it, but he had always liked the story of King David and Absalom's revolt. Sometimes the words of the lament: "O my son Absalom, my son, my son Absalom, would God I had died for thee, O Absalom my son, my son!" used to come into his mind in moments of inexplicable sadness, long before he himself had become a father.

As if through a veil, he heard the voice of the middle-aged woman, with traces of an unidentifiable accent, something Eastern European, reading from her notes the story of the birth of Samson and the events of his life. Then she took off her reading glasses for a moment and asked: "The interpretations now?" Shai nodded, and Michael sensed the lecturer's tension, his growing excitement as the woman resumed reading. She quoted the rabbinical exegetes in a deliberate voice, and as she proceeded, Tuvia Shai's fists tightened. Finally she said; "That's all as far as Samson is concerned," and Tuvia Shai opened his mouth and said, in the kind of voice one would use to tell children a story: "What's it really about, the story of Samson? Have you ever thought about it?" Michael followed the students' eyes. Some of them looked at the door and some shifted uneasily, but Shai didn't wait for an answer. "Have you ever thought about the contradictions in his character? Have you thought about the fact that he is a secret Nazarite consecrated to God, both a judge and a man who hides his light under a bushel? I want to remind you"—his voice rose and he waved his finger in the air—"that he doesn't tell his parents about the lion, he doesn't boast about it anywhere." He looked at the students and then at the window, which should have overlooked a distant view but actually faced nothing but another building. "Have you thought about the fact that he is an adulterer who is betrayed twice in the same way by two different women, his wife and Delilah, and that this contradiction reaches a climax—when? Where do we find the climax of the contradiction in his character?"

"In his death," said the second young man quietly, looking down at his feet and then lifting his clear blue eyes to Shai, who smiled at him affectionately, confirmed his words with a nod, and said: "Yes, in death his figure takes on almost mythical proportions. Think about it, the blind giant, surrounded by mocking Philistines, praying for one last consolation before his death. Picture it: there's certainly an element of the sublime, the tragic, in the picture." He looked at the students as if to make sure that they understood. Michael didn't take his eyes off him but didn't succeed in catching his eye: the man behaved as if Michael weren't there.

"What I want us to think about here is that in the Bible, the figure of Samson the Hero is presented on the one hand as a Hercules and on the other as slightly ridiculous." Michael observed the students. They were writing feverishly. The man sitting next to him kept his hand under his chin and gazed straight ahead: he wasn't taking notes. "What I want us to keep in mind"—Shai's voice rose again after a momentary pause—"is that the Bible presents Samson's hair as a metonymy—a part representing the whole—for his special bond with God, the bond that gives him his supernatural strength. In the mind of the reader, the hair comes to represent the strength itself. Samson's bond with God, along with his weakness regarding women, a weakness expressed in foolishness or at least naïveté, creates a stunning contradiction. Twice"—Tuvia Shai held up two fingers—"twice he is betrayed by women he loves. This isn't simply stupidity; there's conceit here too—it never occurs to Samson that his strength can be taken from him. What the Bible is actually describing is a man who has undergone a certain process over the years. A process as a result of which he comes to identify the divine strength in him with his own personality and forgets its divine origin." Again Shai looked around him and Michael saw the hands arrested as the students stopped writing, and the sudden light shining in the young male student's blue eyes. "For Samson," said Shai in a low voice, "the loss of his hair means the loss of his bond with God, the breaking of his ascetic vows, this is what the loss of his hair means to him, and consequently, ladies and gentlemen, consequently also the loss of his supernatural, superhuman strength."

Tuvia Shai looked around him with what could only be described as a look not of triumph but of pride, by someone who has solved a complicated riddle and shed light on his surroundings. "I can't see the connection," protested a young woman. Her broad back, the only part of her Michael could see, moved irritably, and the light in Tuvia Shai's face went out for a moment. "Patience," he said to her and smiled. "We won't leave until you can see the connection. We're deciphering a multidimensional structure here, we're looking for the third text, let me remind you. It takes time."

"Can you tell us the name of the poet?" asked a young woman in a green headscarf, and Tuvia Shai's face became animated again as he said in an amused tone: "Not yet; to avoid prejudice, only at the end, although I'm sure that some of you know already." And then he went on to talk about Absalom. The man next to Michael searched feverishly through papers he had taken out of the briefcase standing on the floor between his legs, and then, in a calm, deliberate voice, read a summary of the plot of Absalom's revolt. Ancient echoes awoke in Michael, echoes of things he had thought he knew but now realized that he had never understood. With a feeling of shock, he heard the details of "Ahitophel's counsel" and understood the meaning of the words "So they spread Absalom a tent upon the top of the house; and Absalom went in unto his father's concubines in the sight of all Israel"; he stole a look at the open booklet on the writing arm of the chair on his left and again saw the words "Conniving cold Ahitophel," and the poem began to stir with life, to stir with something he had not seen in it before. Something evil and terrible, which he wanted to understand.

Tuvia Shai's voice, too, seemed to be conniving as he said: "You've got all the data now; all you have to do is see the picture clearly," and he confronted the students sternly. They waited, their pens poised. When he wasn't examining an invisible point on the wall or the text on his table, Tuvia Shai would bring light into the blue-eyed student's eyes by looking at him. "Absalom," said Shai, "Absalom killed Amnon for raping Tamar. The act had been planned for a long time; it is not the act of a hot-tempered man. He broods about it for two years, and at last, when he avenges his sister Tamar, only then does it become clear how much rage there is in him. But isn't it also clear that he performs the act that should have been performed by his father, King David?" He glanced at the poem and whispered: "Three years! For three years David's beloved son sits in exile in Geshur, and then it's Joab who initiates his return to Jerusalem, Joab and not David! And the reconciliation between them is particularly cold, something that is stressed by the repeated use of the words 'the king' in the description of this exceedingly chilly reconciliation."

Michael touched the tiny microphone in his shirt pocket. He wondered what Alfandari, sitting in the car and recording the voices, thought about all this. Then he considered the monotonous voice of the Tuvia Shai he thought he knew, the one he had interviewed in his office. Now the same man was suddenly full of life, of emotion. And the things he was talking about! But, he reminded himself, this lesson was prepared long before anyone here had been murdered. Look at him, though: wouldn't he be capable of smashing someone's face in in an attack of rage? Was this the man without qualities? And was he really unaware of his, Michael's, presence? Was it possible that he didn't realize the side of his character that was being exposed here? The potential? Tuvia Shai's eyes, pale and watery, looked straight into Michael's, as if he had read his thoughts. There was no fear in them; the emotion was unmistakable: it was happiness, excitement at the solution, at the ability to put everything into words.

"The end of Absalom is a tragic and ironic end," said Tuvia Shai.

"He who was so in love with his hair dies precisely because of this hair."

"There's a midrash about it," said an older woman who had been silent up to now. She was sitting in the middle of the horseshoe, and Michael saw the excitement in her face.

"Yes," said Shai happily. "Do you remember it?"

"The sages say, in the tractate *Sotah,* I think," said the woman, in a pleasant voice, "that 'Absalom took pride in his hair and therefore he was hanged by his hair,'" and Tuvia Shai nodded vigorously. It was unmistakable: his face virtually beamed with happiness.

"Now we can get into the poem itself," said Shai, and Michael found himself listening to a long discussion of a figure of speech. "Zeugma," wrote Shai on the blackboard, and explained at length how the meaning of the poem was a product of its syntax and structure. "Despite the syntactical facts, which are ostensibly intended to emphasize the presence of the speaker in the poem," said Shai, wiping the chalk off his hands, "we get the sense that the subject of the verse is to be found precisely in the syntactically subordinate part of the sentence: Samson's hair, Samson's life. And the speaker disappears from the awareness of the reader. In other words, the object clauses in the poem are substantivized—that is, they become substitutes for the noun." Michael didn't understand exactly what Shai was talking about. He felt confused; his interest in the poem slackened. The others seemed completely absorbed in a world he thought he had understood, where people were now speaking a different language. Tuvia Shai spoke enthusiastically, and the students wrote energetically. One of them lifted her head, made a face, hesitated, and then raised her hand. "Just a minute," said Shai, "I'll be finished soon," and speaking almost at dictation speed, he continued: "Samson's hair is the object of reference, and everything else relates to it. It's the initial phrase— 'I've never really understood'—to which everything that follows is grammatically subordinate; it's this phrase that enables the sentence not to exhaust its energy." Then he turned to the student and with a gesture gave her permission to speak.

She was sitting opposite Michael, a girl in her early twenties with a pretty face. Her nose was full of freckles, and her eyes, dark and shining, were revealed as she pushed a fringe of hair off her forehead and said in an agitated voice: "I don't know how the others feel about it, but it simply ruins the poem for me, all this talk about syntax."

Tuvia Shai didn't smile. With a completely serious expression, he said: "First of all, we haven't finished yet, and second, Tamar"—it was the first time he had addressed anyone by name—"we've been talking about syntax all year, and third, I promise you that if this poem is worth anything, nothing will ruin it for you, not even a syntactical analysis. But perhaps you'll tell us your opinion again at the end?"

Someone in the room sighed, someone else smiled kindly. The two women in the headscarves exchanged a glance of mutual understanding and then regarded the young woman with indignation and contempt. She blushed, pouted, and said crossly, "I don't know," and looked down at her pen.

"It's the speaker, Tamar, it's the speaker," said Shai as if revealing a great secret. Michael looked at him, and gradually he began to understand. "It's the speaker in the poem who confronts the biblical stories and questions them. The statement, ultimately, is about the first-person speaker, and it is made by means of the choice of details from the biblical story and their setting between the opposition 'I've never understood . . . I have no trouble. . .' We learn about the speaker, about his character, through the change in the status of the allusion, and its being understood by the speaker or not understood by him. Do you remember the essay by Culler?" The clear-eyed young man nodded, and Tuvia Shai looked at him and said: "When a certain intention is declared by the speaker, we have a point of gravity, which dominates the interpretation." The room held a silence of concentration. Tuvia Shai pointed to the booklet and, taking a deep breath, said: "The poem places in a situation of choice a sequence of details that ostensibly—I stress *ostensibly*—follow necessarily from each other. In other words, an examination of the change in the status of the allusion on its way from the Bible to the poem and its location in the architectonic structure of the poem will enable us to understand what the speaker is saying about himself."

And what are you saying here about *yourself?* Michael asked silently, and again his eyes met those of the lecturer, who didn't blink but embarked on the lengthy statement the entire lesson had clearly been leading up to. "Only now that we've done all the spadework—investigating every allusion and all its possible interpretations, examining the use made by the poem of syntax and structure, and the way it selects the details of the biblical stories—only now are we in a position to decipher the change in the status of the allusion within the poem. The only element of the biblical story of Samson introduced into the poem is the 'immense secrecy' and 'ascetic mystery' of his hair"—now again Michael heard words like "signifier" and "signified" and wondered wearily what Shai was getting at. Then his attention was recaptured by: "'the constant fear of loss of locks'—this fear is not expressed in the Bible, either directly or indirectly. The presentation of the fear in the poem is a result of the point of view of the speaker, who thinks that if all his own strength came from his hair, he would be afraid to lose it. The poem changes Samson's weakness in the face of female temptation into a real fear of women, a fear that contradicts the risks taken by the biblical Samson. The poem interprets Samson's weakness with regard to women not as the inability to withstand temptation but as castration anxiety! Samson is presented as someone whose fears are for his own virility!" Again the triumph in his eyes, very like that of Balilty when he had discovered some detail or other, the triumph of the successful detective. Michael would never have imagined that Tuvia Shai could experience this feeling. "The subject of castration," continued Shai, "comes out clearly in a second reading: why the taboo against talking about his hair? Is it a sexual organ? And that dread of his, whenever Delilah lightly strokes his hair, characterizes Samson as a man constantly preoccupied with guarding his hair. In other words, the poet perceives Samson's strength as primitive, infantile, despite the mystic element inherent in it." Even the possessor of the freckled nose looked at Tuvia Shai with intent concentration, making an effort to understand.

"Excuse me," said the turbaned woman. "Would you mind repeating the last sentence?"

"What was the last sentence?" Tuvia Shai asked with a bewildered expression, as if he had been awakened from a hypnotic trance.

"I didn't understand it properly," the woman in the turban insisted.

Tuvia Shai repeated the words "castration anxiety" and "metonymy" a couple of times and went over his last sentences again. She nodded her head and wrote energetically, saying: "I understand," in a tone that made it clear to Michael that she hadn't understood a thing but had given up trying.

One of the women in a headscarf whispered something to her neighbor, who smiled and said something in reply that made her blush and fall silent. Shai resumed his lecture.

Michael listened attentively to the exposition describing the "change in the status of the biblical story of Absalom in the poem." Tuvia Shai stressed that Absalom's hair was red, which connected him by association with David, who was "ruddy and fair of countenance," and in the end he said: "All the feelings and qualities attributed to the hair in the poem are additions to the source. We don't find them anywhere in the biblical text." And then: "By connecting the associations evoked by the allusion to Ahitophel's attitude toward Absalom, which is expressed in the averting of his eyes from his hair, the poem creates an explicit erotic link between Absalom and Ahitophel."

"Eroticism again!" protested the woman in the headscarf. Shai ignored her and continued: "Another outcome of the syntactical discontinuity is the additional attribute accorded to Absalom, 'the reason for David's love,' which is equated with the hair—in other words, Absalom's beauty. In other words: David loves Absalom for his beauty!" And then: "And this 'glorious hair' is the 'perfect motive' for everything—the uprising and afterward the death." Now Tuvia Shai clasped his hands behind his back and turned to the window. His words had been deeply engraved in Michael's mind, and they went on echoing there all day long. What did you learn today? he asked himself after listening to them over and over on the tape, especially the final words: "The poem reveals a hidden layer that deals with the tremendous effect beauty has on people. The emphasis, both in the biblical story and in the poem, is on Absalom's beauty as a characteristic that ostensibly explains the terrible crime—the threat of patricide, the realization of incest—and ostensibly justifies the incomprehensible behavior of David. The explanation stems from the unique power possessed by the beauty that admires itself without any conflict, hesitation, or doubt. The average person is limited in his capacity for relating to his own realized, physical beauty. And at the same time he has a longing, a yearning, for concrete beauty. This yearning leads both to pining after manifestations of such beauty and to an attitude of exaggerated respect for them. People long to identify with such beauty, partly because the identification creates the illusion that the beauty of the object of the identification is imparted to the identifier. A person who shelters under the shade of such beauty and identifies with it feels, too, that some of it rubs off on him." Tuvia Shai then sat down, bowed his head, and continued in a monotonous voice: "In other words, the speaker in the poem sees Absalom's beauty as a beauty that possesses a terrible power, stronger than everything else—stonger than the evil and the coldness of Ahitophel, stronger than the father and king, sweeping away everything with it. This is an inhuman beauty, not superhuman but inhuman, and therefore it cannot be withstood. The uprising is presented here as the power of the flesh. As if this revolt is the opposite of human. This is a beauty that cannot be controlled by moral values. It causes the outbreak of primordial forces. The revolt against the father-king is presented in the poem as the inevitable result of Absalom's superior beauty. The sublimity of his beauty puts him outside human values. The realms of the absolute are inhuman. 'And afterwards the terebinth'—the triumph of beauty and youth ends in the gallop to perdition."

He raised his head and looked at the students, who stopped writing, and then with particular compassion at the freckled girl, who gazed back at him with eager eyes. Michael asked himself if she, at her age, could understand what had been said. He himself felt full of a great respect for the poet Natan Zach and for Tuvia Shai. Something had turned over in his stomach as he listened to this interpretation. He knew, too, that Shai had exposed something vital that related to himself, but Michael felt unable to tie up the connecting threads.

"The speaker exposes himself through his understanding and not-understanding. He is not moved by the gap between Samson's miraculous strength and his weakness. The superiority of divine over human power does not move him. He is moved by destructive, devastating beauty, not by the emanation of divine power from human beings. Samson's strength does not have the inertia of destruction, and therefore it does not impress, it has no meaning for the speaker. Samson's strength does not destroy basic relationships like that of father-son, king-subject, and so on. The destructive power that appeals to the speaker's heart is an unrestrained destructive force, which reaches the primordial level in the hearts of people who usually obey a moral code but cannot withstand this irresistible force and are swept by it to perdition. This perdition," and Tuvia Shai looked straight into Michael's eyes—"is not only Absalom's. We remember the twenty thousand people killed in the war in the forest, we remember Ahitophel, who committed suicide, we remember David's terrible lament—the most powerful lament in the Bible—for his beloved son. In order to put an end to David's lamentations, Joab is obliged to rebuke him by saying that he would have preferred all his subjects to die if only Absalom had lived." There was a silence, until Tuvia Shai went on: "Do you understand, ladies and gentlemen? That's the third text. Thank you." And he sat down.

"But who's the poet?" asked the woman in the turban.

"Zach," said the clear-eyed young man, looking lovingly at the booklet next to him. The woman in the turban began to write. "Natan Zach?" she asked again. Nobody replied.

Michael remained seated. He saw the pretty freckled girl leaning over the seated Tuvia Shai and heard her say: "The seminar paper on allusion," and then the older man say something to him about a signature on his attendance record for the Education Ministry, and someone ask about a tutorial that was held during the first semester, and someone else inquire about the bibliography. Tuvia Shai had already resumed his dull, lifeless expression. Michael asked himself what force of devastating, destructive beauty Tuvia Shai worshiped. Suddenly he understood how Shai could see the relations between his wife and Tirosh as justified. He lowered his eyes to the poem, the booklet still open on the writing arm—the older man was standing next to Tuvia Shai, who was writing something on the slip of paper the man had handed him—and then he noticed something else. Yes, he thought, but not everybody admires that beauty the way you described. It's not exactly the way you said. Joab, for example, doesn't admire it and isn't bowled over by it. Why? Because he's an army captain. He's a hero, without any feelings of inferiority. There's nothing weak or wretched about him.

He looked again at Shai, who gathered up his papers as he listened to the older student. The picture grew clearer. Michael felt that the time he had spent in the class had clarified for him above all Tuvia Shai's view of the world.

Who admires it, that beauty? King David, and Ahitophel, and the speaker in the poem, and you too, Tuvia. Why? Because you dread above all the wretchedness of existence, the awareness of the wretchedness of existence, that's what's at the bottom of it. The identification with beauty, the yearning for the sublime, these things enable you to deny the non-beautiful. Now I understand the role Tirosh played in your life. I still have to find out if you were capable of murdering the source of your identification with beauty. I have a feeling that you weren't. But go and explain all that to Ariyeh Levy. I wouldn't even be able to explain it to Shorer. Or maybe I could.

Michael left the room before Shai had time to get up and come over to him. He gave up the idea of the interrogation. Accelerating his pace, he made for the public telephone he had previously noticed in the corridor.

12

When Tzilla finally answered the phone, she had nothing new to tell him. Eli Bahar had not yet returned from Tirosh's house; the polygraph technician was testing Yael Eisenstein. "Ariyeh Klein's looking for you," said Tzilla. "He phones every hour and begs to talk to you—he sounds desperate. I had to restrain myself from telling him where you were." Michael promised that he would contact him. "He's at home all day, till half past three, and then he's coming here for the polygraph," she reminded him. Michael was on the ground floor of the Humanities Building. Near him, at another telephone, a young girl was standing and whispering into the mouthpiece. He looked at the silk trousers and T-shirt she was wearing, and she sensed his eyes on her and turned around.

And what have you got to tell me? he thought as he dialed Ariyeh Klein's number. The initial digits identified the neighborhood as Rehavia. Naturally, where else, he thought, with a mother in Rosh Pinna, salt-of-the-earth, pioneering stock—where else would he live but Rehavia? The line was busy; Michael remembered that Ariyeh

Klein had three daughters, and he asked himself how long it would take to get through. He looked at his watch and waited. Fifteen minutes later, at a quarter past one, the line was free and Ariyeh Klein answered the phone. "Mr. Ohayon," he said with a sigh of relief. "I've been looking for you since yesterday; it's of the utmost importance that we should speak." Michael noticed the pure, correct Hebrew of a native of Rosh Pinna. But he also remembered the friendly informality of Klein's lectures, their meeting in the corridor on Mount Scopus after the discovery of Tirosh's body, his terror in the face of death, and the clever eyes of this big man—all this banished the hostility aroused in him by Rosh Pinna and Rehavia and the polished Hebrew. The main reason why Michael accepted Klein's invitation to go to his house in El Harizi Street was curiosity, the childish curiosity that came from not yet having overcome entirely the teacher-pupil relationship between them. He didn't deny to himself his wish to become familiar with the man, although he knew that this was not the reason he would give to his teammates if they were to ask him.

Alfandari said nothing when Michael informed him: "We're going back. I'll take my own car from the Compound. See that Tzilla gets today's material; I want it typed up right away, and I want Tuvia Shai brought in for another polygraph test. I never said anything to him about it being inconclusive." By the way Raffi tightened his lips, Michael knew that he was being criticized. "You think we should arrest him," he said.

Alfandari stared ahead at the road, as if he were driving in the dark.

"He's not going to run away," Michael consoled him.

Only after parking the station wagon in the lot at the Russian Compound did Alfandari say: "No. I know he's not going to run away," and added hesitantly: "I'm sure you know what you're doing."

Michael smiled at him and hoped that the smile did not betray his embarrassment. "Tell Tzilla I'm at Ariyeh Klein's place," he said as he turned toward his car.

He found the house easily and took the path through the back garden, which led to the entrance. As he rang the bell, he felt his breath coming quickly. He was tense, constantly fingering the little recording device in his shirt pocket. The morning's fatigue was gone. He seemed to be hearing sounds from the house, but he wasn't sure until the door opened and he identified a string instrument and a piano. He was not familiar with the mysteries of chamber music. When he was sixteen, Becky Pomerantz, his first lover, had told him that this type of music demanded a certain maturity, and she had played only one such record for him—the "Trout" Quintet by Schubert. He didn't know the music now being played in Ariyeh Klein's house, but he could tell that it wasn't coming from a record. As if to confirm this, the music stopped, and loud, girlish voices took its place. When Ariyeh Klein led him to his study, next to the entrance hall, he remarked, "My daughters are practicing," in an apologetic tone that tried to disguise his pride, and then he shut the door of the room behind them.

"The door is usually left open; the women of the household are in the habit of popping in and out," said Klein, "and to tell the truth, I'm usually glad of it." To close the door, he had to pick up the stack of books acting as a doorstop and move them away. Then he sat down heavily in the chair behind the big desk, which was covered with papers, open books, offprints, and coffee cups.

Books were everywhere: on the shelves lining the walls, stacks and stacks of them on the sunken floor tiles, some next to the shabby armchair where Michael sat, gratefully sipping the strong coffee Klein had prepared. A large window opened onto the garden, and the air in the room was laden with the scents of damp earth and flowers mixed with the aroma of a vegetable broth. Compared to the heat outside, it was pleasantly cool in the room, the coolness characteristic of the high-ceilinged rooms in the old houses of Rehavia.

On Klein's big face Michael read perplexity and pain, and the gentleness and vulnerability there contrasted oddly with his size. The upper half of his body rose broad and sturdy above the desktop, and Michael looked at the thick arms, the gray hair above the high forehead, and the large hands with their long, delicate fingers.

"We didn't send them back to school; it didn't seem worth it in the middle of June," apologized Klein when the strains of a violin were heard again. It was the first violin in the family quartet, he explained with suppressed pride after sending away his youngest daughter, a girl of about eight, with fair hair and milky skin, who had knocked stubbornly on the door until he opened it and whispered a few words in a firm tone, after which she disappeared, waving the undersized violin she was holding in her hand. His wife, Klein explained, played the cello, and the eldest daughter played the piano. The middle daughter, he said, smiling, refused to take any interest in classical music and fought for her right to play pop music—"but," he concluded complacently, "we nevertheless have a quartet—I can handle both the violin and the viola."

Michael struggled between the wish to behave in a businesslike manner and the desire to get to know Klein. Michael had fulfilled the requirements of what in his day was called "basic studies" by taking courses in the departments of Hebrew Literature and French Language and Literature. He had landed in Klein's course by chance. It would never have occurred to him to take medieval Hebrew poetry, but he had been advised to attend Klein's lectures as a complement to a tutorial on Muslim conquests in the Middle Ages, and since the hours had suited his schedule, he had found himself in the big, crowded hall attending the introductory course. During the first lecture he had realized, once more, the truth of the cliché that the subject didn't matter: what mattered was the teacher. Thanks to Dr. Klein, Michael had learned that there was life in the poems of Shlomo Ibn Gabirol and Yehuda Halevi, texts that had seemed lifeless and tedious to him in high school, and so, in his third year, he had also attended a seminar conducted by Dr. Klein. Now he looked around him, stunned by the chaos of empty coffee cups and scattered papers; there was even a child's dress lying on one of the bookshelves and an unfinished jigsaw puzzle on the floor, and he breathed in the delicious aroma of the vegetable soup that wafted in around the closed door. He noticed the Persian miniature on the desk, and the fruit trees outside the window beyond Klein; he remembered the flower beds in the front garden and felt a mixture of envy and disbelief. The shadow of a thought along the lines of "It's too good to be true" crossed his mind. There was an incongruity between the lived-in warmth of the room and the earnestness all the books signified. He managed to read *Carmina Romana*, the title of the book lying face upward on top of the pile next to the armchair. Underneath it he glimpsed Cyrillic letters on the brown and dusty spine of another book. All this testified to a breadth of culture that gave rise in him to an unwilling reverence. He looked at Ariyeh Klein and thought that he was looking at a modern Renaissance man: a man of letters, an intellectual who was also a family man, a gardener, and a cook (he offered Michael a bowl of his vegetable soup with the same simplicity with which he had offered him a cup of coffee and the glass of cold water he had put before him without even asking), and in the final analysis, thought Michael, the complete opposite of Tirosh.

Now he had to find out, he thought, the significance of Klein's specialization in the Middle Ages and how this choice expressed the contrast between him and his murdered colleague. In his ears he heard the rich, musical voice of Tirosh, as opposed to that of Klein, the clear, strong, passionate voice he remembered from the lectures in the big lecture hall in the Mazer building on the old Givat Ram campus.

Klein coughed, looked at him across the desk, and said hesitantly: "Um, I've been looking for you since yesterday because there are certain things I have to tell you," and with an apologetic smile, he added: "I remember you from the seminar on Hebrew and Arabic poetry of the twelfth century."

Michael looked at the thick lips, which quivered slightly before Klein went on speaking. "I wasn't sure, um, that the people I spoke to would take what I had to say seriously. Perhaps that was unjust. I thought they were too young to be familiar with the vicissitudes of academic life." Again he coughed, in evident discomfort, then he continued: "I'm afraid I have certain prejudices with regard to policemen, which I find it difficult to overcome."

Michael blushed but said nothing.

"It's all very vague. I don't have anything you might call meaty, only impressionistic trivia," warned Klein.

In the distance, loud female voices and the sound of breaking glass were heard. Ariyeh Klein inclined his head, smiled apologetically, and took a gulp of coffee from a cup without a handle.

"I wanted to tell you that Iddo visited me in New York, he even stayed with us in our house at Fort Schuyler in the Bronx. A big old wooden house on the shore of Long Island Sound; my uncle, who was in Israel at the time, lives there. Iddo stayed with us twice: for a week at the beginning of his trip to America, and for three days before his return."

"How long was he there all told—a month?"

Klein nodded.

"He was there in connection with his Ph.D.? For only a month?"

Klein briefly explained the research grant from the Institute for Contemporary Judaism that Tirosh had obtained for Iddo. "He spent the first week at libraries and meeting specialists in the problems of minorities in the Soviet Union, especially Jews, of course. He met refuseniks too. He was busy and excited," said Klein with a tolerant smile, and added: "as we all tend to be when we discover new source materials in our field of research." And then he resumed in a brisker tone: "During the last week of his stay, Iddo traveled south, to North Carolina, to meet a jurist active on behalf of refuseniks and dissidents in the Soviet Union. The lawyer had a lot of material concerning the people in whom Iddo was interested, particularly Ferber. I don't know if you're familiar with Ferber's poetry."

Michael maintained his poker face.

"Anatoly Ferber was Shaul's discovery. He discovered many other poets too, in Israel, but he also liked 'discovering' unknown foreign poets and translating their poetry from German, or Czech, as he did in the case of the poet Hrabal." Klein glanced at Michael questioningly as he pronounced the name.

Michael shook his head to confirm that he had never heard of the poet in question.

"But Anatoly Ferber was his discovery with a capital *D*," said Klein, leaning forward. "I myself think, and have always thought, that it was part of the myth Shaul carefully constructed for himself. In my opinion, Ferber's poetry lacks, um, the originality Shaul attributed to it. The truth is that the poems are quite mediocre, and if they possess any importance, it derives only from the historical context. But it was impossible to say this to Shaul without risking a long lecture on the history of the Hebrew language."

The thick lips quivered in a kind of smile, and then, as if the events of recent days had been recalled, tightened again. Klein sat up in his chair. "Even before Iddo set out, the lawyer told him on the telephone that he had someone who knew Ferber staying at his house, someone who had been with him in prison and even knew how he had hidden his poems. He knew Hebrew and was familiar with the poetry, and this was quite a startling revelation, because Tirosh had said that he found the poems in Vienna, a fascinating tale in itself, and that no one in the camp where Ferber was incarcerated had understood Hebrew. In brief, Iddo was beside himself with excitement; I can still see the gleam in his eyes." Ariyeh Klein sighed and took another sip of coffee.

"How did he discover the lawyer?"

"It was by chance, through one of the librarians at the Jewish Theological Seminary, where he spent some time during his first week. I don't remember the details, but Iddo told him over the phone that he was a Ph.D. candidate from Jerusalem, working on research, and the lawyer invited him to come and stay with him."

Klein arched his eyebrows and looked at the large photograph hanging on the wall between two bookcases, a photograph of a bald man with a broad face, wearing a suit. The face looked familiar to Michael, but he couldn't place it.

"Iddo went to Washington and called me from there once, and then traveled to North Carolina, to a university town called Chapel Hill. Have you ever been to America?"

Michael shook his head and said: "Only to Europe." He asked if he could smoke.

"Certainly, certainly," said Klein and, without looking, unearthed a glass ashtray from behind a pile of papers. It was clear that he knew exactly where everything was.

"Everything I've said is in the nature of an introduction to the essential problem, which is Iddo Dudai's condition when he returned from North Carolina. You would have had to know him to perceive the immense change that had taken place within him." Klein was silent for a moment, as if conjuring up the image of Dudai, and then he continued: "Perhaps you are asking yourself how we came to be so close even though he wasn't my student—my doctoral student, that is. Naturally, he had taken classes with me and even participated in seminars, but our relations went beyond that. You couldn't help admiring his seriousness as a scholar and his intellectual integrity. He was an honest, clever boy, though he lacked the lightheartedness appropriate to his age; there was no playfulness in him, but there were no depressive tendencies either. You could say that he was an uncomplicated person, psychologically speaking, although he was definitely sensitive. But not given to moods. Ofra, my wife, was very fond of him, and he came here often. Shaul didn't like it. He was in the habit of making slighting remarks to me, and behind my back, about what he called my 'family-mindedness.' The fact that I invited people like Iddo or Yael Eisenstein to my home and introduced them to my wife and children, that they ate at my table, was in his eyes an 'obvious residue of provincial life in the colony of Rosh Pinna.' Naturally, when Iddo wrote to say that he was coming to the States and asked my help in finding somewhere to live, I invited him to stay with us. We were living in a spacious house with a separate wing for guests; we had a lot of people staying with us during the year. It was on the grounds of the Maritime College, where my uncle taught navigation. The Jews are a peculiar people," interjected Klein, lacing his fingers together, leaning back in his chair with a sigh, and turning around to look out the window at the garden.

A silence typical of a Rehavia afternoon ensued, punctuated only by the chirping of birds and the strains of music. Klein went on looking at the window behind his desk, and Michael wondered why he didn't get to the point. Then Klein turned around and said: "I need to explain the background, as an exposition, in order to stress how strange Iddo was when he returned from North Carolina. He arrived late, at about eleven o'clock at night; I remember because I was worried—his car might have broken down on the road, and Iddo had only his school English. I waited up for him. As soon as I opened the door, I asked him what was wrong, because his face was pale and there were dark rings under his eyes, and for a moment I thought he'd been mugged, although his clothes weren't torn and there were no apparent bruises on him. He said that he was just tired, and I can vividly remember the strange, dull look in his eyes as he said it. But I accepted his explanation, that he was tired." He then asked, "May I?" and pointed to the pack of cigarettes on the desk. Michael hurriedly gestured with his hand as if to say, "Please do," lit a match, and leaned toward him to light the cigarette.

"I gave up smoking five years ago," said Klein in embarrassment, and took up his story. "He didn't come down to breakfast in the morning. I drove off to teach without seeing him. I naturally assumed that he was still sleeping. Ofra and the children were out of town; they didn't see him that time. It's all still sharp and vivid in my memory. When I came back I found him sitting in the dark living room. I don't know if I'm explaining properly." Klein sighed and exhaled white smoke. "You understand, there was nothing wild and romantic about Iddo, there was nothing extreme, and I've known him since his first year at the university; he was always pleasant and polite. Even when his daughter was born he didn't act excited. He was a reserved person; next to him I sometimes felt loud; there was something restrained and balanced about him. And all of sudden he's sitting in the dark. When I switched on the light, he started and said he hadn't noticed the darkness. He looked tormented. I sat down opposite him and asked him what the matter was, several times: 'Iddo, what's wrong with you?' and at last he blurted out: 'Ariyeh, how many years have you known Tirosh?' and I answered what everyone knew: that we were the same age, that we met during his first year in Jerusalem, and that we'd been close ever since. But Iddo wasn't listening; he asked again if I *really* knew him. I tried to reply ironically, but he angrily brushed it aside. There was suddenly something frightening about him, as if he was in deadly earnest, like a character in a Hermann Hesse novel.

"I asked him about his impressions of Washington, about his

meeting with the lawyer and with the man who knew Ferber from the camps, but he replied tersely, in a way uncharacteristic of him. 'Fine, fine,' he repeated several times, and then he asked me again if I really knew Shaul Tirosh, and again I tried to ask if it was ever possible 'really' to know someone, but he refused to accept this line and obstinately asked me again. In the end, I said—and this was the truth—that I thought I knew him as well as a man like me could know a man like him, that in my eyes he was the exemplar par excellence of nihilism, whereas I had tried all my life to be the complete opposite, which is one of the reasons I chose to specialize in medieval poetry."

Again Klein glanced at the photograph of the man in the suit, and then he noticed Michael's questioning look and said: "Shirman. It's a photograph of my teacher Professor Shirman. Did you know him?" Michael shook his head vaguely, and Klein went on from where he had left off: "I chose medieval poetry—and I'm familiar with modern poetry too—because of its rigorous order, because there we don't have to dwell on the question 'What did the poet mean?' It was the pure classicism that appealed to me. I couldn't stand the tedious drivel of the students of modern poetry, the interminable arguments, the shocking ignorance. After all, how many times in our lives do we have students like Iddo Dudai?

"I spoke to him, to Iddo, so frankly because I could sense that he was in great distress. And I spoke a lot about the differences between us, Shaul and me. But in the end I said that I could assure him that I knew Shaul Tirosh well, with all his weaknesses and virtues, and he looked at me with terrible bitterness and said: 'I want to tell you that you don't know him at all, you only think you do,' and I tended to agree, mainly because I was dying of hunger, and when I saw that he was in no mood to go out to dine, I suggested that we move into the kitchen. And there, while I was making a salad, he stood behind me and asked me if I thought that Tirosh was a good poet. And I remember looking at him for a moment—I thought he had gone out of his mind—and telling him that Tirosh's poetry was his justification for living, the thing that made it possible for him to live such a lonely life, and that in my opinion, as Iddo knew, he was a great poet.

"He burst out laughing, very uncharacteristically—Iddo didn't laugh much, and this, moreover, was laughter of a different order, there was something demonic about it—and again I asked him: 'What's going on?' and he said: 'Nothing's going on.' I remember the words and the precise tone, because it was an answer so typical of Shaul, of the way he talked, and again I asked about the lawyer and the man from the camps, and he said: 'One day I'll tell you, but not now,' and then he told me that he was going to try to put his flight forward. With a great effort but without much success, I tried to feed him and talk to him about other things, but he wasn't there. I don't know"—Klein ground out the stub of the cigarette—"where Iddo had been the night before, somewhere between North Carolina and New York. It was clear that he had been through some great crisis, something terrible had happened there, but I don't know what it was, because in the two days before his return to Israel he would disappear from the house early in the morning and come back late at night. When I drove him to the airport I tried to make him talk, and he said: 'First I have to talk to Tirosh,' and those were the last words I heard him say."

"And did you talk to the lawyer?" asked Michael.

"No; I don't know him. But perhaps I should have. . . . Now I think. . . " Klein looked at him in alarm.

"Have you got the lawyer's name and address?" asked Michael urgently.

Klein nodded eagerly, then looked around him in despair. "I've got them, but I'll have to look. Should I look now?"

"It can wait for a minute," said Michael, and then he asked Klein to explain just how well he had known Tirosh, and he could sense the emotion that underlay the response: "As you know, you're not the first person to ask me, and to tell the truth, lately I've been thinking about it constantly. Up to the past few days I thought that I did—that I knew Shaul, that is. I've known him since he arrived in the country. We studied together, when the university was still housed in the Terra Sancta Monastery. He used to come to our house at least once a week, until a few years ago."

"What happened a few years ago?" asked Michael, and noticed again the tremor of the thick lips, which, he instantly decided, were Ariyeh Klein's most expressive facial feature.

"It's hard to define," said Klein slowly, "but I think that our ways of life became increasingly different. He grew more extreme, and I too, in a sense, grew more extreme in my own way of life, and there were resentments accumulating over the years as well: students' complaints about the grades he gave them when I was head of the department, obligations he failed to fulfill, arguments on questions of principle at department faculty meetings—arguments that ostensibly had nothing to do with our personal relations, but as you know, it's difficult to sit at the same table and eat a friendly meal with a man when you've just attacked the articles of his faith and he's defended them fanatically. There were very few things on which we agreed, and the truth is, I'm afraid that if you knew us both, you would have been surprised by the ties that once existed between us rather than by the fact that we drifted apart. You have to understand: there was no drama, no fight, no actual breaking off of the relationship; only a gradual weakening of the ties. His visits became less frequent, and when he did come there were islands of prolonged silence." For a few seconds Klein was silent, as if seeing the picture before his eyes. "Ofra, my wife, claimed that he despised us for our bourgeois way of life, but I'm inclined to think that there were other things behind it. There's no doubt that ever since he stopped writing, his life has become increasingly empty. There are many things you could have said about Shaul, but everyone would agree that he was a discriminating judge of poetry, and no one will persuade me that Shaul thought his latest, political poems were any good. He must have known their true value. And if he was unable to write, what justification did he have for his existence? His existence as it was, that is, lonely and pleasure-seeking, always unsatisfied. What could we offer him except a mirror in which to see his own barrenness?" he said softly.

Michael asked abruptly: "Perhaps he simply found other friends? Like the Shais, for example?"

Ariyeh Klein blushed and said nothing. Then he lowered his eyes and said: "Perhaps; I don't know," and raised them again. In his open eyes Michael read the intelligence and the sadness and also the disgust, and he didn't know whether the latter was directed toward Shaul Tirosh, or toward Tirosh's relations with Tuvia and Ruchama Shai, or perhaps, Michael feared, toward himself and his questions.

There was a persistent buzzing sound from the direction of the desk, and Klein dexterously moved a pile of papers aside and lifted the receiver of the telephone it had concealed. "Just a moment," he said, handing the phone to Michael. Eli Bahar's voice came over the line.

"Are you available?" asked Eli.

"I'm listening," said Michael, and heard that the cylinder in Tirosh's house was indeed an ordinary cylinder of domestic cooking gas.

Michael looked into Ariyeh Klein's face, and for a second their eyes met, after which Klein resumed looking discreetly at the opposite wall, as if to demonstrate that he wasn't listening to the conversation.

"Okay. What's happening now?" said Michael.

"We're going through the papers we brought down from Mount Scopus, Alfandari and me. I haven't got a clue where Balilty is. Tzilla's helping us with the papers. We asked Shai to come in for another polygraph; he didn't answer. Are you coming back here from there?"

"I don't know," said Michael, "but I'll be in touch. What's it now, about half past two? So I'll contact you at about five."

Klein looked worn out by the passion with which he had spoken about Iddo Dudai. He smiled when asked about the poets Tirosh had offended.

"You want to know about his relations with unknown poets?"

"Yes, more or less. How did it work? Did people send him manuscripts?" asked Michael.

"By the dozen," replied Klein. "He was always complaining about it, although of course he enjoyed it too. Sometimes he showed me manuscripts. He always handed the prose on to Dita Fuchs. During the past few years he himself read only poetry."

"Yet we found on his desk a note about the last chapter of *Shira*."

"*Shira*? You mean Agnon's *Shira*?" Klein pursed his lips in surprise. "What did Shaul have to do with Agnon? He never worked on Agnon." And then he added doubtfully: "As far as I know."

Michael asked about procedures—how the manuscripts were sent and how they were returned.

"The senders attach an address or a telephone number, unless someone you know personally actually hands you a manuscript," explained Klein. "And in contrast to seminar papers, Shaul responded quickly to manuscripts. He was always busy searching for gifted young poets; he never hid the fact that he wanted to be what I called an *arbiter poeticum,* to influence the Zeitgeist."

Michael referred to Tirosh's role at the Café Rovall in Tel Aviv, and Klein smiled for a moment and then said firmly: "No, compassion wasn't his outstanding quality; especially when it came to art, he could sometimes be cruel. But I never held it against him; I believe that people engaged in art risk exposure, and part of that exposure is to artistic judgment. And as far as that's concerned, Shaul had no rivals; he was a first-rate critic."

The telephone rang again, and Klein picked up the receiver and listened. His face softened, and then he sent a worried look in Michael's direction and said: "Try to calm yourself. I'll get in touch with you as soon as I can."

"That was Yael Eisenstein," he said after replacing the receiver. "As you know, she's a doctoral student of mine. She's been questioned again, and the polygraph test had a bad effect on her; she's very vulnerable."

"Oh, yes?" Michael heard the hostility in his own voice. He was fed up with Ariyeh Klein's protective, paternal attitude toward his students, and he wondered how much Yael Eisenstein's beauty influenced the big man who sat opposite him, playing with a paper knife.

"Did you know that she was once married to Shaul Tirosh?" asked Michael. Again a faint blush appeared on Ariyeh Klein's face. He looked at Michael cautiously and protested: "Years ago; that's all past and forgotten," and laid the paper knife down carefully on the desk.

"Was it generally known?"

"No," said Klein, wiping his face with his big hands. "I don't think so. Shaul never spoke of it, and Yael too preferred, um, not to remember."

Michael was silent, and Klein looked around him uncomfortably, but finally he gave in and looked into the policeman's eyes.

About fifteen years ago, Klein said—he could work out the exact date if it was important—he was coming out of a classroom in the Mazer Building on Givat Ram, when he found a young girl dressed in black waiting for him next to the gallery balustrade. He remembered exactly where she was standing, he said, running his tongue over his lips. She wanted to talk to him. He had never met her before, and he invited her into his office because she had an air of desperation about her. She told him how she had met Shaul. "When she mentioned his name," said Klein, smiling, "I thought she was one more victim, like all the others who were always falling in love with him. But she seemed younger than the rest, more vulnerable, and, in general, different."

You mean more beautiful than all the rest, Michael interpreted. Klein went on to tell him about the period when Tirosh's girls would come and cry on his shoulder and he would comfort them. Michael's lips tightened for a moment, and he asked himself if he was jealous, but he said nothing and listened patiently to the story of the "special young girl" whom Tirosh married during his sabbatical in Canada, after he had made her pregnant, how he had withdrawn into himself, and how, without saying anything, he had forced her to have an abortion, to let go of him, and to return to Israel alone and humiliated. "He treated the whole thing like a game," explained Klein in astonishment. "He invited her to Canada, and then he changed his mind, he simply changed his mind." He shook his head in incomprehension.

Michael asked why Yael had wanted to talk to him that first time.

"As soon as she had recovered from the abortion, she got on a plane and flew back to Israel; she simply ran for her life. Apparently she felt the need for support from someone who was close to Shaul Tirosh. I gave her all the support I could, I spoke to her for hours, in the end I even wrote to Shaul about her. I had the impression," he explained apologetically, "that I had influence over him, that Shaul respected me." Yes, Shaul had cooperated and had not opposed the divorce, but ever since then the barrier between Tirosh and himself had grown higher. And he had always had a special relationship with Yael after that, as if he felt guilty toward her. Klein's face clouded over.

Michael asked for an explanation of this guilt.

"It's true," stammered Klein, "she wasn't the only one he made pregnant—there were two other two cases—but she was so young and so anxious, so fragile," and Michael remembered the gentle voice that had answered: "just something years ago," when she was asked about her relations with Tirosh.

Aloud, he contented himself with asking why she had kept it a secret.

Klein shrugged his shoulders and replied that Tirosh didn't like being reminded of his guilt and Yael had suffered a severe trauma then, what with the abortion and the humiliation, "even though afterward she behaved as if it was all over and forgotten."

Again there was a silence, which Klein broke by saying philosophically that there were people who were unable to bear the ugliness of existence. People like Yael, he explained, suffered at the sight of a trash can. Dirty dishes in the sink, blood, body secretions, the smell of sweat in a bus, beggars, a peeling wall—"all these things are ugly to her," he said passionately. "You can't just put it down to self-indulgence. If you knew the way she reacted, you would understand. Sometimes I ask myself how she manages to exist at all. There are people like that," he said persuasively, "and there are others who live for beauty, like Tuvia Shai, which is a completely different phenomenon." Michael felt his body stiffening and asked for an explanation.

"A few years ago I was with Tuvia at an academic conference in Rome, and I went with him to the Capitoline Museum. We were looking at the busts of the Roman emperors, and I turned to Tuvia to say something to him about the face of Marcus Aurelius, and Tuvia wasn't there. I looked around and saw him standing next to the 'Dying Gaul.'"

Michael nodded. He remembered the statue, the smoothness of the marble, the muscles in the arm of the figure trying not to fall to the ground.

"I didn't dare approach him," said Klein. "I stood to one side and looked at the expression on his face. It was one of utter self-abandonment. I've never seen his eyes so alive, so full of expression, as they were at that moment in the gallery, when he was alone, on his own, carefully stroking the marble. I understood a lot of things then."

"What, for example?" asked Michael brutally, and stole a look at his watch before fixing his eyes on Klein again.

"His attitude to Shaul, his joy in his company. Tuvia isn't moved by the beauty of nature—a mountain landscape or a sunset at sea. He seeks the perfection of art. At lunch after our visit to the gallery he could speak of nothing else but that—the perfection of art. He paid no attention to the food, he drank the wine as if it were water. He spoke like a man trying to revive a memory connected to a beloved woman," and Klein stopped himself—perhaps he felt exposed—and fell silent, directing at Michael a sad and mocking look.

"You alluded before to Tuvia's private life," Ariyeh Klein continued hesitantly. "Not many people would be capable of understanding the situation. Perhaps now you'll be able to see the well-known facts in a different light, perhaps you'll be able to understand Tuvia Shai's total self-abnegation vis-à-vis Shaul Tirosh the poet, his willingness to give his all. He would have given Shaul his life, if he had wanted it, never mind his wife."

"I wanted to ask you something else, in the light of what you've told me about Iddo Dudai," said Michael, as if he had not heard what Klein had just said.

Klein looked at him and waited.

"Did Iddo Dudai play you the tapes of his interviews in America?"

"No," said Klein carefully. "He only told me that he was going to record them."

"And he never played you a tape or a copy of one?" Michael peered intently at Klein.

Klein shook his head a few times and then said, "No."

"Because we have the tapes, and there's no interview with a lawyer in North Carolina; there's nothing like that at all."

"Perhaps he didn't record that interview?" ventured Klein.

"Why should he record everything else and not that?" insisted Michael, staring at Klein, who appeared embarrassed and confused.

"I have no idea," said Klein. "Would you like me to look for the lawyer's number now? It could take hours in this mess."

"Not necessarily this very second, but sometime today." Michael reflected for a moment and then added: "When you find it, call me. If I'm not there, give the number to Tzilla Bahar."

There's something genuine about you, despite all the lofty talk. But why do I have the feeling that you, too, are hiding something? thought Michael as he started his car and looked back at Klein, who was standing at the window. And then he remembered that all the time he had been with Klein, he hadn't thought once of Maya, and he felt a sudden pang of loneliness. Again he looked at the flowered curtain waving in the window, and then he put his hands on the blazing-hot steering wheel.

13

Inside the Russian Compound building the heat was as stifling as it was outside. Michael went into his office and found Eli Bahar rummaging through papers that he was extracting from a big plastic bag.

"Is there anything new?" asked Michael, and he took a swig from the bottle of juice Eli handed him. "I've got something new to tell you," he went on, without waiting for an answer, and put the bottle down. Eli Bahar looked at him expectantly.

"You remember the boxes of cassettes? With the space for one more?"

Eli nodded.

"He had an encounter that either he didn't record or that he did and the cassette's missing."

"Klein told you?"

"Yes. He knows about a meeting that Dudai traveled eight hours there and back to go to. He returned in a state of collapse, and I've no idea why."

"And Klein doesn't know what went on there?"

"No. He only knows that he met a lawyer and some Russian Jew who was staying with him."

"Okay," said Eli with a sigh. "You want me to leave this stuff and go and search the place again?"

Michael nodded. "And search his office on Mount Scopus again too."

"But we've already taken all this stuff from there," said Eli in despair.

"Take Alfandari with you. I want to talk to Ruth Dudai again too, so you can go and get her and bring her back here with you first."

"Assuming she's there," said Eli doubtfully.

"She'll be there. She won't be going anywhere in this heat with a baby," Michael assured him.

Michael spent the next hour going through the transcripts of the cassettes that had been found in the home of Iddo Dudai. He scanned the typewritten pages filled with place names, dates, and the complicated names of people unknown to him. Only when Tzilla came in did he realize how much time had passed.

"She's here," said Tzilla.

"Can you wait for Balilty in the conference room? I'll manage with Mrs. Dudai on my own," said Michael, and handed her the transcripts. Eli Bahar brought Ruth Dudai into the room and practically deposited her in the chair opposite Michael. "I'm off," said Eli.

At six o'clock there was nothing left to do. The interview with Ruth Dudai had led nowhere, Eli Bahar had not yet returned from Mount Scopus, Tuvia Shai was undergoing a second polygraph test, and Michael sat idly in his office. The telephone didn't ring. The polygraph man can report to Tzilla, he said to himself as he went down to his car.

The air was cooler, but his movements were slower than usual, and he turned into Jaffa Street with cars hooting behind him and drove mechanically to Givat Ram, where he parked in front of the almost empty campus.

He walked slowly through the gate and stared at the well-tended lawns, where no one sat anymore, and the old pictures rose before his eyes—the dozens of liberal arts students who used to lie sprawled on the grass between lectures or who were on their way from the library to the cafeteria, the green grass dotted with their bright clothing, the paths where everyone would stroll, as if there was all the time in the world then. Then, before they moved the humanities to Mount Scopus. Only five years ago, thought Michael, you never saw science students here on the lawn; they were all in the back wing of the university, poring over their experiments in the laboratories. And now that all the buildings had been turned into laboratories, the science students walked on the paths with a brisk, purposeful efficiency that made Michael wonder what purpose people could have in a world that no longer seemed to have purpose. He stopped to look at the new name on what had once been the Lauterman Building: it was now the Berman Building. There were piles of broken chairs in the entrance lobby, but he didn't go inside, remembering that on a previous visit he had seen that the rooms had been converted into offices. What had been wrong with this campus that they found it necessary to build the monster on Mount Scopus and turn Lauterman into a ghost building? What kind of generation was growing up inside that stone fortress? he asked himself again, and then he shook himself and hurried toward the National Library building.

The first thing that struck him was the smell. The same smell of books and bindings and wood and people still permeated the catalogue room, and then he noticed the boxes of cards, the red cards for the general reading room and the blue cards for the Judaic and Oriental Studies reading room. There were innovations too—computer terminals stood on the round black counter, and behind them sat middle-aged women who answered questions patiently and politely. His movements grew swifter as he stood in front of the catalogue cupboards and pulled out the drawer labeled "Ti-Tr" and began writing the names and catalogue numbers of poetry books on the request cards. Remembering his student years—when he would wait eagerly for some rare item, only to find a red slip awaiting him in the reading room with the words: "Not found in the stacks"—Michael Ohayon ordered all the copies, taking particular care to request the reserved copy, marked by the letter *R;* he asked for Tuvia Shai's *A Commentary on Tirosh* as well, inserted all the cards into the slot with the word "Requests" engraved above it in black letters, and asked how long it would take for the books to arrive. The student behind the counter said: "At least an hour," and Michael sighed—that hadn't changed. He turned toward the stairs leading up to the library floor and then retraced his steps to the catalogue room and searched feverishly through the works of Agnon. He ordered two copies of *Shira,* one of them the first edition, and went back to the stairs. In the library, the ghostly atmosphere of the campus disappeared, although the old cafeteria on the ground floor was no longer there, and his heart again suffered a pang. And it was in the Judaic Studies reading room—where he paged through various literary journals, reflecting on Israeli endeavors to be part of the international scene and wondering at the titles of the articles, which seemed utterly obscure to him ("Semiotic Connections and Bound Combinations," "Emotive Functions of Free Indirect Speech")—it was there that he was seized by murderous rage against Maya and her husband and the world at large, and for this he didn't reprimand himself. Only anger, Michael Ohayon knew, would help him to mobilize the energy required to investigate this case, and he would have to mobilize all his powers of concentration, to be at his best, in order to succeed in penetrating an academic discipline of which he was almost completely ignorant—because a common reader like himself, he knew, was ignorant indeed of the mysteries of contemporary literary criticism.

For hours Michael sat in the reading room, poring over articles and footnotes. Once, he raised his eyes and saw before him Professor Nechama Leibowitz, whom he regarded as one of the giants of the old world, and when he saw her walking toward the librarian's counter, inclining her head, with its eternal brown beret, and heard her gruff voice attempting to whisper to the librarian: "But it doesn't mean me, that's not my book, it must be my brother's," and saw the kindly smile illuminating her face as she returned to her place, he sighed a sigh of relief and went back to studying the critical and interpretive essays on Tirosh's poetry and the essays by Tirosh on other poets, especially unknown ones. He paid particular attention to Tirosh's column, devoted to criticism of contemporary literature, in the quarterly *Directions*—it was entitled, often only too aptly, "Notes from a Poisoned Pen"—and applied himself to understanding the aesthetic criteria of the man who had heaped praise on poets who were completely unknown at the time and with whose names and work even Michael was now familiar. And the venomous barbs directed at poets of whom Michael had never heard, these, too, he studied.

Not all the poems praised by Tirosh spoke to Michael's heart. Some of them seemed to him a conglomeration of unintelligible words. But he recognized Shaul Tirosh's power to determine the "poetry map" of Israel, and acknowledging this power induced in him a tension he could not understand.

On a sheet of paper he had obtained from the young librarian, he wrote down the names of the poets and writers whom Tirosh had attacked with ruthless cruelty.

In the first numbers of the magazine *Literature*, Michael found two articles by Tirosh, which examined, with his customary seriousness, the poet Shaul Tchernichowsky. The opening paragraphs reviewed the criticism of Tchernichowsky's poetry, and in a few lucid sentences Tirosh demolished the accepted interpretations of his lyrical poems and set forth a new critical direction, which to Michael's own surprise caught his interest. Then he opened the first-edition copy of Agnon's *Shira* and saw that the last chapter was indeed missing. He leafed through the unfinished novel, set the volume aside, and turned to the fifth edition, the additional copy he had ordered out of habit in case the other copies were out. He glanced mechanically through the book, not expecting to find anything. But as he turned the pages, he suddenly saw the heading: "Last Chapter." While he read the chapter, Aharonovitz's words rang in his ears. He also read attentively the note by Emuna Yaron appended to the new edition: "At the same time that my father was writing *Shira* he also wrote the story 'Forevermore.' After *Shira* was published, Raffi Weizer of the Agnon Archives came across a handwritten page connecting 'Forevermore' with the novel. In other words, at some stage 'Forevermore' was taken out of *Shira* and turned into a separate story. In 'Forevermore' the scholar Adiel enters a lepers' hospital and never comes out again; he stays there forevermore."

Michael was horrified. The description of Manfred Herbst entering the lepers' hospital filled him with terror. He thought of the accidental way in which he had discovered the chapter and wondered why he hadn't continued to discuss the question of the last chapter with Klein. He sensed that there was something he needed to understand in what he had read, but he didn't know what it was. Above all, what confused him was the feeling that this last chapter described something terrible, almost revolting. Agnon had not left in the connecting bridge to the last chapter, and so although Michael knew what the end would be, he was unable to explain why. I don't understand how it connects with Tirosh, he thought as he passed through the periodicals reading room, after indicating the pages he wanted to copy.

In the periodicals reading room, he found the literary supplements in whose pages Aharonovitz and Tirosh had waged war for months on end. The war had begun with an academic argument about Yehuda Amichai's lastest book of poetry, and it continued in bitter personal attacks by Aharonovitz on Tirosh's method of criticism, which went so far as to include a remark expressing explicit reservations about his poetry, alongside a general appreciation of its value. ("There is no need for any further evidence in order to point out the flawed nature of his poetry, poetry whose importance, of course, is not in any doubt. The essential flaw that undermines his poetry and sets it on feet of clay—or, to use his own imagery, on 'feet of melting snow'—is the lack of any organic connection between its parts, any affinity between its structures and its contents, which may, in themselves, be compared to a conglomerate—a terrifying but random collection of details from every field and corner of the world. . . .") Michael noted the difference between the style of Aharonovitz's writing and the Talmudic style of his speech, and he smiled to himself.

He couldn't help enjoying Tirosh's retaliatory articles. Again he sensed the mockery, the venom, the cold, ironic stance indicating the writer's remote invulnerability. After reading the comments accusing Aharonovitz's academic work of triviality, Michael marked these passages, too, for copying.

Then he went to the general reading room, where he was greeted by the librarian, a buxom, pleasant-faced brunette, who remembered him from his student days. She handed him the pile of books he had requested; they had all arrived, with the result that he found himself with three copies of *White Poems* by Tirosh and two of *A Commentary on Tirosh* by Tuvia Shai. He began leafing through the latter, dwelling particularly on the introduction, which was completely impersonal and listed the accomplishments of the poet and his unique contribution to Hebrew poetry. "An entire generation of poets," wrote Shai, "sees itself as belonging to the poetic tradition created by Shaul Tirosh." And then he saw the dedication: "To Shaul, if you find it worthy."

Quite by chance Michael remembered the story Maya had told him about a manuscript of "The Waste Land," which T. S. Eliot had apparently sent to Ezra Pound along with the words "if you want it." And he remembered Maya's interpretation too, her shining eyes as she asked: "Don't you think it would make a wonderful dedication?" No, he didn't think so. He also thought that Tuvia Shai's version of this expressed his utter abnegation before Tirosh, an abasement that aroused Michael's anger and made him feel uncomfortable.

He left the reading room, sat down opposite the painter Ardon's huge stained-glass window, lit a cigarette, stretched out his legs, and tipped his ash into the only ashtray in the entrance hall, ignoring the annihilating stare of the well-known professor who walked past him and looked pointedly at the "No Smoking" sign.

The unfamiliar sweet aroma of another cigarette wafted toward him from the end of the row of chairs. He turned his head and saw Shulamith Zellermaier, a cigarette between her lips and what appeared to be a professional journal in her hands. A pile of papers lay on the chair next to her. She sat with her legs apart, the hemline of her blue skirt failing to hide her thick thighs, and he saw the profile of her round face and her untidy gray curls. She sighed loudly, put the journal down with a thud on the adjacent chair, and turned her face toward him. Her eyes met his, her face took on a confused expression, and then, recognizing him, she asked loudly from the other end of the row: "Aren't you the policeman?" Michael nodded, then stood up and moved over to sit on the chair next to the pile of papers. "So what are you doing here?" she asked, and without waiting for a reply, she added: "I've already had the polygraph. A curious business, the lie detector or, in other words, truth machine, which is of course an oxymoron, if not pure nonsense." Michael tried to remember what "oxymoron" meant, and as if in response, she went on: "It's a contradiction in terms. How can it be possible for a machine to measure an idea as abstract as truth? Especially in view of the fact that the word 'poly' means many, and the etymology of 'poly-graph,' from the Greek, is 'to write a lot,' and as the man explained to me, the machine measures and writes down physiological reactions such as pulse rate, perspiration, blood pressure, and similar variables in order to identify the psychological state of the person taking the test. But what has this to do with truth? Can't you see to it that people refer to it correctly as a polygraph and abolish the fallacious notion of a truth machine?" Before Michael had time to reply, she continued: "I understand that you are in charge of the investigation?" Michael nodded and lit another cigarette, whose smell prevailed over the sweet aroma of Dr. Zellermaier's brand.

"There's an article of mine in here," she said, her fingers playing with the wooden beads around her neck. "I found five misprints. What's the point in proofreading?" Angrily baring her large, prominent teeth, she handed him the American journal containing her article, "Death Motifs in Talmudic Literature." He glanced at the article, and when he handed back the magazine he asked her how long she had been teaching in the Hebrew Literature Department.

"A long time; almost as long as you've been alive. And if you want to discuss the tedious question of why I'm not a professor," she said without looking at him, "you can ask Mr. Tirosh, may he rest in peace, who never recommended me once on behalf of the department. In spite of all my publications."

Michael asked her why Professor Tirosh had opposed her professional advancement.

"Och!" she said and pursed her lips over her protruding teeth. "He treated me like a curiosity, and my specialty, popular literature, like a collection of old wives' tales. Every year he would propose cutting the lectures down to one or two hours a week, on the grounds that the subject wasn't scholarly enough. But he never succeeded in obtaining a majority for his proposal, which in my opinion stemmed from nothing but a desire to torment me personally. He liked seeing me angry. He said so on numerous occasions. I can still hear his voice: 'Shulamith, you're magnificent when you're angry,' and then he would go on to quote Alterman: 'Your magnificence, alewife, exceeds that of elephants, your girth overflows, and who dares embrace it?' He never quoted any further. I don't know if you're familiar with 'An Evening in the Old Inn of Poems and a Toast to the Alewife.'" With her projecting eyeteeth, she really was magnificent in her anger, thought Michael.

"In any case," she went on, looking into his eyes, "I didn't kill him. Even though there was no love lost between us, as you've no doubt gathered, although I must say that I always respected him." Michael asked: "And who do you think did kill him?" and Shulamith Zellermaier closed her legs, lit another cigarette, and answered in her gruff voice: "I'm more interested in who killed Iddo, and although I'm a detective fiction fan, I haven't the faintest idea." She tightened her upper lip and fell silent.

Michael caught her eye and said: "Not even after the last departmental seminar?" and was rewarded with an appreciative look, which he could not help enjoying. He liked her, this big woman, who had something both masculine and virginal about her.

"At the last departmental seminar," she said reflectively, "Iddo criticized Tirosh's poetry, which no one had ever done before him. Although in my opinion, too"—she lowered her voice—"his political poetry isn't worth the paper it's printed on. This shows you that Iddo Dudai was a true intellectual and a brave man."

"And the attack on Ferber?" asked Michael, and she pulled her pleated skirt up and straightened her legs as she said: "It wasn't exactly an attack. It was a question of something Tirosh had discovered, which is a separate matter. When he was still a new immigrant, a student at the university, still struggling with Hebrew and as yet unpublished, he went to visit his mother in Vienna, and he told me more than once about how he met a Russian émigré who gave him the pieces of paper on which Ferber had written his poetry, and how he had deciphered it. You have to understand that poems hidden in a labor camp require a lot of work to ready them for publication; I know from my own field how much work you have to invest in those bits of paper. The fact that the poems are mediocre, perhaps even a little primitive, didn't stop Shaul from marveling at the fact that they had been written at all, in Hebrew, by a young man in a labor camp in the Soviet Union—it made a terrific impression on him. He didn't even address the question of their artistic value, which was most unusual for him. You know, I once showed him some poems by a blind student of mine, first poems, and he gave them back to me with expressions of polite disdain. The circumstances were of no interest to him, probably because it wasn't his student. Iddo questioned something that was supposed to be self-evident, that the historical circumstances made the accepted poetic criteria irrelevant, and he was right to question it. But who could have murdered Iddo? Tirosh was already dead, and so was Ferber." She smiled as at a private joke, and then her face clouded. "And Tuvia," she began hesitantly, and then went on confidently: "Tuvia would have tried to convince Iddo of his mistake, he would have been angry, he was angry, but Tuvia isn't capable of harming a fly, and he certainly hasn't got the sophistication to tamper with gases and air tanks and so on. The boy who questioned me yesterday and the day before told me about it; he asked me if I knew anything about scuba diving." She snorted in amusement. "But Tuvia is a tragedy of another kind." Again her face clouded. "Don't make any mistake about Tuvia: he's a complex person with high moral standards; you shouldn't be misled by cheap gossip," she said reprovingly and sank into thought. Then she roused herself and stood up with a profound sigh. "Time to get back to work," and with surprising agility she collected her papers and the two old books buried beneath them, threw the cigarette into the black cylinder that served as an ashtray, and without another word strode off in the direction of the Judaic Studies reading room.

Michael returned to Tirosh's poems. Like a diligent student, he copied out sentences and underlined images with a compulsiveness that mystified him. The fact that his own library included all Tirosh's poetry had no meaning for him now. When he walked into the Judaic Studies reading room, he had entered the temple of the Hebrew Literature Department. He knew that he had to immerse himself in the world of these people, knew it was there that he would find the solution. The more he read, however, the more he felt that he was learning nothing pertinent to the investigation, that there was something almost self-indulgent in remaining there. But, he reminded himself, there's still the business with *Shira*. Tirosh took hardly any interest in prose; why did he write "the last chapter" on that notepad? Was he really going to write an article about it? At least I know now that there is a last chapter, and I also know what it's about. But that's all I know. Yet an inner voice, faint and frightened, told him that there was something else he had understood from reading the chapter, something that was related to Tuvia Shai's class that morning, something connected to Herbst's ability or compulsion to follow Shira into the lepers' hospital. There are some people who follow things through to the end, he thought, but why does he connect it to leprosy?

He read in Tuvia Shai's book and then returned to the poems. Again he had the feeling that only there would he find the end of the thread. He knew that he would not be able to share this feeling with the other members of the investigation team; they wouldn't see the connection. He himself couldn't define it either, but ever since watching the film footage of the departmental seminar, he had sensed its existence, sensed that the poems were alive and breathing, sensed their power, as if they were the blade of a knife. Slowly a feeling of dejection seeped into him. You're deceiving yourself, he scolded himself as he read. There's nothing here, nothing new. And from time to time he raised his eyes and stared up into the spaces of the reading room, and the pictures rose before his eyes again. He didn't fight them.

The sight of Ruth Dudai at her husband's funeral, her face during questioning, her tearful voice as she admitted that she had waited for a phone call from Shaul Tirosh ever since Friday afternoon, the details about the baby-sitter she had asked to come, how she had sat and waited with her in the flat, how at last she had sent the girl home when, by ten o'clock, he still had not called. How she had called his home every hour and heard only the phone ringing in an empty house. "It began not long before Iddo went to America," she said in the tearful voice, "but I was never actually with him." And he remembered the cold voice in which Eli Bahar had asked her: "You mean you never went to bed with him?" and the hurt look she gave him through her tears, the blush on her round cheeks and the embarrassed nod, when Michael himself repeated Eli's question. "It began when I asked him to help me with my Ph.D. thesis, because I wasn't getting any real help from my supervisor," she said, and described the subject of her thesis, which was something in the field of aesthetics. "He had offered to help me ages ago, but I felt uncomfortable about accepting, and I was afraid of him too. He came to visit us once when Iddo wasn't at home, and he sat on the armchair and leaned back," and she launched into a detailed description of how he had crossed his hands behind his head, of the gesture with which he had raked his fingers through his hair, the anguished look he had given her, the embarrassment and anxiety she had felt, how her hands had trembled when she was making him coffee; how he had hinted that his relations with the opposite sex had nowhere left to go, and she knew that he was talking about Ruchama. And then she quoted his statements about his loneliness, and Michael now heard her voice echoing in his ears as she asked if he understood how flattered she had been when he appealed to her as the one who would "rescue him from his loneliness," and he remembered, too, how he had believed her when she said: "It's absurd to ask me if I killed Iddo. We only got married quite recently, and we were good friends until he went to America. It was that trip that spoiled everything: nothing would have happened with Shaul if he hadn't gone away in the first place; and then he came back so weird—up to then he was a very square person; and I'm not exactly a free spirit either. But I don't believe that I would ever have become seriously attached to him, to Shaul; it was more like a spell he cast on me, something hypnotic. The truth is," she continued in the same imploring voice, "that I felt relieved when he didn't call on that Friday, five days ago, only five days ago," and she burst into tears again. Sitting in the reading room now, Michael remembered how they had asked her repeatedly about Iddo's experiences in America— Eli Bahar's persistent question: "What happened to him over there?" and her ceaseless sobbing and her answer: "I don't know, I really don't know. I asked him and he didn't say anything, really." And then the pile of cassettes to which Eli Bahar and he himself had listened, seven tapes of interviews with refuseniks and Jewish dissidents, poets and intellectuals living in the United States. As they listened to heavy voices reading poetry into Iddo Dudai's recording machine, he could visualize the serious, attentive young man whose intelligent face he had seen in the film—the same face he had seen on the beach in Eilat, bloated and dead. Each tape was labeled with the place, date, and time, as well as the name of the speaker. Hours of recordings that shed no light on anything.

"How many cassettes did he have?" Eli Bahar asked Ruth Dudai, holding the two boxes.

"I don't know; I didn't count." Michael remembered the reply and the helpless tone in which it was given. "There's room here for eight, and we only found seven," insisted Eli. Michael had been listening in the next room. "I don't know," repeated Ruth Dudai, and she mumbled it over and over: "I don't know, I don't know."

Again Michael thought of all the hours of fruitless searching, of the neat files he had found in the Dudais' bedroom, of the big desk that took up most of the space in the room—of the overcrowded bedroom that doubled as a study—and he returned with a sigh to Tirosh's articles.

When they were about to close the library, he felt a gnawing hunger and remembered that he hadn't even had a cup of coffee. The new canteen that had been opened in the Levy Building, close to the library, was shut, and Michael found himself returning to the parking lot. The air was cooler, but his car was still hot, and he heard the radio crackling through the closed window even before he inserted the key in the door. Control reported that Tzilla wanted him to get in touch. He returned to the campus and dialed the number in the administration building's public telephone alcove. Tzilla answered, her voice anxious. "I couldn't find you anywhere," she complained. "All of a sudden you disappeared, and I'm stuck here with all the papers and the tapes; everyone's gone."

"I'm on my way," said Michael reassuringly, as he looked into the darkness beyond the glass door. He went back to his car thinking about gas cylinders, air tanks, carbon monoxide poisoning, and the possibility that Tirosh might have murdered Dudai.

But why? he asked himself. A tenured professor, a famous poet, an intellectual and an aesthete, doesn't murder his doctoral student simply because he attacks his poetry at a departmental seminar. However gifted Iddo was, he could hardly have posed a serious threat to Tirosh's position. Had there really been some kind of confrontation between them? And if Tirosh was the one who had poisoned Iddo's air tank . . . who had murdered Tirosh? And how would Tirosh, the intellectual and poet, have come by the necessary know-how? And where had he obtained the carbon monoxide?

By then Michael was already in the Russian Compound lot, and he parked his car and glanced at the building and the illuminated squares of the windows and walked with measured steps up to his office. Tzilla was sitting there under the fluorescent light, poring over the papers from the same plastic bag Eli had previously been dealing with. She looked at him with an exhausted expression. "Why don't you go home and rest," said Michael gently. "It won't do anyone any good if you kill yourself." She raised herself from the chair with an effort and looked at him uncertainly. "Go on!" he scolded, and she smiled and left the room.

At three o'clock in the morning, the black telephone rang, causing him to jump up from his chair. Excited and out of breath, Eli Bahar said: "I couldn't wait to come up and tell you in person. We found it!"

"What? What did you find?" asked Michael nervously.

"Come and see, we're downstairs, me and Alfandari, next to the conference room, we found a safe."

"Where? Whose safe? Talk like a human being, can't you?"

"We've got the papers here. Tirosh had a safe-deposit box at the bank."

"Where did you find the papers?"

"We're here, downstairs, come and see. In some file of poems. It was with the stuff from the office, not the stuff from the house," explained Eli breathlessly.

Michael ran down the two flights of stairs, and even though he knew that there were people working in many of the rooms, the sound of his footsteps had a terribly lonely ring in his ears.

Eli Bahar looked at him apologetically and happily. "Sorry I didn't come upstairs to you. I called you without thinking, as soon as I saw the beginning."

"Where was it?" asked Michael again.

"In these papers here," said Alfandari in his pleasant voice, handing him a stiff cardboard file containing thin printed pages. Michael looked through them, smiled, and said: "Nice work."

"The National Bank," said Alfandari.

"What's the time?" asked Bahar.

"After three," replied Michael thoughtfully. "It'll take two hours to get the court order. Where's Balilty?" he asked them.

"Why? Who wants to know?" asked Balilty, smiling triumphantly as he appeared in the doorway.

Michael handed him the safe-deposit box ownership documents.

After a whistle of admiration, and with a rare serious expression on his face, Balilty asked. "You want me to get a court order?"

Michael shrugged his shoulders.

"I'll be back in an hour. Who's the judge on duty today?"

They didn't know.

"Okay, never mind. Should we wake the bank officer or wait till morning?"

"We'll wait till morning," Michael decided.

14

At six in the morning—after spending the last working hours of the previous day with Balilty, who had kept compulsively humming the tune of the popular song "The Answer to the Riddle"—Michael Ohayon stood in clean clothes in front of his bathroom mirror, carefully scraping a razor over his face. Again and again he thought of Ariyeh Klein's words, which he had replayed over and over on the little recording device lying on the table between Balilty and himself, and as he wiped his cheeks with a towel, he came to a decision.

"Tell me, do you know what the time is?" complained Avigdor, the head of the Criminal Identification Division, answering the phone in a sleepy voice. "Can't it wait for a more civilized hour?"

"Look, it doesn't have to be a big tank; there's something called a laboratory bottle, a little cylinder like a miniature soda siphon, which contains two hundred grams, but. . . ."

"Yes, I know. I used to use laboratory bottles when I taught chemistry at the university. Nobody woke me up at home at six in the morning then. . . . Ohayon, how many years have I been in charge of Forensics in Jerusalem? Why don't you trust me? I've already told you a thousand times that it doesn't make sense—it's an insane idea. The thing's quite simple. You could go into your garage, seal it, turn on the car engine—and you've got CO. In my humble opinion, you won't find anything that way. . . . Ye-es, there's something in what you say"—for the first time, there was a note of hesitation in Avigdor's voice—"but your man would have to know some chemistry. Altogether he'd have to know some chemistry for the whole business: to think of the gas in the first place and to think about the fact that if he filled it up in the garage it would smell. It's true what you say, that it's only when it's produced in a laboratory that the gas is odorless. You don't need to look for a diver, you need to look for a chemist, but the idea of chemical suppliers is absurd. Any laboratory—"

"I've checked the laboratories at the university and in the hospitals," said Michael wearily. "I want to examine all the orders over the past month. How many cylinders like that would you need?"

"Five, six; not many. But believe me—"

"I'm sending someone to you this morning. Give him a list of the places and he can check them out. After all, what have we got to lose?" asked Michael, looking at the empty vase next to the telephone, and thanking Avigdor before he replaced the receiver.

He glared at his watch and waited for the hands to move: when they finally reached half past six, he permitted himself to dial Emanuel Shorer's number.

"Where?" asked Shorer in a wide-awake voice.

"The Café Atara; it's around the corner from the bank," said Michael.

At half past seven, the two of them were sitting silently in the Atara, next to the big window that overlooked the side alley, as the waitress, chatting in Hungarian to an old woman sitting beside the center aisle, placed their breakfast before them: omelets, rolls, little cubes of butter, saucers of jam, and orange juice.

"Did I wake you?" asked Michael, staring at his omelet.

"Nonsense," said Shorer, and asked: "When did you get the court order?"

"This morning at half past four."

"So what's all the fuss about? You could have let people sleep."

"That's just what I did," said Michael defensively.

"Well? What else is new?" said Shorer.

Michael summarized his conversation with Klein and described the discovery of the safe-deposit box. He wondered whether to say anything about Agnon's *Shira*, but a vague dread prevented him from doing so. Besides, he didn't know exactly what to say about it. Finally he summed up with the words: "And so I think there's a new, different lead."

"And what if he didn't order it in Israel?" asked Shorer. "There are chemical suppliers all over the world. Are you thinking that he kept empty gas bottles or brochures from chemical suppliers in his safe-deposit box?"

Two men came into the café and sat at the counter. Michael glanced at their dark suits and narrow ties, and he straightened his shirt collar.

"Let's think a minute," said Shorer paternally, sipping the coffee the waitress had brought. "How can a literature professor get hold of carbon monoxide? How would you do it?"

Michael set his coffee cup down carefully in its saucer. "I told you, we checked with all the laboratories, and none of them reported anything missing. The only remaining avenue was the legal one: ordering it from a supplier, by phone or mail. But either way, somebody has to receive the parcel, somebody has to pay, the supplier has to know who paid, whom he has to send it to."

"Yes," agreed Shorer, crumbling the blackened matchstick Michael had put in the ashtray, "that's exactly the problem. Why on earth would someone planning a murder so carefully take the trouble to leave tracks if he could get hold of a not very rare gas in other ways? And even if we're talking about small containers, somebody has to receive them too, sign for them, and so on."

"I've got an idea about that," said Michael stubbornly. "But not now. First I want to see the safe-deposit box, and after that . . . You'll agree that it won't do any harm to look into it."

Shorer beckoned the waitress and pointed to his empty cup. She called out "Café au lait" in the direction of the open kitchen door and returned a moment later with the coffee. "The problem with Tirosh," said Shorer, "is that he lived completely alone. I understand that you have hopes for the bank box, but I have to say I'm pessimistic."

"Up to now I haven't found any clues," Michael admitted. "No phone number of a chemical supplier, no brochure, no chemistry books. But still I'm sure; I can feel it in my bones. In any case, I intend to keep trying." He looked again at the big clock, which said eight o'clock. Emanuel Shorer asked for the check and glared at Michael, who quickly put his wallet away. Shorer paid the waitress, and she rummaged in the leather pouch hanging from her waist and counted out the change, which was left on the table.

The two men in suits paid for their espresso, and Michael saw them walking down Ben Yehuda Street in the direction of Zion Square. There were only a few people about on the pedestrian mall; the shops were still shut. When they reached Zion Square, they saw Eli Bahar standing in front of the National Bank branch, talking tensely to the two men from the café. The shorter of the two, it turned out, was the bank manager. At the entrance, two women and a man formed a little queue, and the sight of the two men in suits sent a flicker of hope to their eyes, which turned to disappointment when the manager opened the door and, with an expression of someone with important business awaiting him, pointed to his watch.

He locked the door behind him after Michael, Eli Bahar, and Shorer entered. With Shorer beside him, the bank manager studied the court order. He then led the three policemen to the safe deposit vault, lecturing them self-importantly about the security arrangements.

Shorer kept discreetly in the background as Michael and Eli Bahar bent over the box. The manager counted the bank notes it contained and scrupulously wrote down each item before returning it to its envelope. Only after Eli obediently signed the form placed before him were they permitted to empty the contents of the box into opaque plastic bags.

The manager held out his hand to receive one of the copies of the court order; the other Michael retained.

Michael checked the inside of the empty black safe-deposit box, then they filed out slowly through the bank's back door. Eli carried the two plastic bags, and Michael kept his eyes fixed on his back.

In his office in the Russian Compound, Michael looked at the black cardboard file that Tzilla had brought back from the forensics lab. Then he looked at Shorer and Eli and finally at the envelopes.

His movements were slow, as always when he was excited.

In these brown envelopes Shaul Tirosh had kept all the important documents of his life: the papers pertaining to his purchase of the house in Yemin Moshe, his Ph.D. degree, the certificate awarding him the President's Prize for poetry, medical records, yellowing letters and documents in a foreign language.

"Czech," said Shorer, and knitted his brows in the effort to remember the name of a translator. Then, with a cry of triumph, he asked for the list of internal phone numbers, dialed, and urgently demanded to speak to Horowitz in the accounting office. A few minutes later, Horowitz hurried in, his pale face shy, a few gray wisps of hair surviving on his bald head. "*Now* you remember," he said with a good-natured smile. "Two months before I retire, you take advantage of my language." He translated aloud the matriculation certificates of Jan Schasky and Helena Radovensky, Tirosh's parents. Then he looked carefully at another document and said: "This one isn't Czech; it's German—a list of grades from the medical school in Vienna, second year. In the name of Pavel Schasky; here, you can see for yourself," and Shorer bent over the document.

When he raised his head, he saw Michael's smile. "We couldn't have asked for anything better. It's all here but the gas itself—all the chemistry," said Michael, and he sank down on his chair, feeling tired and weak.

In a brown paper bag and in white envelopes they found foreign currency: Swiss francs, dollars, pounds sterling, and even Jordanian dinars. From another envelope Michael drew a string of bluish pearls with a diamond-studded clasp and held it in his hand, together with a pair of matching earrings. For a moment he sat there looking at them, and then Eli Bahar cried triumphantly: "Here it is!"

The will, signed by a notary, was in a separate envelope. Michael read through the concise document a few times, held it out to Shorer, and then dialed the black telephone and asked Tzilla to come into the room.

She stared at the will for a moment or two and gave it back to Michael. Her cheeks were flushed.

"This doesn't leave us any choice," said Eli Bahar, pushing his hand into his hair. "She can bring a lawyer if she likes." And in an aggrieved tone: "I told you from the beginning that I didn't like the look of her."

Michael nodded at Tzilla, and she looked at him questioningly.

"Okay," he said. "We have to locate her and then bring her in. Are you ready?"

Tzilla nodded vigorously, opened the door, and bumped into Manny Ezra.

"Where are you going?" he asked nervously, and looked behind him.

She looked past his shoulder and smiled pleasantly at the thin, bespectacled young man who came forward and stood in the doorway next to Manny Ezra.

He was wearing a police uniform, with a sergeant's stripes on his sleeve. "Illan Muallem, sir," he said to Michael Ohayon as he handed him a letter.

"Why is he in uniform?" Eli asked Manny, and Manny stifled a snicker and said: "He thought that maybe we were strict here in the big city."

Illan Muallem shifted his weight from foot to foot. "He's from the Ofakim police," explained Manny. "He's our assistance from the Southern District."

"Lucky Balilty's not here; he would have eaten him alive," said Eli Bahar, taking hold of the sergeant's arm. "Come on, kid; we'll organize you coffee and something to eat," and he led him out of the room.

Michael turned to Manny, explained briefly how to set about checking all the purchases of carbon monoxide over the past month, and asked him to make a list.

"With him? With that Muallem?" asked Manny incredulously.

"I assume he knows how to talk on the telephone," said Michael coldly, feeling a pang of pity for the humble figure in the ironed uniform.

When they had all left the room, Michael opened the cardboard file that had arrived from the forensics lab and leafed through the flimsy sheets of paper on which the poems were typed. Then he lit a cigarette and studied the forensics report that Tzilla had laid on his desk. The report stated the make of typewriter on which the poems had been typed and the kind of paper: "rice paper," Michael read in Pnina's neat handwriting. There were also notes on the flaws in certain letters, on the kind of ink used by the typist to vowel-point the poems by hand. A special note reported that Tirosh's fingerprints had been found on the poetry typescripts, along with other prints, which had been blurred due to "careless handling by forensic staff."

"A leaf flew up / fell / on my white shirt / then into darkness / slipped / in silence," Michael read, and then went on carefully turning the pages, seeking some detail that would reveal the identity of the poet, and as he read, his embarrassment grew. It was impossible, he thought, simply impossible that the writer had not been aware of their banality.

With a certain enjoyment, he noted the comments in Tirosh's handwriting, which he had learned to recognize during the several days. "Closed metaphor," he had written next to the line "I didn't know if I'd locked the door after you'd gone." Although Michael knew that literary theory distinguished between the writer and the speaker in a text, he decided that the poems had been written by a woman. Turning the flimsy pages, he saw more comments by Tirosh, with elongated question marks and the words "no" and "not like that" in narrow, elongated letters. On one of the pages, within quotation marks, Tirosh had written, in red ink: "Not thus and not of this is it fit to write," and Michael wondered whom the poet-professor was quoting. He remembered Klein's appreciative words about Tirosh's critical abilities and realized their validity. He also assumed from the nature of the comments that Tirosh knew the poet he was criticizing.

Balilty entered the room, puffing and panting as usual. "It's a pity Shorer's left already," he said. "I've got something interesting for him, and for you too."

"There's no such thing as coincidence," muttered Michael as he put the file down on his desk. "If Tirosh kept the record of his safe-deposit box in a file of poems, there has to be a reason for it."

"If you say so," said Balilty, shrugging his shoulders. "I'm not saying it's impossible to find out who wrote those poems, but at the same time, a person can put something somewhere if someone comes suddenly into the room, and he doesn't know that he's going to be murdered soon either. But I'll find out for you, don't worry."

It cost Balilty a serious effort to concentrate on what Michael was saying and to listen until he was finished. He took the cardboard file and looked at his boss, who drummed his fingers on the desk. Balilty licked his lips and tucked his shirttail into his belt with a characteristic gesture.

Michael had the impression that he had gained weight over the past few days: his belly seemed to stick out more than usual and peeped through his shirt. "What did you want to say?" asked Michael.

Balilty smiled smugly. "What's the time now?" he asked rhetorically as he looked at his watch. "Only half past ten; not bad for half past ten, but I have to tell you the truth, I've got connections, and I didn't start working on it today either, I smelled something fishy at once, but after you played me the tape of that professor of yours, I was sure, and luckily I got onto the right man."

"What are you talking about?" asked Michael tensely, his mind on carbon monoxide.

Smiling triumphantly, Balilty replied: "About the gynecologist of that porcelain doll, what's her name, Eisenstein."

"What about her gynecologist?" asked Michael on cue.

And Balilty began with his usual opening: "Ask and I'll tell you," and grew graver as his story progressed. He mentioned the name of the gynecologist, threw out a couple of hints regarding the tortuous methods he had adopted "in order to avoid getting involved in the bureaucratic problems of medical confidentiality," and waxed lyrical in praise of the medical secretary of said gynecologist, whose private clinic happened to be situated "right next door to my sister-in-law, my wife's little sister, Amalia, I introduced you to her once, maybe you've forgotten."

Michael hadn't forgotten. Friday dinner at Balilty's: his fat wife, her shy smile, the intelligence officer in a patriarchal pose at the head of the table, the candles burning in the corner, the spotless children, the statement: "Eat, eat, nobody in the world makes *kubbeh* like my wife," the heat in the room, the heavy food, and Balilty's sister-in-law, Amalia, young and shy, with her dark ponytail, brown eyes, and sweet smile, whom Balilty had tried desperately to fix up with Michael Ohayon. He even remembered her shy voice when she said: "I've heard so much about you from Danny."

"I don't know if I can use it without a court order lifting medical confidentiality," he reflected aloud when Balilty had concluded his exposition, and Balilty flushed and protested: "What's the matter? Have I ever given you incorrect information?"

"That's not the point," replied Michael in a conciliatory tone. "She was already demanding a lawyer at the initial interrogation, before we knew anything. Can you imagine how she would react if I brought the subject up in interrogation now?"

"But even the polygraph people told you that her responses were inconclusive, hers and Tuvia Shai's, and Ariyeh Klein's too. There's no reason not to get a court order and to use it in the meantime," urged Balilty.

"Who said that Klein's test was inconclusive?" Michael leapt from his seat.

"Okay, relax; the guy from the polygraph told us. But not terrifically inconclusive; we'll just have to ask him to go over it again, with all that mix-up over when he arrived, where he was, exactly, all that stuff."

"What mix-up?" asked Michael suspiciously. "There's no mix-up! He came back on Thursday afternoon—what's there to get mixed up about?"

"Okay, I don't know, maybe they didn't prepare him for the questions properly, we'll ask him to do it again. What's there to get so upset about? He isn't the only one who'll have to do it again." And Balilty smiled a small, knowing smile. "I know he's your man and all that."

Michael Ohayon nodded his head and looked questioningly at Balilty, who hadn't stopped sweating since he entered the room.

"Anyway," said Balilty slowly, "anyway, to get back to what's more urgent at the moment, it won't be you who gets in trouble; it'll be the secretary who gets in trouble, or the doctor, not us. And by the time you get to court, you'll have admissible evidence, I promise you. Apart from which, you can arrest her already."

Michael sighed. "You know how much I value your work, Danny," he said, and out of the corner of his eye he saw the intelligence officer's face softening, "but I'm constrained by the law. I'm not saying I won't use the information, but I'm not sure what will happen. The way things stand now, she's got at least one motive for murder, if not more, but I don't like the feeling that we're not covered by the law."

"Okay, should I copy this stuff and give it back to you? Or what?" asked Balilty as he stood up with the cardboard file in his hand.

Michael nodded and looked at the file.

"Ten minutes," said Balilty, leafing rapidly through the pages on his way out of the room.

The white telephone rang even before Balilty shut the door behind him. On the other end of the line he heard Tzilla, breathing heavily. "She refuses to come," she said despairingly. "She says that we'll have to use force to bring her to 'that place,' and I don't know what to do. I tried everything possible. I told her that the police van would come to take her away and God knows what, but she won't come."

"Where are you?" asked Michael.

"At Mount Scopus. She's working in her office. I don't know what to do. Should we bring a van and take her by force? Do you want to arrest her?"

"No," he said firmly. "I don't want to arrest anyone yet, but find out if Klein's there."

"He's here," said Tzilla. "I saw him next to the secretary's room when I arrived. Should I talk to him?"

"No. I'll get in touch with him myself. Wait there."

"University," said the switchboard operator in a bored voice. Michael asked her for the secretary of the Hebrew Literature Department.

"Hello," said Adina Lipkin nervously, and Michael asked to speak to Professor Klein.

"Who wants him?" asked Lipkin.

"The police." Michael heard the sound of his voice with satisfaction.

"He was here until a minute ago, then he went out for a minute. I can go and find him, but only if it's urgent, because there are people here, and the question is if it wouldn't be possible to leave him a message."

"No, it wouldn't," said Michael sternly.

"All right, but you'll have to wait," said Lipkin.

A few moments later he heard the familiar voice saying a brisk "Hello" and then: "Klein here."

Michael spoke for a few minutes and heard the breathing of the man on the other end of the line, who said "Yes" several times and, once, "I understand."

For a long time Michael looked at his watch. The minute hand moved slowly, and the ashtray filled up with stubs. His legs were stretched out in front of him, and he watched the smoke rings he was making and saw Yael Eisenstein's face inside them. He couldn't concentrate on anything but the coming interrogation. Balilty came back after ten minutes, as promised, to return the file, looked at him, and went out again without saying anything.

Any minute, thought Michael, the door would open, and the fragile, flowerlike figure would stand there, and he would have to ignore the fragility and the beauty.

He concentrated on the image of the murder. The dark shadow hitting the long face again and again, the fall backward. The pathologist's calculations of the murderer's height allowed for too many variations. The lengthy, exhausting work of the forensics team at the scene of the crime, all their measurements and calculations, had come up with nothing. A murder committed in a burst of rage, he said to himself, isn't planned in advance. A murder like that, he explained to the contending voices, doesn't take place because of an expected inheritance. He imagined the delicate, Madonna-like figure of Yael Eisenstein holding the statue of the Indian god Shiva, the god of fertility and destruction, and the image rose vividly before his eyes. He could see the white arm, the face twisted in terrible rage, the eyes bulging furiously, and he could feel what she was feeling . . . perhaps, he warned himself.

He thought about the vulnerability of a person capable of such rage. Such a person would have to desire something passionately, with a terrible force, and also to hate this passionate desire. Perhaps, he said to himself, perhaps it was Yael.

But not because of the inheritance, he said to himself. Because of something else, something I don't know.

By the time the door opened, he knew that he would have to gamble.

Tzilla came in, and he made haste to put into a drawer the black cardboard file that Balilty had returned.

"She's here," said Tzilla, wiping her forehead. "The heat outside's terrible. She's waiting with Klein; he wants to know if he can come in with her, and I said I'd find out. What should I tell him?"

"Tell him I want to talk to her alone at first. Afterward, maybe."

Michael Ohayon turned on the tape recorder as soon as he saw the slender figure standing in the doorway. She was wearing a black knit outfit again, although not the same one as before; this one was made of a looser weave. Her arms seemed particularly thin, and a narrow string of pearls encircled her white neck, white on white, and again Michael was seized with guilt for what was about to happen, a guilt he silenced with other voices.

He kept his face expressionless and pushed the ashtray toward her as she lit a cigarette.

"You wished to speak to me," she stated coldly.

"Yes." Michael sighed, "I want you to describe again your movements on the day Shaul Tirosh was murdered."

"I've already told you," she said angrily. "At least three times I've told you."

"I know and I'm sorry; every time there are different reasons. We're not interested in harassment for its own sake."

"No, not for its own sake," said Yael Eisenstein, and she shook the ash off her cigarette with a violent movement.

"I'd like to clarify again what time you arrived at the university on Friday less than a week ago."

She tilted her head and looked at him scornfully. He kept his eyes fixed on her face. He felt no anger, only pity and exhaustion.

"How did you know that you should ask him that question precisely?" Shorer had inquired years before when they were listening together to the tape of an interrogation. "Tell me, how did you already know at that stage?"

And Michael had explained, with an embarrassed effort: "I sense the person, I get inside his mind, I think like him, I hear him speak, and then I often know. Not the facts, perhaps, but the principle."

"That's dangerous," protested Shorer. "It's impossible to interrogate a person when you identify with him; you need violence, hostility too, when you're questioning a murder suspect."

"It's the only way I can do it," Michael had said apologetically. "It's only when I identify with someone that I know which way to go. There's a lot of pain in coming close to people like that, especially for me, in the mere fact of the closeness and, mainly, because it's coming close to them for the sake of tormenting them, but it's the only way I can know."

Now he asked again, with nagging insistence, about her movements on that Friday.

She replied in detail, repeated that she had arrived in time for the department faculty meeting, then gone to the library, and then taken a taxi home, as she called her parents' house.

"And when was the last time you saw him?"

She shook her head, like Yuval as a baby refusing to eat, turning his head from left to right. "To put it plainly," she said quietly, "it's none of your business," and she lit a cigarette with a shaking hand. Again he noticed her slender fingers, free of rings and yellow with nicotine.

"Your fingerprints were found in his office," Michael warned her.

"So? What does that prove? That I was once in his office? Okay, I heard you."

"And you weren't in his office on Friday?"

She stared at him. "I've already told you."

Michael turned the matchbox between his fingers and endeavored to appear paternal.

"I wish," he said slowly, "that you would trust me more."

"I wonder why. Perhaps because you only want what's best for me?" she said sarcastically.

He smiled a wise, tolerant smile. Then he said quietly, giving his voice the requisite note of intimacy: "I'm truly sorry about the misery and humiliation you suffered at the hands of Shaul Tirosh."

"What are you referring to?" she asked and a delicate pink began to suffuse her cheeks.

"Would you like me to remind you?"

She was silent.

"I'm referring to your marriage and divorce and abortion and also—"

"Who told you?" Her face was flushed, and her voice choked. "Did Ariyeh Klein tell you?"

Michael smiled sadly, "Klein didn't have to tell me."

"I don't know what you're talking about," she said, but he caught a glimpse of the tears shining in her eyes before she lowered her head.

"I know that years have passed since then, but humiliations like that must be hard to forget."

Silence.

"Especially," Michael continued, stressing every word, "since I realize how unhappy it must make you to know that you'll never be able to have children as a result of what happened then."

She lifted her head. "How can you possibly know something like that?" she asked in a horrified whisper. Her lips twisted.

"I try to imagine how you must have felt. The misery, and especially the humiliation. You're not the only person Shaul Tirosh humiliated, if that makes you feel any better."

She didn't react. The pale face looked at him stiffly. He read fear and terrible rage in it. She didn't move, only stared fixedly at him.

"I can imagine the conversation between you. He humiliates you, as usual, with his refinement, his reserve; perhaps you even tell him about your gynecological problems; and he, as always, responds with cynicism. What did he say to you? That in any case you're not cut out for motherhood? That in any case you're not a woman? What, exactly, did he say to you that made you hit him so hard, that made you want him to die?"

She stood up and ran to the door, and Michael only managed to stop her when her hand was already on the door handle. He pried her fingers off the handle, one by one, and taking her slender arm in a firm grip, he led her back to her chair and lowered her into it.

I wasn't mistaken, thought Michael, and permitted himself a moment of triumph before he went on talking.

She sat limply, as if she no longer had any will, frightened and helpless. He knew that from now on it would be easy.

"What *did* he say to you? You know there's no point in trying to run from here. What did he say to you, when you were in his office, that made you strike him with the statue? And hit him again and again?" He asked himself if this was the right moment to say something about manslaughter, if she cooperated, as opposed to murder with malice aforethought, and decided to refrain.

"It was terrible to see him fall, to leave him there," he stated as if he had been there himself.

She looked at him and averted her eyes, shook her head, and

finally she took an embroidered handkerchief out of the little leather bag hanging from the back of the chair and soundlessly blew her nose. It was years since Michael had seen a woman blow her nose on an embroidered handkerchief, like a well-brought-up little girl.

He was on the point of repeating his question, when she said in a voice even softer than usual that she wasn't the one who had hit him.

"But you were in his room," stated Michael.

"Yes, but only on Thursday."

"And you quarreled with him."

She nodded.

"What was the quarrel about?"

"Something personal."

"More personal than the fact that you can't have children?"

Yes. In her eyes. That was how she saw things. And in any case, she had never told Shaul about it.

What, Michael asked himself, could she consider more personal that her gynecological problems? And he felt that he should know, that he had to guess, urgently, as if his life depended on it. He thought about her life, her work at the university, her reclusiveness, her avoidance of traveling by bus, her diet of yogurt and fruit, her monotonous wardrobe that never changed according to the dictates of fashion, about the intelligence information Balilty had unearthed about the psychoanalytic treatment she had undergone—four times a week, Balilty had said, taxis there and back—about her loneliness, especially about her loneliness. You're losing the rhythm; sense her. Don't ask yourself what's personal by your standards, ask what's personal for her. And with a rapid movement, he whipped the black cardboard file out of the desk drawer.

"I understand that what really hurt you was his attitude to this," he said, and handed her the poems.

She gripped the file tightly and said nothing.

I read them. They're awful. They're so bad they're embarrassing, thought Michael. Aloud he asked: "Was it because of his criticism of your poems that you became enraged and hit him? Was this the humiliation that made you lose your head?" She wept soundlessly. It was supposed to melt his heart, thought Michael. "You must answer me," he said quietly.

She didn't hit him, she said. She was in his office on Thursday, in the morning. Ruchama Shai had been waiting outside; he could ask her, Ruchama, how she had looked when she came out of the office. She had left the poems there with him because she couldn't bear to look at him for another minute. She felt frozen, she said. She had never been capable of reacting violently when someone hurt her, she simply came apart, and he had never, never insulted her as he did then, when he returned her poems. He sat behind his desk and he tried to be tactful, she said, which was insulting in itself. She had never shown the poems to anyone, she sobbed, not even to Klein. Actually, she had only started writing this past year, and she had no way of knowing their worth. At first he had tried to be gentle, but being Shaul, he couldn't help getting in a few digs, and in the end he said impatiently: "You haven't got a future. You can't write; you need a womb to write." Perhaps she would have hit him if she'd had the strength, but her first impulse was to throw herself out the window of the sixth-floor office.

Michael didn't take his eyes off her. He listened intently to every word and saw the scene before his eyes. A couple of times he asked himself if he believed the story he was hearing. He didn't know the answer. She looked exhausted.

He had two questions, he said.

And again, like lightning, anxiety lit her face.

Had Tirosh ever tried to start with her again?

Yes, she admitted. He tried and she rejected him. He had been angry, but not for long.

The second question: Could this serve to explain the sentence: "If only this might make some slight amends for what it was not in my power to give."

"Could what serve? Explain what? What are you talking about?" Her wide eyebrows arched, and she stared at him incomprehendingly.

It was no longer "What are you referring to?" thought Michael. Now she was genuine, as if everything was already known. Or perhaps she wasn't genuine, perhaps he was being led astray by his so-called "intuitions"?

And after a slight hesitation: "Perhaps you know something about the will left by Shaul Tirosh?"

She shrugged her shoulders. "Will? What will?" she asked without fear, only surprise.

"Did he ever talk to you about it?"

She wasn't interested in such things, she replied.

"Nevertheless, taxis, analysis, medical treatments, food . . . What do you live on?" he asked, thinking about the monthly sum regularly deposited in her bank account. This was one of Balilty's achievements, displayed with a flourish at a team meeting.

She worked, she replied, and she received support from her parents every month.

"But," he said carefully, "as I understand it, your father went bankrupt in '76, and since his last heart attack he hasn't been working."

She was silent, and he waited. Moments passed before he addressed her: "Come on, you've said far worse things today. If you don't care about money, you shouldn't have any difficulty in speaking about it." He was unable to prevent the impatience from showing in his voice.

She swallowed her saliva and explained with some embarrassment that the apartment was registered in her name and that her father had managed to transfer money to America "before the crisis, a large sum, I don't know exactly how much, but I live on the interest, and although my father says there's nothing to worry about, I can't help feeling uneasy about transgressing the law."

Michael laid the photocopy of the will in front of her. At first she stared at it uncomprehendingly, and then she bent her head and peered at it. Then she picked it up with a trembling hand and raised it to her eyes. Laying it on the desk again, she groped inside her gray leather bag, removed a pair of eyeglasses in square black frames from their case, put them on, and resumed reading. Finally she put the document down on the desk. The glasses gave her face a more mature, intelligent look, and she looked straight at him, her blue eyes clear and focused. It was impossible not to see the anger in her face. Again her lips tightened with the movement that had already become familiar to him.

"You knew nothing about this?" asked Michael, and he replaced the document in the brown envelope without taking his eyes off hers.

She shook her head. "But I'm not surprised, not at all," and a spurt of tears blurred the lenses of her glasses.

"Why are you crying?"

She shook her head. "You wouldn't understand. Nobody would."

Michael sighed. "So explain it to me. Maybe I'll understand if you explain."

"He couldn't leave me even my hatred. He had to make an apparently noble gesture—how typical. As usual, he wasn't thinking of me, only of himself—despite what he writes here about his unfailing admiration for me. Who'll believe me?"

There was a long silence.

"I'm afraid," said Michael, leaning forward, "that we'll have to do a polygraph test again; perhaps this time it will be different: we'll know exactly what to ask. You have nothing to fear—if you've told the truth, of course."

She wasn't afraid, she said, she was ready for it, if only they believed her.

"We'll let you know the exact time. This time you'll be asked about painful subjects: your marriage, divorce, pregnancy, the poems, the will. Nobody wants to humiliate you, but we're investigating a murder here, two murders."

She nodded and asked hopefully: "Is that all? Have we finished here?"

"For today we've finished," said Michael. He stood up, his hands and legs trembling, as if he had lifted a heavy load.

She reached for the black cardboard file.

"I'm afraid that will have to remain here, for the time being," he said apologetically.

"But you won't show them to anybody," she said anxiously. He walked to the door and she followed him hesitantly, glancing back at the poems lying on the desk.

Klein was waiting at the door, looking like a man who has entrusted his daughter to the mercies of a witch doctor. He looked at her face, at the traces of tears evident on the white cheeks, and Michael said: "I'd like to talk to you, if you can spare a moment."

Klein looked at Yael, as if seeking her permission.

"We can take her home, if that's the problem," said Michael.

"She can go home by herself," said Yael, taking off the glasses and pushing them into the gray bag hanging over her arm. Her eyes were quiet lakes again, her look was vague.

Klein looked at her in concern and said: "I'll accompany you outside."

Michael Ohayon went back into his room and turned on the tape recorder. He was tired to death and his body ached, but with nothing of the pleasantness that comes after physical labor. He looked despairingly around the bare room and asked himself when he would be able to get into bed and not hear another sound. It was only two in the afternoon.

15

"As I recall," said Klein, beginning to clear the pile of books and papers from his desk, "I wrote the number in the address book we had in the States: not the address, just the telephone number. But God knows where I put it, " he muttered, and opened the desk drawer.

He examined every piece of paper he took out of the deep drawer, occasionally smiling or raising his eyebrows in surprise. "As a rule," he said to Michael, "I remember where everything is, but I haven't had time to sort out my papers since we returned, what with all the commotion and the fact that my wife and the girls only arrived on Saturday night, but I remember seeing it, the address book, and I know for certain that I put it somewhere here in this room. I just don't remember where."

It was three in the afternoon, and Michael sat and smoked while Klein searched slowly for the telephone number of the lawyer whom Iddo Dudai had met in America. The house was still. Michael pricked up his ears, but he couldn't hear the female voices or the sounds of music.

"I'm surprised that she didn't show the poems to me; I thought I we were close," said Klein, raising his head from the drawer. "Maybe because she knew that I would spare her, that I would be tactful in my criticism," he concluded, and resumed rummaging.

Michael contemplated the big man, whose papers were piling up on the desktop, and thought of Klein's first reaction to the poems an hour earlier in the Russian Compound, when he returned after accompanying Yael outside. He remembered the big face, flushed and sweating from the heat, over the black cardboard folder, the big hand delicately turning the pages, the grimace with which he had slammed down the poems on the scratched wooden desk, and then the impatient expression in his eyes as he waited for Michael to explain. Now, smoking in the still house while he watched the slow search for the address book, Michael remembered their conversation.

"Do you know these poems?"

Klein leafed through the flimsy pages again, shook his head, and said: "No. Am I supposed to know this stuff?"

"I thought she'd shown them to you."

"Who?"

"Yael Eisenstein; she wrote them."

Klein looked at him with conspicuous disbelief and studied the poems once more. Finally, when he raised his head again, Michael saw in his eyes the embarrassment and insult of not having known. "Are you sure?" he asked.

"You can ask her yourself."

Klein wiped his face with his hands, took a sip of water from the yellow plastic cup Michael had brought him when he entered the office, and stared at him sadly.

"I thought she was talented," remarked Michael.

"Very, very talented," said Klein enthusiastically. "Serious, thorough, perceptive, discriminating, and very clever."

"In that case, how do you account for this?" said Michael doubtfully.

Klein banged the plastic cup on the table, sending drops of water flying, and replied: "What's one thing got to do with the other? She's talented at research, not at creative writing. They're two separate things."

"Yes, I realize that. Obviously, that's not what I meant."

"What did you mean?" asked Klein wearily.

"I meant her taste: how come she didn't see for herself how bad these poems are?"

Klein nodded and smiled. "It's got nothing to do with talent," he pronounced. "A person can't judge the value of his own creations, except, sometimes, with the perspective of hindsight. There are exceptions, of course, but generally speaking, especially when it's a question of literature, and especially when it's the first time, there's no way of knowing. The writer is too absorbed by what he is writing, too involved with his feelings, and so on. You need a certain distance in order to be able to judge your own creation. But," he said, wiping his brow, "don't jump to any conclusions. She's a very gifted scholar, and it doesn't diminish her a bit"—he took another sip of water—"that she aspires, like the rest of us, to create." His voice died away gradually and then rose again as he said passionately: "I believe in the value of scholarship in the field of art in general and of literature in particular, but inside every good scholar there's a frustrated artist; in other words, every good literary critic dreams of writing 'real' literature himself."

Michael suppressed the urge to ask if he, Klein, too had tried his hand at writing something "real."

"Sometimes they try, usually when they're younger," Klein continued, "and there's often an inverse proportion: the more sophisticated the scholar, the more involved he is in his research, the harder it is for him to create. And that's what astonished me so much about Shaul. His artistic judgment, his powers of discrimination, his profound literary understanding—and at the same time he produced great poetry. What more could a man wish for himself?" He gazed sadly at the window behind Michael's back.

"What do you mean, astonished you?"

Klein played with the yellow cup. Once or twice he opened his mouth and took a breath, as if about to speak. At last he slowly said:

"I knew Shaul Tirosh for over thirty years. For a whole year we lived together in one apartment, when we were students. So I don't doubt that there were years when he was close to me, very close." He bowed his head and examined his hands. "And I want you to know that I'm saying this precisely because I was fond of him. Shaul had a lot of charm, the kind of charm possessed by people who use the whole world as one big mirror to confirm the fact of their own existence, which is why they go to so much trouble to charm it. But at the same time he possessed a surprising degree of self-awareness. He was capable of not relating to himself seriously. In spite of the facade of theatrical gestures, in spite of the total nihilism, he had the rare ability to see himself in an ironic light. I well remember moments when we were alone together, when we were still young. 'We know you, Shaul, my friend,' he would say to himself in my presence. 'You'll sing her a serenade under her window, in order to watch yourself serenading a woman under her window.' And don't forget, either, how interesting and erudite he was, how discriminating his taste was. But this isn't what I wanted to talk about. What were we talking about?" He paused for reflection. "Yes, we were talking about the rare combination in one man of eminent scholar, critic of contemporary poetry with a rare understanding of literature, and great poet into the bargain. In my opinion, it is a contradiction in terms—and then, on top of it, think of his nihilism."

"Nihilism." Michael repeated the word reflectively.

"His women, for example," said Klein, and fell silent.

Michael waited.

"People say that Shaul loved women. But that isn't so. I've never understood—ahem—the psychological roots of the phenomenon, but of one thing I'm certain: Shaul didn't love women. But what can I say, after everything that's been written about Don Juan—except that in his case we're not even talking about hatred of women as such. I don't know, I'd say there was a constant search for new stimuli, there was something hungry there, a hunger for confirmation, confirmation of his worth. There were moments when he would be filled with anxiety that he didn't exist. The big riddle here is the poetry. I don't understand how out of that abyss, that void of negation, great poetry could be created."

Michael then asked him if he had ever seen Tirosh's will.

"No," said Klein, "but Yael told me about it just now, on the way to the taxi."

"And what do you think about it?"

"Well, I was surprised, of course, but not for long. On second thought, there's nothing surprising about it. I find it hard to believe that Shaul felt any real guilt toward Yael, but he was capable of generous gestures from time to time, outbursts of generosity that sometimes were embarrassing. When my first daughter was born, he bought us the furniture for the nursery. Or Nathaniel Yaron's poetry collection, which he published at his own expense, I've never understood why."

And then he seemed to understood what Michael was driving at, and he said carefully: "I wouldn't jump to any conclusions, if you asked me."

"I am asking you."

Klein shook his head emphatically from left to right. "She couldn't conceive of anything even approaching murder. If you spent a few hours with her in ordinary circumstances, you'd realize that I'm right."

"Not even if he demolished her poetry? If he humiliated her?"

"No. She's capable of harming only herself, her own body, and she's actually tried it a few times."

"Professor Klein," said Michael slowly, "do you always have such close relations with your female students?"

Klein was not taken aback; his face did not change color; he smiled good-naturedly and looked at the policeman with a fatherly, almost pitying look. "Ahem, I wouldn't jump to conclusions here either. I think that on the rare occasions when our lives touch the lives of others, we should accept the contact and welcome it. What else does a man have in the world but relationships with others? I mean real relationships, affection and understanding and friendship, consolations of that kind." Again he wiped his brow. "I don't intend to try to convince you of how 'pure' my relations with Yael are. She is a significant person in my life from many points of view, and I have no intention of discussing them now. I presume you aren't implying that I committed murder for her sake. Obviously you could say that I'm not objective about her, but you're not objective either, if you don't mind my saying so."

"Is there anyone, in your opinion, who would be capable of committing murder for her sake?"

Klein made a face and said something about her loneliness, her reclusiveness. "And altogether," he said impatiently, "I haven't the faintest idea who could have murdered Shaul. And I certainly haven't any idea who could have murdered Iddo. I couldn't even begin to imagine."

Really? Michael silently wondered. Couldn't you really begin to imagine? Or perhaps you're afraid of even imagining it? Then he began to discuss details of the Iddo Dudai case. Klein knew about Shaul Tirosh's early medical studies, but he attached no importance to them.

"And in the matter of your polygraph test," said Michael casually, although Balilty's remark, which he had noted at the back of his mind and verified with the polygraph technician, had been nagging at him all day long, "you know that it hasn't been proved conclusively that you're telling the truth?"

Klein nodded. "He told me, the man who did the test, that the results were inconclusive." Michael looked into his eyes but could find no anxiety or tension there. "I can't explain it," said Klein in embarrassment, "but naturally I won't object to being tested again, it goes without saying." Michael sensed himself inclining his head and examining the big face, the body language, and coming to the conclusion that there was nothing out of the ordinary. It could wait until the next day, after the polygraph was repeated, he said to himself.

When Michael asked him about the telephone number of the lawyer whom Iddo Dudai had met in the United States, Klein gave him a startled look. "Oh, I forgot," he said in confusion. "It completely slipped my mind. Is it really so urgent?" He stressed the word "so."

"You yourself said that he came back in a state of shock," Michael reminded him as he stood up, "and when he returned to Israel his behavior had changed. It's clear that something happened there that's in some way connected to his death. Not to mention the fact that there's no tape of his meeting with that lawyer."

"Tape?" asked Klein in confusion, and recollected: "Ah, you mean that tape."

"You yourself told me that he recorded all his meetings. We found seven cassettes, all of them with labels saying when they were taped, who took part in the interview, and where it took place. We listened to them all. There's nothing there about a lawyer in North Carolina or a friend of Ferber's." Klein opened his mouth as if to say something, but Michael continued: "It's not only that. He had two of those boxes for storing cassettes, with room for four cassettes in each—they're supposed to protect them—and one of them has only three cassettes. The fourth one's missing."

Klein said nothing, his face thoughtful.

"Among other things, I want to ask you if you know anything about the meeting between Dudai and Tirosh."

"What do you mean?" said Klein in surprise, reviving. "Of course they met. Are you referring to some specific meeting?"

"I'm referring to Dudai's visit to Tirosh's house. He told you he wanted to speak to Tirosh first, didn't he? Do you know if he spoke to him?"

Klein shook his head. "I wasn't here; you'll have to ask the others."

I did ask the others. I thought they might have told you things they didn't tell me, Michael had thought again when they were in the car, on their way to Klein's house in Rehavia. Now he heard Klein's voice thundering in the study.

"I don't understand," he cried in despair. "Where could I have put it? It was a little notebook with a red cover, and I didn't send it by air freight with the other things. I remember that Ofra, my wife, made a special point of it. It was in one of my suitcases. I unpacked it right here in this room. It contained all the papers that I didn't want to send on ahead. And I remember that I put it somewhere in this room." Michael followed his eyes, and the books scattered everywhere, the crammed shelves, the old typewriter with a sheet of paper in it, standing on the floor near the desk, filled him with apprehension.

Klein did not remember the lawyer's name. "But," he said, with sudden animation, "Ruth Dudai will know!"

Michael explained that she didn't know anything about the meeting, and he remembered her tears when he had aggressively asked her: "How did you interpret the change in his behavior? The change in his attitude toward Tirosh?" Weeping, she said that she had thought the changes were due to her relationship with Tirosh and that she had preferred not to say anything and not to ask any questions.

"And among his papers? Iddo's papers?"

"We didn't find a thing, not a clue," replied Michael, and he knelt down next to a pile of books. There was no other possibility, he insisted; they had to find the address book.

"Maybe it's somewhere on the shelves, between the books," said Klein hopefully, and Michael looked at the bookshelves. "You can help me," said Klein, and suggested that they begin with the shelves next to the desk. For the next hour they ran their hands over the dusty books on the shelves, but there was no address book to be found.

Klein proposed a break, "to have something to drink," and they went into the big, white-painted kitchen. Klein stuck his hand through the window to the branches of a large lemon tree and plucked a leaf, rubbed it between his fingers, and noisily smelled them. Then he picked a few lemons and opened a drawer. "You need a special knife for these lemons," he said, beginning to describe the lemonade he was about to make. And then he looked inside the drawer and burst into loud, uninhibited laughter, waving a red notebook the size of a small book in his hand. "You see? Would you believe it?" he asked in amazement and began paging through the address book. "All my connections in America," he said.

Michael wrote down the telephone number on a piece of paper that Klein gave him and put it carefully into his shirt pocket.

"Now we're entitled to a glass of fresh lemonade," and Klein placed a tall glass, in which slices of lemon and mint leaves were floating, on the large wooden table in front of Michael.

Without knowing why, Michael suddenly asked: "How could you tell right away that the poems were no good?"

"And you yourself, couldn't you tell right away?" asked Klein, cutting thick slices from a loaf of dark bread.

"Yes, but what must they have in order to be good?" Michael persisted, and he knew that he wanted to hear the teacher's voice of long ago. He wanted to relax his vigilant, policeman's attention to the subtle nuances of the conversation. He wanted to rest.

"Under other circumstances, I could explain the criteria to you," said Klein, stirring three eggs with a practiced hand in a small white bowl, "but that's not what interests you at the moment."

"No," admitted Michael, "that's not what I wanted to talk to you about today. But now that we're on the subject . . . I've always wanted to understand what a poem must have in order to be good."

"You want a lecture on poetry? Now?" Klein glanced at him and placed a dab of margarine in a pan. Michael couldn't see the expression on his face. Klein poured the eggs into the pan, and strewed them with crumbs of cheese, and bent over the stove to lower the flame. "Will you spread the butter?" he asked, and without waiting for a reply, he put the sliced bread, a knife, and a dish of butter on the table and began to cut up vegetables.

"How would you feel if I asked you whether man makes history or history makes man? Which, by the way, is a question I often think about. In other words, I'm prepared to say a few things on condition that you remember they're likely to be superficial. This is a subject for a long seminar, one that has been addressed by the greatest aestheticians," he warned as he peeled an onion, wiping his eyes.

Michael nodded, but Klein had already begun to talk: "First of all, you have to understand that whatever I say is susceptible, in the last analysis, to a certain subjective bias, which is not to say that every reader is free to interpret a poem as he sees fit but refers to the relativity of universal standards of judgment." His voice became didactic, even authoritative. Cutting cucumbers into thin slices, he said: "The criteria are context-dependent; they rely on readers sharing the same cultural and political environment, more or less, as the poem."

Michael nodded again, but Klein was standing with his back to him and did not notice his assent.

"The poems Yael wrote are bad because they lack certain things." He moved to the stove, turned the omelet over, set a large empty plate before his guest, slid half the omelet onto it, and sat down opposite him at the big wooden table, which had seen better days. Between them stood the salad bowl, with onion rings and Greek olives decorating the tomato cubes and slices of cucumber.

Klein chewed a piece of bread and continued. "First of all," he said, "understanding a good poem requires a process similar to that of detection, which is referred to by various academics as hermeneutic: in other words, a good poem enables the reader to experience the discovery and deciphering of hidden meanings, which become clearer the more deeply he penetrates into the text. This process is made possible by the presence of certain basic elements in the poem—which exist not only in literature, by the way, but in all works of art. The first of these is symbolization—in other words, the use of an idea or an image that intersects with, or is contiguous with, or incorporates, another idea or image. Do you want coffee?" asked Klein, dipping his bread into the salad dressing. Then he stood up and filled the electric kettle at the end of the marble counter. "You understand," he said when he resumed his seat, "when Alterman writes: 'Your earrings dead inside a box,' the reader hears other things in this expression: he hears the joie de vivre that is no longer, the femininity that was once alive and is now stiff and frozen. It's about loneliness, about waiting for years in a house that is perceived as a prison. . . . It's about dozens of things!"

He looked at his interlocutor as if seeing him for the first time. "And there's another component," he continued, "which is called condensation. A great work of art can contain several ideas, several universal experiences, in one idea. Leah Goldberg defined a poem as a 'dense utterance,'" he said, grinding black pepper onto the omelet on his plate. "And the two things, the symbolization and the condensation, are interconnected." Now he cut himself a block of salty cheese and bit into it. "A sentence like 'Death came to the rocking-horse Michael' in Natan Zach's poem contains within it the personification of death, associations of childhood by way of the rocking horse, and condensation too, because of the allusion to the well-known children's song about the little boy called Michael. The symbolization and the condensation permit abstraction and openness in other areas."

Klein took a deep breath. "Now listen. The third basic element existing in every good work of art is called displacement, the transference of emotion from one area to another. This enables the artist to achieve generalization. A marvelous example of a poem based on displacement is Ibn Gabirol's 'See the Sun.' Do you know it?" Michael made haste to swallow a piece of tomato drenched in green olive oil and then nodded. A gratified expression appeared on the face of the teacher of medieval Hebrew poetry as his erstwhile student quoted the poem in full:

"See the sun at evening time: red
as though it clothed itself in scarlet.
It disrobes the north and south,
it covers the west with purple.
And the earth, now left naked,
seeks refuge in the shadow of the night, and sleeps.
Then the skies darken, as if covered with sackcloth,
mourning the death of Jekuthiel."

"I even remember what a 'girdle' rhyme is," said Michael in an amused voice.

"You understand," said Klein, "that to describe the sunset as a process in which the earth is orphaned by the sun, and then, at the end, in a few in words, to make the connection between the bereavement of the world and the grief of the speaker—that's displacement! And it's this that gives the experience of the speaker in the poem colossal dimensions."

He finished his omelet greedily and piled salad on his plate. "So you see," he said finally, leaning forward after putting his fork down next to his plate, "they're all interwoven. In every good metaphor you'll find these three factors somewhere, but there has to be a delicate balance among them. A metaphor, or a symbol, should never be too far removed from the object it represents, like"—he coughed deeply—"ahem . . . 'The butter's cheeks are red, winter is lusty.' There may be symbolization here, but I can't follow it because the metaphor's too open, it allows for an almost unlimited associative field." He stood up and went to make the coffee.

The little coffee grinder made a terrible noise, and he went on talking only after examining the ground beans. "Although a metaphor, or symbol, should also be original and innovative, making the reader see familiar things in a new, different light. After all"—he brandished a copper *finjan*—"the subjects that concern the artist are always the same; they never change. Have you ever asked yourself what works of art revolve around? Around love, sex, death, and the meaning of life; the struggle of man against his fate, against society; man's relations with nature and with God. What else?" Now he held a small coffee cup in his hand and poured water from it into the *finjan*, carefully spooned in coffee and sugar, stirred, placed the *finjan* on the gas. He stood with his back to Michael again, stirring busily. "The greatness of art lies in the possibility of dealing yet again, but from a different point of view, with the subjects that are common to all mankind. If an artist produces symbols that are too far removed from the subject, with metaphors that are too 'open,' the processes I have described won't be able to take place. And the same holds if they're the opposite, if they're banal. I'm talking about the banality of metaphors, but I'm also referring to analogies, rhymes, syntax, grammatical structure, the sequence of the lines, everything that goes into building a poem. Poetic 'talent' is the ability to achieve the delicate balance, which is so rare, between the original and the familiar, the hidden and the revealed, the symbol and the object to be symbolized."

With a rapid movement, Klein removed the *finjan*, from the flame and set it on the counter, and, his hand steady, poured the coffee into tiny cups of white china, rimmed with a gold band. "The metaphors

Yael used were incredibly banal, 'closed,' as Shaul commented, which means that they leave no room for the imagination, for associations. Not only because they're trite but because they lack the necessary dialogue between the concrete and the abstract. Amichai's poems, for example, are based on precisely this kind of play. Take a line like: 'In the place where we're right, flowers will never bloom in spring,' or, if you want a particularly subtle example of the counterpoint between the concrete and the abstract, look at Dan Pagis's poetry, in a line like: 'And He in his mercy left nothing in me to die.' The interplay between the concrete and the abstract isn't made explicit here, but it's inherent in the text, making the impact more powerful, in one of the most shocking poetic statements I've ever read."

Klein gulped down the steaming coffee and licked his lips. "There's no evidence of any of the things I've mentioned in her poems, and I'm sorry to say that apparently there never will be."

At five o'clock Michael Ohayon left Klein's house, and Klein accompanied him to his car, humming a familiar tune. It was only at the Terra Sancta junction, at the intersection of Agron, Aza, and King George streets, waiting for the traffic lights to change, that Michael identified what Klein had been humming as some of Sarastro's aria from *The Magic Flute*, an opera of which Maya was particularly fond.

It was still hot, and the streets were full of people who were looking neither for corpses nor for murderers.

"Your son left a message for you. He was here and said that if you came back in time, you could meet him at the Society for the Protection of Nature. It's next to the Mortgage and Loan Bank, you know." Avraham from the control center pitched his voice low. Michael did know, but what was "in time" supposed to mean? Until when would Yuval be there? "Until six, he said. He left here only a minute ago," explained Avraham, who concluded by assuring Michael that there were "no problems." Michael returned to his car and drove off to the Nature Protection Society.

He parked next to the bank and entered the large courtyard of another of the palaces built by Prince Sergei. A passerby unfamiliar with Jerusalem could never imagine what lay hidden behind these big buildings, thought Michael. A huge gate was set into the wall facing the street, and when you passed through it you stepped into another world, bemused in the inner courtyard, as if the ghosts were beckoning you to enter the splendid edifice.

At first Michael sat on a tree stump at the entrance to the palace and waited for Yuval to conclude his business in the bungalow in the courtyard, where the Society for the Protection of Nature had its office. Then he began wandering around the yard, kicking the dry soil. One wing of the building housed the Agriculture Ministry, but Michael was drawn into the other, the derelict wing of the palace, where he found himself contemplating the boarded-up windows covered by cobwebs. It was dark inside the rooms, but nevertheless he was able to make out the fresco, patterned like a Russian carpet, that covered the ceiling of the big salon. There was an old bathroom, with the remains of Armenian tiles and a bathtub standing on four clawed legs, as if it were borne on the back of an iron tiger. The soles of his sandals creaked on the big floor tiles. He went into another room and gazed in wonder at the papers scattered over the floor. He picked up a yellowing sheet and studied the Cyrillic letters penned there. He had often regretted the fact that he had not continued his study of the Russian language, but the Latin he needed then for medieval history had left him no time for other languages. He dropped the paper, and it fell onto the carpet of derelict pages.

He emerged from the palace into daylight. It was almost six, and the light was softer and paler now. Yuval was standing at the door of the Society for the Protection of Nature and looking around him. When Michael approached, the worried expression left the boy's face. "I didn't know if I'd manage to catch you. I need money for the hike I told you about, to the Judean Hills."

"Is that all?" asked Michael, placing his hand on a shoulder that was growing broader by the day.

They went into the office together. A young man in shorts was holding forth enthusiastically about a rare type of bird he had recently spotted. Michael thought of his friend Uzi Rimon from the diving club as he made out the check and handed it to a girl in jeans. She smiled at him sweetly and gave the receipt to Yuval. The boy folded it and put it into his back pocket, and an expression of relief spread over his tense face.

Michael felt bad. It had been days since he had seen his son.

"Let's park the car in the Compound," he said when they stepped out of the office, "and go and sit down somewhere."

Opposite the Mortgage and Loan Bank, next to the rear gate of the Russian Compound, stood the policeman on guard, who opened the gate obediently.

When they stepped out of Michael's dusty Ford Escort, Yuval said: "Get a load of the kind of car that's being parked here nowadays!" He laid his hand gingerly on the fender of the elegant white vehicle. "What is it? Look, even the seats have class."

Michael bent over the car. "Alfa Romeo GTV; there are only two of them in the country. It doesn't belong to any of us."

"So who does it belong to?" asked Yuval eagerly.

"To somebody who isn't going to be using it anymore." Michael sighed and turned the door handle. The car wasn't locked. "I don't believe it," he muttered. "They've left the car open and the key inside. Yuval looked at him imploringly and opened the door on the driver's side. Michael got in next to him and lit a cigarette. Yuval half turned the single key in the ignition and examined the dashboard, pressed the glove compartment button, peeped inside, and said in a disappointed voice: "It's empty."

Michael smiled. The boy had always been a car nut. Even as a small child he would diligently cut pictures of cars out of the illustrated magazines in his grandparents' house. Michael's former mother-in-law, Fela, had made a point of reading the German and English press. She always had the latest copies of *Time* and *Newsweek,* as well as *Burda* and other fashion magazines, in the colored straw basket next to the grand piano. Yuval would hang on to her dressing gown and ask: "Can I cut this one now, Granny, can I now?"

Yuval pressed the radio button, and the sound of piano music was heard. "Listen to that tone!" he said, and pressed another button.

"Why waste it on classical music!" But by then Michael had thrown his cigarette out the window and pounced on the radio.

"They didn't check the tape," he said to Yuval, who looked at him uncomprehendingly. Michael pressed the appropriate button, and the tape ran forward and then backward. There was no sound.

"Stay here a minute, don't touch," he said to Yuval, and he ran to his own car, where he activated the radio transmitter. And then he returned, panting, to the Alfa Romeo.

Yuval said nothing, but the gleeful expression had faded from his face, giving way to sober concern.

"Who does the car belong to, Dad?" he finally asked, but Eli Bahar was already standing at the window, pulling a thin glove from his pocket and saying to Yuval: "Excuse me for a second."

The boy got out, and Eli, with a gloved hand, removed the cassette and put it carefully into the nylon bag in his hand.

"You can come with me, if you like," said Michael. "We're going to National HQ."

"For how long?" asked Yuval suspiciously. "How long will it take?"

"Not long," promised Michael. "And after that maybe we'll do something."

"I haven't got much time," said Yuval. "I promised someone I'd help her with something."

Michael looked at the serious face, noted the downy cheeks, and smiled. He wondered what Yuval had to help her with so urgently— the long vacation had just begun—but he said nothing. "By eight we'll have finished twice over," he promised solemnly. Eli Bahar took Yuval by the elbow and led him gently to the Ford.

"It's pure chance I'm still here," said Shaul from Forensics, carefully dusting the tape with powder. He left the room and returned several long moments later. "There isn't a single print on it. As if no one's ever touched it. What do you say to that?"

"I'd like to know how they removed the label without leaving any sign, " said Michael. "Someone put a lot of work into it. And I can tell you at a glance that it's a perfect match with the cassettes Iddo Dudai brought back from the U.S."

"In other words, you think it's the missing tape?"

"That's what it looks like, but let's try listening to it. Have you got a tape player here?"

"Be my guest," said Shaul, taking a tape machine out of his desk drawer.

"Dad, that cassette'll take an hour to play, I want to be there at eight."

"Yuvali, I don't intend to listen to the whole thing; it'll only take a few minutes, you'll see," said Michael, and he noted the pouting lips and disappointed expression that he had seen so often before.

Eli Bahar turned on the player. There was no sound. After a few silent minutes on Play, he pressed Fast Forward and about ten seconds later again tried Play. Again, no sound. In this way he quickly sampled the entire first side. The second side produced no sound either, until the moment when Yuval had opened his mouth to protest and Michael was laying a soothing hand on his arm to indicate "One more second." Just then the room filled with the sound of a hoarse, elderly voice declaiming in Hebrew, but in a heavy Russian accent: "At dawn violets wilted in your skin." A cut-off syllable in another voice followed, and then there was silence again. For a few minutes none of them said anything. Yuval's eyes, too, were fixed on the little tape player.

The tape ended. Michael pressed Rewind and then Play, and the words were repeated, again followed by the cut-off syllable in a different voice.

"What was that all about?" asked Yuval.

"It's a line from a poem by Shaul Tirosh," replied Michael, and he went on listening to the blank tape.

"That's it," he said at the end. "Not another word. There seems to be nothing else on the cassette, but have someone play it all to make sure."

Shaul examined it and said: "It's a TDK. You can get them here, but they make them abroad, in Japan."

"They do everything abroad," said Michael dreamily, "murder investigations too."

"What are you talking about?" said Eli Bahar, looking at him anxiously, as if he had gone out of his mind.

"This is a recording of a conversation between Iddo Dudai and an old Russian, a recording made in America, and you don't need to be a genius to conclude that the odds are very much in favor of it being the one missing cassette. It's from Iddo Dudai's trip to North Carolina, and somebody erased it. Why?"

There was silence in the room again. Eli Bahar bowed his head, and Michael said angrily: "I would think that after the car of a murder victim was found, at least it would be properly examined."

Eli didn't react.

"So what do we do now?" asked Shaul in a Talmudic singsong.

"That's the question," replied Michael. "Come on, Yuval. It's already a quarter to eight, and tomorrow's a big day."

The phone rang when they were at the door. Michael had no intention of stopping, but Shaul, who had picked up the receiver, said: "Just a minute, he's here; you're lucky you caught him. It's for you," and he put the receiver down on the desk. On his way to the desk, Michael heard his son's despairing sigh behind his back, but then the excited words at the other end of the line overwhelmed Yuval's complaint. "Good, bring him in now," he said at last, and wiped his hands on the sides of his trousers, first one and then the other. Eli Bahar looked at him anxiously.

"What's happened?" asked Shaul. "Why are you so pale?"

Michael did not reply. "I'll drop you off on the way," he said to Yuval. "I have to go back to work."

The boy's face expressed a combination of anger and resolve: to behave with dignity and not show his disappointment, but to make sure that his father realized how he felt about its always being the same—the time to relax together that was always promised and never came. All of this was expressed with a twist of the corner of his mouth, a twist that Michael knew only too well, together with the whole spectrum of emotions it represented. But now he saw nothing except the fog that filled his mind. "How many times have I told you," he heard Shorer's voice echoing in his ear, "to be careful of hunches, never to follow them up without covering your ass?" And later, on the way back to the Russian Compound, he heard Ariyeh Levy's hoarse laughter and saw the gleam in his little eyes. "So you've messed up again! I told you it wasn't a university here. Did I tell you, or didn't I?"

16

Eli Bahar, too, listened to Balilty's report. Michael was sitting behind his desk, his face expressionless and his body still. "Alfandari's gone to get him," said Balilty, finishing. "They'll be here in a minute. You don't look in such great shape to me."

Michael ignored this comment. "Tell me again. Everything, from the beginning, slowly," he said.

"Why don't you tape me?" asked Balilty, beginning to smile, but Michael waved his arm impatiently and Balilty's smile was abruptly nipped in the bud.

"Where to start?" he asked, and stared at the ceiling. Then he began again, this time speaking deliberately, glancing sideways as if for confirmation at Eli Bahar, who sat next to the desk, looking at him intently.

"You know that we checked his story," said Balilty. "Alfandari spoke to his mother; he drove up to Rosh Pinna specially on Monday. You said not over the phone, so he went in person. You heard what he said at the meeting: that she's one of those pioneering types, eighty if she's a day. He's got a brother in Safad, and a sister in Sede Yehoshua; they're quite a close family. He's the middle one. Anyway, his mother told Raffi that he arrived at her place on Thursday night and drove from there to the airport on Saturday night, so Raffi went over her story with her and he believed her. You can trust him, and he says that I would have believed her too. It's a big house, with a lot of land, and a big fence around it. So I don't know, maybe Raffi's right and nobody saw anything. Anyway, he wasn't satisfied—Raffi, that is—because the next-door neighbor wasn't there when he arrived to question the mother and the first thing Ariyeh Levy asked was if we had spoken to the neighbors. So this morning we drove up again, me and Raffi. I had something to do in Tiberias, anyway, not connected with the case. This time the neighbor was at home. Another one who wasn't born yesterday, half deaf and doesn't know what's going on, but his son was there too, character himself, about fifty, and what did he say? He said that on Thursday night, when Klein's supposed to be there already if he came straight from the airport, at about eleven, she comes knocking at their door, Klein's mother, her name's Sarah, and asks if he, the neighbor's son, who doesn't live there—he was only visiting and was just about to leave for Haifa, where he lives—listen to this: she asks him if he can come and see what's wrong with the telephone. Her phone doesn't ring loud enough and with her being hard of hearing at her age, she was afraid she wouldn't hear when it rang. So naturally I ask myself why she has to go and ask the neighbor's son to come and fix the phone for her if her own son is there. And so I ask the neighbor's son, his name's Yoska, if Ariyeh Klein was there at the time. Nu, of course he wasn't, he says, otherwise she wouldn't have needed him, because Ariyeh can fix anything. There was nobody home except her. That's what he said. Before that I spun him a yarn about why I was asking him; it was all very friendly; he didn't have a clue about what he was telling me. So then I asked him when did Klein arrive, and he said he didn't know but that when he finished fixing the phone his mother persuaded him not to go back to Haifa and to spend the night with them, so he stayed and slept over, at his parents' house. It was pure chance he was there today too, I caught him there by chance; he brought his kids to visit their grandparents, that's what he said. Anyway, so I asked him when Klein arrived, and he said he didn't know, he left early on Friday morning and drove home to Haifa. Okay?" Balilty sighed and stole a glance at Michael, who sat tensely and said nothing.

"Well?" Eli Bahar spoke for the first time since entering the room.

"Well, so like I said, Raffi and me went back to Klein's mother's house and told her to come with us. And she said why on earth should she, and I warned her about perjury and asked her why she didn't ask her own son to fix the phone if he was at home, and then she saw she was trapped, but she didn't say a thing. She didn't tell a different story either. She just stood there as if she was posing for a monument and said she didn't have anything else to tell us and she wasn't going any-where with anyone and if we wanted to we could take her by force. Do I look as if I was going to take her by force? I said to her: Okay, lady, if that's the way you want it, you can have the local police force right here on your doorstep. We disconnected that phone of hers and got a local cop to keep her incommunicado, so she couldn't warn the professor, and drove straight back here."

"So he wasn't really at Rosh Pinna?" asked Eli Bahar.

"He wasn't there on Thursday night. And his flight got in at two o'clock in the afternoon. So it seems to me that we should ask him where he was. If you have no objections."

The door opened, and Raffi Alfandari's head peeped into the room. "He's here. When do you want him?"

"Let him wait," said Michael.

"Let him stew for a bit," added Balilty nastily, and Raffi's head disappeared.

"When did you get back from there?" asked Eli Bahar.

"Just now, five minutes before I got hold of you at Forensics. We didn't even have time to eat. It's a long drive from Rosh Pinna. Raffi did it in three hours flat. And while I was phoning you he went to wait outside Klein's house, so the bird wouldn't fly the coop. So what do you say to that little story, eh? Here's a guy that everyone's crazy about, the great man himself, and like your boss says, you should always talk to the neighbors."

Balilty fell silent and looked at Michael, whose face was still blank and whose body was frozen. Beginning to squirm in his chair, Balilty said: "I'm dying of hunger; let's grab a bite on the corner and bring the boss something too. Eh, Ohayon? What do you say?"

Michael said nothing. At last he made an undefined movement with his head, which Balilty chose to interpret as consent. "What should we bring you?" he asked hesitantly.

"Nothing, thanks. I'm not hungry, I've already eaten today," replied Michael, when he noticed them standing and waiting at the door. The taste of the onion at lunch rose in his throat. When they left he dialed Shorer's number. There was no reply. He tried his number at home, and there was no reply there either. Finally he put the phone down and told himself that nobody else could do the job for him. He tried to banish the anxiety and confusion fogging his mind. Nobody was to blame, nobody had misled him, only he himself was responsible, and now he felt betrayed. Ariyeh Levy was right, he had been taken in by the good home, the old family, the modern Renaissance man. And maybe he had a story, maybe there was some simple explanation. So why did his mother lie? What did Klein have to hide? he asked himself as he dialed the number of the room next door and told Alfandari to bring the man in.

Klein stood in the doorway. He was wearing the shirt he had been wearing a few hours earlier, the short-sleeved striped shirt that emphasized his big arms. Next to him, Raffi looked shorter than he really was. Raffi left the office excitedly, and Michael knew that he would be in the next room, listening to every word.

Michael felt his face stiffening, sensed his eyes emptying of expression.

Klein too, for the first time since Michael had met him at the university, when he came into the room with his voice booming, looked tense. His face was pale, and he responded to Michael's mute invitation and sat down, facing him, on the other side of the desk. Again the taste of the onion, accompanied by the taste of Greek olives, rose in Michael's throat, and he felt nauseous. He sought to suppress his panic, to ignore his anxiety, to erase the thought that in one minute everything was going to collapse around him and there would be no escape from the knowledge that he had been deceived by his own wishes, that he had lost his better judgment. This thought would not let him be; he tried to will anger to replace it, but the anxiety flooded everything. He attempted to relax his leg muscles, but he couldn't even stretch the legs out in front of him. The air in the room was stifling. Looking behind him, he saw that the window was open, and then he turned back to Klein, who was sitting silently opposite him. Finally Klein cleared his throat a few times and asked in his bass voice: "What's the problem?"

Michael looked at the thick lips, which were dry now, and asked him quietly when he had returned from America.

"I told you. On Thursday afternoon. Surely it's easy enough to check," replied Klein in a tone of puzzled surprise, but Michael noticed that his hands had clenched into big fists. His arms were folded on his chest, and beads of sweat had broken out on his forehead. Michael registered every detail. "Look at the body," he would explain to his students in the Police Academy, "it's the body that talks." Klein's body was shouting. Every movement bespoke apprehension. Yet the cultured voice lacked any trace of indignation. Michael knew that Klein had lied, or more precisely—he consoled himself—withheld information, but he still could not help feeling awed by the man. Someone else should interrogate him, he thought; I'm too involved. But I also want that someone to be gentle with him, to show respect; there's nobody suitable for a man of his caliber, I can't hand him over to Balilty or Bahar.

"And tell me again, please: why did you fly separately? You and your family?"

"What's wrong?" asked Klein, and passed a parched tongue over his lips. "What's wrong all of a sudden?"

"Just answer the question: why did you fly separately?"

"Because of my daughter's end-of-term party in America. The middle one, Dana. As I told you. She wasn't willing to give it up, and I couldn't wait. My mother was expecting me; I promised her. And besides, there was no room for me on the flight that arrived on Saturday night. Ofra and I never fly together—it makes her anxious."

"But she flew back with all your daughters?"

Klein said impatiently: "Yes, I already said so."

"Okay, we'll leave that for the moment. You said there was a rental car waiting for you? At the airport?"

Klein nodded. His arms were still folded on his chest, as if in an attempt to hide his clenched hands. "I ordered it in New York."

"Why didn't your family come to meet you? They hadn't seen you for nearly a year, your brother, your sister, even your mother; why didn't they come to the airport?"

Klein took his hands from his chest and rested them on his knees, so that his shoulders rose and the upper half of his body stretched and lengthened. Michael waited.

"Complicated family matters. That's what we arranged, that they would come to my mother's on Saturday. I don't like to be a nuisance."

"Are you sure that that's the reason?"

"Meaning what? What other reason occurs to you?"

"To give you freedom of movement, for example?" said Michael quietly, with contradictory wishes in his heart. Let him lie, let him go on lying, he thought; then I'll be able to get angry. At the same time, he also wanted him not to lie, for things to be the way they had been a few hours before, for him to remain a good guy.

But Klein said nothing.

At last Michael asked the question he was afraid to ask. "When, exactly, did you get to Rosh Pinna, to your mother's place?"

Klein crossed his arms on his chest again. "I've already told you," he replied and compressed his lips into a straight line.

Michael waited, but Klein remained silent.

"We know that you weren't there on Thursday night," said Michael finally. He couldn't bear the thought of Klein lying. "When *did* you arrive there?"

After an eternity, Klein sighed and said: "It makes no difference when I arrived there."

There was a long silence. Michael looked directly into Klein's eyes, and Klein put his elbows on the desk and cupped his face in his hands.

"Can you explain why, exactly, it makes no difference?"

"Because it's not relevant," said Klein, looking up and down into Michael's eyes. "You'll have to believe me that it's got nothing to do with the murder."

"Professor Klein," said Michael, feeling the anger begin to well up, "you'll have to be a little more forthcoming for me to give you any credence. When, exactly, did you arrive, and why isn't it relevant?"

"I arrived in Rosh Pinna early on Friday evening, and I'm telling you that it's got nothing to do with the case. Why can't you just believe me and leave it at that?"

Later, when he listened to the playback, Michael heard the furious sound that had burst out of him, jackal-like, shameful in its self-exposure. Only then did he realize just how hurt he had been.

"Professor Klein," he exclaimed, stressing every syllable, "I'm investigating a murder, two murders. Of a young man you were fond of and attached to and of a man who was close to you for many years. I'm asking you!"

Klein wiped his forehead with his hand and looked into Michael's eyes again, his own eyes wide open, seeming more than anything else sad and serious.

"I'm sorry you don't trust me, really sorry," he said in the end.

"It's not a question of whether I trust you, not to mention the fact that you already lied once. It's a question of facts. Your mother lied—why did you make her lie? Things people say are meaningless unless there are facts behind them. What's it got to do with my trusting you? Respect, affection, none of that means a thing if I don't have the facts. If we're talking about trust, it's you who didn't trust me!"

Klein looked as if he were hesitating, pondering what Michael had said. At last he said: "You're right. But after I tell you, you'll see that it has nothing to do with the case, nothing at all."

Michael waited, without putting any more pressure on him. At last Klein said: "It has to stay between us. Do you understand? It has to. Promise me."

Michael nodded.

"Do you promise?" repeated Klein, and this childish insistence astonished Michael. He thought of Raffi listening in the next room, of Balilty and Eli Bahar, who would no doubt soon join him there, of the team meeting, of the typed transcripts of the entire conversation, which Tzilla would place before him the next morning, and he said: "I promise." For some reason, he didn't add the usual formula: on condition that it turned out to be unconnected with the investigation, etc.

"Because other people are involved too," said Klein as if he had read his thoughts. "It's not only me."

Michael nodded but said nothing. Again he felt his confusion, his contradictory wishes. What could Klein's secret be? He was dying to know.

"I met a woman I had to meet," said Klein at last, clenching his lips. Then he added, almost in a whisper: "And that's the reason I asked my mother to lie. I didn't tell her what it was about."

That's all? You too? You old lecher, thought Michael in disappointment as he saw the arms crossing on the chest again.

"I'll assume that she's married," he said.

The thick eyebrows rose. "Why should you assume that? She's not married."

"So why the secrecy?" asked Michael, confused. "On your own account?"

Klein's face was very pale; its expression resembled the one Michael had seen the day, an eternity ago, when they both sat on the bench, in the so-called square, next to the mailboxes, after the discovery of Tirosh's body. Michael wanted to return to the fraternity, equality, the wordless sympathy he had felt then; he wanted to go back to the lunch they had eaten together in Klein's kitchen.

"In the end, yes, on my own account, although there are a lot of other people along the way."

"How long were you with her?" asked Michael carefully.

"Until Friday afternoon. I left Jerusalem at half past two."

Michael lit a cigarette. "And you say that you went there from the airport and you were there until the next day?" he asked, looking at the charred match he then placed in the ashtray filled with butts.

"Do you have to know everything?" asked Klein.

"Were you there the whole time?" insisted Michael.

"Since you've already come so far, there doesn't seem to be any point in hiding anything." Klein sighed. "Yes, all the time except for the two hours I spent with Shaul Tirosh, on Thursday evening."

I don't believe it! said Michael Ohayon to himself. I don't believe it! How could I have slipped up so badly?

"Where?" he asked aloud. "Where did you meet him?"

"In a restaurant," replied Klein. His voice was calm, his arms, too, had relaxed. Now his forearms were flat on the desk. At first his fingers were parted, then gradually, they came together.

"What restaurant?" asked Michael.

"That's part of the story," said Klein slowly, "and as I've already told you, it's got nothing to do with—"

"Professor Klein!" Michael's voice rose in angry impatience.

And only then did Klein tell him the whole story. He told it not like a someone who had been broken but as a man who had come to a decision. There was no need to ask any questions; he told him everything, down to the last detail.

"Give me the name and address, please," said Michael at the end, and he carefully wrote down the lady's name and her address. It seemed to him that he heard a door open in the corridor. They were on their way to bring her in, he knew, and it was already after midnight.

"How can a person hide a story like that for twelve years!" Balilty stopped the tape player and whistled. "And in Jerusalem!" And then he added: "I swear that if you'd given me one more day I would have ferreted it out. How old's the kid? Five? I don't understand it—how could the guy have gotten in so deep? And with three daughters at home? Maybe he planned it on purpose, to have a son from the other one? And you thought he was such a saint! A saint with a mistress!" He gulped down the rest of his coffee, shook his head, and sighed loudly. Suddenly he jumped to his feet and exclaimed in excitement: "Wait a minute—isn't 'Malka' Mali Arditi? Mali from the restaurant? I don't believe it!"

"What's the matter with you?" asked Michael impatiently. "Who's Mali?"

"Who's Mali?! What a devil, what a devil!"

"Who?" asked Michael, staring curiously at Balilty. "Who . . . what? Tell me slowly."

"You remember that time when we went, after that guy what's-his-name's trial, to that restaurant over there, next to that bar in Nahalat Shiva?" Michael nodded. "And it was shut," said Balilty, "and we went somewhere else—where, I don't remember. Never mind, it doesn't matter; what matters is where we ended up. What matters is if she's the one I think she is, then I just don't believe it—that woman's so terrific that I just don't know. Wait till you see her, how terrific she is, but not only terrific from the point of view of gorgeous—she can cook! Boy, can she cook! You've never tasted anything like it," said Balilty, and he passed the tip of his tongue over his lips with an expression of extraordinary gluttony. "She stuffs a carrot so even the carrot's mother wouldn't recognize it, and the way she spices zucchini, and if you give her some meat, what she does with a piece of lamb! And she's Klein's mistress? I don't believe it! So maybe it's not her," he said hopefully, and went back to listening to the tape.

Klein was put in the conference room, with Manny Ezra to watch him. Balilty listened to the tape again. They were waiting for Eli Bahar, who had gone to bring her in.

"First of all," said Michael when she was sitting opposite him in his office, "I'd like the details."

Mali Arditi looked at him with a smile that lit up the whole room, and then a clear, uninhibited laugh which shook her full, round shoulders—later described by Balilty with the words "There's something to take hold of there"—and her large breasts. Then she pulled up a strap of her dress, a stringlike band that had slipped off her shoulder. "A strawberry-blond doll," Balilty had said, and that was an understatement, thought Michael as he looked at the thick auburn curls, which she now gathered into a twist as she went on laughing. She belonged to the rare breed of redheads whose skin was free of freckles. The exposed skin at the top of her breasts and on her arms was smooth and dark—"mocha mousse," said Balilty when he saw her at the end of the corridor. "That sonofabitch Klein, how did he do it?"

"I'm not angry anymore; it doesn't last long with me, anger. Dragging a person out of bed at this hour of the night! . . . What do you mean, the details? You'll have to tell me what you want, sugar."

Michael was stunned. He tried to ignore the overt sexuality, which couldn't be called vulgar. She looked at him with an amused expression and smoothed her cheek with a broad, white-nailed hand. He had the distinct impression that if they had met under different circumstances she would have made short work of him. In his wildest dreams he couldn't imagine this woman waiting faithfully for Klein, crying into her pillow at night when he didn't arrive, doing all the things done by his image of "the other woman." This woman didn't belong to anyone.

"When did he arrive at your place?"

"I'll tell you exactly, just a minute." He looked at her neck as she raised her head to the ceiling and knitted her arched eyebrows, which were a little too thin for the big face. Their color, too, was auburn, like her hair. Michael followed the movement of her hand, which came to rest on her ample décolletage. "It was on Thursday, Thursday at about four o'clock."

"And when did he leave you?"

"He left on Friday. We went to get the kid from his friend's house, and at half past two he brought us home and drove to his mother's."

"And between Thursday and Friday he didn't go out of the house?"

"You're cute." And again that pealing laughter, which sounded completely crazy in his office in the Russian Compound. She doesn't belong here, he thought, but he looked at her poker-faced, or so, at any rate, he hoped. "So uptight. Why do you take everything so seriously?" And then her face grew grave, as if she had decided to "get down to business," and her brown eyes, almond shaped and full of life, looked at him with a stern expression as she said: "He wasn't out of my sight the whole day and night. And we didn't coordinate our stories, if that's what you think. He met somebody, but that was in the restaurant. I opened the restaurant for them and they sat there, the two of them, because I didn't want the other guy in the house. My flat's above the restaurant. You know where it is?"

"And who was the man?" asked Michael, and offered her his pack of cigarettes. She took a cigarette, looked at it absentmindedly, and leaned forward for him to light it.

"You'll have to ask him that, sweetie; we don't talk about each other's lives. We never have and we're not about to start now. You heard the man: he told me to tell you where he was, that's all, not who he was with."

Michael saw in his mind's eye the scene that had shocked him earlier, the voluptuous redhead in the conference room, gazing at Klein with a look full of sympathy and understanding. "Tell him where I was," Klein had said in his presence, and then she had smiled for the first time, an intimate, understanding smile, after raging all the way there, according to Eli Bahar.

Now she signed a copy of her statement and agreed without any hesitation to undergo a polygraph test. Then she was taken home. Klein remained in the conference room.

"I know her," said Manny Ezra. "She lives next door to my sister-in-law's sister. She's got a little restaurant in Nahalat Shiva; they specialize in stuffed vegetables; she inherited it from her parents. She's a real character—doesn't give a damn about anything. The check you get has nothing to do with the menu—she makes people pay whatever she feels like. And she opens the restaurant whenever she feels like. I've eaten there. What can I tell you? One thing's sure—she knows how to cook. Where did he pick her up? And the kid, is it his?"

"Apparently," said Michael thoughtfully.

"How did he do it? I want to understand, how did he do it?" protested Balilty.

"Wonders will never cease," said Michael Ohayon, who was preoccupied by the very same question.

"Should I bring him here?" Manny asked, and glanced at his watch. "Eli's talking to him now. It's three o'clock in the morning. Do you want him now?"

"Yes," said Michael. "Bring him here. I need the material for the meeting in the morning."

The building was surrounded by silence. He stood at the window and stared into the darkness. There were lights on in all the offices, and he could hear a typewriter somewhere. The air now was damper, but it was still hot. Klein was led into the room and Manny closed the door behind him silently.

"Now you know," said Klein gloomily.

"She didn't want to talk, your lady friend, about the man you met, until you asked her to. Did she sit with you? Listen to your conversation?"

"Mali hears what she wants to hear and knows what she wants to know. The best thing about her is her total ability to live and let live. In exchange, all she asks is to be allowed to live too. I've no idea what she heard. She was in the kitchen. There's a window between the kitchen and the restaurant. It was closed, I think, but if you make an effort you can hear," said Klein.

"She's coming in tomorrow to take a polygraph test. Are you prepared to tell her to talk about your meeting with Tirosh?"

"I'm prepared to ask her—you can't exactly 'tell her' to do anything."

"Let's return to that meeting. Who initiated it?"

"I did," said Klein hoarsely.

"I want to understand. You come back to the country after nearly a year abroad, you go to see your . . . son and his mother, and you make an appointment with Tirosh?" And tell me that it has nothing to do with the murder, thought Michael angrily.

Klein shook his head. "I'll explain everything. But I want you to promise me that what I tell you won't leave this building. Because I've already realized that it can't remain just between the two of us."

"If you had told me in the beginning, it could have; if you had told me of your own free will," said Michael bitterly.

"You have to understand my side of it too," pleaded Klein. "It's not exactly the way you see it." They both sat in silence, and Michael struggled between his tremendous curiosity to know how Klein had ended up in this situation, living this double life, and his knowledge that it had nothing to do with the investigation—not to mention his wish to let Klein go on stewing in his embarrassment, as well as his wish to be close to him and at the same time fulfill the need to keep his distance, to maintain his reserve and superiority.

"My relationship with Mali goes deep, and naturally I love her and the child. It's not some little extracurricular affair."

"How old is the boy?" asked Michael in a cold, businesslike tone.

"Five"—Klein sighed, averting his eyes—"and he has another family, which wouldn't be able to accept the situation."

Michael tilted his head to one side and looked at Klein, who shifted his weight uneasily in the chair and then said: "You're ignoring the fact that all this could be extremely destructive. My wife's not made to cope with this kind of thing; it would devastate her. She wouldn't be able to understand that it's possible to live two separate lives, without the one negating the other. There's no need to see everything in such uncompromising colors," said Klein despairingly.

Michael sternly suppressed the urge to ask for an explanation of the "two separate lives." He still didn't know how he felt about Klein, he couldn't isolate the sense of disappointment. Inside him there was a vortex of emotions, dominated by the suspicion that had come into being after the complete trust he had felt for Klein had been betrayed. He remembered that he had tried to ignore the results of Klein's polygraph, and he felt like a fool. He didn't really know him, he said to himself, nothing was what he had imagined, nothing apparently fitted his idea of the man. But only apparently, he knew in the depths of his heart; in fact everything fitted perfectly. What was it he had said, Klein, about integrity? Perfection? It was a long time ago, actually it was that very afternoon—what had he said? That people weren't perfect? Only art attained perfection, that's what he said, thought Michael, and what I have to do is stick to the matter at hand, to the facts, and to stop philosophizing. "What, exactly, happened with Tirosh?" he asked after strenuously silencing the inner voices.

"It's quite simple to explain," said Klein, "but it isn't easy for me to expose myself. You understand," he said, and leaned forward, "I've been keeping the affair with Mali a secret for years. Nobody knows, not even the child." He looked around him in embarrassment. "He doesn't know that I'm his father. I've never spoken about her; there are only a few people who know that there's anything between us, and nobody knows the real nature of the relationship. My wife has never met her. There are people who go with me to eat at her restaurant sometimes. That's how I met her. Tirosh took me there the first time, and later on he found out."

"Found out?" repeated Michael. "When did he find out?"

"I don't know when, and I don't know how. All I can tell you is that he never spoke to Mali; he didn't find out from her. It had to have been before I left for America. From what I understand today, he might even have used a private detective. He would have had his work cut out for him, because we don't meet on a regular basis, Mali and I, and we're always very careful. Or so I thought."

"How do you know? How did you know?" asked Michael.

But Klein ignored the repeated question, as if he did not comprehend its significance. "Just before my return, I received a letter from him. To his credit, he sent it to the department, to Columbia University, and not to our home address. The letter hinted clearly that he knew. He was always looking for another side of me, for 'subterranean currents,' as he called them. You see, my way of life drove him wild, because it never occurred to him that there were any cracks in it; he imagined it as other than it really was."

"Do you have the letter?" asked Michael, knowing in advance what the answer would be.

"No, of course not. I tore it to shreds as soon as I'd read it. You don't keep such things."

No, thought Michael. I wouldn't have kept it either. And aloud he said: "But you remember what was written?"

"Of course I remember," replied Klein, and wiped his brow. "It invited me, in a would-be witty vein, to meet him tête-à-tête as soon as I returned, 'in view of information shedding a new light' on my character. I remember the expression. Naturally, I was furious and also worried. Shaul wasn't exactly the soul of discretion. But I hoped that nobody would believe his story if he told it."

"What did he want of you?"

"I asked myself the same thing," said Klein, his face twisting in anger. "When I read the letter I thought it was only jealousy, or a feeling of triumph over my bourgeois way of life, as he called it. But after we met, or during the conversation itself, I sensed that there was something else behind it."

"Tell me again, from the beginning," said Michael, not for the first time that night, though he couldn't remember when he had said it first or to whom. "What did he say to you?"

Suddenly Klein looked very tired. On his full face Michael saw wrinkles he had not noticed before. His skin had a yellowish tinge, or perhaps it was the fluorescent light, thought Michael. He remembered the man's confident, reassuring voice when he had spoken to his wife on the telephone a few hours earlier.

"Now I see again how he succeeded in destroying everything around him," said Klein reflectively. "Destroying everything—he was always good at that. I have no idea what he wanted. As usual, he beat around the bush; he was an expert at innuendo. He talked about Iddo. He kept asking me what Iddo had said to me when he visited us in America. I told him that Iddo had undergone some kind of crisis, that something had happened to him, I didn't know what it was. He kept coming back to it. Then he asked me if Iddo had left me anything in writing. I asked him what he meant by 'left me anything' and why he didn't go to Iddo and ask him himself. But he spoke obscurely about 'something for safekeeping,' if Iddo had left me something for safekeeping, and then he asked me if I had seen the cassette—"

Michael interrupted him: "So you knew what I was talking about when I asked you today about that tape?"

Klein looked at him guiltily and dropped his eyes. "Well, I didn't really know, but I didn't not know either. Before, this afternoon, I got into a bit of a panic for a while. You have to understand that during the conversation with Tirosh I was very tense. . . ." His voice trailed away.

"You were tense," Michael repeated in the most neutral tone his dry throat was capable of producing.

"Well, I was afraid that everything was going to explode. I was too nervous to think of all the implications, as you called them before. In any case, he brought up the business with Mali, and he said—this bit I remember vividly—'You look after me, and I'll look after you.' I asked him what he was getting at—it's not that I didn't ask, even though I was in a panic—and he said: 'When it's necessary for you to know, you'll know, I promise you, and if Iddo speaks to you, tell me.'"

"In other words," said Michael Ohayon, "you weren't exactly overcome with grief when you saw Tirosh dead."

"You know," said Klein hesitantly, "I don't expect you to believe me, but that's not quite the way it was. I mean, I wasn't really afraid, I don't know why, but I felt sure that if he ever did bring things out into the open, I would be able to cope with the consequences." He looked at Michael, who remained silent.

Again Klein cleared his throat and said in embarrassment: "Perhaps I even wanted it to come out, who knows? A human being is such a complicated creature. . . ."

"And you maintain that you didn't kill him?" Michael suddenly shot at him, and Klein looked at him and crossed his arms. He shook his head several times and said in a serious voice, weighing every word: "No, of course not. I saw him on Thursday, and on Friday he was still alive. Besides, I don't believe that you really think I had enough of a reason to do such a thing."

"It was you yourself who just said that he destroyed everything, no?" asked Michael with suppressed anger. "And as for your claim that you didn't see him again, we'll have to check the time that you arrived in Rosh Pinna on Friday afternoon."

"But I told you. . . " Klein began to protest, then fell silent. "Okay, I can't really expect you to, but believe me: I couldn't have hidden away on Mount Scopus, and there's no way of getting into the campus without being seen. I didn't set foot in the university until Sunday."

"Are you positive that Iddo never left you a cassette?" Michael suddenly asked, after a brief silence.

Klein shook his head. "Of course I'm positive. I couldn't have any possible reason for hiding it, and I promise you that I don't know the first thing about whatever Iddo was threatening Shaul with, I haven't the faintest idea."

"I want to clarify this point again," said Michael, as if they were dealing with some scientific problem. "Were you afraid that Tirosh would blackmail you? That he would use his information about your double life?"

Klein shook his head firmly. "No, I wasn't afraid. If you'd known Shaul you would understand."

Michael waited for an explanation; Klein looked as if he was trying to formulate, to his own satisfaction, what he wanted to say.

"Listen," he said slowly, "Shaul—how should I put it?—felt humiliated in advance; there was something that was bothering him. Perhaps he even wanted my help, though of course he was unable to put it into words. He was always humiliated in advance, in spite of his confident appearance, and his arrogance, and the . . . the information he discovered about me apparently wasn't intended for external use, you can forget about blackmail or any melodramatic nonsense along those lines. It was intended for one thing only: his feeling of triumph over me, that I wasn't perfect either, that I, too, had some blot on my copybook, some weakness. So he would feel less humiliated. I don't know if you can understand this, if you've known people like that."

The sky was already pale when Michael took Klein back to the conference room, after preparing him for the polygraph test. Then he sat in his office and began listening to the recorded conversation. The team meeting was to take place at eight o'clock, and Tzilla had already typed and organized the material. Michael was beyond exhaustion, anxious and tense in anticipation of the meeting, of the remarks his C.O. would make. He still had no idea who was telling the truth and who was lying, and in the midst of his confusion and uncertainty, a new anger at himself began to well up. You idiot, he said to himself almost aloud, with your fantasies about integrity and perfection, you suddenly seem to have arrived at a new morality.

He buried his face in his hands and rubbed his eyes. So what? the inner voice continued, just because a man leads two lives, suddenly he's got no integrity? What are you, king of the bourgeoisie? And what about Maya? Nevertheless, he felt a grievance against Klein, although he didn't know exactly what it was. He suspected that it had nothing to do with the murder, or with the lie. It was his own very private lament that even Klein did not live an impeccable life, that even he was touched by something not completely clean. Why couldn't anyone be simple and right, the way a person was supposed to be? he asked himself. Why? Not even one single person? And then Tzilla came into the room, with a cup of coffee and a fresh roll on a tray in her hands, and a green file under her arm.

So tell them we've got prints—it won't be the first time. See what they say, how they react. You want me to draw you a picture?" said Ariyeh Levy impatiently. "And Klein's not getting out of here, definitely not before the polygraph. Every day there's another lead—it's enough to drive you crazy." The subdistrict commander took a sip of coffee and everyone waited silently.

Michael was still tense because of the anticipated reactions to the business with Klein, but to his surprise, no one had made fun of him. But nobody knew about the lunch in his kitchen, he thought, about the feeling of friendship, the wish for closeness. Actually, he suddenly reminded himself, none of them would understand, anyway. The fact that he had a few sleepless nights behind him made him particularly vulnerable. Everything had surfaced during the meeting, including the heartbreak over Maya. "I want another meeting today, before you leave, and you can go and order the traveler's checks now. The rest we can leave to Personnel. What do you say?" Michael said, and turned to Avidan, the departmental investigations officer, who nodded a few times.

At half past nine the same morning Ruchama Shai sat opposite him, blinking her eyes and looking belligerently at the tape recorder. "I've never heard it," she said for the second time. "Never."

"It's a fact that we found your fingerprints on the cassette," insisted Michael.

"Well," she said, twisting her fingers, "I can't explain it. I didn't see Shaul after Thursday morning, and even then I only saw him in his office at the university, and I wasn't with him in his car. I don't know how to explain it."

Michael removed the cassette from the tape player and put it on the desk in front of her.

A glint flickered in her eyes. "I'm not sure," she said with a frightened look, "but I may have seen it before, I don't remember where. Maybe in Shaul's room, maybe at his house. I don't remember. Maybe with Tuvia? No, I don't know. I'm not sure it's the same cassette either, but it seems to me that I saw something like it—with Tuvia's things perhaps, when I took the keys out of his briefcase? I saw a cassette somewhere, it did look like this one—it didn't have anything written on it either." She spoke in all innocence. Michael examined her face and realized that she herself didn't understand the significance of what she was saying.

He asked himself how, if at all, the cassette had come into Tuvia Shai's possession, and then, on a sudden hunch, he asked her: "Do you know when your husband met Iddo Dudai before he was murdered? Before the faculty meeting, I mean? Before Friday morning?"

Ruchama Shai examined her fingers, and then she said: "Well, they met at the university too. They probably met every day."

"Too?" Michael pounced. "What do you mean 'too'?"

"After the departmental seminar on Wednesday night, Iddo came to our house. He wanted to talk to Tuvia, but I don't know what they talked about, because I went to bed." The words came out quickly, as if she refused to weigh their potential for help or harm.

Again Michael examined the childish face, the drooping mouth; he saw the puffiness under the eyes. He knew that she spent most of her time sleeping. All the fears, all the horrors of the past week were channeled into sleep. "To work and to sleep. No shopping, no cooking, no people, nothing! She behaves as if she's very sick," Alfandari had said, reporting the finding of the surveillance detail. "That's how she's been living for more than a week. Except for the sound of footsteps, you'd think there's nobody alive in the house. They don't talk to each other at all, and on the phone he only talks about work. Only he; nobody calls her up at all," said Alfandari, describing what he had heard on tapes. Michael thought they were behaving like people who had lost the taste for life.

He remembered Ruchama's words during one of the interrogations: "Once, before I met Shaul, I wasn't even aware of the possibility of losing something. Now I know that I have nothing left to lose."

Her face looked like an illustration of this statement: the face of a person without expectations, someone who had nothing left to lose.

After he dismissed her, Michael glanced at his diary. Sunday, the twenty-ninth of June. Tuvia Shai had asked for his "appointment" to be postponed to one o'clock. He had a conference hour, he explained politely to Tzilla.

Now Ruth Dudai was about to enter, and Michael had the distinct feeling that nothing was going to happen, that he had nothing more to learn about these people, with whose way of life, whose anxieties and miseries, he had become so familiar during the past week.

He could have predicted the nervous movement with which Ruth Dudai looked at her watch immediately, after entering the room. She complained, in the cultured tones he had come to know, that she was in a hurry, that she should have been at home already, that the sitter had to leave, that she hadn't even been allowed to mourn properly.

Michael looked at the full face, the blue tricot dress exposing the round shoulders, the brown, intelligent, sad eyes behind the round glasses, and he remembered last Saturday, when he had knocked at her door with Uzi Rimon. The expression on her face had hardly changed during the days that had passed since she had been informed of her husband's death. Her complexion was fresh. Despite the intelligent sadness in her eyes, there were no signs of sleeplessness. "I know you'll say that not everybody reacts in the same way, that some people only break after a long time," Balilty had commented doubtfully, "but that one is some tough cookie." And at the team meeting he had reported on her surveillance: "There's always some dame with a kid there; I think she's moved in—some friend of hers from the army. Her parents have arrived in the country too; there are always people there. She's never alone for a minute."

Now she contemplated the cassette without touching it. She didn't know, she said; it looked like the others. Iddo kept them with him; she couldn't have touched it. She had no idea how her fingerprints came to be on it.

No, she didn't know the voice that had quoted the line from Tirosh's poem. "I told you," she said wearily, "I've already told you a thousand times, that Iddo didn't tell me anything about what he did in America. He came back completely crazy."

She didn't know what time, exactly, Iddo had come home after the departmental seminar. Late. She had awakened when he turned on the bedroom light.

"I didn't ask him anything about anything. If I asked him any questions, he would answer impatiently and irritably, and I felt so guilty." At this she burst into tears. "I was so glad when he went off to scuba dive; I thought he would get to relax. I thought he would calm down, that he would be more pleasant afterward, and besides"—she sniffed and took off her glasses—"there was the question of Shaul."

Michael understood her embarrassed silence. He could hardly expect a woman in her position to recount how she had arranged, joyfully, to meet her lover when her husband was away from home. "And I wanted Iddo out of the house," she continued, "because he was simply unbearable. And now I feel so guilty!"

She laid her head on her arms, folded on the table, and sobbed. Michael looked at her arms and neck, at the locks of hair escaping from the thick rubber band encircling her ponytail, at her skin, fresh as a baby's, and thought that it wouldn't take more than a couple of years for her to find someone to console her, that she wouldn't be alone for long. He was unable to find a drop of pity for her in his heart.

"In the matter of the air tanks," he said slowly, "was Tirosh ever there again, in the basement?"

"I've already told you. How many times do you have to ask? How am I supposed to know? Anyone can go in and out of the basement. He certainly didn't say anything to me about it. And anyway, what are you trying to imply? That he tampered with the oxygen? What do you think, that he wanted me so much he was prepared to get rid of my husband? That's simply absurd," she said, wiping her eyes. "Apart from which," she continued in a flash of illumination, "he died before Iddo, so how could he have—" And suddenly she fell silent. Then she said hesitantly: "What are you trying to say—that he went into the basement and filled the tanks before that? Why? Why would he have? The basement was open, that's true, but I don't know, one of the neighbors could have seen him, and anyway, why would he do it? Tell me why?"

Michael was about to tell her that all the neighbors had been questioned and none of them had seen anything, when the black telephone, the internal line, rang.

"We've got the list. And before you see Shai, I want to show you something," said Raffi. "There's something very peculiar here."

"I've finished here," Michael replied. "You can come in now." Before he could say anything to her, Ruth Dudai dropped her wet tissues into the wastepaper basket underneath his desk and rose heavily and uncertainly to her feet.

Michael accompanied her to the door and peered outside. Tuvia Shai was sitting in the same posture as on the previous occasions, staring in front of him with a dead, apathetic look. At the end of the corridor, Raffi appeared, holding a cup of coffee in each hand and a cardboard file under his arm. He stepped nimbly into the room, and Michael closed the door behind him and looked at the thin file folder.

"Just like I said at the meeting this morning, we were close. He's a character, that Muallem."

"What's the peculiar thing you found?" asked Michael, as he looked at the long list inside the brown file.

"See for yourself—it's really weird," said Alfandari, and sipped his coffee.

Obediently Michael ran his finger down the list of all the orders of carbon monoxide for the last month. Alfandari had arranged the list alphabetically and marked all the orders from Jerusalem in red. There were a few suppliers in the Tel Aviv area and others in Haifa and its environs. Marked in red, Michael noted, were orders for large cylinders from a private medical laboratory and from Shaarei Tzedek Hospital, and for two small cylinders of carbon monoxide gas from "Professor A. Klein, Hebrew University, Jerusalem."

Alongside the name of the supplier was the date of order; it had been placed two weeks before Iddo Dudai's death, when Klein was still in New York.

"How was it paid for?" asked Michael, gripping his coffee cup tightly.

"I drove to Tel Aviv this morning, without Muallem, to see the supplier in person," said Alfandari, pushing back the fair lock of hair that was falling, as usual, onto his forehead. "He told me that the order had been paid for in advance by cash in the mail. The secretary remembered exactly, because usually they send a bill and are paid by check. But this time the customer sent money inside the letter that ordered the gas. It was all in an ordinary envelope."

"Where was it sent to?" asked Michael, and Raffi Alfandari replied: "To Professor A. Klein, care of the Hebrew Literature Department, Hebrew University. And I've already checked: it was a rather small parcel but not small enough to fit into his mailbox, so what they do in that case, the university, is put a note in the person's mailbox, that there's a parcel for him at the campus post office, and he goes to get it. But he was out of the country, of course, so I went to the post office and checked for that date, and a parcel did come for him, and somebody took it. But search me, I don't know who it was—the signature was illegible, some foreign language."

"Didn't you talk to the post office clerk? Try to find out?"

"Of course. The clerk at the counter doesn't remember; the ID number's there, but she admits that she isn't too strict about asking for the card and checking and so on, because everyone she sees works at the university. Well, from now on she'll check. The number written there doesn't belong to any of the people concerned."

Michael drummed his fingers on the desk and thought aloud: "Since Klein was abroad, who knew that he was supposed to get a parcel? Who took the note out of his mailbox? Who was responsible for emptying it?"

"I don't know," said Alfandari. "Not that I didn't try to find out, but the department secretary wasn't there, and nobody else could tell me."

"What about the girl who helps her?" asked Michael impatiently.

"She's on leave, studying for her exams somewhere, at home maybe. You want me to look for her?"

"How do you know she's on leave?"

"That big woman, Zellermaier, was standing next to the office. She was in a temper."

"What about?" asked Michael, and heard a detailed description of Shulamith Zellermaier's annoyance at the fact that the department secretary "'couldn't find any other time to go to the dentist except when Racheli's on leave, and how is everything supposed to wait until tomorrow?'" Alfandari sounded amused. "She's a character, that one," he said.

Michael dialed Klein's home number. There was no reply. He tried his office on Mount Scopus; no reply there either.

"Well," said Alfandari, and leaning back in his chair, "in any case, he was in America." And then he sat up. "People can fly back and forth, of course," he said slowly, "but that sounds too complicated, to come all the way from New York two weeks before he has to come back anyway, and then to do it all again—it doesn't make sense."

"No," said Michael thoughtfully. "We checked the flight records; he really did arrive on Thursday afternoon. But now we'll have to find out if he left New York for two or three days two weeks before that." Raffi Alfandari looked at Michael patiently, and Michael sat up straight, his expression becoming decisive. "The question is," he said, "who took the mail out of his mailbox during the entire year?" And then: "I think I know who it was."

"But Mrs. Lipkin's at the dentist," Raffi reminded him.

"Visits to the dentist don't really last forever," said Michael. "She'll be back. Ask Tzilla to keep phoning to find out when she arrives. And get hold of her assistant. She doesn't have to come all the way here; we can see her there too. We'll be a lot wiser after we've spoken to them. And now for Dr. Shai."

Alfandari collected the empty coffee cups, glanced at the sheet of paper that Michael folded neatly and put into his pocket, and headed for the door. "Nice work, Raffi," said Michael. Raffi waved his hand dismissively, and Michael knew that his praise was too little and too late.

But he didn't have long to beat his breast: the next minute, Tuvia Shai was again sitting opposite him. Again Michael had the distinct impression that the man was not afraid, that he was uninterested in what was happening around him, that his spirit was elsewhere. He made no complaint about the repeated interrogations. Michael showed him the cassette. Shai looked at it and said nothing. The expression on his face did not change as Michael inserted the cassette into the tape player. But he shuddered abruptly at the sound of the heavy, croaking voice that erupted when Michael pressed the button, and then he immediately resumed his former expression.

"You know it," Michael stated.

Tuvia Shai shrugged his shoulders. "I know all Tirosh's poems. Every word of them."

"That's not what I mean," said Michael, and waited.

The man opposite him made no attempt to break the silence.

"I mean that particular voice. You know it; you've heard it before."

Shai did not reply.

"The fact is," said Michael Ohayon, "that your fingerprints were found on the cassette."

The pale eyebrows rose politely, but not a word was said.

"I take it that you don't deny having touched the cassette."

"Then you take it incorrectly," replied Shai. "How do I know whether I touched it or not? Who am I, as opposed to a fingerprint?"

"Your wife maintains that she saw the cassette in your briefcase on Thursday morning," said Michael as if he had not heard the protest.

Tuvia Shai shrugged his shoulders.

"Not to mention the fact that you told me explicitly that you met Iddo Dudai for the last time at the department meeting."

Shai nodded.

"But you didn't tell me about the meeting you had with him after the departmental seminar, at your house. When Dudai explained the meaning of his strange behavior at the seminar."

Tuvia Shai kept quiet.

"A very noble decision on your part—to keep quiet. You don't demean yourself by actually lying. But I'm afraid, Dr. Shai, that it's a decision you aren't at liberty to make. Your alibi is very weak."

Shai suddenly opened his mouth and said heatedly: "If I'd murdered him, I would have taken care to provide myself with a more sophisticated alibi. I'm sorry I didn't know that I should have noticed people and been noticed by them."

Michael ignored the sarcasm. He inclined his head, lit a cigarette, and looked at a face that was becoming more and more familiar to him.

"So what did you talk about with Iddo Dudai after the seminar?"

"About personal matters," replied Tuvia Shai, and his lips pursed in an expression of childish obstinacy, which made his face look grotesque. For a moment Michael could see the child he had once been, an unattractive, old-looking child.

"I'm afraid you'll have to be more specific," he said, hearing the faint sarcasm in his own voice.

"Why? It's not relevant to the murder," protested Shai, and his voice broke as he said angrily: "And please don't tell me that you'll decide what's relevant to the murder and what isn't."

Michael nodded and looked into the small eyes of nondescript color.

"He asked my advice about whether to continue his studies," said Shai at last. The words seemed to escape his lips against his will.

Every attempt to clarify the meaning of this sentence ran up against a blank wall. Shai refused to elaborate. He repeated: "Iddo didn't give reasons; he just said he was undergoing a professional crisis."

Michael returned to the fingerprints and to the elderly hoarse voice with the Russian accent, but Tuvia had nothing to add. He didn't remember having touched the cassette. He had never heard the voice before. He didn't know the cassette belonged to Iddo.

No, Iddo had not spoken to him about Tirosh. Not one word. Neither about the man nor about his poetry.

Michael returned to the question of the alibi.

"I've already told you dozens of times. I don't understand—Shulamith Zellermaier doesn't have any witnesses either; neither has Ruth Dudai or some of the others. Normal human beings don't worry about exactly what time it is every minute of the day, or who saw them where. They don't spend their time looking for witnesses."

"How do you know about Dr. Zellermaier?" asked Michael, and for the first time he saw a look of embarrassment on the man's face. Tuvia Shai shrugged his shoulders, a gesture that was rapidly driving Michael out of his mind.

"Her name is the first one that occurred to me. We happened to be talking about alibis in the office, and she said that her father had been sleeping, so who would vouch for the fact that she was at home? She laughed, but Dita Fuchs didn't laugh, and I saw the panic on poor Kalitzky's face and Aharonovitz trying to remember exactly when he finished his shopping. In short," he said angrily, "you've stirred up all of us to such an extent that people are scrutinizing their actions through a microscope without having done anything wrong."

The black telephone rang. Michael picked up the receiver, listened to Tzilla at the other end, and finally said: "Please tell her that I'm leaving now."

He stood up and said to Tuvia Shai, who bowed his head: "I'd like you to come with me now, to go over the route you took on Friday, the way you say you often walk home on Friday afternoons after the Cinematheque."

Shai rose to his feet and, with surprising docility, preceded Michael to the door and was escorted into another office to wait.

"We'll begin at the university, in Tirosh's office. I have to have a few words with Mrs. Lipkin, anyway," said Michael as he started the Ford's engine.

It was already after two. Adina Lipkin, Michael knew, would wait for him even if he arrived after working hours, but nevertheless he found himself exceeding the speed limit in the Wadi Joz area.

And waiting she was, her hand on her cheek. She said nothing about the dental treatment, but her expression conveyed suffering and self-sacrifice without end.

"The key to Professor Klein's mailbox?" she asked, flustered, and removed her hand from her cheek. "I don't understand; he's back in the country."

"And what happened when somebody asked for it when he was abroad?" asked Michael.

"Ah," said Adina Lipkin, "that's another matter. I took his mail out myself, every single day."

Michael could see the ritual in his imagination. As if she had read his thoughts, she said: "At one o'clock, after making myself a cup of coffee—I would be exhausted from the consulting hour—I would empty his mailbox and sort out his mail, without opening it, of course; I only opened official, university mail. Once every two weeks I would send him his letters. That's what we had agreed." She looked at him as if to say: That's all for today. The interview's over.

But Michael persisted: "You're sure it was only you? Nobody else opened his mailbox?"

"If they did," she said carefully, "they would have had to get the key from me."

"And if you weren't here?" asked Michael.

"That could never happen. Even if I have a fever I come to work. I can't leave everything to take care of itself." Adina Lipkin looked aghast at the very possibility. But then she raised her hand to her cheek again. "There were a few times when I was absent from work, when I had to go to the dentist—he only sees people in the morning. But then I simply didn't empty the mailbox. I let it wait till the next day."

"Where did you keep it?"

"The key? Here, next to the master, in the first drawer, because in the second drawer—"

"In other words, anyone could have taken it out?" Michael interrupted, and saw her vacillating between the obligation to answer him and the pressing need to finish her sentence. Finally she nodded her head: everyone knew where the key was kept.

"And Racheli?" asked Michael patiently.

"Racheli knows the procedures," replied Adina Lipkin, like someone who had tamed a pet animal. "She herself never opened the mailbox."

And with perfect timing the door opened and Raffi said: "She's here."

Michael glanced outside and looked at the little figure in the summer dress and plaited sandals, her eyes big and liquid, a bundle of papers under her arm. Then he went out into the narrow corridor to join her. Raffi Alfandari walked inside and shut the door. Michael and Racheli stood at the juncture of two corridors. Michael peered around the corner. Nobody was there. Racheli leaned against the wall, her face pale.

"I want to ask you something," whispered Michael.

She waited in suspense.

"About the key to Professor Klein's mailbox," Michael continued in a whisper, and looked around him. There was still nobody to be seen.

She bent down, quickly set the papers she was holding on the marble floor, and straightened up and again leaned against the wall.

"What about it?" she whispered. She raised her head in order to look into his eyes; he had to lower his eyes in order to meet hers.

"Did you ever happen to have to take his mail out?"

She was silent for a few seconds, and then she nodded her head, saying, "Yes, of course. There were a few times when Adina wasn't there and I took his mail out myself." She peered around her apprehensively. "Although Adina didn't tell me to."

"Now try to remember if he received a parcel recently—a notice from the post office requesting him to pick up a parcel," said Michael.

Again she was silent for a few seconds, and then she said: "I don't remember, because after I emptied his mailbox I put the mail on Adina's desk. I didn't really look at it."

Michael remembered the bench around the corner, in the "square," and smiled to himself as he said: "Let's go and sit down for a minute." She picked up the bundle of papers and followed him obediently to the bench, where she flopped down as if her strength had suddenly deserted her. He sat beside her.

"Think hard for a minute, try to concentrate. Did you ever give the key to anyone else?"

He heard the pleading tone of his voice and noticed her regarding him with surprise. Then she blushed and said in a clear voice: "That's actually not so hard to remember. About two weeks ago—no, three weeks; I can check—Professor Tirosh asked me for the key, twice, one day after the next, because he'd written an article in collaboration with Professor Klein and he wanted to see if it had arrived. He came in the middle of the consulting hour. I was too embarrassed to ask him to wait; he's the head of the department after all—I mean, was."

"And did you see the article? Did he find what he was looking for?"

Racheli shrugged her shoulders. "I don't know," she said. "He didn't say anything to me. He returned the key, but it didn't look to me as if he'd found anything there."

"How long did it take from when he took the key until he brought it back?" asked Michael, and he felt his back stiffening so that it became hard for him to breathe.

"That's it: I forgot to ask for it back—there was a lot going on in the office—and he only brought it back the next day. I remember because I phoned him; I was afraid Adina would see that the key was missing," said Racheli in embarrassment. "I know I shouldn't have given it to him, but I couldn't refuse him, could I?"

"When did this happen, exactly? Is there any way you can check?"

"I don't remember the day, but Adina was at the dentist two days in a row; it was when she had her bridge made. She wasn't here for two days, so it won't be difficult to find out," said Racheli, and looked at him. They were sitting very close to each other. She gave off a sweet smell. She's so young, thought Michael, her face is so innocent and her eyes so full of yearning. It's a pity she's so young, he thought; how sweet she smells. He stood up with a sigh. Racheli remained seated on the bench.

They drove to the Cinematheque, and Michael parked the car. Again Tuvia Shai stated that he had left there at about half past four. They began walking down the path from the Cinematheque toward the Jaffa Gate.

"How long does it usually take you?" asked Michael.

"It depends," said Tuvia Shai. Michael stopped and looked at him skeptically. "Sometimes one hour, sometimes two. Depending on whether I stop or not."

"Is there a regular place where you stop?" asked Michael.

Shai replied slowly: "There are a few places. You want to see where I was on Friday?"

They walked in silence. Only once did they exchange a few sentences. "Did you know that he was working on *Shira?*" asked Michael, stressing the first syllable of the word.

"*Shira?* You mean the novel by Agnon?" Tuvia Shai stopped and looked at him.

"That's how we understand it."

"Not as far as I knew," said Shai disbelievingly.

"So how do you explain the note we found on his desk?"

Shai did not reply. He looked at Michael with interest and went on walking. After a few minutes he suddenly said: "In any case, he never wrote anything about Agnon. And who told you that he was referring to Agnon's *Shira?*"

"Aharonovitz told us," said Michael, stealing a glance at Shai's face. For a moment Tuvia Shai slowed down, as if he were about to stop entirely, and then he quickened his pace again.

"Aharonovitz gets ideas into his head!" Shai muttered. "Well, maybe he's right, but I for one knew nothing about it."

"And suppose it's true; what do you think he could have meant?"

"I don't know," said Shai hesitantly, and Michael caught his quick sidelong look. "I don't understand it myself. But that doesn't mean that Aharonovitz is wrong."

"I hear," said Michael when they were close to the main road of Ramat Eshkol, "that a memorial evening is being planned for both Tirosh and Dudai next month."

Tuvia Shai nodded.

"Are you organizing it?"

"No; apparently Klein's doing it."

"But presumably you'll speak, no?"

Shai shrugged his shoulders. "Probably, among others," he said without looking at Michael.

At half past four, after an hour of rapid walking, they were on Ammunition Hill. Here Tuvia Shai stopped. They had made a detour around René Cassin High School, and now Shai pointed to one of the mounds of dry earth: "I sat here for a long time."

"How long?" asked Michael, lighting a cigarette.

"I don't know exactly. Perhaps until it grew dark."

"We set out from the Cinematheque at half past three, and we arrived here at half past four, an hour's walk. You left the Cinematheque at about half past four? You arrived here at half past five, let's say. It's summer now. It gets dark late. Are you trying to tell me that you sat here three, four hours?" asked Michael with patent disbelief.

Tuvia Shai nodded.

"What did you do here all that time?" asked Michael curiously, as if the question were of purely academic interest.

"I thought. I needed to be alone."

"Alone?" repeated Michael.

Shai was silent.

"What did you think about?"

Tuvia Shai looked at him angrily, as if he was intruding on his privacy with a question no one had the right to ask. Then he appeared to be deliberating. He smiled, a private smile. "Look how beautiful the city is from here," he said in his colorless voice. "You stand here on the hill and see the street emptying. The light fades. The noise dies down. It's beautiful."

Michael Ohayon regarded him in silence. "Tuvia isn't moved by the beauty of nature," he remembered Klein saying.

He asked Tuvia Shai where he wanted to go from here.

"Back to the university," he replied. His shoulders slumped, as if to say: It makes no difference to me.

"The picture is as follows," said Michael, beginning to conclude the team meeting as Ariyeh Levy smoothed his hair disapprovingly and wiped the sweat from his forehead. "There are still a few details we have to wind up, like the signature for the parcel, which we've given to a handwriting expert, because the people at the post office don't remember who signed, and a couple of other things. But the main conclusion we can say we've come to is: Tirosh murdered Iddo Dudai. The motives for the murder of Dudai and of Tirosh himself are related to whatever was said here"—he indicated the empty cassette—"and the ordering of the gas cylinders puts the lid on it. All that's missing is the motive itself, but we've got a lead on that too, even if it's not a clear one."

"What's not clear?" said Arieyh Levy with contempt. "You said yourself that Dudai had something on Tirosh."

"Yes, but what was that something?" said Balilty.

"So how do you see it?" asked Eli Bahar, his face tense. "You think he really went into the basement and fixed the tanks? And if he hadn't been murdered, how was he going to get away with it? What was he thinking of? What was so clever about it?"

"There are some things it's impossible to explain," said Michael. "I can't tell you what he was thinking, but he must have been sure his plan was the height of cleverness. Every murderer thinks so."

"No," insisted Eli, "I mean something else: If he'd asked them to send the cylinders to the main post office, not to the university, and given some fictitious name, there would have been less chance of getting caught. Why did he need all that business with the university post office and Klein's mailbox—that's what I don't understand. It's as if he wanted us to find out."

Nobody said anything for a minute. "Maybe he was trying to

incriminate Klein," remarked Avidan at last, turning his eyes to Ariyeh Levy.

Levy sighed and looked at Michael, who paused for a few seconds before remarking: "I don't know what he would have said if he had lived, but Columbia University in New York says that Klein was teaching there until the last minute and he never missed a day's work, so at least we can be confident that he didn't kill Dudai."

"Not by himself, at any rate. Maybe he had a partner, maybe Klein and Tirosh together. . . ," began Balilty, but nobody took any notice of him.

"There's no chance of finding the empty cylinders, I suppose?" asked Tzilla.

Alfandari shook his head. "After three weeks? Have a heart," he said in a gloomy voice, and Michael looked at him. "Not that we didn't check the garbage bins, and the municipal dump too, but it was hopeless from the start," continued Alfandari. "We looked everywhere—inside his house, in the toolshed in the yard, at the university, everywhere. Zero."

"Maybe Klein and Tirosh did do it together," repeated Balilty, and laughed. "Maybe Dudai had something on both of them."

"That's enough speculation," said Ariyeh Levy sullenly. "Let's hope we'll have more to go on after Ohayon comes back. There are a lot of unanswered questions. We still don't know who killed Tirosh— that's something else the head of the SIT hasn't explained yet—but everyone works at his own pace. . . ."

"We have to talk to the Cinematheque people again, to double check Tuvia Shai's alibi," said Eli Bahar. "I'll go there again today; I want to talk to the projectionist. He's been on army reserve duty all week, and I still haven't managed to get hold of him. I don't know any of the types who go there—and on Friday afternoon too."

"All kinds of culture freaks go there; it's a left-wing hangout," muttered Ariyeh Levy.

"We can't very well advertise in the paper that we want to talk to people who were there," said Tzilla, giving Eli an encouraging look.

Very hesitantly, Michael said: "From what Klein said, it seems that the poems are connected to the murder."

"The poems!" shouted Ariyeh Levy, and stood up abruptly. "Maybe it really is time you took a break and got your head sorted out. I ask you—the poems!"

Nobody reacted, but a rare expression of concentrated thought appeared on Balilty's face.

When Michael returned to his office after the team meeting, Eli Bahar was waiting. He had with him a thick brown envelope and a green plastic wallet. "The flight leaves at eight in the morning, and they're seven hours behind us. So you'll get there in the morning and save a day. Here's the ticket"—he handed him the plastic wallet—"and your passport's ready. Shatz will be waiting for you at Kennedy Airport. Don't forget your passport," and he removed it from the brown envelope. "There's money here too, and they told me to remind you to bring back receipts for all your expenses and not to forget to confirm your return flight, in exactly one week. Why are you laughing?"

"Maybe it's the heat and the exhaustion, but you're talking to me like a mother hen. You've become just like your wife, in no time at all."

Eli Bahar protested in embarrassment: "I lived in New York for two years and you've never been there, and believe me, you're in for a shock, landing at JFK. But I didn't mean to. . . ."

"No, actually I think it's nice," Michael reassured him, "but I suppose I haven't really taken it in yet, the fact that I'm taking off tomorrow and Yuval's still on that hike. He's coming back tomorrow. If you don't mind, maybe you could get in touch with him and tell him about the trip, and also that I'll call him from there."

"No problem," Eli replied. "We'll look after him. Anything else?"

"Keep at them while I'm away; keep at Klein too. And don't get sloppy about the SIT meetings, and see that Tzilla types up the surveillance reports at the end of every day, so I can see them when I get back. And if anything comes up, call me. And tell Tzilla to get Racheli, the secretary, to sign a statement. And ask Klein again, just to be on the safe side, if he ordered the gas, if he knows anything about it. Try to rattle him a bit."

"No problem," said Eli Bahar when he had finished writing everything down with the childlike seriousness so familiar to Michael, in the handwriting that always touched his heart.

"You should try to get some sleep before the flight. It's already ten o'clock, and you have to be at the airport at six in the morning; you haven't got too many hours left. And if you wait for an answer from Forensics about the signature at the post office, you won't have time to sleep," said Eli in embarrassment, and he blinked his eyes as if in anticipation of a rebuke.

In fact, Michael wouldn't sleep that night. The handwriting expert had explained in detail that the vague scribble before them could have been forged by Tirosh. He had pointed to the letter *K* and said: "I don't think Klein would have written it like that, even to disguise his handwriting. It's impossible. He's left-handed in the first place, and his handwriting possesses certain special features. On the other hand, though I wouldn't be prepared to swear to it in court, it could very well be Tirosh's writing."

Eli Bahar drove Michael home and, despite his protests, insisted on returning to take him to the airport in the morning.

At 2:00 A.M., after packing a small suitcase and realizing that sleep was out of the question, Michael spread out minutes of all the Literature Department meetings of the past year on the kitchen table. At five in the morning, Eli Bahar found him shaved and ready. His eyes were red, but he had a new understanding of the relations among the department faculty members. He had noted nuances and undercurrents that hitherto escaped him, and reflectively, he summed up his conclusions to Eli Bahar on the way from Jerusalem to Ben-Gurion Airport. Eli listened in silence.

"Very interesting things, minutes. And it's interesting, too, how after you know the people and understand what they're talking about, you can imagine the whole situation, picture the individual attitudes. You can learn a tremendous amount from them. For instance, you read a discussion that's ostensibly about whether the students should be examined at the end of the year in a course called Basic Concepts or whether the exercises they've handed in during the year are enough to evaluate them. I read the minutes of an entire meeting devoted to this subject. And what I learned from them, for example, was Tirosh's dominance, his habit of insulting the other speakers. Or the tension between Zellermaier and Dita Fuchs. Dita Fuchs says something, and Zellermaier always contradicts her sharply. And Kalitzky invariably chimes in to defend Fuchs with grotesque chivalry. The weirdest things." Eli concentrated on driving. Michael looked at him and reflected on the delicacy of his profile, the slight, classical curve of his nose, the long lashes, things he had scarcely noticed before.

"You understand," said Michael as they got out of the car near the glass doors of the airport, "Tuvia Shai supported every proposal Tirosh made this year, even the provocative ones. But at the last meeting he didn't say a word, according to the minutes, not one single word, and on the vote they took about changing the structure of the department and holding some workshop, he abstained."

Eli Bahar did not react.

"You don't understand," said Michael, taking hold of his arm. "What I'm trying to say is that Tuvia Shai's behaving as if the world doesn't exist, has nothing to do with mourning for Tirosh. There isn't a single department meeting where he doesn't appear in the meeting's minutes at least once, and always in support of Tirosh. In the last meeting's minutes he's mentioned as being present, but not as saying anything, not one word. And that meeting took place before anyone was murdered. Tsippi Lev-Ari took the minutes, and I checked with the other minutes she recorded, and although she looks sloppy, her minutes seem to be full and accurate."

A twinkle appeared in Eli Bahar's green eyes, and finally he said: "Maybe he had a headache at the last meeting?"

Michael fell silent. He had the feeling that they had exchanged roles during the last few hours, that Eli Bahar had stepped into his shoes and the pattern of their relationship had been turned upside down. Eli noticed Michael's reflective gaze and apologized: "It's just that I'm astonished at your indifference. A guy's flying to New York for the first time in his life, and he's got nothing to say about it?"

"Who's going to be in New York?" muttered Michael. "I'm in the middle of a case—have I got time for sightseeing in New York?"

"But still," said Eli, "but still."

The board showed a change in the departure time, the flight to New York having been advanced fifteen minutes. The terminal was hot and humid despite the air-conditioning. For the first time, Michael looked around him and took in the typical sights: three young girls with their parents, who were checking their passports every minute. An ultra-Orthodox family with a large brood of children, all of them holding on to the hem of their father's black coat, the father's face hidden by his broad-brimmed black hat; his tired-looking wife, her belly sticking out and a baby in her arms, endlessly fiddling with the luggage—the stereotype of a Mea Shearim family. Students with heavy backpacks beside them; the queue in front of the luggage check; the nervous murmurs of the people surrounding him, the shouts of the porters, and the silence on the upper floor; the smell of the fresh coffee he and Eli sat drinking silently in a corner of the big entrance hall as they watched people, carrying plastic bags from the duty-free shops, go through the security check. The repeated blare of the loudspeaker, announcing departures and arrivals.

"Actually, like a lot of people, I really like airports," declared Michael. "The smell and the noise and the feeling that you're already in another country. Every airport has a different smell, just as every country has a different smell."

"I envy you, getting out of here for a while, especially to New York. I'd give a lot to spend a week in New York now," said Eli wistfully.

"Even on a case?" asked Michael.

"Even on a case. I wouldn't care. You know how many years it's going to be before I'll be able to afford a trip abroad?"

"Nira's father, my ex-father-in-law, had an old Polish saying: 'A horse crosses the ocean and remains a horse.'"

Eli smiled. "I know you claim that all the people in the world are basically the same, but we'll see what you say after New York."

18

He woke up when the pilot announced in Hebrew and English that they were circling Kennedy Airport, awaiting permission to land.

It was impossible to see anything because of the heavy smog. Michael touched his cheek and felt the stubble, then saw the long line in front of the toilets and decided that it was too late to shave.

He thought of the bloated face and cold gray eyes of Shatz, who had been head of the Investigations and Crime Fighting Division during Michael's first years on the force. His ambition and his greed had been legendary. Even Balilty, Michael remembered, used to complain about his crudeness, his brutal attitude toward his colleagues. Shorer had called him "the corpse climber." Michael thought of Balilty's remark at the end of the last team meeting: "Don't give Shatz my regards. And take my advice, don't buy anything from him. He's got a whole sideline in electrical appliances. Anyone who meets him in New York comes back with all the latest gadgets. And be careful not to go to a nightclub with him," he said with a sardonic smile. "He might corrupt you. . . ."

The thought of Shatz pushed the dream of Maya aside. He couldn't remember the details of the dream, but the sense of oppression did not leave him for a long time after they landed. Before falling asleep in the plane, he had glanced at the young woman sitting next to him. She had fair hair, and he could smell the faint scent of Nina Ricci's *L'air du Temps*, a perfume Tzilla often used. No, she didn't look at all like Maya.

He thought about the period after his divorce. Every flight had been a romantic adventure then. Leaving the country was always connected in his mind with being with a woman, any woman, without making any fateful commitments. But ever since his last meeting with Maya, he couldn't even think of a woman without feeling oppressed. During the day, when he was working, thoughts of her nagged him like a headache, a dull, constant pain. At night, in bed, he let the thoughts overwhelm him. Then he would surrender himself to the images and return in his memory to her touch and her voice and the smell of her skin, the sound of her laugh. Again he would hear things she had said, funny things or infuriating things or words of love. He had never taken a vacation with her, he had never traveled to another country with her. In fact, he thought, when he sensed the interest of the woman sitting next to him, he had never spent more than twenty-four hours at a time with her. And she had hardly ever spent the whole night with him either. She almost always had to rush home after a few hours.

It was this trip that had brought up the missed opportunities, he explained to himself. But he was not consoled by the explanation. It did not banish the feeling of loss.

At the airport, they did not spare him the formalities. They checked his papers as if he were some illegal immigrant, although they did not bother to search his luggage. "The Americans don't cut any corners; you can't fix anything with anyone. I may know everyone in the airport, but with these bastards it doesn't mean a thing, even with my connections I can't get you through without an examination," said Shatz, sweating in his cream-colored safari suit as he led him outside. Michael did not react; he was tired and dazed.

The car was a large one, like in the movies. "An old Pontiac," said

Shatz, as he gripped the handle and opened the door for Michael. "Normally I'd take you directly to La Guardia Airport, but I want to give you at least a look at Manhattan before you disappear into the boondocks."

As they drove off, Shatz launched into an enthusiastic speech about the advantages of his fantastic job. "There's only one representative here of the whole Israeli police force, and that's yours truly. It was hard work to get here, pal, very hard work, I can tell you. Not everyone could do it. Boy oh boy, what a town!" His monologue, a startling combination of Hebrew, English, and Arabic, included remarks about their surroundings. From time to time he pointed out sights, mentioned names, indicated directions. The farther they got from the airport, the greater was the shock.

"Ninety-four percent humidity and ninety degrees in the shade—a real stinker," reported Shatz, "but believe me, pal, it's not as bad as Tel Aviv. Here everything's air-conditioned, but *everything!* Look at this car—isn't it something?"

As far as Michael was concerned, he was in hell. The hot, humid air that hit him in the face before they got into the car, the broad, multilane roads, the greenish-gray light, the distant skyscrapers, familiar to him from movies and photographs, the huge cars sliding past. He looked at the dozens of limousines racing by. There were people sitting behind those opaque windows, he thought, and marveled at Shatz's skillful maneuvering among the hundreds of speeding yellow cabs passing everything in their way.

They drove for a long time, and Michael lost his orientation. On the way, Shatz said to him: "We'll make it back to La Guardia in time. Your flight to North Carolina leaves from there, and you'll have to return to Kennedy from there too." Michael looked at the man's profile. If his face hadn't been so fat, you could have called it handsome. But the fat, and the greedy, cunning expression, and the sweat pouring off him despite the car's air-conditioning, made him repulsive.

"Not that I understand why you don't want to stay in New York for a day or two. I could have taken you to a club. You know what goes on here?" he asked in a salacious tone, and stole a look at

Michael, who was gazing out the window. "Okay, if you can't you can't. But believe me, I wouldn't tell anyone if you happened to change your mind, hey?"

"I won't," said Michael without turning his head.

"And when are you going to do your shopping? Don't buy anything at the airport; all those duty-free shops rob you blind, believe me. On Lexington there are some shops I could show you where you wouldn't know what to pick—they've got everything there. I could get you something, if you want, and save you the hassle, what do you say?"

Michael muttered something about discussing it when he came back.

"You're nervous, hey? Listen, your guy, the lawyer, he's expecting you, but the other one, the Russian, he's still touch and go, and the lawyer's at the hospital with him all the time. It wasn't easy getting hold of him, believe me."

Michael looked outside and thought of the greenish-gray that dominated the movie *Blade Runner,* the endless drizzle that had depressed him more and more as the violence and alienation of the world created on the screen became increasingly apparent to him.

"But what are you going to do about jet lag? You have to be alert for your interviews. From what I've read in the papers, you haven't made a hell of a lot of progress up to now."

"It's a difficult case," said Michael without taking offense.

"But you're the star, hey? You're the current darling over there. You'd better watch out though; stars fall fast with them. Don't take me as an example—nobody can touch me."

"Perhaps you can tell me something about this lawyer. What do you know about him?"

"Sure I can tell you a few things about him; I've got connections here. I thought you wanted to wait until we got to the airport—you've got time until your flight." Shatz stole a glance at Michael and began talking in a monotone: "Well, what's there to tell? Max Lowenthal, sixty-one years old, Jewish, born in Russia, but his parents came to America when he was a baby. Graduated from Harvard Law School but nevertheless lives in some hole called Chapel Hill, a university town in North Carolina. He teaches in the law school there, and he's also very active in the ACLU. You know what that is?" Michael confessed that he had no idea.

"It's an organization—the initials stand for American Civil Liberties Union. He's a civil rights freak, a real weirdo. He could be a rich, successful lawyer anywhere else, but he sits there in the South instead. Though he's *loaded,* believe me." Shatz noticed the incomprehension on Michael's face at the English word and explained: "Stuffed with money. He's got a big house in Chapel Hill and a summer house on an island, and what hasn't he got. And every year he goes skiing in Switzerland. He donates a lot of money to the UJA too. We've got a file on him here: he's always been active in all kinds of causes, traveled to Russia a lot and sat in the back of the buses in the South when they were reserved for blacks—you know the type. We've got them in Israel too," and Shatz sniffed contemptuously.

"And what's his connection with the Russian?"

"I don't know, exactly, but he had a lot of connections in Russia, this Lowenthal; he even wrote a book about the Russian Jews, and he smuggled all kinds of manuscripts out of there. He'll tell you himself. The Russian's name is . . ." Shatz rummaged in his memory and finally took a piece of paper out of the inner pocket of his safari jacket and glanced at it as he drove: ". . . Boris Zinger. He was in the same camp with some other Russian, a poet, the guy whatsis, the young one from the university, Dudai, was interested in. Lowenthal got him out after thirty years in some jail or camp in Russia; I've got it all written down," he said in the aggressive tone of one who suspects that his reliability as a source of information is being called into doubt. "Just a minute, I have to concentrate on the turnoff to La Guardia now," and they were both silent until Shatz parked in a huge lot. Then he hurried on ahead of Michael into the airport, examined the flight times, and said with satisfaction, wiping his face with a used tissue he took out of his pocket: "You've got over half an hour. Come on, I'll buy you a drink."

When they finally sat down on two stools at the bar, after covering vast distances inside the terminal, Michael insisted on ordering a coffee with his beer, and as he drank the tasteless liquid he looked at Shatz sipping his scotch and wondered whether he had ordered the drink to impress him or if he was really in the habit of drinking hard liquor in the morning. Shatz cleared his throat and said: "He's a wreck, that Zinger, a real wreck. He's got some problem with his heart, and Lowenthal was very uptight about him meeting you. It was only after I explained the situation, after I told him about your case, that he agreed, but on condition that it was in small doses and that he decided on the timetable. I arranged for him to meet you there. It's a hell of a long way from the airport to that town. Listen, since we're talking about it, what's your story with that cassette? Is it true you had evidence and you wiped it out?"

"No; where did you get hold of that rumor?" asked Michael, trying, he didn't know why, to disguise the hostility in his voice.

"I don't know, I heard it somewhere. I heard there were a lot of fuck-ups in the case. That you had a whole cassette and only one sentence was left. So why didn't they erase the whole thing? That's what surprises me about it: if someone erased it, why didn't they erase the whole thing?"

It was clear that he was waiting for an explanation, and against his will—afterward Michael blamed the weather and the panic aroused in him by the big city; even though he wasn't actually in it, he could feel its frenzy in all his nerve ends—against his will, he said: "It wasn't exactly evidence, but something that could have provided a new lead. It's a cassette that someone erased in broad daylight, somewhere where he apparently wasn't supposed to be. So he was in a hurry, or somebody disturbed him in the middle. It was inside a car and—"

"He erased it inside a car?" said Shatz sharply. "How? the tape decks in cars are only for listening; you can't record with them, or erase either."

Michael smiled. "If you saw the car you'd understand. An Alfa Romeo GTV—it's got a stereo system big enough for a dance hall. It can do everything."

"Is that so," said Shatz slowly, taking it in. "Who's got a car like that in Israel?"

"Shaul Tirosh had one," said Michael despite his dislike of Shatz's gossipy inquisitiveness.

"I heard that the gentleman in question left tracks leading him right to those gas cylinders," said Shatz with a sly expression on his face. He narrowed his eyes and chewed an ice cube.

"Tell me," said Michael angrily, "how did you hear everything so quickly? Who told you those things?"

"Much more easily than you think. I've got a brother; you know him."

"Me? Your brother? Where do I know your brother from?"

"Think about it for a minute. We don't look alike, me and my brother, but we're brothers anyway." Shatz laughed, and Michael felt the blood rising to his face. "Meir Shatz the historian is your brother?" he asked incredulously.

"It's a fact, whether you like it or not," said Shatz, roaring with laughter. "And we're close too; he brought me up. We were orphaned at an early age, and he was like a father to me. Are you shocked?" he asked with open enjoyment. And then he added: "That's why you've got standing with me, because of what my brother told me about you. You don't have to be so shocked. He's the intellectual of the family, but I have my role too. I take care of the practical side. You think he would own an apartment today without me?"

"None of that explains how you came by all that information so quickly," said Michael.

"My brother's got a friend—you know him too: Klein, Ariyeh Klein—and he told him a few things. I talk to my brother on the phone almost every other day. With my job, I'm telling you, I've got God by the balls." He ordered another scotch.

"Still," continued Shatz, "When you think about it, there are a couple of things that don't add up. A guy fills diving tanks with CO, and he doesn't take the trouble to cover up his tracks, he trips himself up like that? Orders the gas in Klein's name? Scribbles some signature? What's it all about?"

"Yes"—Michael sighed—"it doesn't make too much sense. What other options did he have, though? He could have broken into a lab, but that would have been even riskier."

Shatz looked at his glass and rattled the ice cubes. When he spoke, his voice was more serious and deliberate, as if he had lost the wish to impress. "I think it was something else," he said slowly.

"Like what?" asked Michael, glancing at his watch.

"I think," said Shatz, "that he was sick and tired, that he wanted to be exposed. I think Tirosh was a burnt-out case."

Michael said nothing. He thought of Graham Greene's novel about the leper colony, and about the last chapter of Agnon's *Shira*. He thought of corruption and decay and of Manfred Herbst following the nurse Shira, whose name meant poetry, into the leper hospital, forevermore. And he looked at Shatz with new respect and thought that again he had made a mistake in judgment. After a long silence, he asked: "You mean he wanted to get caught?"

"Frankly, I wouldn't put it exactly like that, but that's the general direction, more or less. I wouldn't mention it at the SIT meeting if I was you, though," he warned.

"Actually, what you say is very interesting. But it doesn't fit in too well with his personality. What made you think of it?" asked Michael curiously.

"I'll tell you the truth," said Shatz, leaning forward. Michael looked at the sweaty hands holding the empty glass, at the manicured nails. "The will made me think of it. It's quite a strange will, isn't it? As if the guy was putting things in order before making his exit, right?" Shatz didn't wait for a reply and, almost in the same breath, went on to say: "I want to ask you something else. Dudai—have you got the exact time when he arrived in Eilat?"

"Really," protested Michael, "what do you take us for? I've got a signed statement that he arrived in Eilat at four o'clock. He left the department faculty meeting at half past eleven. In his own car. The director of the diving club spoke to him at quarter past four. Even if he flew—and we checked that he didn't—I don't think he would have had the time to deal with Tirosh and get there by four."

"Pity," said Shatz. "I had a theory."

Michael looked at him and thought again of the man's image in the police force, of the impression he himself had had of him until the last few minutes. He felt guilty and ashamed of having snubbed him from the first minute. Now he wanted to take it back, to somehow express his approval, but Shatz looked into the mirror opposite them and said in his old voice: "Well, buddy, your flight's leaving soon. We'd better get moving." He glanced at the check and left some bills on the table with a practiced, confident gesture, then led Michael to the departure gate for his flight. "I hope you're not shocked when you hear the way they speak down South. I don't know what your English is like, pal, but it's hard even for me to understand them, and I've been here for three years." He laughed. "Call me from there if you like, if you need anything. Maybe you'll change your mind and we'll go out and have a bit of fun together on your way back."

19

There were three of them. Jews, of course. We're talking about 1950. One of them had emigrated with his parents to Palestine, to Eretz Israel, in the mid-thirties, when he was still a small boy. His mother became very homesick for Russia, and when she saw that there was no hope of realizing the ideals she had dreamed of, she took her son and returned to the Soviet Union. We're talking now about the period just after World War Two but before the establishment of the state of Israel. Anyway, she chose to return to Russia. The victorious Red Army attracted her, Stalin attracted her; God knows, today we're a little wiser, so it's hard for us to understand what attracted her." Laughter. "By then her young son was sixteen years old. There were a handful of similar cases, of Jews who emigrated back to Russia from Palestine, each of them a story of its own. Almost all of them regretted it. So this woman took her son back with her to the Soviet Union, and they lived for a couple of years in Moscow. And when Anatoly Ferber was eighteen, he decided to cross the border with two friends his age and go back to Israel. It wasn't the most legal thing in the world, as you know." A deep breath. "There were the three of them. Ferber, whom you're so interested in—he's probably the hero of your story—had of course grown up in Tel Aviv, had a Hebrew education—his longing to go back is easily explained. But it doesn't explain his influence on Boris. Our friend Boris is the hero of *my* story: thirty years in Soviet jails and under house arrest and it's a wonder he came out of alive, not to mention the state of his heart, his diabetes, kidneys, and God knows what else.

"Boris was the second. They reached Batumi, a Russian port on the shore of the Black Sea, seven kilometers from Turkey. And there they were caught. Boris claims that they were caught because the third member of the group informed on them. A guy called Duchin. At night, when Boris was burning with fever, when he was staying here, so many years later, with me, he would always talk about Duchin. But he didn't even try to track him down when they let him out of jail. Go and understand human beings.

"They were together for seven years, your Anatoly and my Boris: three years in the Lubyanka in Moscow, two years in the Perm prison in Mordovia, and then in Magadan, in northeast Siberia, a labor camp, what they call in Russian *katorga*. They were there for two years. There people have to toe the line and work like dogs. I can't begin to describe the suffering to you, because it's indescribable. Maybe you've read Solzhenitsyn's *One Day in the Life of Ivan Denisovich* and *The Gulag Archipelago*. That book actually describes Magadan, but maybe these details aren't important to you at the moment. In any case, it was there in Magadan that Anatoly Ferber died. What did he die of? Pneumonia. Believe me, dying of pneumonia was no problem, with the hunger and the work and the miserable excuse for medical treatment they had there. Antibiotics already existed in the world. But not there. That's one of the things I've been fighting for all these years, not only to let them go but also to let them live. It wouldn't be correct to say that Anatoly Ferber was a real dissident. All he wanted was to return to Israel. But in the labor camp he apparently became a dissident, because they sentenced them to five years at the beginning and then to another five—it was during those years that Ferber died—

under Article 58-10: Anti-Soviet Agitation, a very common charge. Anyone can decide what constitutes anti-Soviet agitation. That's the story. Later on my Boris was transferred to the Butyrki prison in Moscow, and he was there for another five years, and after that he was in the Lubyanka again. And another four years in Lefortovo prison, also in Moscow. From then on, he lived in a town near Moscow, under house arrest because he had become a hero and mentor of the younger dissidents. It was only recently that I finally succeeded in getting him out of the country. Don't ask me how, but I brought him here, to my house, and he's been under medical supervison ever since. He wants to go to Israel, of course, but in his condition I doubt if he'll make it. His English is very poor, but we speak Yiddish and a bit of Russian, and with the young fellow who was here three weeks ago, the one you said died in a diving accident, he spoke all night in Hebrew."

Michael sat in his hotel room, translating into Hebrew the words of the lawyer coming out of the tape recorder. Now he stopped writing and listened to his own voice describing the circumstances of Iddo Dudai's murder. The American lawyer, Max Lowenthal, uttered exclamations of shock and horror. The word "devastating" occurred several times, and Michael opened his English-Hebrew dictionary to look it up.

He sat at a desk in a large, comfortable room painted white and brown in the Carolina Inn, a colonial-style building close to the campus and the hospital in the university town of Chapel Hill. They had brought him there after Max Lowenthal and the ill Boris Zinger had signed preliminary statements in the presence of two policemen, produced for the occasion by Lowenthal. Once Michael had stressed the importance of Boris's statement as evidence, the lawyer had no need of any further explanations—although he did express some doubt as to the admissibility of this evidence in court, since the local policemen could not understand a word that was said. They might be capable of understanding the words of his own statement, Lowenthal had said, laughing, but he doubted very much if they would be able to comprehend Zinger's biblical Hebrew. The tape came to an end, and Michael

Ohayon peered out of the big window, which overlooked the street. The town was utterly tranquil. In New York, Shatz had complained, you heard the noise and the traffic all night long, even on the twelfth floor, but here all that was audible was the chirping of the crickets. The air-conditioning was on in the room. Michael opened the window and breathed in the heavy, moist air saturated with the sweet smell of magnolia blossoms. The whole place looked like an immense forest, giving way here and there to occasional buildings and narrow streets. He couldn't fall asleep. When he returned home, he decided, he would see a doctor about his insomnia. Then he sat down and listened yet again to the tapes he had recorded during the day. At the hospital, Lowenthal had repeated his warning before allowing him to go into Zinger's room, exhorting him not to ask about conditions in the prisons where he had been incarcerated, to be as gentle and tactful as possible. The Jewish community in the nearby city of Charlotte was paying the bill for Boris's hospitalization, explained Lowenthal, which made the private room and all the necessary treatments possible. The man was completely broken inside. He was only fifty-five, Lowenthal said with a sigh, but he looked like a ruin, though better than he did when he first arrived.

His condition was so sensitive, said Lowenthal, that any excitement put him at risk. In fact, it was after the conversation with Iddo Dudai that he had been rushed to the hospital. During that interview he had been obliged to return in his imagination to all the terrible events that even he, Lowenthal, had not dared to ask him about.

Michael turned the cassette over and went on listening to Lowenthal's lively voice. He remembered the long, narrow face, with its small lips. A pampered mouth, he thought when he first saw him, until the American naïveté that had made all that wide-ranging work possible filled him with awe. Lowenthal told him about his activities without either boastfulness or modesty, speaking matter-of-factly, like someone explaining how he had come upon some information. After all, he had written a book on the subject, he asserted. Soviet Jewry was the issue closest to his heart, he said passionately, bursting with youthful energy. Back home, thought Michael, such intensity existed only among the right-wing religious fanatics of Gush Emunim and the handful of Trotskyists in the group they called Avant-garde.

Now this side of the tape came to an end, and Michael prepared to listen for the second time to the recording of his conversation with Boris Zinger. First the tape player emitted a creaking sound—Lowenthal sitting down on the hospital bed, like a son next to his father—and then Michael heard Lowenthal addressing Boris in fluent Yiddish, mixed with some words in English. *"Vos?"* the emaciated man lying on the big bed said. "What?" It was the only word of Yiddish Michael understood. The bedside table had held vases of flowers, candies, a Yiddish newspaper, and a Hebrew Bible. A television set hung from the ceiling.

"I'll tell him that you're another literary scholar. That there's a revival of interest in Ferber's poetry. It'll make him happy. Not a word about murder and trials." Then Lowenthal had allowed him at last to enter the room.

The body lying on the bed was ruined, as the lawyer had said. But the eyes! Like those of the prophets I imagined when I was a child, thought Michael as he looked into the deep brown eyes, full of ardent feeling and wisdom. Lowenthal plumped the pillows, and the man raised himself to a sitting position and leaned against them. A mane of white hair surrounded his shriveled face, which was an unhealthy pink color, and his smile was warm and full of life.

Now his voice came over the tape recorder, and Michael thought again, as he had in the hospital, that on his way back, too, he would not linger in New York but would hurry straight home.

"Anatoly," said Boris Zinger in a voice full of longing and supplication, and he began to quote lines from "Requiem in a Black Square," except that he said "Red Square," and Michael suddenly realized that he knew exactly how Iddo Dudai had felt on that night when he returned to Klein's house from North Carolina. It was shocking to think of Tirosh changing words that might have betrayed the source of the poems. Now Boris Zinger spoke, sometimes in Yiddish, which Lowenthal would translate without being asked, but for the most part in fluent Hebrew.

In a low voice, which now sounded to him strangely stilted, Michael asked his first question, about Boris's Hebrew. Anatoly, explained Boris, spoke perfect Hebrew, and it was he who had taught the language to him. For whole days at a time he taught him, and in the camp, he, Boris, had learned Anatoly's lines by heart, "so that if anything happened, God forbid, if Anatoly didn't live," he would be able to preserve them. The prison authorities didn't know anything about the Hebrew, "they weren't interested in poetry there." The hotel room filled with peals of childlike laughter, which seemed totally inappropriate to the figure Michael remembered, to the face with its sunken eyes. For a moment he had asked himself if the man was sane. "So how did it work?" asked Michael. "Did Anatoly write the poems down, or did he just remember them?"

"Both," said Boris. "He wrote them on pieces of newspaper, and he remembered them. But there is no point in explaining how people write in *katorga*. There are ways. All kinds of ways and systems."

The tape player was silent for a few seconds, and then Boris went on speaking, in a lower, less enthusiastic tone. There were camps, said Boris, where it was possible to obtain paper; you only had to know where to hide it. There was a boy with them in Perm who had learned Pushkin by heart and who spent his days and nights writing down his works. But in any case, it was impossible to rely on the written word; you had to learn everything by heart.

"Where did you hide the manuscripts?" Michael heard himself asking in his Israeli accent, which sounded strange next to the Yiddish with an American accent that Lowenthal interjected from time to time and to Boris Zinger's Hebrew with its heavy Russian accent.

"There are places," and Zinger had looked at Michael fearfully.

But Michael insisted, gently. He even drew his chair closer to the sick man's bed and repeated the lie he had agreed on with Lowenthal: the Institute for Contemporary Judaism wanted to document everything, they wanted a picture of Boris too. And slowly, as if he was still afraid, Boris elaborated.

There were all kinds of places to hide writing. Inside the hollow iron legs of the beds, where no one looked. And in the place where they worked chopping down trees, they hid it there too, in the cracks in the walls of the cabin. But that wasn't important—the hoarse voice rose—it wasn't important. He, Boris, knew all the poems by heart, anyway. He was Anatoly's secretary, and again laughter. And then the coughing. So on their way to work, and at night after the day's work was over, especially when it was impossible to get warm, and it was almost always impossible to get warm, Anatoly would begin to recite the lines, and he, Boris, would repeat them, until he had them by heart. Under those conditions, said Boris—and Michael recalled the haunted expression of someone remembering and banishing the memory, but hanging on to it for a few minutes too—under those terrible conditions, they needed it.

"Needed what?" Michael listened in embarrassment to his own stupid question, the answer to which was so obvious, and he remembered Boris's forgiving smile. Max Lowenthal said: "What? What did he say?" Boris Zinger translated Michael's question, and it was Lowenthal who explained: they needed to transcend themselves, needed things that were beyond the body, outside the cold and the hunger and the daily body searches, beyond the pain. There were solitary people there, but they, he and Anatoly, had each other. Like brothers. More than brothers, they were souls that complemented each other. Anatoly created, and Boris remembered. In those days, they were at the beginning of the road, today there were dozens of people in the Soviet Union copying the manuscripts, so that everything need not depend on one person; but then . . . And again there came the sound of Boris's laughter, now mingled with sobs, and Michael, who knew the tape almost by heart now, waved his hand as if to rebuke himself for his sentimentality.

"Perhaps the muses are silent when the cannons roar," said Max Lowenthal suddenly, "but when everything has been destroyed, even without cannons, when people are crowded together in one hut, or one cell, when there's no privacy, when you go out to work in the dark and come back in the dark, when you're being watched all the time, day after day, year after year, when you discover that your main thoughts are of bread or cold or exhaustion—then your only refuge is an external reality. First there were Anatoly's poems, and then Boris had something to live for: to take care of Anatoly and to learn the poems by heart. Four hundred and thirty-seven poems. And then Anatoly died. Of pneumonia." Michael heard Lowenthal's American accent coming out of the tape player. "And that's something you won't hear about from Boris. They don't talk about things like that," he added with pathos.

The tape player emitted sobs and murmurs in Russian and Hebrew and Yiddish, "A beautiful soul . . . a great heart. . . "

Michael pressed the button. The voices were silenced, and he returned to the ordinary world.

Outside the window, the darkness was absolute. The sights and sounds of the day echoed in his mind. The Southern accent of the two policemen waiting in the hospital corridor. To his relief, he had understood every word they said. They spoke to him slowly, as if he were dull-witted as well as foreign. They didn't comment on his accent.

He remembered the amazing sight he had seen outside the big white hotel. Across the road was a girls' dormitory, "a sorority, for girl students only," explained Lowenthal, and made a face.

On the large veranda opposite the hotel entrance, ten girls had sat on wicker chairs around a circular table. They were wearing wide, dark skirts, and they had white gloves on their hands. They were sipping from delicate cups. Michael and Lowenthal stood next to the fence surrounding the round, Southern-style veranda and watched ten extended pinkies rise into the air along with raised teacups.

"In the South you can see everything," said Lowenthal dryly. "They're still living in the last century," and he described the rite of passage they underwent at the age of eighteen: the ritual of "coming out" into society. "Debutante," Michael said, recalling the word used to describe such girls.

He himself had come here from Boston, Lowenthal said proudly, and he had chosen to live in the South and work there in the civil rights movement. "That represents exactly the kind of nonsense I'm here to oppose," he said, pointing to the girls on the veranda.

A quiet, pleasant breeze blew into Michael's room, but the air was still humid. The moon above the magnolia tree pierced his heart with its beauty. All day long, Michael had felt as if he were being dragged against his will into another world. He shook himself and returned to the tape player.

"What did you do after Anatoly died?" he heard himself say in the quiet, careful voice he had adopted throughout the interview.

Boris had recited the poems over and over again, until he knew them by heart. In the last analysis, he knew that he was the only witness to the poems, the only source, and he was aware of their value, their greatness. The task of his life, his vocation, his mission, was to get them out. And when he received an additional sentence, he said, and was transferred to a camp outside Moscow, he was very worried.

For five years, said Boris, he had worked at befriending a man in the camp near Moscow—not a prisoner but a worker, an illiterate plumber. He had taught him things, given him advice on his love life, and also bribed him with every means in his power, with all kinds of goods he had received or stolen. "The man was a simple kulak," explained Boris apologetically, in his heavy Russian accent, "but there was no alternative. It takes years to get to know someone in those places. People don't trust each other. Everyone's suspect. I was afraid that I, too, would die soon. And I took my soul in my hands, as Anatoly liked to say, and gave the poems to the kulak. You know, in Russia there's no censorship of internal mail. If you're not a convict, you can send anything inside the country. I gave him the address of someone I had known as a student in Moscow, before I was arrested. A man who had recently arrived in the camp told me that he was still in Moscow, living in the same place. And so I tried, hoping that my old acquaintance would be able to pass everything on to somebody in Moscow who would be able to get it out of the country."

"All the poems at once?" Michael heard his own voice asking.

No. There were ten parcels, and the poems inside were in very small handwriting. Now there were mutters in Yiddish again. The tape player emitted Boris's cough and Lowenthal's attempts to conclude the interview at this point: Michael could finish the rest later; now they had to let Boris rest.

"Perhaps I could have just the essence now?" With a faint feeling of embarrassment, Michael heard his own voice and then Lowenthal's impatient reply: He himself, Lowenthal, had received the poems, from a Jewish student in Moscow, in 1956, when the first rumblings of the thaw were being heard. It was during his first visit there.

"In '56?" asked Michael.

"I know it sounds strange. It was very early for someone like me, who wasn't a Communist or even a member of a front organization, but my involvement with civil rights got me in."

"You weren't working for the CIA, were you?"

"I certainly wasn't. Not then or ever. But I've discovered that the most incredible things happen to those who don't know they're incredible."

From Moscow he had flown to Vienna, and there, he said with flashing eyes, he had met that talented youngster who later became an important poet in Israel. It had been at an anti-Communist conference at which both of them were student representatives. He had shown him the poems. Shaul Tirosh, said Lowenthal proudly, was the man to whom he gave the manuscripts. They sat at a café—he could even remember the taste of the strudel, but not the name of the café. Even then he had felt a need to share his experiences, explained Lowenthal, and so he had shown the poems to Tirosh. Tirosh was very excited and immediately offered to take them back to Israel with him. He told Lowenthal that he worked in the Hebrew Literature Department at the Hebrew University, that he had connections in the literary world, and he held the little pages with such love that he, Lowenthal, was sure they would be in safe hands. Tirosh translated a few lines for him, right there in the café, and even he, who didn't understand the first thing about poetry, was impressed by their power. He knew that he could trust him, Lowenthal repeated, and sure enough, Tirosh had published the poems in an annotated edition. Unfortunately he himself, as Michael knew, had no Hebrew, and so he was unable to enjoy the fruits of his endeavors to the full.

Here Michael interrupted to ask Lowenthal if he had shown Boris the book Tirosh sent him.

There was a moment's silence, and then Lowenthal said in embarrassment that he didn't know how to explain it, but the book had been lost a few years earlier. In a near whisper, he added that he had shown the book to someone who knew Hebrew and that this person had not been particularly impressed. And so, he said in the same embarrassed tone, he had not been overly concerned about losing it. He was silent for a moment and then said that the young man, Dudai, had promised to send him another copy.

At this point Michael took the book he had brought with him out of his briefcase and handed it wordlessly to Boris. Boris stroked the cover with joyful excitement and then opened the book and leafed through it. The only sound coming over the tape player was the rustle of the pages.

Michael vividly remembered the expression of confusion and dismay that spread over the sick man's face as he failed to find the familiar words, the words he had preserved all those years and known by heart as if they were his daily prayers. He repeated the words "This isn't. . . " a few times and then said: "The young man, Dudai, said it was all right, that everything was all right," and Michael thought of how Iddo must have had to restrain himself in order not to reveal anything to Boris, or even to Lowenthal.

Then Zinger's hoarse voice rose from the tape player, uttering a spate of quotations. Once more Michael heard the familiar, typical images of Tirosh's poetry, together with the famous line: "At dawn violets wilted in your skin," pronounced in the same way as on the cassette in the forensics lab in Jerusalem. A flood of quotes from "Apollo Appeared to Me by a Blasted Tree," and from the long poem "On the Last First Man": "Under the thin skin hides the warm flesh and the blood. . . " and "In the yellowing skeleton of the living man the dust sings a siren song. . . " and, afterward, "For if there is a spirit in man it is a withering wind. . . ," and then Michael heard his own voice, tensely interrupting the compulsive stream of quotations with the question: "Is that what Ferber wrote?"

And the man's outburst of rage. "What is this?" he cried several times. And then the groans of pain and the sobs.

Then Lowenthal's pampered mouth tightened sternly, and he seized Michael by the arm and dragged him out the door and into the corridor.

With a grave expression on his face, Lowenthal demanded an explanation of what had been said inside the room. Finally he asked Michael if there was a suspicion of plagiarism, and Michael nodded.

Now the tape came to an end.

In the mid-sixties, Lowenthal explained to Michael, as they sat in the elegant hotel dining room, the manuscripts began streaming out. Until then everything was sporadic, dribs and drabs. Manuscripts were smuggled out via channels that had been carefully checked in advance. They had to make sure that the source in the Soviet Union would not come to any harm and also that it wasn't a trap. Lowenthal stuck his fork into a piece of sweet potato and lifted it to his mouth. He resumed talking before he had finished chewing: "That's why the whole story is so fantastic, because in 1956 I was a total innocent. If I'd known then what I know today, I would never have smuggled Ferber's manuscripts out of Russia. Only a lunatic or an idiot would have done what I did then." He stared in front of him and shuddered, and then he continued speaking as if he were lecturing to a historical committee: Today there were ways of smuggling manuscripts, and for obvious reason he couldn't go into all of them in detail. One example, he said, wiping his mouth with the white linen napkin, was a network set up in Italy by anti-Soviet left-wing Catholic activists who belonged to a group based in Milan. One of them was a librarian in Bologna, said Lowenthal in a dreamy voice. He himself knew only this librarian, who was able to get mail in and out of the Soviet Union. Lowenthal would receive the mail in America, in a parcel sent to his home from Bologna, and he would inform them of the exact date of its arrival.

"Whom did you inform?" asked Michael.

The librarian in Bologna. Lowenthal would also inform him of the state of the manuscript, and after showing it to Russian experts, he would pass on their opinion. Once the connection had been established, many manuscripts began to arrive. "You won't believe it"—

Lowenthal laughed—"but some of the manuscripts were sent in the Vatican diplomatic pouch. The Vatican has representatives in Moscow, and they made the connection. There are other ways too; journalists, for example. They use the diplomatic mail of their countries' representatives in Moscow, sometimes even without the knowledge of the embassy people. They had an arrangement with someone at the American end, who would pass the stuff on to me. Sometimes it was a journalist, sometimes, I guess, someone from the CIA. Or someone on the Russian desk in the State Department. . . .

"There's another method too," he said with renewed energy after an interval in which he polished off the rest of his chicken. "People who traveled a lot to Russia, like a Swedish biologist I met called Perla Lindborg. She went there several times a year, and she would send me the material from Stockholm. I can tell you her name now because she's dead. And there was someone else, an Austrian physician who sent material from Vienna. It's also possible via Hong Kong, but. . ." Lowenthal looked at Michael dolefully and acknowledged that now he was trusted. They had begun to trust him after a number of Russians had given him manuscripts they had smuggled out of the Soviet Union. Lowenthal shook his finger at Michael. "There are things you may not know about," he said. "Did you know that the YMCA Press in Paris prints smuggled manuscripts by Soviet dissidents?" And without waiting for a response, he added that an anti-Soviet publisher in Frankfurt smuggled manuscripts out of Russia, published them, and deposited the royalties in a Swiss bank for the authors' accounts. In 1972, Lowenthal had flown to Frankfurt and given money to the people there. They had sent the money—royalties for smuggled manuscripts—by an unknown route to the authors in the Soviet Union. After that there were no more problems with regard to his trustworthiness. When he arrived in Russia in '73, they knew that they could reply on Max Lowenthal one hundred percent. Even Andrei Sakarov had called him up and asked to meet him. By then there were no more questions. Why was he telling Michael all this? asked Lowenthal rhetorically. "So that you'll understand what a complicated industry it is today, what a complex operation, and you'll realize how primitive I was in 1956. I was careless, unsophisticated, I didn't know anything. It was my first visit to the Soviet Union; how could I know? If I'd smuggled Ferber's manuscripts out ten years ago, fifteen years ago, it could never have happened. But then? You'll never believe it if I tell you what I did then. I took those little pages, covered closely with that tiny writing, and I felt like a master spy. The night before I left, I undid the waistband of my trousers"—here there was a demonstration: Lowenthal opened his narrow leather belt and exposed the inner lining of the waistband of his trousers—"I flattened out the papers"— he smoothed the tablecloth to illustrate his words—"crammed them in and sewed the lining up again." That was all he could think of doing then. Half the night he spent sewing, he said, chuckling, he wanted so desperately to succeed.

"Yes." Michael heard his own voice on the tape player in his hesitant high school English. "Yes, but why did they believe that they could trust you then?"

Lowenthal had studied Russian history for his B.A. He was very eager to visit the Soviet Union, and when the thaw set in in 1956, there was a big youth festival, and he went to Moscow for the first time in his life. It wasn't a good time for an American to be in Moscow, but he went anyway. Laughter. It was a peace and friendship festival—again Lowenthal uttered a shrill, nervous laugh, which was intended to be ironical—and there were students there from all over the world. In Gorky Park the Jew approached him.

You had to understand, he said heatedly, that he was completely green; he not only took insane risks but also was full of fears. You had to beware of traps, but to the same extent you had to beware of aiding and abetting reactionary groups. He wasn't out to destroy the Soviet Union; he was only interested in the issue of human rights, especially where Jews were concerned. His parents had emigrated to America from Russia; he had family there. The Jew who approached him in Gorky Park knew that he was Jewish, and he knew his family. It was this man who told him that Boris Zinger was responsible for Ferber's manuscripts, that Ferber had died in prison and that Boris was still alive. The young man worked in a publishing firm and knew Lowenthal's cousin. The same publisher brought out *One Day in the Life of Ivan Denisovich,* but this of course only happened later. When the man first came up to him in Gorky Park, he only told Lowenthal to be at a spot in Sokolniki Park the next day at five. Lowenthal fell silent, as if reconstructing the episode. The next day he received a bundle of Russian newspapers, with an envelope inside them. In the envelope were masses of poems, in dense, tiny handwriting. He still remembered the hurried, tense voice of the Russian Jew and his pale face, his frightened, darting eyes and broken English, as, for the first time, he heard the names Ferber and Zinger. Actually, when you came to think of it, that was the start of his profound involvement with the lives of Soviet Jews. It was then that he began to take an interest in the fate of Boris Zinger, began to exert pressure for his release. It took a long time, and in the meantime Boris was moved from one prison to another, but in the end Lowenthal succeeded, and they let him go. After thirty-five years, he said with a sigh, but then his eyes gleamed again: it was really tough to get anyone out of the country, yet he had finally managed it, and they had saved him at the last minute, his poor health having been a factor in his release.

Michael remembered the suspicious look that appeared in Lowenthal's eyes when he asked why they hadn't passed the poems to someone from the Israeli delegation to the festival.

"But they were under surveillance all the time," he replied impatiently, as if it was too obvious to need saying. "It would have been too dangerous."

From Moscow, Lowenthal had flown to Vienna, and there, he said, dropping his eyes, he had met Tirosh. It would never have occurred to him then, he said furiously, that someone like Tirosh . . . These days, for example, he notified people at the other end immediately of the receipt of a parcel, and they kept tabs on everything, but at that time he knew nothing. "How could I have known?" he pleaded. "I was so young too, and he looked so European, so refined and respectable. I was so glad when the book came out; how could I have known that it wasn't the right book?" Michael did not comfort him.

He would have the entire statement translated into English, said

Lowenthal before they parted, and get Boris's signature on it in front of police witnesses. If Boris survived the shock. He hoped that Michael would be able to spare Boris the shock of exposure to these painful matters, but as a man of the law, said Lowenthal with a little smile, he could not withhold his cooperation. Especially since he felt guilty, responsible. God knows, Tirosh had seemed so reliable, so serious, so charming, and Lowenthal had only been a young student. How could he have known? So who was actually the author of the poems in Ferber's book? he asked suspiciously.

Michael shrugged his shoulders and carefully, slowly spoke a sentence he had often read in English-language books: "Your guess is as good as mine." Lowenthal remained silent.

And then, in parting, he said words that echoed in Michael's mind at three o'clock in the morning in the Carolina Inn as he sat in front of the silent tape player. "There's no fate worse than that of a mediocre artist," said Lowenthal dispassionately, in a tone of melancholy philosophical wisdom.

Michael remembered the pained expression on Shaul Tirosh's face when Iddo Dudai asked the audience at the departmental seminar: "If this poem had been written here, in this country, in the fifties or sixties, would anyone of you have considered it a good poem?" and he knew now who had written the poems published in Israel under Anatoly Ferber's name.

He closed the window and thought that if he succeeded in falling asleep, he would be able to sleep for five consecutive hours before returning to the hospital.

20

They all spoke at once: "Tell him we found prints on the car," said Balilty insistently. "What do you care? What have you got to lose?" "I still don't think it was because of the poems," said Alfandari looking around in embarrassment as Tzilla trod heavily from chair to chair and set an additional sheaf of papers in front of them. Eli Bahar repeated the question "What can we do now?" and Ariyeh Levy peered again at the pile of papers in front of him and rubbed his hands on the table. Suddenly his shout silenced them: "Maybe we could hear from the head of our team? Maybe he's got some suggestions—eh, Ohayon?"

Everything was blurred: the voices on the tapes buzzed in his head, and his feet still didn't feel firm on the ground. He tried to shut himself off from the voices in the room, but they continued to penetrate the thick fog. He remained silent.

"You can say what you like, and you can go on talking until tomorrow, but there's no meat," said Ariyeh Levy in a strained voice. "As far as I'm concerned, it's just another lead. You want me to tell you how it's going to sound in court? With what you've got, we can't hold him for more than forty-eight hours—or maybe you've forgotten where you are?" Michael maintained his silence.

"What do you intend to do?" roared Ariyeh Levy. "Has the cat got your tongue—or are you afraid we won't understand what you're saying after all the time you've spent hobnobbing with poets and university professors?"

"I'm not sure how to go about it," said Michael at last. "He's not the kind of guy that if I said something to him about fingerprints and so on, that's what would break him."

Not even the C.O. spoke now. A few seconds went by, until Balilty, who could never endure a prolonged silence, asked in a measured tone: "So what *will* break him?"

"Something else," replied Michael slowly, and saw the fog in which he was enveloped spreading to the others. The excitement in the room now became a hum of suppressed suspense, the voices growing more restrained.

Eli Bahar said despairingly: "Look, I was with him for forty hours all told over the past three days. The guy's out of it. I've never seen anything like it. You saw for yourself, from the tapes; you heard it all. It's impossible to get through to him. You talk and talk and he's not there."

"There's a way to reach him," said Michael, "and I intend to take it. But don't ask me for any explanations in advance; you'll have to trust me."

"But what about his wife?" protested the C.O. "Why can't you talk to him about her? What's going on here?"

Balilty nodded vigorously and then raised his head to the ceiling and said: "In the last analysis, whichever way you look at it, that story with his wife had to get to him. With all due respect for all your theories, it's just not possible that a man—"

"Okay. Bring him in and we'll see what happens," said Michael, ignoring the critical looks of his colleagues. Ariyeh Levy expressed the general skepticism: "I want something. I want proof. I want him to break down and confess—I've had enough subtleties. Think of a court of law, not a university," he said, and left the room.

Michael looked at Shaul, who activated the recording devices. "We don't want to miss anything," warned Balilty, and Michael felt the whole wing of the building turn into one giant ear.

He switched on the tape player. Boris Zinger's hoarse, trembling, excited voice filled the room. Tuvia Shai folded his hands, but he couldn't stop them from shaking. He listened to the recording, and as the flood of words poured forth, his face paled. When Zinger's groans of pain rose from the tape and the question "What is this?" echoed in the room in the Russian Compound, Michael leaned back and examined Shai's face, which remained blank.

"You see," said Michael after a long silence, "I know the whole story."

"What story?" inquired Tuvia Shai, pursing his lips.

"As soon as I came into possession of the evidence, I asked myself about the motive. When the interview with Zinger was over, I asked myself who would be hurt most by the theft, the fraud perpetrated by Shaul Tirosh. Who would be really devastated by it, I asked myself, to the extent of an outburst of violence leading to murder? The only answer to my question was you. When I thought of how you had given up your life, and not only your own life: your wife's life too; how you had become wiped-out people. . . " Michael collected the papers strewn over his desk and arranged them in a neat pile in front of him. He waited for a reaction, but Tuvia Shai remained silent.

"I know that Iddo Dudai spoke to you and played you the tape of his interview with Zinger," said Michael. "I can imagine how you must have felt after your conversation with Iddo. When it became clear that Iddo had been murdered, you knew who was guilty. You knew very well that Iddo had spoken to Tirosh, that there had been a confrontation, but you only found out about it on Wednesday night, after the departmental seminar. Iddo was broken by it, but not you. The only people who knew about the plagiarism were you and Iddo, and this is the common factor that explains both cases, both the murder of Tirosh and the murder of Dudai. The plagiarism. When Iddo confronted him, Tirosh denied everything and said that any lunatic could say anything. Iddo turned to you and asked you to help him prove it—after all, it's not every day that the recipient of the Presidential Poet Prize is exposed as a fraud." Michael carefully examined the pile of papers in front of him. Shai looked at him and said nothing.

"Once, a few years ago," said Michael slowly, "I knew a girl who was studying philosophy."

Tuvia Shai looked at him patiently.

"This girl," Michael continued, weighing every word, "was studying Kant. She was very keen on Kant. There's no question about it, he was great, right?"

Shai looked at him in bewilderment but nodded faintly.

"I'm not telling you this because of the philosophy," said Michael, glancing around him. "I'm telling you because it's relevant to what we're talking about."

"I imagine so," said Tuvia Shai skeptically.

"This girl knocked on my door one day and told me in tears that Kant was right. She said that 'everything is transparent' and spoke about the impossibility of knowing 'things-in-themselves.' Do you understand what I'm saying?"

There was no mistake about it: a new expression flickered on Shai's face, part interest and part embarrassment. He shifted in his chair.

"Then I understood," Michael went on carefully, maintaining a friendly, undramatic tone, "that there are some people who internalize abstract subjects like philosophy, internalize them so profoundly that they come to govern their lives."

Tuvia Shai said nothing, but Michael knew that he was listening to every word.

"You know this yourself," stated Michael, "but what I couldn't decide was whether she had simply gone out of her mind or whether. . . "

"She hadn't gone out of her mind," said Tuvia Shai with an authority which he had not possessed even at the departmental seminar, in the lecture Michael had seen on the television film.

"I ask myself," said Michael, and he felt his mouth becoming dry, "if you, too, haven't gone crazy."

A faint flush appeared on the pale cheeks, and the lips began to tremble.

"You understand," said Michael Ohayon, and leaned forward, "when I think of how someone must feel who's devoted his life, his wife, his whole being, to one man, and his idol turns out to have feet of clay—I think that all he can do is go mad. Lose control over his actions."

"Nonsense," said Tuvia Shai heatedly. "You're talking nonsense."

"You understand," Michael went on as if he hadn't heard, "after I spoke to Boris Zinger I realized that a thing like this could drive a person out of his mind. Not everybody, but some people, people who take their principles seriously."

"I don't know what you're talking about." Tuvia Shai's voice shook.

"I thought: How does Boris feel? He did it for Anatoly, devoted his whole life to him, and you heard yourself what he had to say. Nobody in the world knows better than you how Boris felt, although, as distinct from you, he was deceived not by the man he loved but by somebody else, and I'm sure that you're moral enough to agree with me that this injustice, at least, has to be rectified."

Tuvia Shai raised his head. In a muffled voice and with an expression of contempt, he said: "Let's leave morality to those who have nothing else to pride themselves on."

"Your alibi's weak," and Michael looked into Shai's eyes. "And the polygraph, you know—it's hard to lie successfully in a polygraph; it works on five parameters at once, nobody can overcome them all. When you succeeded in controlling your sweat and your pulse rate, your blood pressure rose. I have to tell you that according to all the polygraph tests, you were lying. But I didn't arrest you until I had the whole story. You murdered Shaul Tirosh because he made a fool of you. Because he exposed the fact that you had devoted your life to something that was a lie."

Michael looked at the new face of the man sitting opposite him.

Gone was the lifeless expression of a faded man. There was a power in his face that Michael had never seen there before. Tuvia Shai said furiously: "Who do you think you are? You understand nothing. You don't know what you're talking about. My life isn't so important; neither is yours. And Tirosh's life wouldn't have been so important either, if I hadn't believed that he was the high priest of art. But how can I expect you to understand such things? A person who belongs to a body that hands out traffic reports and breaks up demonstrations can't understand such things."

Not for the first time that morning, Michael thought about Dostoyevsky, about Porfiry and Raskolnikov. Am I like Porfiry? he asked himself as Tuvia Shai spoke. The only thing motivating me now is getting proof that will stand up in court—and my own curiosity. But you couldn't say that I don't feel any sympathy for him; there's something about him that demands respect, he thought as he looked at the man's face and listened to his words. But I mustn't show it so openly, he warned himself. I have to get him to talk. To give him the feeling that I really don't understand but that it's in his interest to make me understand, since I already *know*.

Tuvia Shai went on talking: "I'm not interested in petty things, the private lives of people like you and me, which doesn't mean that I'm in a hurry to go to jail—why should I be? But my motives and Boris Zinger's aren't the same. I understand him, but unlike me he's bound by the rules of ordinary morality, and he was Anatoly Ferber's disciple. I was never a blind disciple. I didn't give a damn for all your rules and conventions, and Shaul Tirosh the man didn't interest me in the least. I wasn't jealous of my wife, and I didn't kill him because he left her. All that presupposes that I put him or her, or myself as the disciple of some person or some theory or other, in the center. I don't put myself in the center. You didn't even realize that I don't feel guilty. You think I'm a psychopath? I'm not. If I'd killed him for personal revenge, I would have felt guiltier. I have no pangs of conscience. I'm sure I did the right thing, even though nobody will understand what I'm talking about—I'm used to that by now. It never bothered me all those years, the image I had as Shaul's shadow. You think I didn't know what people thought? But there's something bigger than all of us. And it's true what they said to you there in the U.S., that thanks to art, human beings are able to rise above the vanities of this world. To put it simply, I gave all of myself for the real thing. I don't expect you to understand my morality; because you represent the police, the blind robot of the law, you wouldn't understand what it's all about."

"Give me a chance," said Michael quietly.

Tuvia Shai looked at him doubtfully, but the need to talk was overpowering. "Do you know why animals have no morality?" he asked passionately. "It's not that they really have no morality; they do have a certain kind of morality. Their morality consists of one supreme value: the instinct to preserve the race. Ask any geneticist—he'll tell you. Human beings, too, possess an instinct for the preservation of the race—the human race. In most people it's expressed in children, in reproduction, in rearing their offspring. But there are a few, a chosen few, who are able to devote themselves to the real thing. The real thing, the only important thing in my eyes, at the level of the preservation of the human race, is art. It doesn't matter if Tirosh was a positive or a negative person, if I loved him or I didn't love him, all that is unimportant and irrelevant. You think Nietzsche was naive? He cherished every kind of human greatness. Nietzsche, too, would have said that Tirosh was a genius and that genius is entitled to special conditions. But when it turned out that he wasn't a genius but was a mediocre creature, someone who for thirty years masqueraded as a genius by appropriating Ferber's great poems as his own and publishing his own mediocre poems as Ferber's, I had to see that justice was done. For the sake of the world, the generations to come, it was necessary to destroy the creature who desecrated the holy of holies." Michael couldn't believe what he was hearing. He fingered the tape machine to check that it was working and said calmly: "Good, that's the ancient dilemma of the conflict between art and morality."

"Yes," Tuvia Shai agreed, and he wiped his lips.

"In other words," Michael continued, "we come back to the banal question of whether a genius is exempt from the moral laws that apply to ordinary individuals—whether he can lie, cheat, use other people to his own ends, and so on."

"If Tirosh had been a real artist," said Tuvia Shai, "giving him my wife would have been a small thing. Or giving him myself, for that matter. In any case, the world would have no meaning without great art. Great art is the only thing that advances humanity, and compared to that, individual suffering doesn't count. I killed him because he didn't advance humanity but, rather, the opposite. I killed him because he brought great art into contempt. All my life I effaced myself in order to serve the highest expression of the human spirit: it was the justification of my existence. You're not the only person incapable of understanding that—nobody's capable of understanding it," he said in the same tone of bottomless contempt.

"And yet," said Michael, "the poems themselves exist. What does it matter, in the light of everything you've said, who wrote them? You should have worshiped the poems, not the poet."

An expression of irritation appeared on Tuvia Shai's face. "You're less intelligent than I thought," he said with a dismissive wave of his hand. He gazed at the window behind Michael's back, and Michael waited silently.

"I wanted to help him." He went on talking, as if to himself. "I wanted to be there for him so that he would be able to create the things I believed he was capable of creating. Not because he was my friend but because I believed he was a creator. And when it turned out that he hadn't created anything—and lied at the expense of art—there was no place left for him in the world. He benefited from the highest thing there is and gave nothing. You don't understand anything! He put himself at the center."

"But you did it in a burst of rage, not with the deliberate intention of executing him in the name of some higher justice. How do you reconcile your defense of art, your crusade on its behalf, with this spontaneous outburst of violence?"

Shai seemed confused, embarrassed. He looked at Michael

appraisingly, and for a moment, as if against his will, an expression of something resembling respect flickered in his eyes.

"Afterward I was sorry," he said. "It's the only thing I had any regrets about. You understand, I feel no remorse, no guilt. It's only that now I've got no goal left, that's all, but I don't feel guilty."

"Perhaps there were personal motives involved nevertheless?" said Michael slowly, with a detached, reflective interest that again aroused Shai's ire. Above all he wanted the loftiness of his motive to be recognized as such.

"Rubbish!" screamed Tuvia Shai. "There was no personal motive! I demanded that he confess and make public what he had done, and he thought that was absurd. He made fun of the whole thing. That's the reason I didn't plan it carefully, the reason I lost control on the spot. If he had admitted everything to the world, returned the prize and all the rest of it, perhaps I wouldn't have had to kill him. But in any case, I don't regret it. Even though it means that I'll have to pay the price, I don't really mind paying it, as long as people understand at last that there are some people in the world whose motives are different from the ordinary motives, who don't act out of jealousy, avarice, revenge, and all the usual petty things."

In a paternal voice, Michael said: "Why don't you tell me exactly what happened."

Tuvia Shai looked at him suspiciously. Michael was careful not to change the expression on his face as he said: "We're speaking now of things that will affect the course of your life, that will determine whether you serve a life sentence for deliberate murder, or are charged with manslaughter and spend a lot less time in prison. I don't know about you, but the difference seems quite crucial to me."

Tuvia Shai wiped his face. It was very hot in the room. He looked around him and began talking in the monotonous voice with which Michael was familiar from previous interrogations.

"After Iddo came to see me after the departmental seminar, and told me, and played me that cassette, I thought of confronting Shaul. I had seen, like everybody else, that Iddo came back from America in a state of disintegration, as you said. But I didn't know why. I didn't have the least idea. I was stunned at the seminar; I couldn't understand what had gotten into him. And when it was over, he came home with me and told me."

"What, exactly, did he tell you?" asked Michael, keeping his tone as casual as he could.

"That he'd been to see Shaul, at his house. A few days after he arrived back in the country. He told Shaul about his meeting with Boris Zinger, with everything it implied."

"And how did Tirosh react?"

"Iddo said that he maintained a 'tragic silence,' but if I know Shaul, he was simply calculating his next moves," said Shai bitterly.

"Why didn't he kill him on the spot?" asked Michael sharply.

Shai blinked his eyes: "You mean then? When Iddo went to see him at his house?"

Michael nodded. "How could he have let him go with that kind of information and waited two weeks until the scuba-diving trip? Does that sound logical to you?"

"You didn't know Iddo. Shaul asked him to give him time, to promise him not to talk about it to anybody until he decided 'how to resolve it.' And Iddo agreed. Anyone who knew Iddo knew that his word could be relied on utterly. With him a promise was a vow."

"In other words," Michael reflected aloud, "Tirosh was waiting for an opportunity, in your opinion? Did he know about the diving in advance?"

"It was well known that Iddo was going down to Eilat at the end of the academic year to finish the course."

"And why did Iddo tell you? In spite of his promise?"

"I don't know," said Tuvia in a broken voice. "I really don't know. In any case, he couldn't keep it."

Michael sighed. "So what happened when Iddo came to see you?"

After hesitating a few seconds, Tuvia Shai began to speak again: "Iddo came to me. Naturally, I at first didn't believe him. My own needs, too, took control of me, but only for a few minutes: until he played me the cassette he'd brought back from America with him.

Iddo asked Boris Zinger if he could recite a few of Ferber's poems onto the tape for him, from memory, and Zinger began reciting Shaul's lines—except that they weren't Shaul's. Finally I believed him. I had no choice. The changes especially were what convinced me: Zinger used words and names that Shaul had changed and adapted to the local scene. Ferber's fir trees became pines, and his wolves were turned into jackals. Iddo argued, correctly, that I was the person with the greatest right, the most power, to stand up to Tirosh and bring the truth to light. 'You'll bring the truth to light,' he said that night, and he repeated it until it stuck in my mind. That sentence rang in my head all the next day and the night after it. And now too, when I think of Iddo, I think of the choked voice in which he said that sentence. I promised him that the truth would be brought to light. Iddo demanded it 'for Ferber's sake,' but I had a deeper motive. 'For the sake of the truth, for the sake of art,' I said to him. For hours after he left I sat reading and rereading the poems. I then read the introduction Shaul had written to Ferber's poems. Suddenly it all seemed so despicable. How could anyone make light of such things, I asked myself, to lie and cheat and steal, and for what? I think that murder is a small matter compared to what he did. Really. I have no regrets."

In the silence that fell on the room, it was possible to hear footsteps in the corridor. The telephone rang, but Michael ignored it.

When the silence lengthened and Tuvia Shai looked as if he had withdrawn into himself and forgotten where he was, Michael said: "And then you went with him to his office at the university, after you had lunch together."

"Yes," Tuvia Shai confirmed, and as if he could see the picture before his eyes, he said with a sigh: "It was hard, the department meeting. To see it all with a clear eye, to listen to the mannerisms, to suddenly know that there was nothing behind the facade. And to keep quiet. It was hard. But he was so absorbed in his own affairs that he said nothing about my silence. He spoke about Iddo at lunch. 'A crisis,' 'a nervous breakdown,' were the words he used. And I'll always remember how he said to me, like some gossiping housewife: 'He's even suffering from delusions, but I don't want to go into the details.'

He had no idea that I already knew. He said that it would be necessary to 'discreetly ease Iddo out,' that 'it was probably the doctorate that broke him.' And I sat there and said nothing; I didn't react. Those hours were the worst. But I wanted to be alone with him in his office. In the day and the night that had passed since Iddo told me, I had structured the whole confrontation. It was all planned. I had no doubt that I would be able to make him do the right thing. I thought, in my innocence, that he would even be relieved at the prospect of exposure. I don't know what I thought, it never occurred to me that he would have the nerve to refuse me. Hubris. We all suffer from hubris."

Again Tuvia Shai fell into a prolonged silence, with a blank, trancelike expression on his face. Michael said slowly: "And then you played him the cassette."

"Not right away. We sat in his office. And he said that he had to go and gave me the papers he wanted me to pass on to Adina. He behaved as if there was no doubt in his mind that I would go on running his errands for him. And that's what I said to him: 'You've got no doubt that I'll always go on running your errands for you?' And he looked at me as if I'd gone mad. And then I asked him if he thought that a great artist was entitled to see himself as exempt from moral restraints, and he put on his amused, ironic look, which had never bothered me before but which at that moment infuriated me. I demanded a serious answer, and he looked at me as if I was a sick man who had to be humored, and said: 'Are you asking if the artist should be bound by morality or if art should be bound by morality?' And he added that we'd often discussed the matter before and he didn't have time to talk about it now."

After another silence Tuvia Shai turned to Michael and asked him: "What do you think about morality and art?"

Michael choked. For a moment he thought of smiling and dismissing the question with a joke, or keeping quiet, but he looked at Tuvia Shai sitting opposite him with an expression of strained expectation on his face, and he realized that if he wanted a confession, a serious debate on the question was unavoidable. And there was nothing he wanted more at this moment than a signed confession. Of all the discussions he had ever had during an interrogation, he said afterward to Emanuel Shorer, this was the craziest question that had ever been addressed to him by a suspect, the last thing one would expect in the situation of a police interrogation. But he didn't have any choice, he said apologetically to Emanuel; he had to answer with perfect seriousness, because Tuvia Shai was testing him.

"At first," said Michael later to Emanuel Shorer, "I thought of turning the question back at him, of saying to him: 'And what do you think about it?' But then I saw that at the first trick I played, the first wrong word I said, he would clam up and I wouldn't be able to get another thing out of him. So I really didn't have a choice," he apologized in embarrassment to Emanuel Shorer, who listened to the recording of the interrogation and, to Michael's great relief, did not make fun of what he heard.

"I don't think a distinction should be made between the artist and art," said Michael to Tuvia Shai with a serious expression.

"In other words?" asked Shai as if he were conducting a class at the university.

"In other words, the things you said about Nietszche are different from what I've always thought. Look, this isn't the kind of thing I think about every day, like you. I don't know if I can define my thoughts exactly." He was silent and tried to concentrate, afraid of exposing his limitations; he wanted to present a thesis that would seem serious and profound. And then he said: "For me art isn't a matter of such . . . not that it isn't important to me; it *is* important. But I'm certain it doesn't mean to me what it means to you. In general, I think that love of others is the main motive for constructive acts." There was a silence. Tuvia Shai waited for him to go on, and Michael asked himself: Oh, yes? Is that what I really think? Who says that's what I think? And aloud he said: "In other words, I think it's more important for a great artist to love than to be loved. I happen to think the same with regard to people in general. A writer who hurts people unnecessarily all his life isn't capable of mobilizing the compassion to create characters of flesh and blood." He remembered something he had once heard in an introductory lecture on twentieth-century literature, and said: "Even Kafka, who depicted human existence as absurd, created a world in his writing, a complete world. And don't tell me that there's no compassion in it. I don't know any work of art that I admire which isn't based, overtly or covertly, as you people like to say, on love and compassion for humanity." He hesitated trying to organize his thoughts. "And also, I think that in a great work of art there's always some recommendation of a way of life." The trace of an ironic smile appeared on Tuvia Shai's face. His eyebrows rose but he said nothing. Michael noticed the subtle changes, but he went on talking with the same seriousness: "Even the absurdists present the absurd as axiomatic, and show the humiliation and all that so we'll see ourselves in a mirror and be able to live differently in this absurd world. In my opinion, this is something that demands a certain level of morality. Perhaps deeper than all the others. You have to live in the swamp and know that it's a swamp. Someone who isn't moral doesn't know that it's a swamp. If he's a complete cynic, he won't be able to describe his world and his suffering in a way that will shock others."

Tuvia Shai regarded him with a glint that Michael later described to Shorer as a "dangerous look in his eye."

"That's what I really think. Without any relation to Nietzsche," said Michael, who wondered whether the man opposite him was about to jump up and attack him.

But Tuvia Shai didn't move. He said quietly: "A very naive view. I disagree with you completely. I don't think you understood Nietzsche, or other books you read either. But it's not bad for someone who works in the police."

There were some things about which Michael never spoke to anybody later. Not even to Shorer. For a long time afterward he remembered Tuvia Shai and the things he said. And he kept asking himself the same question. Was there any substance in what he himself had said? Which of them was right, he asked himself, without trying to find an answer. Of one thing he was certain, and he already knew it during the interrogation itself: Tuvia Shai was not insane. Even though Michael was inclined to believe in his own declaration of faith, he felt sure even as he made it that in reality, in human history, there were things that justified Shai's point of view. Later too he did not come to any definite conclusions.

"I know you disagree with me," said Michael Ohayon. "And I know that of the two of us, the expert on aesthetics is you."

"It's not a question of aesthetics and ethics. It's a question of what I'm prepared to do for the sake of what's important in my eyes and what you're prepared to do. You work here," and Shai waved his hand to take in the room around them, "and live your little life, and you think that you're making a difference in the world. I, on the other hand, was prepared to efface myself completely, turn my life to dust and ashes, for the thing that was important in my eyes."

"But still, you couldn't control yourself," said Michael, trying to bring the conversation back to the scene of the crime.

"It's not that I couldn't control myself," said Tuvia Shai. He had fallen so quickly into the trap that Michael understood how strong his need was to talk, now that the wall of muteness had been breached. "If Shaul had been ready to expose himself and be punished for the sake of the truth," said Shai, "if he had understood what I was talking about, I would have left him alone. But he laughed. I explained the situation to him, and he laughed. But when I played him Iddo's cassette he stopped laughing. He had a portable tape machine in his office, on which he sometimes recorded his lectures. I played him Boris Zinger reading what had passed for so long as Shaul Tirosh's poems, and he stopped laughing. But his face showed a kind of careful cunning, like the expression he had when he was planning to make a play for a woman. And then he said to me: 'Tuvia, you were always insane. Not everyone knows, but I know that you're insane. Nothing is important enough to justify your destroying me so completely. I thought you loved me.' That's what he said to me. And then I realized that he didn't understand anything either and that he thought I loved him personally, for what he was. And I told him in so many words: 'Nothing will stop me from exposing you, but I want you to acknowledge that art is greater than both of us, and truth is greater than both of us, and to do it yourself. I never loved you. You yourself are of no importance whatsoever.' And then he looked at me very seriously and said: 'I have no intention of admitting anything to anyone, and you're leaving that cassette right here in this room. Nor will you expose anything. You can just forget the whole thing.' And then I took the little statue, quickly, before he had a chance to realize what was happening. He was standing next to the window and looking out—it's a pose he was particularly fond of—and he turned his face to me, and then I hit him again and again, because he didn't know the difference between what was important and what wasn't and he was going to destroy the cassette to prevent himself from being exposed."

"But that's what you did yourself, later on. You destroyed the cassette to prevent yourself from being exposed. You didn't bring the truth to light," said Michael wearily.

"And that's the main reason I'm talking to you. I'll go to prison as long as it helps bring the truth to light," said Tuvia Shai, and he began to shiver.

"And after you killed him you went to the movies?" asked Michael without sounding surprised.

He described how he had left the building, and that he hadn't even thought of being afraid. There were no bloodstains on his clothes. He put the statuette into a plastic bag and removed the cassette from the tape recorder. He explained that from that moment onward his feelings had been paralyzed. "If a fire had broken out I would have gone on standing there," he said. He didn't take the trouble to hide and nobody noticed him. When he finally left Tirosh's office, it was after half past one, and he took the car and drove it to the parking lot of the Hadassah Hospital on Mount Scopus and listened one more time to the cassette before erasing it. And then he had noticed that it was getting late and he would be late for the movie. It was only then that he wiped off the fingerprints, with the cloth Tirosh kept in his glove compartment. Afterward he threw it away in Wadi Joz.

"You could have gone home, no?" asked Michael.

"I didn't think of it," said Shai in surprise. "I don't even know why I had to see *Blade Runner*." And then he was silent.

It took several hours to draw up the statement. Tuvia Shai insisted on formulating his motives himself. He went back with them to Tirosh's office on Mount Scopus and reconstructed the murder to the satisfaction of Emanuel Shorer, who had come into Michael's office just as Tuvia Shai finished talking.

When Balilty suggested again, as usual, that they should "go and celebrate at some place with style," Tzilla warned him with a withering look. She knew Michael Ohayon's moods. "You can talk to him in a few days' time," she said, and glanced at Michael. "Do me a favor, leave him alone now."

That evening Michael sat with Emanuel Shorer in the Café Nava. Shorer stirred the sugar in his tea. Michael stared at his coffee.

"What are you thinking about?" asked Shorer, and smiled.

Michael didn't answer. He held the glass cup in both hands and went on staring.

"By the way, I forgot to ask you," said Shorer. "What was that piece of paper on the desk? Did you ever find out what it meant? You know, the one you told me about, about the last chapter of that novel by Agnon. Do you understand it now?"

Michael shook his head. He had not told any of the members of the special investigation team about Manfred Herbst and the nurse Shira. He was tired and depressed. As always, he had no sense of victory. Only sadness and a longing to curl up inside a woman's body and sleep for years.

Shorer sipped his tea and looked at him, and finally he said: "I've been meaning to tell you for some time now, that for a person who believes you should love the human race, or that it's more important to love than to be loved, you don't seem to be doing such a great job of it." There was no rebuke in his voice.